MW01093121

THE WOLVES OF WINDSOR RIDGE

(MATT BANNISTER WESTERN 4)

KEN PRATT

The Wolves Of Windsor Ridge

Paperback Edition
Copyright © 2019 by Ken Pratt

CKN Christian Publishing
An Imprint of Wolfpack Publishing
6032 Wheat Penny Avenue
Las Vegas, NV 89122

christiankindlenews.com

All rights reserved. No part of this book may be reproduced by any means without the prior written consent of the publisher, other than brief quotes for reviews.

Characters, places and incidents are used fictitiously, and any resemblance to actual persons, living or dead, business establishments, events, or locales is entirely coincidental.

Paperback ISBN 978-1-64119-617-8
eBook ISBN 978-1-64119-616-1

Library of Congress Control Number: 2019934702

This book is dedicated to my son, Keith Pratt. His brutal honesty, opinions, viewpoints and feedback have been very much appreciated and a great help with this story. It is a blessing to me to have a son who takes as much interest in my writing as I do. Keith will be graduating from high school this year, and it is an honor for me to see the amazing young man he is becoming. I am very proud of you, Keith.

"A wise son brings joy to his father, but a foolish son grief to his mother."
Proverbs 10:1

ACKNOWLEDGMENTS

First and foremost, I want to thank my wife, Cathy. A man's wife has the unique position to either encourage or discourage her husband. I am lucky enough to have a wife, who despite her Alzheimer's condition, still encourages me, and that makes all the difference in everything, not just writing. And for that, I thank my wife for believing in me.

I want to thank, Allie Green, whose knowledge and overall input on the story certainly helped to make it better.

I want to thank Andrew Worley, who was a listening ear, and his feedback was invaluable. Again, it wasn't uncommon for me to text or call after midnight to run through a scene and ask his opinion. A friend tolerant enough to listen like that is hard to find, and I am very blessed to have one.

And finally, I want to mention a special note of appreciation for Lauren Bridges, Rachel Del Grosso, Mike Bray and the rest of the team at CKN Christian Publishing for their work to make this book possible.

THE WOLVES OF WINDSOR RIDGE

PROLOGUE

Branson, Oregon. June 1883

MATT BANNISTER STOOD in the center of his U.S. Marshal's Office and looked around him with a small smile on his face. It had been less than a year ago when he'd sat alone in a small shack in Cheyenne, Wyoming, and pointed his own revolver at his head. He had reached the end of a long downhill spiral that left him hopeless in a life full of emptiness and regrets. Fifteen years after running away from his home, he had become one of the most famous deputy marshals in the west. That fame, which young men dreamed about, meant absolutely nothing when his finger was on the trigger. He wanted to end the loneliness that never left him for long. The only purpose he possessed was the ability to track down men who would kill him in a second if they weren't too afraid to die themselves. On that summer's night, the only thing that saved his life was an unexpected knock on the door. The knocker was his pastor, who had stopped by. After a long discussion, the minister convinced Matt it was time to go back home and see his family.

In December, Matt did go back home to Willow Falls, Oregon, to spend Christmas with his family. He had prayed he wouldn't run into his old girlfriend and her husband, his old best friend, Tom Smith. However, some prayers are simply not answered the way we hope they will be. His former fiancé, Elizabeth Smith, was kidnapped by the Moskin Gang on Christmas Eve. Matt was forced to join up with Tom to bring her home. The experience had turned out to be the greatest blessing of Matt's life so far. Because for so many years he had been haunted by the pain of losing Elizabeth to Tom, and for so many years he'd lived with his anger toward them, and the guilt of his own betrayal. And now, because of that unanswered prayer, he could put all those hurts behind him. He could see what he missed by running away from his pain and could now look forward to the future without any shame, pain, or fear. He had no reason to return to Cheyenne.

Once he decided to stay, Branson's Elite Seven, the seven biggest entrepreneurs in Jessup County who controlled the city and county politics, used their political ties and friends in persuasive places, to petition the federal government to appoint Matt as a U.S. Marshal—based in Branson, of course. In the meantime, it was already decided that Matt would be the Jessup County Sheriff at the very least, if not be appointed to a U.S. Marshal's position. Having that in mind, the Elite Seven invested in building the new marshal's office, using the finest craftsmen and materials. The beautiful office was built for Matt. He was appointed as a U.S. Marshal and given county sheriff's responsibilities and jurisdiction over Jessup County, as well. Law in Jessup County had historically been distributed between town sheriffs, who worked together when necessary. But there had never been a county sheriff until now, and he was a U.S. Marshal. Matt's life had turned so completely around in a year's time, it was almost unbelievable to Matt.

He had been blessed to rejoin his family and welcomed home with open arms. To secure a position he had never dreamed of having, in the last city he ever expected to live in was such an amazing thing. Instead of a cold shack he was hardly ever home enough to sleep in, he now had a very nice brick house he actually enjoyed living in. What a tragedy it would have been if he had pulled the trigger that night and missed what the Lord had planned for him. Life was good! Occasionally, though, you have to get through the rougher times to reach the unimaginable blessings on the other side of the darker times of living in this world.

Matt sighed. "Thank you, Lord," he said after reflecting on the past year. It had been a hard one, but worth every moment to be where he was now.

He stepped out of his office, closed and locked the door behind him. As he turned to face the street, he paused to see three young ladies, all wearing beautiful dresses and ornamented hats of various styles, walking toward him. His gaze lingered on the most beautiful lady he had perhaps ever seen walking nearest to him on the boardwalk. His gaze locked onto hers, and hers to his like an invisible connection between them. She had a soft, oval-shaped face with brown-almond eyes. Her hair was dark and very long, but he couldn't tell if it was straight or wavy because it was tied up in a carefully weaved bun circling her head underneath her ostrich-feathered hat. Her lips formed a shy smile as she lowered her face behind a fan as she and her two friends drew near.

A wagon stopped in front of the marshal's office, and a

balding man in his mid-fifties with a gray beard began talking immediately. "You must be the famous marshal, Matt Bannister, yeah?"

"I am," Matt said looking at the older man and the younger man sitting on the bench seat beside him. Both men were dressed quite plainly, and did not appear to be a threat or show any sign of aggression. Matt turned his head back to the three ladies and noticed the other two ladies smile at him as they neared.

"Hello, ladies," he said, while keeping eye contact at the lady wearing the ostrich-feathered hat. She glanced up into his eyes for the brief moment it took her to take the three steps to reach him.

"Hello," she said with a touch of discomfort in her voice. Her two friends giggled.

The man on the wagon spoke loudly. "My name's Jack Schwartz, and this is my boy, Dustin. He's single, ladies! Hell, so am I come to think of it," he called out to the three ladies and then laughed.

"Pa, darn you!" Dustin exclaimed as his face reddened. He was in his mid- to late-twenties.

One of the ladies, a heavier one with dark, shoulder-length hair and a round face, turned back and answered, "Too bad we're not. Except Christine. She is single, but unfortunately for you, she likes the marshal!"

Matt's head lifted with interest to watch for any reaction that might show which of the three ladies Christine was. It didn't take long.

The one Matt had made eye contact, with the ostrich hat, gave her friend a soft shove and said loudly enough to be heard, "Helen!" The one named Helen laughed and glanced back at Matt with an approving smile.

Matt smiled slightly, and the words *I wish* passed

through his mind. He knew only two things: she was a beautiful woman, and her name was Christine. Everything else was a mystery because he had never seen any of these women before.

Jack Schwartz laughed and hollered back to the ladies, "My boy's got a couple of dollars for a romp in the back of the wagon. I get to watch! 'Cause that's all the money we got!" He laughed while he looked at Matt, expecting Matt to laugh. Matt didn't laugh.

"Pa!" Dustin exclaimed again.

"Creep!" Helen yelled back at Jack and kept walking. Christine looked back at Matt and then glanced away again.

Matt frowned, embarrassed by the immature actions of a much older man. He was about to say as much when he heard his cousin, William Fasana, speak to Jack as he walked in front of the wagon toward Matt. Matt's older brother Adam was with him.

"You're barking up the wrong tree there, pops. Those women dance at the new dance hall. If you want their business, it'll cost you a mite bit more than a couple of dollars on a buckboard. You'll find a streetwalker later tonight if that's all you got. You might go away with far more than two dollars' worth of syphilis or some other dripping love token, though," William said. He wore a gray suit with his double reversed gun-belt holding guns with ivory handles. His blond, curly hair was long, and he had a neatly trimmed goatee.

"Are you Buffalo Bill?" Dustin asked curiously.

Adam Bannister laughed. He was a big man with dark, bushy, long hair that fell to his shoulders, as well as a long and thick beard. "No, he's little Willy Hickok. Wild Bill's little brother," he joked.

"Really?" Dustin asked.

William shook his head. "You must be from out of town. You sound too gullible to be from around here. No, my name's William Fasana. I'm the cousin of these two...guys."

"My name's Jack Schwartz, and this is my son, Dustin. I'm the sheriff of Loveland, Oregon. That's why I wanted to introduce myself to the marshal here. We're both lawmen, you know. We're just down here in the lowlands collecting some goods but need to get on back. You know a town without lawmen can get pretty wild, but me and Dustin do a good job keeping the peace. I'm getting a little too old to run much anymore, but if you need a good hand for a deputy marshal, Dustin's your guy!"

"Oh. Well, you'll have let me know where Loveland is, because I'm not sure," Matt said.

Dustin spoke quickly, "Up by Huntsville. We're a small mountain community in the Wallowas. We do a lot of hunting up there, so I'm pretty experienced with my guns. I shot a grizzly not long ago. I killed it with one shot. You probably don't know how steady your hand has to be to kill a grizzly with one shot! If you need a good rifleman, I'd take a position with you."

William Fasana stared at Dustin and slowly asked, "There's not many women up there, is there?"

"No, there's not! That's another reason we're here." Jack laughed.

Adam smiled. "Just a word of advice...don't! Especially if you're going to use introduction lines like you tried on those three ladies. Those ladies didn't look like prostitutes to me. They looked like very fine, upstanding citizens, and you questioned them as if they were ravaged streetwalkers looking for two bits to eat on. You do that to every woman you see around here you won't get out of this town...Well, you'll be busted up if you do."

Jack scoffed. "I know a whore when I see one." He laughed to himself.

"Well, nice to meet you two, but we have to go," Matt said, motioning to his brother and cousin.

"No, we don't," William said with a humorous expression on his face. "So, how big was that grizzly? Was it a cub?" he asked Dustin.

"No! It was probably two thousand pounds and ten or twelve feet tall."

"Wow. One shot, you say? How far away do you think you were?"

"Just one shot," Dustin emphasized by raising one finger. "I don't miss with my Sharps. It was probably two, maybe three hundred feet away. Have you ever killed a bear with one shot from that far away? I'll bet you haven't. Well, I did. And that's why I say, if you need a good shot for a deputy, I'm your man," he said to Matt.

"I'll keep you in mind," Matt said without any interest.

William pointed at Adam. "Adam here could shoot a ribbon off the tip of a running squirrel's tail at a hundred yards."

"So could I," Dustin replied quickly. "But I said three hundred feet, not a hundred yards."

Adam smirked. "Well, that's good shooting," he said before William could say anything else. "I hunt up there in the Wallowas myself. You gentlemen have a great day."

William widened his eyes. "Yeah, that is good shooting. Wow! You know, Adam was our sharpshooter in the cavalry, but I bet you could out-shoot him like I could a child."

"Yeah, maybe. Probably, if I used my Sharps. Where do you hunt at?" Dustin asked Adam. "Maybe I could join up with you and be your guide. I could show you some places outside of Loveland where not many people have been to. And the game's good!"

Adam smiled. "If I come through Loveland, I'll look you up."

"Nice meeting you two lawmen. Take care now," Matt said, waving them off.

After a few moments of William encouraging Dustin to talk about his shooting abilities, the father and son from Loveland drove off and left the three men standing in front of the marshal's office.

Matt looked at William and spoke irritably. "Why do you do that? Why do you encourage people to keep talking all the time? And it's not everyone, either. It's just the annoying ones you do that to. Why?"

William laughed. "For my own entertainment, Matt."

Adam smiled at his cousin. "Do you think I should have invited him to join Uncle Luther and me on our hunting trip? He could probably show Luther how to hunt and how to make jerky too, is my guess."

William chuckled. "If I know anyone, it's Uncle Luther. And I'm telling you, he'd bust that boy's Sharps over his head and wrap its barrel around his throat just to shut him up. You don't show Uncle Luther anything when it comes to hunting or making jerky!"

"By the way, Matt," Adam asked, "do you want to join us for our annual hunting trip? You've never been up there with us, so it would be fun for you, I am sure. And Uncle Luther would love to have you there."

"When?"

"In early August. What do you say? You could shoot an elk or two, maybe a few deer. You can shoot whatever you can find or whatever finds you, depending on your luck."

"Maybe, but I won't commit to it right now. I don't know

what's going to happen from one day to the next around here."

"Well, we've been going to Windsor Ridge for a long time. It would be good if you could go once. It's where our grandfather camped and hunted with Uncle Luther, and now he's sharing it with us. So far, I am the only one to ever go, though."

"If I can, I'd like to."

William shook his head. "Matt isn't going to go, Adam! He's been living on the ground for fifteen years, when he wasn't in his Cheyenne shack. I saw his shack and, trust me, it wasn't as nice as your chicken coop. Now he has a cushy job, a fancy new Davenport in his warm house, and clean clothes for once in his life. No, he's more like me now, and will never hunt again! Why hunt, Adam, when you can just order a steak?"

Adam shrugged. "I'm a rancher and sell those steaks, William. But I sure as heck prefer wild game to my raised stock."

"What are you guys doing down here, anyway?" Matt asked curiously.

Adam spoke. "A horse breeder from California is passing through with several hundred horses and is having a special auction tomorrow. I wanted to go over and look at what he has to sell. He has some good stock. Anyway, that's what I am doing here."

"I'm just following him," William offered.

"Do you two want to join me for lunch? My treat."

"Are you going to buy me a drink to go with it?" William asked.

Matt looked at William. "If you're respectful to the waitress, I will. If you start talking to her like that ass on the wagon just did, then not a chance."

Adam shook his head with a deep frown. "That guy was a creep. Kind of like you," he said to William.

William laughed. "I have more style than he had. I don't need to holler out at the female species. I just wink and smile."

"And they go weak in the knees, right?" Adam asked sarcastically.

Matt spoke before William could answer. "No. It's the sun glaring off that pretty blond hair that blinds them, and they stumble," Matt teased his cousin.

William held up the palms of his hands in surrendering fashion. "Okay, before you two get going too hard on me, can we go get something to eat? And I will treat the waitress with the utmost respect. But if you guys see her spit in my soup, let me know, huh? I can't say I was so respectful the last time I saw her."

Adam frowned. "You don't even know who it is yet."

"It doesn't matter. I treat them all about the same. Ask Matt. He's the one who won't buy me a drink if I'm not...behaved."

"Well, you have money," Adam pointed out.

"Yeah, but it's cheaper if Matt buys, or you. Geez, I'd even let your brother Steven buy, if he ever offered. But he doesn't offer anything, except a free carrot, maybe."

~

Three Weeks Later
Branson, Oregon

RICHARD McKENNA WAS a good-sized man with broad

shoulders and thick muscles from his many years of lifting hundred-pound grain bags and barrels at the mill. He had begun working for the Premro and Sons Grist Mill at seventeen; he was now forty-five years old and still working at the mill. His name was Richard, but his family called him Dick. To everyone else in town, he was commonly known as, "Deuce McKenna," because he weighed over two hundred pounds and could carry two one-hundred-pound bags of grain at once. He could fight like a badger when he needed to and had whipped many men in the saloons over the years, but he wasn't a gunman. And he wasn't feeling all that strong or powerful now.

He took a deep breath and then sighed heavily. "If he gunned down Possum and his wife like that, then boys, we have to do something. If Jesse doesn't trust us, it's just a matter of time before we're all dead, too. I don't think anyone's ever just left the Sperry Helms Gang, do you, Pick?"

Pick Lawson had spent most of his years running from the law in the Midwest and knew a thing or two about handling a gun and life on the run. He had moved to Branson a few years ago to get out of Kansas and as far away from there as he could. He had followed his friend Cass Travers to Branson and teamed up with the Sperry Helms Gang, which was led by two cousins, Morton Sperry and Jesse Helms. Both men could be as brutal and dangerous as any outlaw Pick had ever met, and he'd met quite a few. Pick had met Deuce in a saloon, and the men became friends.

After some time, he introduced Deuce to Morton Sperry. Two years ago, Deuce joined the gang now and then when an extra hand was needed—or a good alibi. However, Deuce had proved his mettle and had become a respected member of the gang and occasional leader when the cousins weren't present. However, in recent months, U.S. Marshal Matt Bannister had taken up residence in Branson. His presence had the gang's leadership spooked. It was beginning to show in some very dark ways that made everyone who wasn't named Sperry or Helms nervous. Pick spat a long stream of brown tobacco juice onto the floor of Deuce's underground cellar where they all sat to talk in private.

"No one leaves if they're not trusted. Those boys aren't going to risk a loose tongue talking about them. The Sperrys like knowing everyone's too scared of them to talk. Possum might have been a nice enough guy, but he was stupid and talked a bit too much about that bank in Nevada last June, and the plan to rob the bank up in Loveland. How stupid do you have to be not to figure out that kind of talk will get you killed? Well, it got him and his wife both killed! This is getting bad, boys. The marshal's in town now, and Morton's not taking any chances. Morton's not stupid either. He and Jessie waited until Marshal Bannister left town, to do the job, but when the marshal comes back from Idaho, he'll be investigating. By then, the trail will be cold. Just like that Natoma sheriff who was executed by the creek has never been solved, and everyone knows who did it. For crying out loud, Morton's little sister and brother talk about it all of the time! Possum talked some, too, but unless you're a Sperry or a Helms, you're expendable. I'll tell you what I fear, and that's if Morton's little brother and sister keep bragging to everyone about being a Sperry. We're the ones who are going to pay for it, one way or another."

Karl Digsby was the newest member of the gang. He'd had the unfortunate privilege of having his first gang outing be as witness to the murders of gang member Possum Overguard and his wife. Morton Sperry, Jesse Helms and Cass Travers murdered the couple in cold blood and then burned their cabin down with the bodies inside. The point was made very clear to Karl that he was to keep his mouth shut or the same would happen to him and his wife. Karl had never seen anything so horrible in his life. He wasn't a criminal, but an employee of the Seven Timbers Lumber Mill, looking for a chance to make an extra dollar or two.

Karl shook his head as he stared at Pick with concern. "Does that mean I can't quit the gang? Because I really don't want anything to do with those guys anymore. I didn't join up to kill people, especially people I know. Not that I knew that man, but I would've gotten to know him. And his poor wife didn't do anything to them!"

Deuce answered sternly, "No, you can't quit! You saw them murder two people, Karl. You're their slave until they say it's the end."

Karl spoke loudly with frustration, "Why did I listen to you guys, anyway? I might not have a dime to my name most of the time, but I never had my life threatened before, either. I'm not a gunfighter, Deuce! Why did you guys even ask me to join this damn gang?"

Deuce raised his eyebrows. "Because you wanted in. You asked us to help you get in, remember?"

"Well, I was wrong! And now I want out."

"I think we all want out," Deuce said simply.

"What made you join up anyway, Deuce? You have everything a guy could want. A great wife, a nice home— you have it all. What made you want to join up with those murdering bastards?"

Deuce frowned. "Oh, I think it was the lure of more money and maybe some excitement. I've been working for the Premro family since I was seventeen. I've helped build that mill for almost thirty years now, and I'm tired. My back is getting weaker, and I ache a lot. After all these years, you'd think I'd be a supervisor or something by now, but I'm just a pack mule. I've watched the Premros get wealthy. I trained Steve Harman ten years ago, and now he's my manager; and I've watched him get wealthy enough, too. I guess I just got sick of being overlooked, and thought with some easy money, I could quit my job and rest my body for a while. I've made some decent money and have some saved up. I've had my fill of excitement too, I think. It would be a good idea for us to be thankful for our jobs and get out of the Sperry Helms Gang, if we can."

"How?" Karl asked, frustrated. "You tell me how we can get out of the gang. If Marshal Bannister was around, I'd go to him and tell him everything I know and get out of the area as fast as I could. But he's not here, and who knows when he'll come back from Sweethome. And there's no way I'm trusting Sheriff Wright. He's as corrupt as they get."

"I know!" a voice said from the other side of the cellar door. It opened, and Deuce's nineteen-year-old nephew, Brent Boyle, walked down the stone steps and then turned back to close the door behind him.

"What in the hell are you doing here?!" Deuce yelled. He stood up in anger. "What do you think you're doing listening to our conversation? I ought to bust your head open for doing that. Do you understand me? Now get the hell out of here! And don't let me catch you listening to our conversations again, or I will beat your hide like a child's!"

It wasn't only his uncle's unexpected anger that concerned Brent, but Pick glared at him with an ugly scowl, as well. Brent had met both men before, but Pick was the one who scared him. Karl was too nice of a man to be frightening. Brent raised his hands in surrender and spoke quickly, "Okay, I'm sorry! It won't ever happen again, Uncle

Dick, I promise. But listen to me. Let's rob the bank and blame it on them!"

"What?" Pick spat out the word with a mouthful of brown juice. He wasn't at all pleased to see the young man.

"We rob the bank! You know, the bank you guys were just talking about. We can all wear masks and call each other their names. If you get away with the money, then they'll be the ones being hunted down. And you know Marshal Matt Bannister will hunt them down, right? There will be no more gang, and no more worries about them while we split the money." Brent Boyle smiled with excitement as he finished explaining his plan to his uncle and his friends.

He was a dark-haired young man with a slender frame and no facial hair to speak of. He wasn't a bad-looking kid, but he had no real desire to work hard either. He had been begging Deuce to introduce him to Morton Sperry so he could join the gang, but Deuce had always refused.

Deuce sat back down in thought. "Who said you could go, anyway?"

Brent gasped. "It's my plan! Come on, Uncle Dick, it's not a bad idea, you have to admit, huh?"

Pick spoke softly. "That might actually work. The key is getting away with it, but if we can, we could set Morton, Jessie and Cass up for a fall."

"What about Joey Helms? You don't think he'd come looking for us?" Karl asked.

"Fine, frame all four of them. We just need another guy."

"Excuse me!" Brent said loudly. "Are you guys blind? I'm right here."

"Forget it, Brent. I don't want you getting into this kind of stuff," Deuce said.

Brent gasped. "I want to! I can either do it with you guys

and learn how to get away with it from you and Pick, or I can just go out with my pals and we'll do it ourselves. I want some adventure, too, Uncle Dick. Trust me, I'm ready for this."

"What do you guys think?" Deuce asked his friends.

Pick shrugged. "I think we need to think about it carefully, but it could work if we hit the Loveland Bank in the morning and get out of there fast. It's a long way—a three-day ride from here to a place we've never been to on the other side of the tallest mountains in Oregon. Possum rode up there with Morton and Jesse to check it out and said it's easy pickin's and there's not much law to worry about. But that's also why he was killed, wasn't it? So, if we *don't* talk about it to anyone else, we could strike it rich and put them guys away. I like your nephew's idea, Deuce. What about you, Karl?"

Karl took a deep breath and exhaled. "Well, I swear. I don't think we have much of a choice, in my opinion. I can wait around for the day when Morton thinks I'm ratting out the gang and kills me or rob a bank and try to get away with it. Even if I went to the marshal and told him what I know and he arrests all three of them, I'd still have to worry about Joey or one of the others in those two families shooting me in the back, no matter where I went. So really, what choice do we have? I guess if we fail, going to prison is better than dying. And it will get us out of the Sperry Helms Gang one way or the other. So, I guess I'm in, but I will not fire my gun at anyone. I'm telling you that right now! I'll surrender if we're caught, but I won't shoot at anyone. Deal?"

Brent scoffed sarcastically with adolescent haste. "Karl, you're such a coward. I'll fight until there's not a man left standing. I won't give up under any circumstance either. Warriors never quit, Karl; remember that."

"Okay, Geronimo. I didn't realize you were such an experienced and battle-tested warrior," Karl said sarcastically.

"I just know what I'm capable of," Brent said arrogantly.

Pick looked at Brent with a doubtful grin. "You'll do as you're told. So, when do you want to do this, Deuce?"

Deuce shook his head. "Look, I don't think we should make that decision tonight. I think we should think about it for a day or two, do some planning and do it right. It's getting to be our busiest time of year at the mill; harvest, you know? But when we pick a week to go, I'll just tell the Premros I need to leave town for a few days. Friday night, I say we all meet back here with a calendar and make plans to hit that bank before summer's over. In the meantime, keep your words few and your noses clean around the gang."

Karl asked, "What am I supposed to do about work? Take time off too? A week's a long time."

Deuce shrugged. "Depends if you want out of the gang or not. We'll plan on hitting the bank on a Friday morning, so we'll leave on a Wednesday. We should be back on Monday. I know some of us might not have a job when we get back, but at least we'll have some money to get by with until we can find new ones. Heck, maybe it's for the best. The Premros haven't done much for me, anyway."

"Don't quit your jobs. We may not get as much as you'd like. I heard the gold up that way has fizzled out," Pick said simply. "Striking it rich would be great but remember the reason we're going is to set those guys up, not the amount of money we take. Whatever we bring home is just extra. Our real success will be Morton and Jesse being arrested or killed trying to fight the law. Deuce is right. Let's do it and do it right." He looked at Karl and spoke pointedly. "You probably won't need to fire your gun but bring your guns anyway and make sure they're loaded, just in case."

Loveland, Oregon.

SARAH PIERCE STARED at the ivory chess set on the decorative hand-carved board with drawer storage for the pieces sitting on the table in front of her. The pieces were hand-carved ivory and depicted a Roman set with carved soldiers as pawns, Roman columns as the castles, cavalrymen on horses the knights and, of course, the queen was of the softest beauty. The Roman emperor was the king. The set was a gift from her parents on her eighteenth birthday four years before. Sarah loved to play chess and had spent the last year teaching her husband, Nathan, how to play the game. Now they sat at the dining table under the light of a lantern on a warm early summer's night, and Nathan was about to win his first game against his young and beautiful wife.

She moved her tall white ivory king backwards onto the last available line. She was tempted to take her arm and knock all the pieces off the game board to remain unbeaten and the retainer of using the white pieces. It had always been "the champion uses the white set and has the first move" for as long as she had ever played. Of course, her father had taught her how to play and they were probably his rules. Nevertheless, she had beaten him at his own game, and had become the family champion. Now her student was about to take her championship title and there was nothing she could do about it, except end it abruptly or lose with grace. The next time they played, she would be using the stained tea-brown pieces for the first time since she beat her father. She took her fingers off her king and waited with a loud, disappointed sigh.

Nathan grinned and put his fingers on a pawn at the other end of the board.

"Nathan, don't be an ass, just end the game!" she said irritably.

He laughed. "Oh, I thought I'd give you a chance."

"With what? I have one pawn against your queen and a castle, among others. End it."

"No, go ahead and try to get your queen back. I'll let you." He chuckled to himself. "Really, go ahead, Sarah."

She looked at him and smiled at his giddiness. "Nathan, if you don't end this game right now, I will knock the pieces over, and no one will win."

"All right," he agreed, released his grip on the pawn and moved a castle down to put her king in checkmate. "Checkmate, my dear. Checkmate! By Jupiter, that sounds good, doesn't it?" He laughed.

"Nice job," she said sincerely.

"So, what's that make me?" he asked, gloating in his victory. "Come on. What's that make me?" he repeated and waited with a cupped ear.

Sarah nodded slowly. "You're the new chess champion of our family."

"That's right! And you know the rule: loser puts them away! I think I'll watch." He giggled.

"Enjoy it while you can, because the next game I won't give you a chance."

"Oh, yeah. Face it, my love, your ruling over the chessboard is now over. I am the champion!"

Nathan's older brother, Cal, looked over from the book he was reading with a smile on his face. "He beat you?" he asked Sarah.

"Yes, he did. But it was my fault. I made a few mistakes..."

"Oh, geez! Just admit it, you got beat!"

"I will not. You had more luck this game than anything else. I may have lost fair and square, but it was luck on your side."

Nathan laughed. "There might have been some luck, but I've learned from the best, too."

"Oh," she said sweetly. "Your weakest link is planning ahead multiple moves at a time. You should always have a planned move ahead and try to read what your opponent's game plan is. You don't ever have a plan. You just play by looking for an opportunity to kill. It paid off tonight, but usually it doesn't. Just like real life, you have to plan ahead a bit and stay the course, even if there are setbacks. Such as you getting my queen so early in the game."

"Oh, sweetheart, I knew if I got your queen, you'd struggle and eventually stumble and fall. You rely on her too much. I do think ahead though. In fact, I'm even thinking about how we can get out of this hellhole and back to civilization." He finished with a smile.

Cal looked up from his book again with a smile. "How's that now?" He lived with Nathan and Sarah in their small cabin and worked at the Loveland Lumber Company with Nathan. They lived in company housing and both worked long hours. Cal worked peeling bark off the trees for easier dragging by the oxen and mules over the skid roads the company had made. Nathan worked as a choker setter for the brand-new donkey engine the company had invested in. The work was hard and didn't pay much, but they had a roof over their heads and food in their bellies. Cal was content with that. Nathan wanted out of the woods and into the world beyond the dark forests of the giant Douglas fir trees of the Pacific Northwest.

Nathan answered promptly, "Cattle drives, Cal. We're horsemen. We should be used to long weeks of being in the saddle. We were in the cavalry, for crying out loud."

"I'm afraid the railroad is putting an end to the cattle-driving business little by little, little brother. Besides, all those old cowboys are now probably fighting for the remaining jobs, and we will never match up against them in their own trade. We can ride, but the cavalry isn't cowboying. We were soldiers, not cowboys."

"No. We're lumberjacks, if you want to be technical. You peel the bark off logs for a living, and I wrap a chain around them. Before that we were gophers, digging a mile deep in the ground for a living. Don't you think there might be something better out there for us? Something with a brighter future than getting buried alive or crushed under a tree?"

"No. I don't," Cal said simply and went back to his book.

"Seriously? You don't think we could find something better than this?"

Cal looked at Nathan and shook his head. "No. And I think you'd be a fool to try. We have it all: a job, good folks around us, a home and no trouble. Why risk changing it?"

Sarah answered for her husband, "He's not changing anything! This is our home."

"Sarah, don't you want a real life where you can wear a nice dress occasionally, or go outside in the winter without freezing to death in six feet of snow? We could do better than this place."

"Where, Nathan? Where can we go where we would have everything we have right now? You tell me that. You can't be a cowboy and go riding off, because I need you with me! I married you to be *with* you, not wait weeks and months *for* you. I won't do that, so that option is gone. We don't make nearly enough money to rent another shack anywhere but here, and before we can leave, we'd have to pay off the mercantile anyway. We are here permanently until we have to leave, and then we'll probably end up in another logging camp, because that's what you'll know by then."

Nathan took a deep breath and exhaled in frustration. "Sarah, I don't want to work in timber camps for the rest of my life. For crying out loud, there's got to be something better out there than this! This company owns everything about us, and it will never stop! If I'm hurt, we lose our home; if I'm fired, we lose our home; and if I quit, we lose our home. It's not our home. We don't *have* a home, Sarah. I don't want to work in timber camps for the rest of my life! I am tired of working bottom-of-the-pond jobs everywhere I go! I'm stuck in the mud and feel like I'm sinking deeper by the day. I don't know how you two can sit in this little cabin and thank God for the roof over our heads and food we spend our pay on; I can't! Thank you for the unfairness of our life and all the garbage that goes with it. Thank you, God, for the crap we have to worry about and laboring my fingers to the bone for absolutely nothing! One of these days that choker chain is going to take my fingers off, if it doesn't snap and rip my head off! I'm not going to pretend I am thankful when I'm not!"

Cal Pierce looked at his little brother and said, "That's too bad, Pliable."

"What?" Nathan asked.

"Have you ever read the book *The Pilgrim's Progress*?"

"No."

"Maybe you should. You remind me a lot of a character

named Pliable. He has a pretty short part in the story, but a significant one. In short, he is excited to be a Christian, until he hit the slough of despond. That moment of sinking into the mud and mire of despair was enough for him. He said... let me look. I am reading the book right now, by the way. Here it is. Pliable's response when it got hard: *'Is this the happiness you have told me all this while of? If we have so much ill speed at our first setting out, what may we expect betwixt this and our journey's end?'* And he quit serving God. That's about it really. Nathan, don't be a pliable guy. You're tougher than that. And mostly, just so you know, I am thankful for where we are because it could be worse, and I am thankful mostly for the contentment and joy I am able to have even through a day of work. Trust me, there's things I'd rather be doing, but I am content right where I am with you and Sarah. You should be, too," he finished, staring at his brother.

"Did you hear anything I said?" Nathan asked, not liking his brother's response.

"Yeah. We were soldiers; we don't quit. So be thankful for what you have and keep laboring until this season of our lives is through. Because someday it will be, and I promise, you will miss it in hindsight."

"No! I won't."

"Yeah, you will."

Sarah took Nathan's hand in hers from across the table. "It's a beautiful night, so let's go for a walk. How about I go get ready, and you put the game away, so we can take a walk."

"Fine." He looked at his brother while Sarah went to their separate bedroom. "I don't quit, either."

"Looks to me like you have. Just because life doesn't go as you had hoped, or seems a bit tougher than you expected, is no reason to give up on the Lord. Maybe He has a plan down the road a bit. Maybe life isn't so much about you and your hopes, but you living a life for Christ for others to see. God is faithful, Nathan. I wish you would just trust him."

Sarah came out of the room and laughed. "And I still haven't put those chessmen away! You see, that's called thinking ahead!"

Outside, Sarah and Nathan walked hand in hand across town to a bridge over a running stream at the town's edge. Tossing small stones into the water as they sat on the edge of the creek, Sarah said, "I don't care where we live or if we ever leave Loveland. I don't care if we're snowed in for months or it gets too hot to step outside. I married you because I love you and wanted to live my life with you, no matter where that is or what you do. I like to think you married me with the same kind of thoughts..."

"Of course, I did! I still do."

"Then stop making me feel like I'm not enough to make you happy. You are my happiness, not where we live or what I wear. All that material stuff is nothing, but being married to the person you love is everything. We don't have a lot, but in my opinion, we have it all in one another. We get by just fine, and we have no big debts. My goodness, Nathan, we are blessed beyond what our righteousness deserves. Let's enjoy it; what do you say?"

Nathan smiled. "Deal. And you're right, we are blessed. Sometimes it's just hard to see when I think of everything."

"I know I like to tease you about thinking ahead when we play chess, but sometimes it's good to be content with right now, because it isn't so bad. I have you, and you have me. And look at how beautiful the stars are up here. I can sit here relaxing to the sound of the creek while looking at the stars with the love of my life. I don't know how it could get better than that. I kind of think this is pretty close to paradise, myself."

"I think you might be right, my love. You might be right." He smiled at Sarah and then kissed her. "I sure love you, Sarah."

1
___

Loveland, Oregon. 1883

THE LOVELAND BANK was the only brick building in the mountain community of Loveland, Oregon. The town nestled in the northern foothills of the Wallowa Mountains. Loveland wasn't more than a logging camp just a few years before, but then gold had been found. Now it was a growing community of miners, lumbermen and a few entrepreneurs coming to make a living in the wild country of Northeastern Oregon.

Jared Bogle was such an entrepreneur. He had left his position at a bank in Spokane for the opportunity of a lifetime: to open the first bank and assay office in the new boomtown of Loveland. He hoped to make a fortune on the gold rush, but he found the lumbermen to be more in need of his bank than the miners who rushed to sell what little gold they found. The gold rush wasn't quite the rush in Loveland it was rumored to be two years before, when he first heard about it and sold everything to come make his fortune. There was gold about, but the rush appeared to be on the other side of the mountain range in Jessup County.

Just when Jared was ready to close his business, take his losses and go back to the city, a broke miner came in to sell out and get what little he could out of his gold claim. He didn't have much gold on his claim, but it did have an abundance of copper. Copper wasn't what he was looking for though. Like most of the uneducated miners, he continued to toss copper ore aside as rubbish in his search for gold.

Jared, on the other hand, knew copper was a valuable mineral that hadn't yet taken the place of gold; but he knew it would eventually. He bought the claim for a minimal price and soon had it evaluated by a geologist. The findings of the geologist in the hard rock were favorable. Jared began planning to invest in a mining operation to pull out the valuable ore before anyone else caught on to the fortune to be made in copper.

Loveland had turned out to be a gold mine for Jared after all, because he was in a favorable position to swindle other broke miners out of claims that showed high amounts of copper. If everything went well for him, he could become the copper king of the Wallowa Mountains and make millions off the ignorance of miners starving for gold.

Jared sat behind the counter of his bank writing a professional letter to W.T. Wittman, the senior partner of Seattle's Whitman and Harvey Ship Builders Corporation. He was respectfully inviting W.T. Wittman to invest in his mining venture. Jared needed capital to purchase the equipment and manpower to begin to pull the tonnage of copper and iron ore out of the mountain. Undoubtedly, the start-up would be expensive, perhaps well over two million dollars to build the roads, a stamp mill, hire the experts to run the machinery and purchase tools to break into the mountain and follow the veins of copper. The geologist had given him very promising news of the potential amount of copper in the mountain but finding investors willing to risk their money to help him extract it from the mountain was a tricky business and involved using the right numbers and the right words. The fact was, Jared didn't know the first thing about mining. He knew numbers, financial numbers, and if he could persuade a few investors to invest, he could then approach some engineers and hire a capable manager to do the rest.

The bank door opened, and Jared looked up to see a placer miner walk in. He was of medium height, a lean man wearing blue canvas pants and a dirty gray shirt with suspenders over his filthy underclothes. The man's shoulder-length black hair was unkempt, as was his long graying black beard. He wore a brown felt hat that had seen better days; its rim was bent in multiple ways. The man wore a gun-belt that holstered a .44 double action Colt. A large knife with a deer-horn handle was strapped to the other side of his hip. In his left hand, he carried a leather pouch.

Jared stood up with interest. Usually, the only reason placer miners came into his place of business was to sell their gold or their claim. "Good morning, sir. How can I help you?"

The man looked at Jared with dark eyes. There was no friendliness in them whatsoever. "Selling gold," he said simply. He set the pouch on the counter. It was closed tightly by threaded leather strings. "There's sixty-three point four ounces in there. I've weighed it twice. Given the gold price is twenty-three dollars and sixty-six cents an ounce, you owe me one thousand, five hundred dollars and forty-four cents."

Jared raised his eyebrows. "Sixty-three ounces! Most

men are happy to find one ounce around here anymore. Where in the world did you find all of that?"

The man looked at Jared for a moment. "You need to weigh it, but in front of me; I know how much is in there."

Jared nodded. "Of course. Let's go over here to the table and have a seat." He walked behind the counter to a table at one end of the counter along the wall. A scale sat on its center between two chairs so that both parties could witness the scale. Stacked along the wall were a few leather-bound ledgers and other books and a pen and ink bottle. Jared sat in a chair and waved at the other. "Have a seat."

The miner had carried his pouch and laid it beside the scale as he sat down. His gaze had not left Jared the entire time.

Jared pulled out a ledger, opened it up, dipped the pen into the ink bottle and then wrote the day's date down on the ledger. "What's your name?"

"Octavius Clark."

"Where are you from, Mister Clark?" he asked as he wrote the name down in the ledger.

"Tennessee, originally."

"Age?"

"Fifty-two or so," he answered, sounding irritated by the questions.

"Are you married?"

"What the hell's that have to do with selling my gold?" he asked sharply.

Jared shrugged. "I'm sorry. I'm just filling out the paper-work. The state took a census last year and changed the ledgers. They want to know who's who, where they're at, and how much gold is being found from where. So, the question is, are you married?"

Octavius answered unpleasantly. "No."

Jared looked at him. "Do you have your claim registration number or any documentation?"

Octavius shook his head. "Nope, my papers all got ruined in the river."

"Where is your claim located? I have an official claims register; I can look up your claim." He reached over and grabbed a larger book.

"I'm up on Juniper Creek," Octavius said.

Jared flipped through the pages of mine claims filed with the state of Oregon; he searched through the names alphabetically and found one claim belonging to Octavius Clark, but it was an older claim on the Metolius River in Central Oregon from five years before. There didn't appear to be an active claim on Juniper Creek for Octavius Clark—or any other claim, for that matter. He turned the book toward Octavius. "Is this your claim here on the Metolius River?"

Octavius nodded.

Jared frowned and turned the book back around to look at it. "They don't have you listed as having any other claim. Did you file a claim on Juniper Creek?"

Octavius nodded slowly.

"When did you file?"

"Last April, I'm guessing. Not long ago. Does it really matter? I'm here to sell my gold, not discuss papers," he said irritably.

Jared flipped to the inside front cover and looked at its date. "This is current from May. Your claim should be in here."

Octavius shook his head in frustration. "Well, apparently, it's not. Are you still buying my gold or not?" he asked.

"Hmm," Jared said, closing the state register. He put it aside and looked back at his business ledger. "All right, I won't argue with a man with gold. However, they do like to know how much is being found where. So, you're up on Juniper Creek. Where are you up there...about where?" he asked and then noticed the cold and fed-up eyes of Octavius staring at him. He added quickly, "It don't really matter, I suppose. Let's weigh your gold." He reached over, grabbed the pouch and untied it. He spoke as he poured the gold slowly onto the scale tray. "There's been some trouble up there, I understand, hasn't there?"

"There's a murderer out there somewhere. He killed my partner when I was out hunting us up some dinner just two days ago. We kept our gold buried under a rock, or I wouldn't have any today. I have had enough, mister. I am cashing out and going home. I buried my partner and came here," Octavius explained.

Jared looked at Octavius, stunned. "Did you tell the sheriff? My word, he needs to go track that killer down! I know there's been what...? Seven murders that I know about, and no one's yet had a single look at the killer. Did you see him at all?"

Octavius shook his head. "No, he was long gone by time I got back. I couldn't track him because he went into the river, and I don't know if he went up stream or down."

"I am sorry to hear that," Jared said as he gently tapped the bag to get all the gold onto the tray. "You know Matt Bannister has a new U.S. Marshal's office in Branson now? You should let him know about your friend. Something has to be done." He set the bag down and looked at the good-sized pile of gold dust and nuggets of various sizes. "Wow, you found the Comstock lode of Juniper Creek! Where is your claim at, if I may ask? If you're not going back, maybe you'll sell it to me." He carefully weighed the gold under the watchful eyes of Octavius.

"It should weigh sixty-three point four ounces," Octavius said in a matter-of-fact tone.

"It does precisely. I was a little concerned about your scale not being calibrated correctly, but it agrees with mine; sixty-three point four ounces precisely."

Octavius spoke pointedly, "I'm not a fool. If you multiply that weight by twenty-three dollars and sixty-six cents, we will also come out at the same price, too."

Jared sighed. "That is the U.S. Gold price. I buy gold at the European gold price, which is eighteen dollars an ounce. That would still give you quite a sum for your gold; well over a thousand dollars. Do we have a deal?"

Octavius took a deep breath. "I just told you, I'm not a fool. The European gold price is twenty dollars and ninety-six cents an ounce. You're already trying to steal what's mine."

The coldness in Octavius' eyes sent a chill down Jared's spine.

Octavius continued, "If you want to make a profit, that's fine, but we'll split the difference. I'll sell it to you for nineteen dollars and thirty-five cents an ounce. You'll make just over a dollar thirty an ounce. I won't go any lower. You tried to cheat me, and I don't like that. So here is my deal: give me my money and I will walk out of here without hurting you."

"What?" Jared asked with surprise. His eyes widened in fear. Octavius, on the other hand, remained as calm as a still pond; however, his eyes appeared to be as cruel as the devil's own.

"You're buying my gold for the price I just set. You shouldn't have tried to cheat me, but that was your choice. You're still making a profit, so go get my money."

Jared nodded nervously. "It's just business, I didn't mean to..."

"Do we have a deal?" Octavius asked in a threatening tone. "I'm not robbing you, but I won't be robbed by you, either." He appeared as threatening as an explosive just waiting to unleash its power.

"We do," Jared agreed.

"I want a bill of sale for one thousand, two hundred and twenty-six dollars and ninety-seven cents. You can double-check my figures if you want, but I am right."

"I will get your money," Jared said with no pleasure in his voice. He was the only assayer, well...banker in the local area, and usually he could get away with undercutting the sellers without any trouble at all. The fact was, most of the placer miners would settle for twelve dollars an ounce, as long as they had enough money to get drunk on.

Octavius Clark wasn't like most of the others Jared had dealt with. He knew precisely how much gold he had and its worth on the U.S. and European markets. Octavius was also a man who simply scared the hell out of Jared. Octavius' eyes were so dark, he couldn't tell where the retina ended, and the pupil began. They were dark, cold and unnerving, and they followed Jared everywhere he went. Jared had a suspicion Octavius might be the most dangerous man he had ever met. He had said very little, but his mere presence was ominous enough to make Jared very uneasy.

He wrote a receipt for 63.4 ounces of gold at nineteen dollars and thirty-five cents an ounce. The sum was precisely as Octavius had said. Jared looked at Octavius in wonder at his ability to calculate the figures so accurately without doing the arithmetic.

Octavius smiled slightly and nodded, as if he knew precisely what Jared was thinking.

2

Deuce McKenna sat on his horse just outside of Loveland, near a tree line, looking at a solidly built wood plank bridge that crossed a shallow creek bordering the town. Just across the small bridge on the left side of the road was the bank, the only brick building in the small mountain community. Quite honestly, it looked out of place, it was so far into the woods. Deuce figured it was made of brick for two reasons: one, to represent security; and the other reason was to protect it in case of a fire.

Loveland was in the northern foothills of the Wallowa Mountains in a wide timber-filled bowl surrounded by tall rolling ridges circling the town. A forest fire could whip down the mountain quicker than a spring river, burn Loveland to ashes and whip right back up the other side of the next ridge, leaving nothing behind except the bank's brick walls. The roof was made of cedar shingles, as were most of the roofs in the small community.

Four other businesses occupied the main street; all were roughhewn board buildings with few windows. The town didn't look like much, but it had a few blocks of forty or so small cabins made of either clapboard or small logs for the lumbermen to live in. There was no school, no church or any other social organizations; there were simply a mercantile, a bank, a blacksmith and a saloon combined with a restaurant. Loveland was rumored to be a flourishing little town recently, or so Deuce and his friends had heard, but now that they had gotten their first look at the place, they weren't sure they believed what they'd been told. They'd heard it was small, but it seemed to be nothing more than a little logging camp with a nice bank.

"It looks too quiet," Pick Lawson said. Pick was in his mid-forties, of medium height and build, with short brown hair under his grey hat. Pick was normally clean shaven, except for a few days' growth of stubble on his face. His nose was slightly curved from once being broken, and his blue eyes appeared dull and empty of life. Pick's oblong face was weathered from a tougher kind of life and bore a long scar down his left cheek from a knife attack many years before. His eyes keenly scanned the empty streets for any sign of life. For being a lumber town, Loveland was eerily quiet. Not a sound came from the town or the woods around it.

Deuce nodded as he tied a sweat-stained white kerchief around his neck. "Yeah, well it's apparently not a bustling town. Listen up, boys. We'll pull our masks on once we get there. Make sure you have your bandana ready to pull up. Karl, remember to bring the ball of twine. I don't know how many folks might be in there. We will ride in and tie our horses at the bank. Brent," he said to his nephew, "you stay with the horses and keep watch. If anything happens, you shoulder that Winchester and cover us as we come outside," he said pointedly. "No shooting unless we *absolutely have to*. Does everyone understand that? We don't need a gunfight. Let's just go in, get what money we can and get out of there."

Deuce McKenna was the oldest of the four riders, in his forty-sixth year of life. He was a tall man with a square build and broad shoulders. He had short, light brown hair under his hat, but it was getting long enough that it covered his mid-ear. Deuce had a round face that appeared to connect to his shoulders via a short neck. He had pockmarks on his face from a severe childhood bout of chickenpox. To hide a large number of pox marks, he wore a full beard to cover some of them. Deuce had deeply inset green eyes that appeared a little too small for the size of his head.

"Uncle Dick," Brent Boyle asked, "what if the sheriff steps out for a morning stroll? Should I shoot him or... what?" he asked with a shrug. Brent was nineteen, fired up and anxious to begin a life of crime. He had brown hair that touched his neck and was of average height, had a lean body and no facial hair. On all accounts, Brent was simply average. Except maybe for the fact that he carried a double reversed gun set he liked to flaunt. He was Deuce's nephew, but unlike his uncle's wiser-aged eyes, Brent's brown eyes flickered with youthful vibrancy and mischief.

Deuce looked at him seriously. "You don't shoot at all, unless it's absolutely necessary," he said sharply. He looked at Karl Digsby. "Are you ready, Karl?"

Karl nodded. Thirty-four years old, Karl was the tallest of the four men. He stood over six feet and had a narrow build. He sported short, light brown hair and a clean-shaven face, except for a light blondish-colored mustache that looked more like peach fuzz than a man's mustache. Karl had rather large blue eyes that seemed a trifle too big for his long, oval face. The one thing that stood out about Karl was that he always looked troubled and under a heavy burden. He was a quiet man, who smiled very little and minded his own business. Like Brent, Karl was a novice criminal, and this was his first bank robbery. Karl appeared more nervous and less assured than Brent did, though.

"Let's go," Deuce said and gently nudged his horse forward. They rode together across the bridge and stopped outside the bank. All four dismounted. Deuce, Karl and Pick tied their horses to a horizontal hitching post, then pulled their kerchiefs up over the bridges of their noses to hide their faces.

Brent stood beside his horse and rested his arms on the saddle. He didn't pull his kerchief up over his nose, but he did keep his face hidden by the saddle as much as he could to watch for anyone coming toward them. His two .44 Colts were secured in his holsters, but his Winchester was ready to be pulled out of its scabbard at a moment's notice. His heart beat with adrenaline and excitement, while his uncle and the others quickly stepped into the bank.

"Don't move!" Deuce yelled as he entered the bank. He held his revolver on the bank teller who stood at a small table counting out cash money to a miner selling his gold; the gold was still on the scale. The bank teller froze in disbelief as he stared at Deuce.

Karl pointed a shotgun at both men at the table as he approached it. "Don't move!" he warned in a loud voice. His adrenaline ran higher than he had ever felt before, and his fear had changed to fierce determination to finish the job and get away before the town could be alerted to their presence. Deuce walked to the table and grabbed the cash Jared had been counting. "I'll take that, and any more you have in your safe. Open it, or you won't live to spend another dime!" he ordered.

Jared stared at the covered face of Deuce and suddenly became aware of the fact that he was more afraid of the masked stranger than he was of Octavius Clark. Jared moved away from the table toward the safe without saying a word; there was no amount of money worth dying for. He reached the safe and began turning the combination lock. "Please, don't kill me." He begged; his hands shook violently.

Deuce said harshly, "Get the safe open, and you'll be fine!"

Octavius curled his lips with his eyes on Deuce. "That's my money! I'd appreciate you giving it back to me."

Deuce looked back at Octavius with an unconcerned expression. "Not anymore! Pick, scoop up that gold over there, too." Deuce looked back at Jared as he tried to calm himself to open the safe again. "We'll take any other gold you have, too. Now open the door!" he snarled at Jared.

"Dang it!" Jared cursed as he had messed up the combination again with his shaking hands. He immediately began spinning the rotary combination dial again.

"Hurry up!" Deuce demanded, putting his revolver to Jared's head. Jared began whimpering while he focused on the numbers.

Pick had holstered his pistol and moved over to the table to get the gold.

Octavius spoke with his eyes burning into Pick, "If you touch my gold, I will kill you!"

"Watch him," Pick said to Karl as he reached down to grab the leather pouch in which to put the gold.

"Last warning," Octavius said in a strangely calm voice.

"Shut up!" Karl demanded. He swung the stock of the shotgun downwards onto the back of Octavius' head. It connected with a solid blow; Octavius fell out of his chair to the floor. Karl hit him in the head again when Octavius tried to sit up and draw his revolver. The second blow to the head left him unconscious on the floor. "Get the gold! I'll take care of him," Karl said and bent down to take Octavius' revolver. He then pulled out a ball of twine, cut off a two-foot-long length and tied Octavius' hands behind his back. Blood dripped from the back of Octavius' head.

Finally, Jared got the safe's door opened and filled a cloth bag with all the cash money he had in there, along with dollar coins. He handed the bag to Deuce along with a metal container about three inches tall by six inches long, which was what he kept the gold in. "That's all I have," he said honestly.

"I got it all," Pick said about the gold on the table while he tied the leather straps of the pouch together.

Deuce waved Jared toward the front of the counter. "You guys tie him up, too, and make sure they're both gagged well and hidden behind the counter. Let's get going," he said and pulled down his kerchief before he walked outside carrying the money and gold. "What's going on out here?" he asked Brent as he opened his saddlebag to put the money inside.

Brent shook his head. "Absolutely nothing. I haven't seen a thing. Not one person. How much did we get?"

Deuce smiled slightly. "We did all right; better than I expected a few moments ago. But now we should get going, and fast. This place will get lively just as soon as they figure out we took their money. Get in the saddle." He said and walked to the bank's door; he opened it and peeked inside. "Let's go, Cass and Jesse! And you can tell your bank friends that the Sperry Helms Gang is back in town! I'm Morton Sperry, and I'll kill you if a posse comes after us. Understand me, fella?"

Jared shook his head quickly from the floor behind the counter, "Of course, sir!"

A moment later, all four men rode out of town unnoticed.

3

The Loveland Sheriff, Jack Schwartz, stood in the bank with a handful of other townsmen, questioning Jared and Octavius about the robbery. Jack Schwartz wasn't an experienced lawman; he was, in fact, a fifty-five-year-old miner, who volunteered for the sheriff's position when no one else wanted it. His gold claim had little to no gold, and he didn't want to work in the timber-falling industry, so he had no choice, if he wanted to survive the winter, than to take the sheriff's position when it came open. Loveland had never had a sheriff, but if they wanted to become a township, rather than remain a logging camp, they needed a sheriff.

Jack Schwartz had jumped on the opportunity and the wage that came with it. For a year now, it had paid him enough to survive on and, the truth was, he didn't have to work all that hard to earn his twenty dollars a month. Other than calming down some of his drunken friends in the saloon on a Saturday night, his job was merely a position to be filled. Building a sheriff's office was in the works, but so far, the fledgling township didn't have the finances to construct a sheriff's office on the main street. Jack's home, a small cabin off the main street by about sixty yards, was the sheriff's office. A poorly-painted homemade sign announced the house as the "Sheriff's Office".

Most days, Jack could sleep in and never leave his cabin, and no one really cared. However, in recent months, there had been at least seven known murders of placer miners in the surrounding area. Of the two murders Jack had investigated, he could not track the murderer or, in truth, see a single sign of him. He had no idea what he was looking for. He was thrilled when the new U.S. Marshal's office opened in Branson. Jack wrote to Matt Bannister about the murders outside of Loveland, but the marshal wrote back and told him to contact his county sheriff for assistance. The problem was the sheriff of Joseph County, named Henry Oswald, had absolutely no respect for Jack and belittled him every chance he got. What made it more humiliating was that Henry did it in front of his deputies and in front of Jack's only deputy, his own son, Dustin.

Dustin didn't have any experience either, but the job did bring in an extra twelve dollars a month. Between the two of them, they lived about as well as anyone in Loveland for doing as little as they did. Jack wished the telegraph wire would make its way to Loveland sometime, because now he would have to ride fifteen miles to Huntsville to let the county sheriff know about their bank having been robbed. He hated the idea of talking with Henry Oswald only to get belittled for his lack of knowledge again.

"So, their faces were covered, huh?" Jack asked again. "I reckon they'll go through Huntsville on their way back down the mountain."

Octavius sat in a chair by the table, holding a wet rag to the back of his head. The bleeding had stopped, but it felt good to hold a cool rag on that knot. His head ached as he stared at the sheriff with annoyance. "There were four of them."

"No. Jared said there were three."

"There are four sets of horse tracks. I went out and looked when I was cut loose. I can track them down easily enough and get our money back, but I need some bullets and supplies from the mercantile. Can I charge it to your account until I bring back our money?" Octavius asked Jared.

"Sure," Jared answered, "but don't you want someone to go with you? There are four of them, you said, and they are hard men. I could tell," Jared said, looking at Jack. "It was the Sperry Helms Gang."

Octavius stood up and dropped the rag on the table. "No, I don't need help," he said simply and put on his old hat before starting for the door.

"Wait a minute," Jack said, stopping Octavius. "Wait for me to form a posse, and we'll all go. It won't take long." He turned to one of the men standing there. "Go get my son, Guy Milton, Levin Barker, the Pierce brothers and Mike Hall. Tell 'em they're officially my posse, and tell 'em to hurry up and get here."

"Old Milt's bogeyed up his back recently, and Levin is taking a load of logs to Huntsville," the man replied nervously.

Jack shook his head. "Well, go get the others. They'll do fine. But tell them to hurry."

Octavius said caustically, "I have no interest in your posse! You guys go your way, and I'll go mine."

"Now, wait a second," Jack said. "I need you to lead us so we can capture them."

"I'm not leading your posse anywhere! But I *am* going after my money."

Jack took a deep breath. "You will lead us, Mister Clark, or you'll find yourself in our jail," Jack said as a threat. He hoped Octavius didn't know they didn't actually have a jail. He continued speaking before anyone could say anything. "There won't be any supplies bought on Jared's account if you don't lead us. That, I promise you. So, your only option is to become our tracker and lead us, and then we'll get your money back. That, or stay in jail while we go."

Octavius glared at Jack and gritted his teeth angrily. Then he sighed. "Fine but hurry up!"

Jack laughed slightly at his own cunning. "All right." He turned to his friend, "Go get those guys, and tell 'em to hurry!"

4

Deuce McKenna led the others out of town at a quick gallop to put some distance between them and any likely posse that would come after them from Loveland. He knew well the only road leading in and out of Loveland connected straight to Huntsville. There were few connecting roads, and there were fifteen miles of wild mountainous land and very little in between, except placer mining claims along the creeks and river. Huntsville, on the other hand, was the Joseph County seat, with a growing population and the county sheriff's office. They had stayed the night before the bank robbery in Huntsville and had spoken to a sheriff's deputy in the saloon about the Loveland sheriff. He had heard from the man's own lips that the Loveland sheriff was an incompetent fool with a homemade badge.

The deputy had laughed as he talked about Jack Schwartz and his son, Dustin, who was the Loveland deputy. They were considered a joke in Huntsville. That was all Deuce needed to know in order to be confident that he could escape any Loveland posse. He also knew there was no telegraph going to Loveland, so any news of the robbery would take at least two hours to reach Huntsville. It was the Joseph County Sheriff's office that scared him, and the very competent sheriff, Henry Oswald.

Deuce pulled back the reins to slow his mount to a stop when they reached the solidly built bridge over the Antioch River. The riverbed was fairly wide and covered with river rock. The water flow itself was low, but it would be easy to lose even a good tracker in the riverbed. Deuce turned his horse off the road into the dry grass and said, "Follow me."

His three men followed him into the tall grass and slowed as he came to the edge of the river. Deuce walked his horse gingerly down a steep, four-foot bank, before making the horse lunge onto the thick rounded river rocks on the dry side of the riverbed. He turned back to watch his friends hesitate to make the plunge down the bank.

"My horse ain't that thirsty yet, Uncle Dick," Brent said from the bank. "But I am, so how about we get into Huntsville and buy ourselves a drink? I know I'd like to grab hold of Mary again tonight. I kind of like her," he added to his new friend Karl Digsby. "She's no Christine, but she'll do for tonight, huh?"

Karl nodded without much interest.

"We're not going back to Huntsville," Deuce said as he watched Pick take his horse down the steep bank onto the rocks. Karl followed Pick with no further hesitation.

"What do you mean, we're not going back?" Brent asked. "I pert' near have Mary convinced I want to marry her, Uncle Dick. I don't, but it doesn't hurt to let her think so. It might save me a few bits to a dollar."

Deuce looked at his nephew, who sat his horse atop of the riverbank. "Hurry up, Brent."

"Well, where are we going then? There's nothing upriver

or down, so where are you going? Like I said, I'd like to see Mary again, myself."

"Brent, get your ass down here and let's go!" Deuce said sharply, losing patience with his nephew.

"Fine, fine," Brent said and kicked his horse. It lunged the four feet onto the rocks and stumbled over loose gravel, before catching itself and coming to a halt.

Pick yelled irritably at Brent, "You don't jump your horse onto rock, you idiot! You're lucky it didn't break a leg or tear something! If your horse gets hurt, you put us all in jeopardy! Do you not have any common sense? Don't do that again!" He turned to Deuce and spoke just as tetchily, "You know as well as I do that these rocks pose a threat to our horses! So, what is it you have planned?"

"We can't go back through Huntsville, so we need to cut across the mountains." Deuce said simply.

"What?" Brent cried out.

Pick cursed bitterly. "Are you kidding me? That's what...? Eighty miles? You want to cut across eighty miles of unexplored wilderness without any supplies? Look at those mountains, Deuce! And you want to cross them?" He pointed at the towering mountains that rose high above them.

"What?" Brent asked again with great reluctance in his voice. "We could be out there for days! We could get lost and die out there! We don't have any food, whiskey or women! We don't even have a tent, Uncle Dick!"

Deuce shook his head. "It's eighty miles going around the mountains! If we cut across them, it's maybe twenty miles, twenty-five at most, until we drop right down into Jessup County and Branson. It's the shortest and safest way home."

"We could eat steak tonight if we go to Huntsville," Brent

offered as a temptation to his uncle. He knew how much his Uncle enjoyed a good steak.

Deuce looked at his nephew. "Brent, stop whining. I swear, you're worse than a woman. There will be food all around us. It's summer, so there'll be berries and deer. Heck, we might even have venison tonight. But we need to go now."

Pick exhaled with frustration and then said heatedly, "I don't like this! I don't like the idea of cutting across fifty miles of who knows what!"

"We will cut fifty miles off our journey, at least, by doing this, and they won't catch us! But we will stand out like pigs in a cattle herd if we go back through Huntsville. Trust me, guys, if Lewis and Clark could navigate two thousand miles of unexplored land and survive, then we can do twenty miles, huh?" Deuce questioned. "The day's passing us by as we stand here. The harder we ride the faster we will get back home."

"Mary's not in the woods," Brent quipped as they started riding carefully over the river rock.

Karl answered Brent with a small smirk. "After we get home, I might come back here and go visit Mary first. I do believe her loyalties are to the first man to flash some cash."

Brent smiled. "Karl, while you're explaining to your wife why you're home late, I will be taking my share and already be halfway back. That's the great thing about being me. I don't have to explain a dang thing to any woman! But you do." He laughed.

Karl shrugged and frowned. "Yeah, that's true."

"Well, boys," Deuce said cheerfully. "All we have to do is get home and we have it made. And best of all, the blame will fall on Morton and Jessie. We have it made, boys!"

Pick wasn't so cheerful. "How about we get home before we celebrate too much, huh?"

5

Adam Bannister moved at an agonizingly slow and careful pace as he climbed up through the thick Douglas fir trees covering the steep incline of the ridge. The sun barely contacted the ground, leaving barren soil, except for a few small grasses, thick ferns and an inch of fir needles on the forest floor. Broken limbs and fallen trees littered the climb but gave Adam a place to sit and rest his weary legs after climbing so far up the mountain's side.

The morning birds chirped pleasantly but were aware of the human intruder in a place where probably no man had been since Adam had made the same climb one year earlier. He looked uphill and saw he had a way to go before he reached the plateau halfway up the massive mountain. He was climbing one of the taller peaks along the southern edge of the Wallowa Mountains. It was a large mountain with a rock cliff face that domed on the top like a monarch's crown. It was easily recognizable and known throughout the valley as Windsor Ridge, the only dome-shaped monstrosity in a long line of towering jagged peaks that made up the entire Wallowa Mountains. Adam had no interest in climbing to the peak of Windsor Ridge. The meadow, halfway up, was where he would find the herd of elk he hunted. It was summer, and the large herds of elk roaming over the Wallowa Mountains went deeper and higher into the mountains to enjoy the rich grass and cool waters of the high country. In the winter, snow drove the large herds lower into the foothills and valley. An easier access into the meadow; a game trail leading around the steepest grade of the mountain, went up the eastern side of the mountain. The grade there was more easily negotiable. The trail remained steep, but it wasn't as grinding and strenuous as the climb Adam was making. It was an exhausting climb, but the reward was that it leveled off at the center of the meadow with good brush and tree cover to keep him concealed. It was there where Adam had shot an elk every year he'd come to this hidden meadow to hunt.

He spent a day and a half traveling from his home outside of Willow Falls, in Jessup County, north to the Wallowa Mountains for this hunt.

Of course, he didn't need to travel so far to shoot an elk, but it was a yearly tradition Adam and his Uncle Luther had made for the last twenty years. Before that, Luther and his father would come to this same mountain meadow to hunt and smoke meat for the winter.

Luther's father, Luke Fasana, had been a trapper in the early days with the Hudson's Bay Company. He had found the meadow while trapping in the Wallowa Mountain range. About that same time, he'd found a bride from the Nez Perce tribe named Tatiana. Coming back to this meadow always reminded Luke of his youth and the excitement of falling in love with his young Indian bride. They had spent their first summer together in the very same opening of grass amidst the tall Douglas fir where Luther and Adam set up their camp every year. It had become a tradition that Luther and Adam loved and looked forward to all year long.

The ride had been long, but once they arrived at their camp, the work was just beginning. Being an annual event, they left the sixteen-pole skeleton of their teepee standing through the winter. After checking the leather strapping that tied the top of the poles together, they unrolled the canvas skin of the teepee and secured it to the poles, creating a twelve-foot-tall and twenty-foot-wide teepee for drying their meat in.

They spent the remainder of the day fashioning a rack of tied sticks to lay the meat over. The rack took up most of the teepee and was built as high as they could reach. It stood on a two-foot block of wood they used as a chopping block as well. The rack they framed was nearly ten-feet tall and stretched across the width of the teepee. It was an A-frame built within the conical shape of the teepee with eight poles creating the basic frame, with smaller poles freshly cut horizontally and then vertically to create a series of racks to lay the meat on. Underneath was a four-foot open space for the two men to stay in, if need be.

The fire pit was small with large river rock encircling it. The fire would be small and made from damp oak and green-apple wood to fill the teepee with smoke. The work of cutting fresh branches and tying them together was tedious, but it had to be done. Luther had learned how to dry meat in the sun, how to make pemmican the Indian way, and how to smoke it in a smokehouse, as his father and other white men did. But Luther found it worked best for him and his taste to make a larger rack that could hold a lot of meat and dry it in the smoke of a teepee.

In August, the teepee would be hot enough, but when he added a slow-burning fire, the meat dried faster and more completely than any other way. The dryer the jerky, the longer it lasted. With the salt and other spices Luther rubbed on his jerky, it just couldn't be beat. Every summer he intended on making enough to last his and Adam's family all winter long.

There were two kinds of people in the world: those who enjoyed beef and other domestically raised meat, and those who had a taste for wild game. Luther and Adam both preferred wild game and looked forward to leaving the world behind and go into the wilderness to get it. Beef, pork and poultry were the common sources of meat sold in every butcher shop, restaurant and inn across not just Jessup County, but everywhere a man went anymore. Most folks in homes outside of town ate their own stock. However, even men like Luther's two sons, who had grown up hunting, preferred going to the butcher shop over going to the woods to kill their own game. Luther wouldn't complain about beef ranchers though. His brother-in-law, Charlie Ziegler; and his nephew, Adam, both raised beef to sell to those butcher shops and beyond. Even so, Adam preferred a good bite of venison over pork, or an elk steak to a slab of beef.

However, now in his sixties, Luther's knees ached more than they once had and limited his mobility as far as climbing up mountain sides went. His days of scaling that steep climb to the meadow above were over. Now his duty was to wait until he heard a shot or two, and then ride his mule up a game trail that circled the eastern side of the mountain on a gentler slope and enter the meadow from its far east corner. He would lead a pack mule and Adam's horse with him, set some wolf traps, and return to camp to prepare meat.

The year before, Luther had stayed in camp and killed a doe with his bow while Adam made his way up the mountain. Luther's weapon of choice was his cherished long bow with metal-tipped arrows. He kept it close at hand in case another doe walked curiously close to camp. It was early, and Luther sat by the fire, drinking a cup of coffee while he waited. He looked up at the steep wall of thick trees that blocked his view of the rest of the mountain. Somewhere in the thickness of trees, Adam climbed alone for the second year in a row.

As Adam neared the top of the steep ridge, the tall Douglas fir gave way to a thicket of leaf-covered birch trees that dropped down into a wide, oblong-shaped meadow. The meadow was a large area of thick green grass that sloped gently toward a small mountain lake set up against the gray granite wall rising seventy feet or so before the Douglas fir trees continued to the crest of Windsor's Ridge. The granite wall continued across the meadow, except for the eastern ridge, where the ground and slope to the top was intact. Surrounding the meadow was an inner circle of birch trees about a hundred yards wide that acted as a barrier between the Douglas fir trees and the meadow.

The country was rough, but incredibly beautiful. Beauty wasn't why Adam climbed halfway up Windsor ridge, though; he was hunting the large herd of elk that made the hidden meadow their summer home.

Adam rested quietly, excitement building in him. Most men hunted for necessity; Adam enjoyed the hunt. He enjoyed the challenge of tracking wild game in its own environment and getting close enough to make a kill. To make it more of a challenge, he carried the first rifle he was ever given. His grandfather, Luke Fasana had given him a Hawken .50 caliber muzzle-loading rifle. His grandfather had given it to Adam on his tenth birthday, which was now thirty-four years ago. He owned more modern long guns, but the Hawken was still his favorite rifle to hunt with.

He would get one shot, and one shot only, with the Hawken to kill his chosen elk. If he missed, he might not get another chance to shoot one, as the elk would scatter and might not be seen again unless he tracked them. Adam had a Henry rifle in camp that shot well and held six cartridges. He could fire that gun rapidly enough, but he thrived on the challenge of hunting with his Hawken cap and ball, like his grandfather used to do.

As quietly as he could, he leaned his rifle against a tree, opened his powder bag and measured the black powder, grabbed his rifle and poured powder down the barrel. He took a half-ounce ball and tamped it tightly in the barrel as quietly as he could. He placed a cap into position and lowered the hammer carefully. He would be concealed within the birch and underbrush for about a hundred yards or so before he would have a clear view of the meadow.

Adam cautiously stepped forward and paid close attention to the breeze, but there wasn't any to speak of. The only things he noticed was the sun at his back shining through the leaves and the birds singing on this beautiful summer morning. He knew there were bound to be a few deer and elk lying in the shade of the trees, but at this time in the morning, he expected to see most of them grazing in the grass close to the lake.

He moved slowly and listened to every sound while stepping lightly in his moccasins. Suddenly, he froze. A cow elk with a spring calf walked out of the brush forty yards ahead of him. He didn't move a single muscle except to get closer to the tree beside him. He watched while they crossed in front of him without noticing him.

After a moment, Adam took a deep breath and began to move forward again, cautious of any movement around him. Slowly, he worked his way among the birch trees and stopped ten feet from the open meadow. He positioned himself next to a tree with a solid branch at the right height to lay his rifle upon. Once he was situated comfortably and had a good view of the meadow, he waited. There were quite a few cow elk and deer grazing peacefully in there, along with a few smaller bull elk. Adam would take a big cow elk if he had to, but he wanted a big bull. Rather than shoot the first elk in sight, he patiently waited and held as still as he could so as not to be noticed.

Forty minutes later, his patience was rewarded, as a massive bull with tall and prominent antlers walked out from the trees on the other side of the meadow. Adam watched it and slowly pulled back the hammer of his Hawken until it clicked. The click of the hammer seemed to echo through the trees, despite his efforts to keep it muffled and quiet. A deer fifty yards away from him lifted its head and looked alertly in his direction.

Ignoring the deer, Adam looked down the sights of his rifle and placed the bead on the big bull's heart. He pulled the trigger before the alert deer could spook his elk. Powder smoke cleared just in time for Adam to watch every elk and deer in the meadow disappear into the trees after the explosive percussion pierced the peaceful silence. Adam smiled at the sight of the big bull lying in the grass a hundred yards or more away, twitching its legs as it died. Adam had hit his target again. He seldom missed with his aging rifle.

Setting the Hawken over his neck and shoulder by its leather strap, Adam walked out into the meadow like a conquering soldier. It took him a few minutes to get to his elk, but when he did, he laid his rifle and gun-belt on the ground. The mature bull weighed at least 1,500 pounds; it was the biggest one he'd shot in recent years. He pulled off his knitted sweater and long-sleeved cotton shirt before he made his cut to clean the massive animal.

Adam had learned long ago to remove his shirts before he cleaned out the viscera from the cavity of the elk. Adam held his knife and cut the skin from the anus of the elk up and around the belly in a circle to expose the large stomach, and then continued cutting the skin straight up past the brisket to the throat. Unlike many other folks, Adam didn't cut the throat, but cut the skin to expose the windpipe, and slit it alone. He punctured a small hole just below where he'd severed the windpipe and then paused to take a breath. The reason he removed his shirt and exposed his bare chest was because now he reached up under the sternum bone with both hands and cut at the tissue holding the lungs and heart to the rib cage, and while he pulled them down to the stomach.

Once most of the tissues had been severed, he reached into the chest cavity for the windpipe, put his fingers into the hole he'd made in the windpipe and pulled down toward the hind legs. By pulling the windpipe all the way down, a large portion of the viscera also came to the belly. With his hands, Adam pulled the remaining organs out of the body cavity and laid them on the grass. With the viscera removed, blood puddled along the spine, which Adam used to wash out any urine that might have leaked into the meat.

Half an hour later, Adam was skinning the elk when he heard a rifle shot from the east side of the mountain. He knew it was his Uncle Luther, who had probably shot another elk or a deer on his way up the mountain. Adam went about skinning his large kill. He had learned how to skin an animal without ruining the hide, by using his hand to slide between the hide and the meat. Once the first few cuts were made, he continued skinning primarily by using his hand to separate the hide from the flesh. He was nearing the end of his job when Luther rode into the meadow on his mule. He was leading a pack mule with a dead doe stretched over its back. Tied to the pack mule was Adam's horse.

Luther looked at the elk with a smile and whistled lightly. "That's a dandy! Where'd you shoot from?" he asked with interest.

Adam pointed in a general direction with a blood covered hand. "Where I always do. The same place you told me to stay put when I was fourteen. It's a good place."

Luther's smile was big as he stepped out of his saddle. "Yes, it is. Well, I shot myself a doe. I'll take it over and hang it in a tree to clean it up real quick." He looked at Adam's blood-soaked upper body approvingly. He had taught Adam how to clean and skin large animals, but he never could figure out exactly how Adam got as bloody as he did. Skinning an elk was a bloody job, of course, but it didn't have to be as bloody as Adam made it.

Adam looked up at the large doe. "It's a good-looking doe; just not as good as mine." He chuckled.

"Yeah, I see that. Now I need you to quarter that monster so we can get it back to camp and get it all prepared and cooking before the day's done."

"I think we'll fill the teepee up, yeah?"

"Well, there's no reason to come all this way to not fill it up," Luther said simply.

"Did you bring my tomahawk?"

Luther chuckled. "Did I bring your tomahawk? Do you think I'd forget that?" he asked, walked to Adam's horse and pulled a steel-bladed tomahawk from Adam's saddle bag. The head was covered in a homemade leather sheath tied together with leather strings. He handed it to Adam, who untied the cover with his bloody fingers.

Adam used the finely sharpened blade to cut through the joints and bones as he and his uncle quartered the large elk into manageable pieces. The tomahawk in the hands of either Adam or Luther could cut through the hip joint in a single swift blow. Skinning, cleaning and butchering didn't depend merely on their physical strength, but they'd both learned the skill to use the sharp instrument in the most effective manner.

Once they had the doe and the elk cut into quarters and tied to the pack mule, they loaded the two hides and the elk's head on the mule as well. They would use every part of the animals they killed, including the viscera and feet. The two men carried their burden over to the northern tree line and spaced them out in three piles as bait for the three wolf traps Luther had brought.

As he finished setting the last trap Luther said, "You know the granite quarry has treated Joel and me pretty well, but I think I should've been a trapper. I missed my calling, Adam. I love being out here under the good Lord's creation. I think tomorrow morning we'll kill us a few wolves. What do you think?"

Adam nodded. "I do. How much is the tannery paying for wolf hides—any idea?"

Luther shrugged. "I'm not sure. But we have a lot of meat to prepare and get hung up, so we had better get back to camp. I'm afraid it's going to be a long day. Dang, we might even have to stay a day or two longer than we expected, to get all of this meat jerked."

Adam smiled. "Well, we have time. But right now, I'm

going to jump into that lake and wash off." One of the greatest pleasures of hunting on a warm summer day was washing all the blood from his body by diving off a rock ten feet above the cold and refreshing clear lake no one else knew about, under the granite cliff of Windsor Ridge.

6

Sarah Pierce was filled with an anxiety she couldn't shake. The morning had started off pleasantly enough; it was a beautiful sunny morning in the northern edge of the Wallowa Mountains. Her handsome husband, Nathan, and his older brother, Cal, had both gone to work at the Loveland Timber Company where they spent many long hours scraping the bark off logs or dragging a heavy chain across the rough ground to wrap more logs.

The boys both worked hard and were often tired when they came home in the evenings to their small rented log cabin. The cabin wasn't much: a simple square cabin with an added lean-to built on, which was Nathan and Sarah's bedroom. Cal slept in the main body of the cabin where they cooked, ate and lived. It was uncomfortable at best, but Sarah worked hard to make the meager structure into a warm and loving home for the two men who made up her only family.

Yes, the day had started pleasantly enough, but then came the news that the bank had been robbed. If ever there was a place one could call safe and free from such crime,

Loveland might be it. However, in recent weeks, several miners had been murdered within a twenty-mile radius of Loveland. The bank robbery was shocking, yet the rumor was that the Sperry Helms Gang from Jessup Valley had done it. Saraho had never heard of the gang, but some of the men in town knew about them, and said they were a tough and murderous bunch of thugs who would rather die fighting than surrender. Sarah's husband, Nathan, and her brother-in-law, Cal, were summoned at work by the sheriff to be a part of a posse. The two brothers came home early and were presently preparing for the journey through unknown territory, hunting a dangerous group of men. Sarah's stomach warned her against letting them go.

"Nathan," she said worriedly, "I really don't like this. I just have a bad feeling. Please tell the sheriff you're not going with him."

Nathan Pierce smiled softly. He looked at Sarah as he counted cartridges for his rifle. He would need to purchase more, as he only had four left. "It'll be fine. I promise."

Sarah stood in the doorway of their little lean-to bedroom with barely enough room to stand up straight. "You can't promise me that. Those men are killers, Nathan, and they will not hesitate to kill you. That's according to Louis, who was telling the sheriff those men must have a plan of escape or they wouldn't be here. They could ambush you men. Besides, I really have a bad feeling. Please don't go," she said with tears of fear in her eyes.

Nathan laid his empty cartridge box down, walked to Sarah and hugged her. "Relax, my love. We probably won't even find them. Most likely, we will just ride to Huntsville and wire the new marshal over in Branson and come back home. Matt Bannister is known for tracking down men like that."

Sarah rolled her eyes with exasperation and said, "What if he joins you? Or has to talk with you about something?" She lowered her voice to a whisper and continued, "You're wanted! Do you think it's a good idea to risk meeting him? Of all the people around here who might recognize your face from a poster, it would be him. Don't go, Nathan! If that gang doesn't kill you, then the marshal might arrest you, if not just kill you outright. It's not worth the risk! I love you far too much to lose you. We're safe here; please...don't risk what we have for something that's none of our business. It's just money. Let them have it."

"He won't recognize me, even if we do meet him. My hair is longer, and I have a beard. Plus, I am twenty-five pounds heavier these days. We won't wait around for him to show up anyway. We'll just wire him and come home. Cal and I aren't in charge; we're just going along for the ride. And if by chance we do have to fight, Cal and I are trained soldiers. That's why Jack asked us to go. But honestly, you know Jack. Do you really think he wants to find those robbers? I say no."

"We can't keep running, Nathan. We have a safe home here. Don't risk it. I am asking you to please stay here with me. I really don't know what I'd do without you. I love you, Nathan."

Nathan smiled. "I love you, too. And I promise everything will turn out fine. Those men are probably long gone by now and look who's leading the posse! Jack and Dustin," he said with a smile. "I know Jack and Dustin are nice fellows, but honestly, we'll be lucky if they don't get us lost on the road to Huntsville."

Sarah laughed despite her anxiety. "Cal can lead them back home if need be. But Cal's not wanted by the law, sweetheart...you are. Cal's not married and Cal's not responsible for me...you are. And I still have a bad feeling, Nathan."

Nathan shook his head. "We'll go chase after them for a few hours and be back by dark most likely. Isn't that right, Cal?" Nathan asked his older brother, who was waiting beside the front door for Nathan to join him.

"Sarah," Cal said seriously, "Jack is the sheriff, and our bank was robbed. He has to at least make it look like he's trying to catch the robbers."

"What if you accidentally run into them?" she asked.

Nathan answered, "We won't. Jack doesn't want to find them. That's the marshal's job."

"And what if the marshal finds you?"

Cal spoke from the front door. "He will be too busy to care about any of us. Let's get going."

Nathan frowned and exhaled deeply. "Walk us to the mercantile?"

Sarah nodded and then hugged him tightly.

7

The Loveland mercantile didn't have a fancy name or much of a selection. A small building with "mercantile" painted across its front, it didn't cater to the wealthy, but supplied the hearty goods hardened loggers and miners needed to work and survive. The shelves were loaded with dry goods, metal pots for cooking, saws, axes, shovels and clothing meant for hard-working men, rather than derby hats and white shirts. It didn't have a big selection of guns, but it carried some firearms, and that was just what Octavius Clark was looking for. He laid a paper note from Jared Bogle on the counter; it was a sanctioned I.O.U. for whatever supplies Octavius would need for the posse.

Lyndall Swanson, the proprietor of the mercantile, read the note and looked from the stranger with a new head wound to the note from Jared. It struck Lyndall as odd that the city-slicker banker would open an unlimited account for a stranger, but what did he care? He would collect from Jared, not the stranger standing before him. Lyndall didn't like the looks of this, and the word "caution" came to mind.

"So, what can I get you?" Lyndall asked curtly. He wasn't one for fake pleasantries.

"Two boxes of .44 cartridges, a new bed roll, blanket, tarpaulin, a new flint, canteen and a...I'd like to get a new horse, but you probably don't have one of those, do ya?"

Lyndall shook his head.

"I'll also need a new rifle and ammunition."

Lyndall looked at Octavius skeptically. "You're making out like a bandit with Jared's money, aren't you?" he asked and turned from the counter to begin to gather the list of items named thereon.

Octavius' eyes flickered dangerously. "They stole my gold and his money. I'm going to get it back. Now if you'll hurry up about getting it all." Octavius was in a rush to collect his supplies, mount his horse and leave before the sheriff arrived with a thrown-together posse. He had no interest in riding with a posse of town folks. They would just slow him down and get in his way. Octavius preferred being alone. The idea of being forced to ride with a group of strangers made him sick to his stomach. He wanted to be alone and track the men down as fast as he could without the law impeding his speed or methods.

"Rumor is, it was the Sperry Helms Gang," Lyndall said as he brought a wooden box of items covered with a new gray wool blanket. He set it on the counter. "That's a bad bunch. It would take a very brave man to go after them alone. I tossed in a pan and some canned goods. You might get hungry on your way," he explained as he unloaded the box on the counter.

Octavius only nodded his thanks and then looked out the window impatiently.

Lyndall continued, "What kind of rifle are you looking for? All I have is up here... I don't have much to choose from." He reached up to a four-gun rack and pulled down a gun. "This here's a Remington repeater. It holds six cartridges of the same .44's you're already buying. It's a good shooter and as deadly as any other," he said as he handed it to Octavius.

Octavius looked it over and down the sights. "What model?"

"1881."

Satisfied, Octavius nodded. "I'll take it. Do you have a scabbard, by chance?"

Lyndall whistled. "Oh, boy, I might have. Let me go look. I had a few once, sold a couple, then the roof sprung a leak and the last one I had got soaked by the water. I didn't notice the leak for quite some time. Let's see. I'm not sure if I tossed it in the back to dry out or threw it away because of the mold on it. Scabbards aren't big sellers up here; most folks already have one when they arrive. I'm surprised you don't. I'll go check in the back and see if I can find it."

Octavius raised his voice to be heard in the back of the store, "I do. But I wasn't expecting to be robbed. I left my long arm in my scabbard at my camp. I knew better, and it's the first time I've ever done that. I just don't have time to go back and get it, is all." He looked out the window again. "If you don't have it, that's okay. I'll tie the knife to the saddle."

"Well, I do," Lyndall called from the back room, where he could be heard moving things around to look for it. "Here it is. Yeah, I have it, but its mildew stained." He came back to the counter carrying a leather scabbard spotted with white, patched, dried mildew on it. It carried a heavy scent of mildew. "I'll give you a good deal on it, since Jared's paying for it."

Octavius frowned., "You didn't clean it when you put it away?"

Lyndall shrugged. "Like I said, no one's wanted one until now."

Octavius scoffed. "I'll take it. Write it all down and give it to the banker. I have to go," he said and grabbed the box of goods, including the bedroll, and started walking quickly towards the door. He stopped and gritted his teeth as the door opened in front of him and the sheriff, Jack Schwartz, walked into the mercantile followed by two other men.

"Ah, just in time!" Jack said loudly. "Good, you got your gear. You get situated on your pony while we grab a few things. We'll be ready to leave in no time. I expect we'll meet up with them in Huntsville, what about you?" Jack asked Octavius.

Octavius shook his head and spoke curtly, "They'd be fools if we did."

"Yeah, but it would be nice if we did. We could toss them in jail and go to the saloon to celebrate! That'd be great, huh?" the sheriff asked with a smile. Then he slapped Octavius on the shoulder as he walked past him towards the counter.

Octavius took a deep breath and went out to put his things into his worn saddlebags. Only one side of his saddlebags was trustworthy, as the other side had a hole in it. If he had thought about it, he would have asked about a set of new saddlebags, too. He didn't have time to go back in to ask now though. He wanted to load his new gear and leave as fast as he could. He knew he could lose the sheriff and the rest of the posse in the mountains. He doubted the sheriff could track a grizzly bear in mud. And by the looks of the two men with the sheriff, neither could they.

One of the men with the sheriff stepped outside with an excited smile on his face. He was tall, with a clean-shaven face and bright blue eyes. He didn't seem like a typical man you'd find in a logging camp or anywhere near a place like Loveland. He wore a tan suit with a dingy, but still white shirt under his vest. His hair was a mixture of light brown and gray. It was cut short and combed neatly with a hair oil of some sort to keep it in place. He wore a newly borrowed gun-belt and a Colt revolver purchased from the mercantile. Octavius had seen that Colt inside.

The man smiled pleasantly, while emphasizing his gun-belt. "Looks good, huh?" He stuck out his hand at Octavius. "I'm John, by the way. John Riggs. I own the saloon over there." He nodded to a plain looking building with the word, "saloon" painted on it. John's smile faded, and his hand went back to his side when Octavius refused to shake his hand but merely passed a glance over John.

Octavius continued to secure the scabbard to his saddle, uninterested in John.

"I know, it doesn't look like much, but when we get back, I'll buy you a drink. It's a lot nicer inside." John spoke of his saloon.

"You're going with the posse?" Octavius asked skeptically.

"You bet! Think I'm going to miss this opportunity? If we end up killing the Sperry Helms Gang, I'm going to line them up in front of my saloon and make a fortune when everyone comes to see the bandits."

"Can you shoot that?" Octavius nodded at John's gun-belt.

"Oh, yeah. I grew up on a farm, so I'm used to killing things."

"Things?" Octavius asked and paused to look John over again. "We're not going after things. We're going after men. Have you ever killed a man?" His stare burned into John, and he already knew the answer.

"No..." John answered uneasily under Octavius' glare. "But I've shot my share of deer and swine. Besides, once we get to Huntsville, we'll contact the marshal, Matt Bannister, if we need to."

"Hmm!" Octavius grunted and went back to securing his supplies and bedroll.

"So, what's your name? Are you new in town, or just avoiding my saloon?" John chuckled.

Octavius turned and looked at John with annoyance. "Mister, might I suggest you stay put? Because, quite frankly, you don't strike me as the kind of man who's cut out for this."

"I won't pretend to be a gunfighter, but we're not going after an army either. There's only four of them and more of us, so I think we'll be okay. Besides, Jack got Cal and Nathan Pierce to come along, and they'll do all of the dirty work if it comes down to that."

Octavius smirked. "Dirty work?"

The mercantile door opened, and Sheriff Jack Schwartz and his deputy walked outside carrying a cloth bag of a dozen pieces of jerky. "Jerky anyone?" the sheriff asked with a smile. "This ought to hold us over until we get to Huntsville."

"No, thanks," John said. "I just had breakfast an hour ago." He normally slept in far later than most everyone else in town.

"I do," the deputy said, holding out his hand. The deputy was nearly six feet tall with an average shoulder width. His brown hair was cut short, and he was clean shaven. He was younger than the other two men, maybe in his late twenties, with an oblong face with large brown eyes that seemed too close together, and a pair of thin lips.

"Here you go, son," Jack said and handed a piece of jerky

to his son. "By the way, this is my son and deputy. His name is Dustin. Dustin, this is our official tracker...what is your name again, Ozzy, Otto...?"

"Octavius," he answered flatly as he looked Dustin over.

"Octavius! I knew it started with an O. Well, we're almost ready. We're just waiting for the Pierce brothers and Mike. They'll be along shortly. They're the real mountain men of our party. Mike's a muleskinner by trade but does a lot of hunting around here. Well, he did, until he hurt his knee a year back. He's never walked the same since then. Now the Pierce brothers, Cal and Nathan, are mighty quiet for the most part, but they are two tough young men. Both are ex-military. I believe it was Nathan who tracked for the cavalry, but it might've been Cal. I don't remember. Either way, they know what they're doing, and we're in good hands with them coming along." Jack said cheerfully.

Dustin looked at Octavius questioningly. "Have you tracked people before? Because this isn't like hunting deer, you know."

Octavius glared at Dustin, and hardness showed in his eyes. "Yeah, I've tracked people down before. Have you?" He looked distastefully at the handmade tin star on the deputy's left lapel. It was cut from a tin can with the word "Deputy" in black paint on it. If Octavius was a laughing type of man, he might've laughed, but instead he shook his head, because he already knew the answer.

"I found a lost boy in the woods. I tracked him for about a mile. He wandered off down a stream and just kept walking. Someone told him if he ever got lost in the woods to just follow the creek downstream."

Octavius nodded silently with a roll of his eyes. His gold was getting farther away by the minute, and he was stuck in a posse of inexperienced men who were perhaps bigger fools then the ones who'd stolen his gold.

"It's true though," Dustin continued. "If you get lost, all you have to do is follow a stream out of the mountains. It'll lead you out of the mountains and into the valley where people are. Did you know that, John?"

John Riggs answered, "The best advice is, don't get lost! If you come upon a stream from the east, just turn around and go back towards the east. How hard could it be? I've never got lost in the woods."

"Me either," Dustin said. "I've spent my whole life in the mountains. I know every inch of these mountains, here. I've killed a lot of game up here," he offered to Octavius.

Octavius ignored him.

Dustin continued, "What about you? Do you do a lot of hunting? My Pa says you're a miner, so you must hunt a bit, yeah?"

"When I need to," Octavius answered without interest. He busied himself with securing his saddlebags.

"I killed a bear about three months ago, just about half a mile out of town." Dustin held up one finger as he continued. "One shot with my Sharps dropped it. Ever killed a bear with one shot? Most folks can't. They have to take four of five shots to kill a bear," Dustin boasted. "That's if they can hit it."

Octavius closed his eyes for a second. He was becoming annoyed with the three men in his company, especially the sheriff's son, Dustin, who kept talking. Octavius was a man who usually had very little to say and preferred silence over worthless nonsense. He understood Dustin might be a friendly guy, and might be curious about him, but Octavius was in no mood to talk idle chitchat about bear, possum or squirrel hunting. He wanted to get moving and find the men who took his gold. He was also irritated that he had missed his opportunity to leave the posse behind him. The more he listened to the men in the posse, the more irritable he became about missing his opportunity. He sighed and looked at Dustin. "Where are you from?"

"Nebraska originally. We had about a dozen acres of our own but tended the wheat fields of our neighbor for a living. After Ma died—she died of consumption—after she died, Pa and I came west. We were in Portland for a while before we came here to strike it rich on gold. The town needed some law, so we sold our claim and became lawmen. What about you? What brings you here?"

Octavius shrugged. "Just selling my gold."

John Riggs laughed, "Not anymore, huh?" he joked.

Octavius looked at John coldly. "I'll get it back."

John added, "Oswald, if you..."

"Octavius!" he said firmly to John.

John chuckled. "Octavius; sorry. But I will cut you a deal. If we catch those bank robbers today, I'll give you a free drink before taking a pinch or two of that gold."

Octavius eyed John like a fox around a hen house. There was no emotion whatsoever in his eyes, except coldness. He turned to Jack. "We need to go."

Jack shrugged, and said loudly, "Yeah, I know it. But we are waiting for the Pierce brothers and Mike Hall. They'll be along shortly. We got time. Heck, I heard the marshal, Matt Bannister, just last Christmas waited a whole night before tracking down and killing the men who stole that woman from Willow Falls. He found them easily enough, and these guys we're after didn't steal a woman, just some money. So there's no hurry. We'll get em."

Octavius squeezed his lips together in frustration. He wanted to get away from the sheriff and his posse as quickly as he could and go find his gold, while the robbers' trail was still fresh. He spoke pointedly to Jack. "I don't care what the marshal did. Those men out there took my gold, and I'm going after them while there's still time and sign enough for me to do it!"

Jack said seriously, "We'll leave just as soon as the others get here. It won't be long. Like I was saying, the marshal took his time, and he found who he was looking for."

"The marshal knew what he was looking for. You don't!" His impatience was beginning to show.

John Riggs chuckled as he asked sarcastically, "How hard is it to follow horse tracks to Huntsville?"

Octavius shook his head, exasperated, and said, "Sheriff, I'm leaving. If you want to follow along, do so, but I'm not waiting any longer. I'm going after my gold." He stepped determinedly up into his saddle with the reigns in his hand.

"Hold on," Jack said, stepping over to Octavius' horse. "If you try leaving us behind, you'll be staying the night in our jail. Without you, we may not find your precious gold or our money. You're not going anywhere without us." Jack nonchalantly grabbed the bit collar of the bridle on Octavius' horse.

Octavius grinned for the first time, albeit with frustration. "They're getting away."

Jack answered in the same cheerful, optimistic tone and smile he'd had all morning. "Oh, they'll hole up somewhere, either in Huntsville or off the road in a meadow someplace. However, I have all the confidence that you'll find them for us, no matter where they are."

Octavius nodded slowly as his eyes grew narrow and mean. "Oh, I will find them; you can trust me on that." His tone didn't hide his fury.

"Besides, you'll be glad to have the Pierce brothers and Mike on your side if a gun battle breaks out. Those are some tough men, and they know their way around a battlefield. So let's be patient and wait a bit."

Octavius glared at Jack. "So you've said."

"Are you hungry?" Jack asked quickly as he still held his bag of jerky and lifted it up to Octavius.

Octavius shook his head.

John Riggs said again with his permanent grin, "Yeah, I've seen Cal draw two pistols at once and shoot the eye out of two hummingbirds from sixty paces at the same time!"

Jack and Dustin both laughed. Jack said, "That's almost as good shooting as the time I shot that twenty-foot grizzly up on Polar Creek. They say you don't ever want to look a grizzly in the eyes, so I laid my rifle backwards over my shoulder and had the boy there"—he nodded at Dustin —"hold a mirror up so I could aim. I got that monster in the heart a hundred yards away!"

Dustin looked at Octavius with a goofy smile and explained, "They're joshing you. But I'm a pretty good shot; I don't miss with my Sharps. My pa bet me once that I couldn't hit a hawk out of the sky, but I did! It must've been three-four hundred yards up in the sky. It was barely visible. Another time, I was hunting and shot a doe running full speed; not many people can make that shot!"

Octavius nodded, uninterested, and looked to the west, the direction the robbers had left town. He already regretted having asked the banker to fund his supplies. He could have easily ridden the six miles to his camp, grabbed his own bedroll, rifle, ammunition, flint and other goods he'd bought, and left to track those men down alone. Instead, he was sitting with a group of fools who were being led by perhaps the greatest fool of them all. Whatever gave these men the impression it would be easy to track the robbers down in the next town, Octavius had no idea. In his experience, most bank robbers didn't ride to the next town and flaunt their money. This posse of town folks acted like they were going on a high-society fox hunt. They knew nothing of what they were setting out to do and, despite his wishes, Octavius couldn't leave them at the moment.

He doubted Jack, Dustin or John would raise a firearm at him if he ran off, but across the street, between the bank and closer to the saloon, stood several other men, many of them older and more experienced who held a significant number of rifles and revolvers. Octavius had no doubt that two or three of those men would be happy to shoot a fleeing suspect. The truth was, anyone new in town wasn't trusted, and he knew how volatile some small towns like this one could be after a crime. He couldn't leave the posse now, but he would do it as soon as he could. He doubted any of them could keep up with him or endure a cold night under the stars without a big fire to keep them warm at night. He shook his head with growing frustration as Dustin continued talking.

"I see you picked the Remington from Lyndall. Remington makes a good rifle, but it's no Sharps. For what it is, I think Lyndall had it over-priced. But I suppose that doesn't matter to you since you're not paying for it. Jared will probably give it to you for a reward, though, if we bring the money back."

Jack laughed while still holding Octavius' horse. "Ah, Octavius isn't going to keep it! It belongs to Jared, so don't make any promises that Jared may not commit to, especially without his knowledge." Jack chuckled.

"I said maybe he would." Dustin said defensively.

"No, you said Jared probably would, which might give Octavius reason to think Jared will. And we just don't know that, so why mention it?"

"It's not even that great of a gun, Pa. I don't think Jared would want it. He's got plenty of other ones that are better. He's got two Winchesters and a Sharps. What about you?" he asked Octavius. "Do you have a rifle?"

Octavius nodded slowly, wishing he could avoid the entire conversation.

"What kind?"

Octavius exhaled heavily. "The shooting kind. Sheriff, can we go, if we're going?" he asked impatiently.

Jack shrugged his shoulders, "Yup, just as soon as our boys get here."

"What kind of rifle do you own?" Dustin asked again, a touch of indignation in his voice. He didn't like to be ignored by anyone.

Octavius looked at Dustin irritably. "I have a Winchester, why?"

"I was just asking." Dustin replied softly. "I know guns, and yours is probably a lot more reliable than that Remington. The last thing you want is having your dinner in your sights and have the rifle jam. I know guns, and your Winchester is a lot better brand than that Remington. That rifle has been sitting in there for sale for a long time. Anyone living around here knows when you're hunting and run across a bear, you need two things: reliability and power. That Remington has neither. I mean, it's good for small game at close range, but beyond that, a guy like you wouldn't need it. But you'll see if we get into a gun fight with those robbers. You'll be better off using your sidearm. You'll be glad I'm bringing my Sharps, and my Pa's got his Winchester if things get bad."

Jack added, "You'll be glad we waited for Mike and the Pierce brothers if that happens, too!"

Octavius looked from Jack to Dustin. "How many gun fights have you been in, son?"

Dustin drew back in defense. "None yet, but we're lawmen, so I'm ready."

Octavius smiled slightly and then snickered for the first time. "Son, I'll bet you my bag of gold that if a gun fight breaks out—and it will—that you'll be the second man to run away or be killed." He pointed at John Riggs. "He'll be the first to run away, and you'll be second. Don't stand here and feed me your line of crap about things you know absolutely nothing about!" he spat out boldly. "I have seen the blood, I've heard the screams, and I've killed men twice as experienced as all of you! Do not talk to me about guns, hunting or how glad I'll be that you're coming with me! I can kill every one of those men on my own. I do not need any of you! Especially you!" he yelled with a pointed finger down at Dustin. He continued, "Your safest bet is to not talk to me anymore! Because, frankly, I don't believe a word you've said! You talk too much. Shut up and leave me alone! This is your only warning," Octavius said severely in a loud voice. He glared menacingly at Dustin.

Dustin's face turned red, as some town folks had overheard the tongue-lashing he'd received from Octavius. He said calmly, "All I was getting at was, I'd be glad to buy that rifle from you when we get those guys. It didn't cost you anything..."

"Oh, for crying out loud!" Octavius vented and turned his head away from. He shook his head in disbelief.

"I'd offer a good deal," Dustin finished.

Jack spoke seriously, "Mister...Octavius..." He couldn't remember the man's last name off the top of his head. "By the way, we're not going after them to kill them, so you can get that idea out of your head. We will arrest them and bring them back for trial. That is our sworn duty to do things right, and I can't condone a hanging party. We may live out in the woods here, but that doesn't make us barbarians."

Octavius held the saddle horn with both hands and laughed quietly to himself. "You are something else. You honestly think you'll arrest those men with this group you have?" he asked with a cynical smile.

Jack frowned. "Well, we're not Matt Bannister, but together we should do all right. We'll do our best anyway." He slapped Octavius' leg and continued happily, "But that's why we have you and them..." he pointed at three men coming toward them. Two rode in on saddles, one on a mule, and the other on a horse. The third walked beside them holding a young attractive lady with his left arm and leading his horse by the reins with his right hand. The man on the mule led a pack mule behind him.

Octavius looked at the three men carefully. All three appeared competent men at first glance. All three seemed to have experience with horsemanship and carried themselves as determined men who had confidence in their weapons, unlike the fools he'd been talking to. The three men possessed a sober-mindedness Octavius immediately had a touch of respect for. They appeared to be capable men.

"Well, it's about time you boys got here! Our tracker was getting impatient, just like a sassy woman!" Jack called out loudly with his usual cheerful smile.

Octavius glared at Jack bitterly and clenched his fist, wanting to drive it into the temple of Jack's head for calling him a woman. He restrained himself, because again, he would not be able to get away from Loveland without being arrested at if he hit the sheriff. However, he had no use for the sheriff at all.

The man sitting on the mule answered. "I had to pack

my animals. I know you guys wouldn't come prepared for anything unless it was a gambling hall with liquor and women," he said loudly. The man was Mike Hall, and he had short, bright red hair and a face red from exposure to the sun. He wore an unkempt red beard, and a wide-brimmed hat sagged on his head to keep the sun out of his eyes. He was not a big man, only about five feet, eight inches tall, and a hundred and fifty pounds with narrow shoulders. He was in his thirties and seemed to smile with ease. Octavius noticed Mike Hall had packed his equipment and supplies like a skilled horseman.

"Octavius, this is Mike Hall. He's a mule skinner up here and knows more about this area than anyone else around these parts," Jack said pleasantly.

"Oh, I wouldn't say that," Mike said uncomfortably. "I run a mule team hauling logs, lumber and goods back and forth on the roads up here. It's nice to meet you, Octavius."

The man astride the horse looked at Octavius suspiciously. He was tall and thin, in his late twenties or early thirties, with long brown hair that fell to his shoulders under a flat-brimmed brown hat. He wore a long brown beard. He had packed his horse lightly and carried a reverse handled Colt on his left hip with an U.S. Cavalry-issued gun-belt. His six-inch knife with a wood handle was strapped on his right hip. He had his Winchester in its scabbard and seemed to be annoyed by the presence of John Riggs and Dustin Schwartz. He did not smile or offer any pleasantries, other than a casual nod to Jack. He seemed to be a sound, solid and a tough man with some fighting experience behind his quiet facade. He nodded at Octavius. "I'm Cal."

Jack continued, "This here's Cal Pierce and his younger brother, Nathan. That's Nathan's wife, Sarah, but I don't think she's coming with us. Are you?" he asked with a friendly chuckle.

Sarah smiled politely, though her anxiety was clear to see as she shook her head in answer to his question.

Nathan Pierce handed his reigns to Cal and stepped forward to shake Octavius' hand. "I'm Nathan. It's nice to meet you," he said. He sounded genuinely friendly, and Octavius turned in the saddle to shake his hand.

Nathan was twenty-five years old with thick, long brown hair and a full, neatly trimmed beard around three inches long. He looked to be a bit shorter than his brother, but broader in the shoulders and quite a bit stronger. Nathan as well wore a U.S. Cavalry-issued gun-belt with a reversed Colt on his left hip and a knife on his right. His mount was also packed lightly for fast traveling and carried his rifle in its scabbard. Nathan, as well, appeared to be much more competent than the other posse members as a fighting man.

"I'm Octavius." He introduced himself as he shook Nathan's hand. However, his eyes went to Sarah. He couldn't stop himself from staring at her. It wasn't that she was so beautiful; it was the fact that she reminded him of his own bride many years ago. Once in a man's lifetime, he meets a certain lady who surpasses all the others. The kind of lady who can work her fingers to the bone to keep her husband fed, healthy, happy, and make his life worth living; not because of wealth or status, but simply because he has her to share his home and life with. Yes, there is a certain type of lady who loves so deeply that her devotion is who she is, and it cannot be bought or stolen away. She makes his joy complete just as he completes hers. Together they are like a pair of fine gloves: neither is complete or worthy without the other. Once in a man's life, he may find the rarest jewel: a woman who genuinely loves him with a fire so bright, the flames never die. And he, if he is wise, will never let her go. Knowing the value of his treasure, he will die to protect her...just as Octavius' wife had died to protect him.

It was uncanny how much Sarah reminded Octavius of his beloved Lucinda. Sarah Pierce was twenty-two years old with dark blonde hair that fell freely to her shoulders. Her oblong face and features were near enough to perfect that she undoubtedly had to be one of the prettiest girls in the area. Her strongest features were her light blue eyes that seemed to shine with joy, despite her blanket of anxiousness. She wore a light blue dress that covered her arms and neck. She clung to Nathan's arm tightly as she fidgeted uncomfortably under Octavius' continued stare.

Nathan, like everyone else, noticed Octavius staring at his wife. "This is my wife, Sarah."

Octavius glanced at Nathan and blinked a few times to clear his thoughts. "Forgive me for staring, miss. You...you remind me of my wife," he said softly.

She said softly with a small smile, "I hope that's a good thing."

He smiled sadly and nodded. "You can't go wrong with it."

"Well," Jack said loudly, "I'll be! I was under the impression you were a bachelor! Who knew ole Oscar was a..."

"Octavius!" he spat out angrily. "I've already told you, my name's Octavius!"

"Sorry. Dang, I knew that, too. I don't know why it keeps slipping my mind," Jack apologized honestly. "I'll remember that, Octavius. No harm meant."

John Riggs chuckled. "You can bring your woman to my saloon while we're gone. They'll keep her warm and busy over there!" He laughed, and then added quickly, "I'm just kidding. Sorry." He continued to laugh.

Octavius rolled his eyes and took a deep breath in an attempt to keep his composure.

Nathan said to John, "That's not funny, John. Not funny at all."

Sarah spoke to Octavius. "If you want, your wife is welcome to stay with me while you're gone."

He looked at her and frowned. "My wife was murdered a long time ago, ma'am."

"Murdered? I am so sorry," she said sincerely.

He nodded but offered no other comment.

"Murdered?" Jack asked. "Who would murder a woman?"

"What she do? I mean, why was she killed?" Dustin asked. "I mean, I've killed lots of things, and will probably kill a man or two today," he said, looking at Sarah, "but I would never kill a woman!" His interest in Sarah was as obvious as a watering hole in the desert.

Octavius stared at his saddle horn, trying his best to ignore the conversation. He would like nothing more than to shove his rifle butt into the mouths of the father and son lawmen to shut them up. But again, until he was out of town, he was at the mercy of these men and had to remain calm and endure their nonsense. That was, of course, if he ever wanted his gold again.

"Knock it off, guys." Nathan said.

"What?" Dustin asked Nathan. "I'm just curious to know why someone would murder his wife. Was it Indians? I hear tell they killed lots of women, but that's all they could kill, at least in our wagon train. We men all had guns, and like I've said, I don't miss."

Octavius began to shake his head in frustration. He peered at Dustin in astonishment. "Are you going to keep asking me until I tell you? For crying out loud, you little rat's ass, she was murdered by a group of Yankee soldiers, if you must know! They came onto my farm and beat me black and blue before leaving me for dead. When I woke up, my wife was already dead from a slit throat. Why'd they kill her you ask...for trying to help me! I was losing consciousness and seen them holding her. She was screaming and fighting them to get to me. I heard my children screaming for me right before I was hit in the head with a rifle butt. They must've thought I was dead. I wasn't even a soldier at the time. I was just a farmer." He glared at Dustin with hard, cold eyes. "But I became a soldier, and a very good one!"

John asked, "Why would they cut her throat when they could have just shot you both? I mean, why were they there if you weren't a Reb?"

Octavius glared icily at John and looked downright dangerous. "They were looking for my wife's cousin, who was raising volunteers. They thought we knew where he was. To answer your damned question, they didn't shoot us because they wanted to keep quiet before they moved on to the next farm."

"So, what'd you do?" Dustin asked.

Octavius slowly turned his attention to Dustin. "I joined the Rebels."

John said loudly, "So you are a Reb!"

Octavius peered at John with his dark eyes. He spoke intentionally. "To this very day. Now I'd appreciate it if we could leave my past behind and go get those thieves who took my gold."

Jack nodded. "Yes, let's go, boys. Saddle up, and let's find us some robbers!" He finally let go of Octavius' horse.

Nathan kissed Sarah and rested his hand on her cheek. "I will be back soon. Keep that fire burning, my love."

She forced a sad smile and hid her frightened tears. "Be

careful and come home to me. Don't take any unnecessary risks. You know what I'm talking about, right?"

He smiled comfortingly. "Don't worry. Pray. Isn't that what you always say to me?"

She nodded. "Yes, but I mean it when I say it. You pray too, okay? Honestly, I have a bad feeling. So, pray and get right with the Lord, so he'll protect you, please."

He smiled wide. "I have to go. I love you, Sarah. And I promise you, I will be praying along the way, just for you."

"No, do it for you."

"I have to go," he said and kissed her one last time before stepping up into the saddle.

"About time," Cal Pierce said to his younger brother.

Sarah said, "Hush it, Cal. You better be praying too. You boys be careful, okay?"

Dustin said, "Don't worry, Sarah. I will be looking after them."

"Thank you, Dustin," she said without much confidence —but friendly, just the same.

Sarah looked at Octavius and approached his horse. She touched his sleeve to get his full attention. "Mister..."

"Octavius," he corrected her gently.

"Octavius. May I ask you did you love your wife?" she asked with soft and anxious eyes.

He looked into her eyes for a moment and then nodded. "Very much."

"What was her name?" she asked.

Octavius squeezed his lips together tightly before saying, "Lucinda."

"Mister Octavius, I love my husband very much; just as much as you loved Lucinda. Can I ask you to promise me that you will make sure my husband comes back home to me?" she asked, tears beginning to fill her eyes. Her light blue gaze never left his.

Octavius watched her eyes fill up with tears of desperation. He nodded wordlessly in reply.

"Promise me that you will do all you can to make sure Nathan comes home to me. Honestly, he is all I have in this world, Mister Octavius. So, promise me that you will make sure he comes back to me alive."

"Sarah, I'll be fine," Nathan said from his horse. He was slightly embarrassed by her pestering the old man to protect him.

She ignored Nathan. "Promise me," she repeated to Octavius.

Octavius looked at Nathan and then back to Sarah. "Young lady, I promise you that he will come back to you alive and well. If I can help him in anyway. You have my word on that, and that means a whole lot more than a promise to me. You'll see him again."

"Thank you. Are you a praying man, Mister...what is your last name?"

"My name's Octavius Clark. And no, ma'am, I am not."

"Well, Octavius Clark, I will be praying for your safety, too. And thank you."

Octavius nodded to Sarah and turned his horse to lead the way out of town.

8

It was nearly noon, and the robbers had close to a two-hour head start once the sheriff had finished gathering his posse and finally left town. The robbers' tracks were still visible in the dust of the road leading out of town. Octavius sped his horse up to a quick trot to follow the long strides of the four running horses. To the best of Octavius' guess, they were about six miles behind the criminals, at least. He didn't care about anything else but finding the men who took his gold, and the man who hit him over the head with that shotgun.

"Hey, what's the hurry?" Jack called out. "They're not going to hop a ship or train before we catch them."

John Riggs chuckled. "Wait up, Otto. We'll run into them at the Blue Saloon. They should be feeling good enough by the time we waltz in to buy us a drink or two before we arrest them." He laughed. "It's only courteous to let them buy us a drink before we arrest them, right?" he asked Jack.

"Well, it would be darned nice of them after making us come after them! But it might be your money they're buying our drinks with," Jack offered.

"I never thought about that."

"Pa," Dustin said, "he isn't slowing down." He nodded towards Octavius, who was slowly pulling farther ahead of them. Octavius then kicked his horse and began galloping away from the posse.

"Hey!" Jack yelled and kicked his horse into a full run to catch up to Octavius. The others did the same. Jack continued to yell, "I told you to stop!"

Octavius looked back with annoyance and pulled his horse to a quick stop. He turned to face the others. He was frustrated, and it showed in his expression. "What?" he asked.

Jack pulled his winded horse to a stop in front of Octavius. "I told you to slow down back there, and then you took off running. What's your hurry? We have all day."

Octavius raised his voice with irritation. "You forced me to come with you. I didn't ask you to come with me! I told you I'm going after these men, and I don't have time to babysit you and your friends. So, either keep up or take your...posse," he said sarcastically, "home where they belong!"

Jack was slightly taken back by the venom in Octavius' voice. His eyes were as dark, cold and furious as any he had ever seen. Jack had to say something in front of his men, but he didn't want to anger Octavius any more than he apparently already had. In a soft tone, Jack said, "Well, if you go too fast, we might miss something."

"I'm not missing anything! Follow along if you want but leave me alone so I can find those men!" Octavius spoke severely and turned his horse back to follow the tracks in the road.

Dustin Schwartz shook his head. "I don't think he knows what he's doing. Cal, you were a tracker. What do you think? You or I should be leading this expedition, not a stranger we know nothing about. For all we know, he could be one of the gang members whose job it is to lead us astray."

"There's only one way out of town, son," Jack said as they followed about thirty yards behind Octavius at a gentle gallop. "And we're on it."

Dustin answered his father, "That's not true, Pa. There are old Indian trails that go clear to the Snake River to the east or the valley to the south. The Indian trails go just about everywhere. I've taken some of those Indian trails to hunt on, and you get to know the territory pretty well. If the Sperry Helms Gang took one of those old Nez Perce trails, well, they might end up right back in Loveland. They probably don't know the Nez Perce made fake trails for their enemies to get lost in the mountains on. You have to know the right trails to take."

"What? What the hell are you talking about, Dustin?" Mike Hall asked with a grin.

"They came this way," Jack said before Dustin could answer Mike. "They're not on an old Indian trail, so obviously, they're going to Huntsville. It's the only place they can go unless they keep going, but they have to stop sometime."

Nathan Pierce said, "Besides, they're not going to risk getting lost in the woods. Speed and distance is what they want right now."

"I just meant they could have taken some old Indian trails. Pa said there was no other way out of town, but there is. Quite a few, actually. There's the main road here, the old Indian trails, and there's plenty of animal trails too."

Cal Pierce grimaced and pointed at the road in front of them. "Their tracks are right there! I don't know who Octavius is, either, but I can tell you, he's following their tracks! You can see their tracks plain as day right there! Four horses running at full gait... Right there, Dustin, not up on the mountain ridge or on an Indian trail, but right there!"

"I know!" Dustin snapped back. "I can see that. I was just saying there are other ways out of town, is all. And they could've taken the skid road up if they wanted to."

"That makes no sense, Dustin!"

"I know. That's what I said," Dustin replied. "All I was saying was this is not the only way out of town. They could've taken a deer trail around the mountains down into Huntsville. It's not so hard to go west, but they would have to know which way that is, or they'd get lost. And I'll tell you, getting lost in the Wallowas is a death sentence. It's no place for greenhorns, that's for sure."

"Fine! They could've went that way, but they didn't! Okay, can we just end it?" Cal snapped.

John Riggs added with a slight smirk, "You know they could have circled back around and waited until we left. That way they're not being followed."

"That's ridiculous," Cal said seriously.

Dustin shook his head and said, "Not necessarily. If they wanted to lose our posse, they could back track and, not knowing the Indian trails, it could happen. I know when I first came up here, it happened to me. But they'll try to hide their tracks, no matter what."

Cal shook his head. "They're not trying to hide their tracks, you idiot! If they were, they'd get off the road! Horses leave tracks, especially in dust, so why would they think they could lose us on a dusty road?"

Dustin looked at Cal with a perplexed expression. "They wouldn't! Especially, since you or I could track them through a swamp if we had to. I'm just saying they could try to hide their tracks. Some people don't know much about the mountains, you know."

Nathan Pierce smiled and shook his head. "Yeah, Cal, they could."

Cal shot a fierce glance at his younger brother. "Don't encourage him! I've already heard enough," he said and pulled the reigns of his horse down to a slow walk. His brother and Mike Hall joined him.

Dustin slowed down as well, but questioned urgently, "What are you stopping for? We're not going to catch up by falling behind."

"Then go! You had better run ahead, just in case Octavius tries to outrun your pa. He'll need you if that happens. We'll be along shortly." Cal encouraged Dustin to leave them.

Dustin nodded. "I think you're right. I don't trust that man. You boys don't linger too far behind. If we run into those men camped by the road up ahead, we may need your guns."

Cal stared at Dustin. "We'll be there. You better catch up with your pa, though. You're falling way behind."

Dustin waved Cal off with a scoff. "Arabians are made for speed. She isn't named Lightning Bolt for nothing," he said proudly of his horse. "I'll see you." He turned his horse and kicked her to catch up with the others.

Cal exhaled heavily and shook his head as he watched Dustin ride away. "He is an idiot! This whole makeshift posse is nothing more than a band of idiots being led by a bigger idiot; who I do not think even wants to find the robbers!"

Mike Hall laughed. "That's why I'm hanging back here by myself, if I can."

Cal wasn't quite finished expressing his built-up frustration. "I swear, Dustin couldn't find his way home from here without someone pointing the way! But he's talking! I guess that never ends, does it?"

Mike laughed at his friend. "Nope. I'm surprised he's not leading us in circles instead of what's his name."

"I'm surprised Jack doesn't let him. He's probably afraid Dustin would find them, what with his tracking skills and all."

Mike shook his head and smiled. "Oh, gosh, I don't know about them two. What do you know about the man leading us?"

Cal shrugged. "I don't know. It's easy to find the tracks on the road, but we'll see. I don't mind going after the robbers, but I really don't want to be talked to death before we find them."

Mike motioned ahead of them. "It looks like we're being left behind."

Cal shrugged. "We'll catch up. It's not like we can't track down our own party on a road."

"We'll probably find John and Dustin lost along the way."

Cal rolled his eyes, unable to enjoy Mike's humor. "They didn't bring any supplies! John's wearing a suit, for crying out loud! They honestly believe they'll find the Sperry Helms Gang in Huntsville sitting in the saloon! Lord forbid we have to chase real killers and stay out under the stars a night or two. Half of this group will turn around and go home!"

Nathan finally joined the conversation. "It would be nice if they did go home."

John Riggs slowed his horse down to a casual walk along with Jack and Dustin, when they caught up with Octavius. "Did you lose their trail?" John asked Octavius, sounding more hopeful than not. He was curious why Octavius had slowed down.

"No!" Octavius answered shortly.

Jack said, "My old nag is about to poop out anyway. I don't think our horses are in any shape to be worked so hard, including yours. If those men are better mounted than we are, we may not catch them."

Octavius looked at Jack severely. "I'll catch them whether they're better mounted or not. They will stop to rest. I won't!"

Jack chuckled. "Well, we'll have to rest, too. Our horses haven't worked this hard in ages. They're already lathered up and out of breath. Except maybe for Mike's mules, they're working mules. But the rest of us, well...we'll have to rest up in Huntsville for the night."

Octavius shook his head in frustration while he gazed at the wooden bridge over the Antioch River up ahead. "You're mighty confidant they're in Huntsville," he said quietly.

Jack nodded. "There's nowhere else for them to go. We're the last civilization around here, and we haven't got much. When my boy and I moved here, the word was folks were finding gold by the handful, but that's all it was: words. Now what gold there was has pretty much died out. We didn't find more than a few flakes on our claim. It works out better for us to be lawmen. At least the pay's a bit more, and we won't starve."

Octavius looked at Jack sternly. He had no idea how the sheriff had linked his history and pay scale to his confidence in finding the robbers in Huntsville. He didn't intend asking, either. Sometimes it was just best to remain silent and not invite conversation.

"Yeah," Jack continued, "the truth is, we don't have a whole lot of crime in Loveland. Mostly it's just fist-fights in

John's saloon occasionally. You know, that feud thing between lumbermen and miners not seeing eye to eye after a few drinks. But fist to eye...now *that*, they tend to see pretty well." He laughed at his own joke. "Usually there's no harm done. Hardly anyone ever gets hurt. And no one around here wears a sidearm, unless they're going hunting. Now people carry rifles out and about, but that's mostly due to grizzlies or wolves. We had a mountain lion maul a prospector once, and a grizzly killed a man last May. Dustin tried to track that grizzly down, but it got away, so, it's still out there somewhere. But overall, we don't get a whole lot of crime. The bank's never been robbed before, that's for sure. There's a first time for everything though. You have to pee?" he asked as Octavius dismounted at the bridge.

Octavius walked into the tall grass beside the road with an annoyed glance back at Jack. The trail where the four horses had left the road and came to the river's edge was in plain sight. "No, I don't have to pee. They left the road, Sheriff. Three of their horses came this way and the fourth..." He tossed his reins to Jack to hold and walked across the road. "Came down this side of the bridge. Wait here," he said, and climbed down the four-foot bank onto the wide riverbed.

"Where's our rebel leader going?" John asked.

Jack answered. "Under the bridge. It seems the Sperry Helms Gang needed to water their horses on their way to Huntsville. We probably should, too, but the creeks just a half mile up the road and a lot easier access than jumping down onto that rock bed."

Dustin looked at the trails through the grass. "Yeah, this where they watered their horses, all right."

Jack said to his son, "Yeah, but they came up this road. They should've known the creek's just ahead. Why they risked injuring their mounts to water here, I don't know."

Octavius had walked under the bridge to the other side and looked intently at the rocks he walked over. His eyes examined every rock for the scrapes of horseshoes.

John Riggs called out with his sarcastic smirk, "You remind me of a dog sniffing around for the perfect rock to mark. Just pee, and let's go!"

Dustin said seriously, "You'll find more leaves up yonder in the underbrush, if you have to relieve yourself."

Octavius glanced up at Dustin and John without saying a word. His displeasure with them was evident by his expression. He continued looking.

"That grizzly my pa was telling you about, I tracked it for about two miles before it disappeared in some thick underbrush. I couldn't press my way through, but that bear sure did somehow..."

Octavius disappeared under the bridge and came out on the south side. He walked south, stepping on the rocks without looking back. Jack smiled to the others and said, "You forgot your horse." He chuckled to himself and turned to John and Dustin. "Do you boys want some jerky?" He pulled the cloth bag out of his saddle bag to get a piece.

"I do, Pa," Dustin said as Nathan, Cal and Mike caught up with them.

Nathan spoke first, with interest. "He must've found their trail down there, huh?"

"No, he's just stretching his legs. He's probably saddle-sore. Those men don't have anywhere else to go except to Huntsville," Jack said with confidence.

"Here he comes," Nathan said to no one in particular.

John touched Jack's shoulder to get his attention. He said quietly, "Maybe you should lead the Reb's horse to the other side of the river, so he has to cross the riverbed and break his ankle on the rocks, if we're lucky. He doesn't seem to like me too much. Although, that goes both ways. I don't like him much either."

"Oh." Jack waved John off. "He may not be too friendly right now, but when he gets his money back, I am sure he will warm up. Heck, you and him might become best friends tonight after buying a few drinks, huh?" He said with a smile, "Isn't that right, Octavius?" as Octavius climbed back up onto the road.

"Huh?" Octavius grunted and then took his reigns from Jack without making eye contact.

"I said, you and John might become best friends tonight after we catch these outlaws, isn't that right?"

Octavius shook his head once and said plainly, "No."

"What did you find?" Cal asked.

Octavius swung up into his saddle and looked at Cal. "They went downstream."

"You mean upstream," Dustin corrected from his saddle.

"No, I said downstream!"

Dustin nodded to the trails leaving the road through the grass to the north side of the bridge. "The trail goes upstream. They wouldn't ride off this side of the bridge if they were going south. There's nothing downstream except the wilderness, and they ain't going there if they're smart. No, they either went straight across the riverbed and back up on the road to Huntsville or went upstream to throw us off their trail. But they're going to Huntsville either way."

Octavius glared at Dustin and nodded slightly. "That explains why you couldn't track your grizzly. They went downstream, so that's where I'm going. You can go north though. That would be fine. In fact, I am almost certain they are going to Huntsville, so if you fellows want to go on ahead and cut them off, that would be great. And I'll just follow behind them..." Octavius kicked his horse lightly to move across the road and near the riverbank's edge. His horse half stepped, and half slipped on the four-foot-tall bank to the river rock below.

"Well, let's get going," Cal said and moved his horse to follow Octavius.

John Riggs frowned. "I thought you said they were going to Huntsville," he said to Jack.

"They are. They're just trying to throw us off a bit."

"Yeah." Dustin agreed with his father. "They probably followed the river for a mile or so and then came back towards the road. They don't want to get lost in those woods, I promise you! There's nothing except predators, even a man-eating grizzly somewhere out there. But you got grizzlies and black bear, wolves, mountain lions and very possibly some renegade Indians running loose. It's no place for a greenhorn, trust me on that!"

Nathan sighed. "Why don't you three ride on to Huntsville, and Mike, Cal and I will trail behind with Octavius. We'll most likely meet you there before too long." He hoped they'd agree with him and ride to Huntsville. Nathan didn't mind people talking or having a conversation, but he had limited tolerance for Dustin and his continuous rambling. Most of the time Dustin was wrong about whatever subject he went on about, but there was no arguing with him. He would somehow turn the conversation around, so it appeared that he had been voicing the other person's point of view all along. It was frustrating, to say the least.

"Sounds good to me," John said immediately. "I didn't plan on camping out."

"No," Jack said slowly. "We'd better go along with our tracker. I don't want him taking all the credit when we arrest those robbers. So, let's just go get this done, boys. We'll still be in Huntsville tonight."

Nathan's hope of a peaceful afternoon was ruined when he heard Dustin say with excitement, "We might even find ourselves a new fishing hole, Pa!"

"We very well could."

John hesitated as he watched Nathan and Mike ride down the bank onto the riverbed. "I'm not much for the outdoors..."

Dustin laughed. "John, for being so far in the mountains, you're too much of a city dweller!"

John nodded. "It was where the dollar was when I moved up here. That doesn't mean I like it. Listen, Jack, I was prepared to ride to Huntsville, not go tromping through the woods."

Nathan turned back to look up at the three men. "John, do yourself a favor and go to Huntsville. We'll meet you there."

"No..." John began to argue without sounding convinced.

"Then go back home. This is the Sperry Helms Gang we're going after. If those men decide to run for the hills, it's going to be a long, cold and hard trip. And I'll be honest. You're not cut out for a journey or a fight like this. We might be chasing them for a day or two, and then have a hell of a fight once we find them. And these are real gunmen; let's not forget about that."

Dustin scoffed. "No one in their right mind would cut across the mountains. There's nowhere to go." He chuckled.

"Maybe they won't, but they *could*!" Nathan emphasized to Dustin.

Mike Hall laughed. "Go home, John. I know you want to."

"Well...I'll meet you in Huntsville," John said. "Hey, if I see them on the road, I'll arrest them on the way!" he said with increasing enthusiasm while the others rode down onto the riverbed and began following the river downstream.

"Yeah, have a beer while you wait for me!" Jack yelled back and then laughed.

John waited on the bridge until the last man was out of sight, and then he turned his horse around and rode home to Loveland.

9

Adam Bannister and Luther Fasana had spent the rest of the day slicing meat from the elk and deer into thin strips of varying lengths and widths. Then they rubbed the strips with Luther's special blend of seasonings and spices. After that Luther took the meat into the teepee and draped them over the racks they'd built. It looked like a maze of horizontal and vertical branches and created enough rack space to fill most of the twelve-foot-wide teepee. The same rack rose nearly to the top, ten feet up. A small fire burned in the center of the teepee where green foliage and uncured applewood would be added once a good bed of coals produced enough smoke. The teepee's rain flap would be mostly closed in order to fill the teepee with smoke. After a few days, the moisture in the meat would evaporate and the meat would be smoked thoroughly and turned into jerky. This technique produced enough jerky to last both of their families through the winter and into spring.

It had been a long day of cleaning, slicing, rubbing and hanging meat. Now both men sat by the fire waiting for their supper to finish cooking. Luther had saved a couple of elk steaks and rubbed them with his spice blend before frying them over the campfire. He had a smaller pan of potatoes and onions sizzling, as well. Luther quietly turned over his steaks, then sat back on his round wood block. Adam also sat on a round wood block across from Luther. Every three years or so, while they waited for the meat to cure, they busied themselves cutting down a tree, de-limbing it, and cutting it into round blocks they would split and stack up for the next few years' worth of hunting trips.

Tomorrow, they would begin felling a tree and splitting logs to replenish their wood pile, but for today, they had enough wood and could rest and enjoy the silence of the Wallowa Mountains.

Luther said, "It's too bad we don't have two teepees. I bet we could fill a second one up tomorrow."

Adam grinned. "We've been blessed for sure. We just finished our last canned elk from last winter. Hazel made a stew with carrots, onions, greens, and potatoes. It wasn't watered down like it is in Lee's restaurant, either. It was thick and hearty, just the way it should be. But when that stew was gone, all we had left was beef. And beef stew doesn't have the same taste. I don't like it. This winter when we go hunting, I'm taking two elk home instead of one. My boys are growing and eating like men now."

Luther and Adam hunted their summer jerky elk in the Wallowas, and hunted closer to home in the winter to more easily preserve the meat.

Luther smiled sadly. "I have plenty left over. I don't have a family to feed anymore, and I'll be danged if my kid doesn't like beef over wild game. Billy Jo doesn't want any elk for her family. I've given some to Charlie and Mary, Joel's kids, too, and I still have plenty. I guess that's what happens when I kill a bigger elk than you, huh?" He laughed at his nephew.

Adam grinned. "Yep, yours was bigger," he admitted. "But not bigger than the one I got today." He chuckled and nodded at the massive antlers set over two tree branches on the edge of their camp. The two hides were stretched out and tied to makeshift frames. The men had rubbed salt thickly on the flesh sides of the hides.

"No, but I'd say we put in a full day though," Luther stated proudly.

Adam nodded. "It's not over yet. Tomorrow, we'll ride up and check our traps. I'd love to catch a mountain lion or a grizzly, but we'll probably wind up with wolves or a coyote."

"We could find room in the teepee for a coyote, but probably not a bear," Luther said.

Adam scoffed. "I'm not jerking a coyote," he said with distaste. "I swear; you'd jerk a slug if you found one!"

Luther laughed heartedly. "No, I would not. But oddly enough, your sister-in-law told me some fancy pants in France and other places eat snails! I don't know why. I asked if they were starving to death, and she said, 'No. Snails are a delicacy!' Can you believe that? People pay good money to eat slugs. Unimaginable to me."

"Who told you that?"

"Regina. Who else would know something like that?" He spoke the words as a fact. "But to get back on subject, I saw a lot of wolf sign all around up there. I am sure we'll get a couple of wolves. There was more sign than I ever remember seeing around here."

Adam ignored him. "Snails, huh? What difference is there between a snail and a slug? What do they fry them up with? Salt and a little bacon grease?"

Luther chuckled and looked at Adam. "I don't know. I've

never tried 'em! But if you want, I can probably find a slug and fry it up for you."

"No. I was just curious if they boiled them like oysters or fried them. I can't imagine they'd just eat them out of their shell."

Luther shrugged. "I didn't ask."

"I thought you might've, since you like to cook and all."

Luther smiled. "No, I didn't. And I really don't *like* to cook, either, but I don't have a wife, so I *have* to. I do like good food though, so I learned how to cook. I don't like oysters though; they're about as close to a slug or a snail as I want to get. You know Joel's going to retire in September and will be going to Eleanor's for a while over in Astoria. He wants to see the Pacific Ocean before his time's up. Have you ever seen it?" He spoke of his older brother and business partner, Joel Fasana, who was retiring from their granite quarry. Joel was planning on spending a month or so with their youngest sister, Eleanor Archer, and her family in Astoria, Oregon.

"While in the cavalry I did. We camped out on the beach for a few days. It was wet and windy the whole time. The ocean's amazing though. The land just ends, and it's blue water as far as the eye can see. It seems to go on forever. I am glad to hear Uncle Joel's going to Aunt Eleanor's for a while to see it. It'll be good for him. What about you, Uncle Luther? Do you ever think about retiring?"

Luther shook his head. "No," he said slowly. "My boys are in California doing okay for themselves, and Billy Jo... Well, she still needs me around here, so I don't reckon I'll be leaving the area. In truth, I can't imagine not working at the quarry either. I enjoy it too much. Besides, your cousin, Robert, is pretty much running the show now. I just advise and do some engraving. These days, he has other people doing the hard work."

"You don't want to see the ocean?"

"I used to," he said, sounding saddened by the question. "Lisa always wanted to see the Pacific Ocean, and we even planned on going a few months after Billy Jo was born. But it never happened." His second wife, Lisa, died giving birth to their daughter, Billy Jo. He continued, "After that, I've never wanted to see it. Still don't."

Adam nodded. "Well, Uncle Luther, you've worked your whole life to get where you are. Your business is in good hands, and you have money in the bank. You might as well take a week or two and go see it. Or at least take a trip to see Luke and David in California. You could take Billy Jo with you. We'll watch her kids if need be."

Luther smiled slightly. "Oh...Adam, sometimes you just hit an age where the best days are simply spent sitting in the woods with fresh game over the fire and the smell of jerky drying. I don't need to see the world; I just like to enjoy the moments each day brings."

"Me too. Don't get me wrong, but it's nice to get away from Hazel and the kids for a few days."

Luther frowned. "Hazel's a good woman. Take it from me, Adam. Love her while you can, because you never know what tomorrow's going to bring. I married the boy's mom, my first wife, Courtney, and I thought I loved her. As you know, she left me for a gambler. He was the first man to offer her another life, and she took it. She just wasn't cut out to be a wife and mother. Courtney and I fought all the time. I hate to even admit this, but she's the only woman I ever even considered hitting. I didn't, but I was tempted, she got me so furious. Anyway, looking back now, I was blessed when she left me. Even though it hurt a lot at the time. But Lisa..." He paused for a moment to consider his words. "Now she was a wonderful woman. I thought I loved Courtney, but I didn't. I did love Lisa. I had her for almost two years before she died. She was the love of my life, just like Hazel is yours. But I took it for granted that Lisa would always be there. She wasn't. I raised Billy Jo on my own." He looked at Adam sadly. "Don't take Hazel for granted, Adam. She's a wonderful wife and mother. You be sure to appreciate her every single day of your lives together."

"I do appreciate her—perhaps not as much as I should, but I do appreciate her," he said sincerely. He then looked at Luther with a slight smile and added, "But I still enjoy getting away from her and the kids occasionally."

Luther laughed. "You should have brought your boys with us. They're getting plenty old enough to hunt with us and learn to make jerky right."

"I was going to, but Jeremiah bet Uncle Charlie that he and his friends could finish Charlie's hay field by this Sunday before the church bell rings. They've been working hard on it, even staying later than everyone else to finish it, but I think they bit off more than they can chew."

"Charlie will do right by them." Luther yawned, reached for the pan over the fire, and stirred the potatoes. "Dinner's about ready. I say grab your plate there and let's eat. Tomorrow's going to be a long day of cutting wood, so we better keep our strength up. I think I may do some gold panning in the creek at some point and see what I can find. I've never had much luck up here, but you never know. I've pulled so much granite out of the ground that I never had much time to look for gold."

Adam commented, "If I found a big enough yield, I'd work it. The problem is finding it. I've panned Pearl Creek and didn't find a trace. I hear even the boom up around

Huntsville has petered out. So, I'm thinking the Blue Mountains hold the gold for whatever the reason, and not the Wallowas."

"There's some up here, just not as much. The Wallowas are bigger and have a lot more granite sticking out of the ground. I'm thinking it's deeper in the ground, like silver is in the Blues, but I don't know. I just wish granite was worth more straight out of the ground. It takes a lot of chiseling work to make a block of granite worth something."

Adam shrugged. "I wish I could find gold or silver on my property. We're struggling with the herd on the ranch. I have seventy head of beeves, which is small even for a one-man show. But I wouldn't mind finding a pot of gold to help us get by this year. I need to buy at least another hundred head to increase my herd. If the market's down next year, I'm afraid I will be selling hides to the Natoma Tannery for a living. As it is, I am doing it for extra money now."

"I know you won't ask, but I could invest in your ranch and buy you some cattle..."

"No, Uncle Luther..."

"Now hear me out. I'll purchase the cattle, you sell them down the road, restock your herd for the following year and pay me back over the next five years. It sounds fair enough to me."

Adam shook his head. "I won't allow you to spend your retirement money on me. You spend your money like Uncle Joel does, by enjoying yourself. You've both earned it."

Luther shook his head. "Adam, I've worked my whole life in that quarry making it what it is today, which isn't much, really, but it's growing. It has paid my dues and then some for all these years. I'm an owner, so my income isn't going to change even if I retire today. My point is, I'd like to help you. You're my family, so let me help you. It would be an investment," he said emphatically.

Adam shook his head and appeared uncomfortable. "I appreciate the offer, but no, Uncle Luther. I don't know how or when, but the Lord will provide for us, without us having to borrow from you or anyone else."

Luther frowned. "Not to sound obvious, Adam, but maybe the Almighty is working through me."

"I don't want to be indebted for five years, Uncle Luther. I don't want to be indebted at all. The Lord knows our needs, and I will trust Him and Him alone to supply a herd. Like I said, I'm just a small rancher. With what I have grazing right now, we'll break even. Next year's herd is up to the Lord; we'll just trust that He will provide."

"You can't expect a bag of money left on your doorstep or a hundred head of unbranded cattle to just appear in your field. Those kinds of miracles just don't happen."

"I'm not expecting a miracle. But I do read my Bible, and God says to rely upon Him, so that's what I'm doing. Like I said, I don't know how or when, but I will trust Him. And I will put my hope in Jesus Christ and wait for Him."

Luther looked proudly at his nephew and smiled. "There's nothing wrong with that, but I'd be glad to help if you need it."

10

Deuce McKenna wasn't the kind of man to be worn out by a day in the saddle, but he was exhausted after a day of forging a trail through the Wallowa Mountains. He had followed the Antioch River for about a mile before the shallows turned into a deep pool of clear water. Deuce and his men had left the river and ridden up a steep, wooded mountain side and continued through what seemed like miles of unexplored timberland full of underbrush. They climbed over one mountain just to descend slowly down the rugged terrain and climb up another one of the vast and steep landscapes that made up the Wallowa Mountains.

Farther to the east lay the impenetrable peaks and ice-capped highlands that would be virtually impossible for them to cross without supplies. Even if they'd brought supplies, the crossing might prove suicidal. Now they were on the western end of the Wallowas where the ridges were daunting and appeared endless, but Deuce knew they could manage these lower altitudes. It would be tough riding, but he was confident they could cross the mountains in good time. Deuce pressed onward up one steep ridge that seemed to rise forever, came down through thick forest, and then followed a ravine for a while, only to repeat the process. They kept going south, turning west, then southeast as they zigzagged their way through the trees and up and down the rugged terrain.

It had been a long day of riding— rugged, hard, riding— and the horses were all exhausted and lathered with sweat. The men found a flat area next to a small trickling stream, when Deuce called a halt to the traveling and decided to make camp. He had no idea where they were exactly, except somewhere in the Wallowa Mountains between Huntsville and Jessup County. If they continued south, they would find their way out of the mountains, but the fact was, they still had a long journey ahead through some equally tough terrain.

He was satisfied with how far they had come, but in the back of his mind, he questioned if he had made the right choice. The terrain was taking a heavy toll on the horses, and the men, as well. He had not seen any evidence of mankind in his path yet, but it was well known that the Nez Perce called these mountains home. He wished he had a map of some sort that showed the trail the Nez Perce might have taken to Jessup Valley from where they were making camp.

Unfortunately, no map like that existed. The only map he owned showed one road going from Huntsville to Branson. That road was eighty miles long, circling the western edge of the Wallowa Mountains through valleys and foothills. However, as Deuce concluded from the map, it was undeniably a shorter distance between Huntsville and Branson as the crow flies.

Loveland lay farther northeast in the mountains than any other town so, by his figuring, Jessup Valley, as it was commonly known, was just thirty short miles away. What he had not counted on was the thick underbrush, low branches, fallen trees and long lengths of mountain sides that seemed steeper and longer than any others he'd ever encountered. The mountains were higher than he'd expected when he decided to cut across them. Another danger he had not considered were the sheer cliffs, deep gorges and the ruggedness of the terrain in general.

The horses had stumbled, jumped logs, scratched their hides on limbs and taken a beating as they navigated the wilds of the Wallowas. On the paper map, he had estimated a meager thirty miles straight across the mountains. However, it would take two miles of vertical riding up and down to travel just one mile of horizontal distance. By the time the sun was nearing the western skyline, Deuce was exhausted, ready to dismount, rest his horse and make camp.

They settled in after making a tie line for their horses where they could eat the thick grass and hydrate themselves overnight with fresh water. Deuce wasted no time unrolling his bedroll but sat his weary body down to rest. He leaned against his saddle and watched the sun going down behind the high ridges above them. He was not the only one beaten down and tired from the day of hard riding, but his first moments of rest were interrupted by his nephew, Brent.

"Uncle Dick, how long until we're in the valley, do you think? I'm thinking we put twenty, twenty-five miles behind us. Do you think the valley is just beyond that high ridge over there?"

To the south rose a series of forest-covered mountains that seemed to roll like waves towards a tall wall of solid granite that peaked above the tallest mountains. There was no way to know what was between here and there, but one thing was clear, and it brought a smile to Deuce's face.

"That's Windsor Ridge, Brent. You can see the other side of it clearly from Branson. We'll just head for it, find a way around that puppy and get home."

"We know where we are, then? So, we should be home tomorrow afternoon, yes?" Brent asked hopefully.

Deuce shook his head. "We'll spend all day tomorrow just trying to get to that mountain. But yes, I know where we are." He grinned.

Pick Lawson spoke with a touch or frustration and anxiety in his voice, "It felt like we rode pert' near thirty miles, but I swear we haven't gotten more than ten miles as the crow flies. We still have a long way to go and nothing to eat along the way. I'm beginning to think this was a bad idea, Deuce. Our horses are banged up already, and if we have to cross country any worse than we have, we might be walking out of here. We should've taken our chances on the main road."

"Ten miles!" Brent exclaimed. "No. We traveled at least twenty."

Deuce shook his head. "I don't know how many miles we've come, but a lot of them were vertical miles. The good thing is, any posse coming after us will have to climb the same terrain and wear their horses out too. If we stay ahead of them, we will come out of this okay."

Brent said, "Pick's right though. We didn't bring any food, and I am getting pretty hungry. We'll have to shoot us a deer tomorrow."

"No, we don't have time to cook us up steaks. We must keep moving and move fast. We won't starve to death if we go a day or two without eating."

Karl Digsby said confidently, "There's lots of berries to

eat along the way. I'll go pick a bunch in the morning. They'll tide us over, anyway."

Pick said, "I should've shot that deer earlier. We could be roasting up some venison right about now, instead of talking about picking berries."

Karl responded wryly, "Don't worry, you won't starve. Tomorrow you can eat as many berries as you want out of my sweaty hat."

Pick frowned at his friend. "All I want is a fire and a slab of meat. The idea of not eating for a day or two doesn't suit me very well. You would think with all the money and gold in Deuce's bag we could afford a meal, but instead we're sitting in the middle of nowhere starving!"

"Well, I need to wander into the woods and water a tree. Be back soon," Brent said, standing up from his side of the fire.

"Beware of grizzlies, Brent," Karl warned with a wink. "They come out at night and are drawn to the edges of firelight, just waiting for a guy like you."

"Yeah, right." Brent chuckled as he walked out of sight. "I'd rather run into a grizzly than a posse."

Deuce leaned forward and said quietly, "Pick, being out here is better than sitting in jail. If we went back through Huntsville, we'd have fifty men chasing us an hour after we passed by. Plus, the sheriff there would wire ahead and chase us right into the arms of the next town's sheriff. I, for one, don't plan on getting caught. You guys heard that deputy in Huntsville. The Loveland sheriff isn't too bright. If all he said is true, they'll never find us up here. So, we have a far better chance of success cutting across these mountains than not. Even if the Huntsville sheriff brings a posse and wires ahead, they'll never know where we will exit the mountains or where we're going. Once we get close to the valley, we will all split up and go home. In the meantime, we gave fake names in the bank, so once we exit the woods into the valley and disappear; the only people who will be blamed are Morton and Jessie, and hopefully Cass, too. I say a couple of days of hard traveling and going hungry are worth every cent coming our way." He then added as an afterthought, although one of great importance, "And we'll finally be free of the Sperry and Helms families once for all."

"Yeah," Pick agreed slowly, "but if they find out it was us, we're in trouble. All of us."

"That's the beauty, though. They never will. No one's going to know it was us."

Pick shifted his position to lean closer to Deuce. "Deuce, I am concerned about your nephew. I don't think he understands the importance of keeping his mouth shut about this. All he has to do is mention this to one of his friends, and we could be arrested or worse. Even if Morton and Jessie are sent to prison, there's other Sperrys and Helmses just as dangerous. Your nephew needs to understand that. There's also Marshal Bannister, who lives right in town now."

Deuce nodded. "Brent knows that. I've emphasized the need for silence all along. He'll be okay."

Pick wasn't convinced. "Just make sure of that, okay?"

Karl said calmly, "Brent will be all right. He is young but he at least has enough common sense to keep his mouth shut."

"He had better," Pick warned.

"Or what?" Deuce asked, growing irritated. "Look, I know Brent is young and dumb about some things. He's not real experienced in our line of work, but he knows the risks. He won't say any more than we will about it, trust me on that."

Pick nodded. "Okay." He sounded hesitant.

Just then Brent walked out of the tree line towards the fire. "No grizzlies, Karl. You can go on out there now if you want. So," he said to Pick, "you think we only went about ten miles or so, huh?"

Pick nodded and said evenly, "I have a bit more experience than you at traveling cross country. And yeah, I'd say about ten miles is all we've come. We did a lot of riding, but we didn't get very far."

Brent sighed. "I was hoping we were closer to home. I'm up for riding all night if it means being back in town by tomorrow night. I was hoping to buy every dance I can with Christine, tomorrow night over at the dancehall."

"Hey...ah...Brent, you do know you can't tell anyone where the money comes from, right? If you start flashing your money around like that, people will become suspicious. So, you can't do that or let anyone know what we did." Deuce said.

"Do you think I'm stupid, Uncle Dick? I'm not going to tell anyone about where I got the money. But I am getting hungry, just thinking about taking her out to dinner," he added with a smile.

Karl yawned. "There's probably some crawdads in the creek we can catch tomorrow. It's not much, but we won't starve."

"Think there's any chance we'll be back in town by tomorrow night?" Brent asked anyone who would answer.

Deuce shook his head. "No. It's going to be a piece of riding just to get to Windsor Ridge. Then we must navigate a way around it. After that, we still have what? Ten, fifteen miles or so of mountains and foothills to cross before we reach the valley."

Brent exhaled deeply. "That means another two or three nights out here without food?"

"Probably, maybe more if our horses don't hold up. They're not used to riding like this either, you know. We'll have to rest them occasionally."

"What if we're being followed? How would we know if we are or not?" Brent asked.

Deuce yawned. "We don't. But we keep moving all the same. Those mountain folks aren't going to be sitting idle when their bank's been robbed. So, let's just keep our fire small, listen to our horses, move as fast as we can and not shoot anything for dinner," he said looking at Pick.

"I'm not stupid, just hungry."

Deuce chuckled. "Me too. But it will be worth it when we get home. Let's just rest up, break camp early and get moving. The faster we go, the faster we'll get home."

"What about a sentinel? Should we keep watch tonight?" Brent asked.

Deuce shook his head. "No one's going to track us in the dark. If they're out there, they'll be making camp too. Let's just relax while we can and get some rest."

11

Cal Pierce rode beside Octavius through the forest as the light began to disappear within the thick trees. They had followed the trail down the river and easily found where the gang departed the riverbed to ride up the steep grade of a tall ridge. Octavius had told Jack that the men they were chasing were not trying to hide their trail. Since then, Octavius had heard Dustin Schwartz repeat the very same line to everyone else in the posse at least twice.

For a man who liked being alone, Octavius could not think of a greater hell on earth than being stuck with the company of a father and son who never quit talking. Worse, they had no idea what they were talking about! It was an aggravation he could barely tolerate, and the more they talked, the more aggravated Octavius became. Twice he had verbalized his frustration to them, but they didn't seem to care; they just kept talking. He would gladly leave them behind or shoot them off their horses, but there were three other men who were far more competent than they, riding along with them.

Cal Pierce seemed the most adept of the three other

men. Cal was a quiet man who spoke very little and smiled even less. Undoubtedly, Cal was a tough breed of man even at his young age of twenty-seven. He was committed, driven and confident in his own skills. His confidence wasn't from back-room street brawling like the many young toughs Octavius had run into over the years, but by the confidence acquired from practical military training and experience. Octavius had no doubt Cal could be the real deal when he needed to be.

His younger brother, Nathan, was a competent horse-man, though not as experienced with tracking as Cal. He asked Cal and Octavius questions occasionally about tracking and seemed to be soaking in everything he could learn. Nathan was clearly a confident young man and genuinely happily married to the love of his life, but behind the joyful exterior there seemed a deep emptiness in his eyes and little peace within him. Cal spoke little and hardly ever smiled, but he seemed joyful despite his sorrowful expression. Nathan, on the other hand, had a handsome smile and quick wit, but the longer Octavius rode with Nathan, the more he noticed Nathan's eyes appeared sad and hopeless.

Octavius liked the two brothers, though. Among other things, he liked that they were as annoyed by the sheriff and his son as he.

Mike Hall was the last of the posse. He intentionally rode behind the rest and hadn't said a word during the whole trip so far. He was obviously a seasoned hunter and maneuvered his mule and pack mule expertly, even on steep grades with fallen trees. He'd had the foresight to bring provisions. None of the others had, and all of them would be grateful to Mike for that. Undoubtedly, Mike knew the mountains and how to navigate them. Mike was quick to ascertain that the gang of robbers was trying to cut across the west end of the mountain range to drop down into Jessup Valley. When they reached that point, the sheriff, Jack Schwartz, wanted to end the pursuit and ride to Huntsville to wire the authorities in Branson.

It was Cal who foolishly pointed out that no one in Jessup County except Octavius could identify the robbers. Octavius and the two brothers insisted on continuing the pursuit, but they encouraged Jack and Dustin to ride to Huntsville and wire ahead. Seeing the others were persistent to continue after the robbers, Jack and Dustin chose to stay with them, to Octavius' great disappointment.

Octavius slowed down to ride beside Nathan. "Your wife seems like a fine lady. She reminds me of my own wife twenty years ago. You're a lucky man."

Nathan looked at Octavius, surprised by the unexpected conversation. The two men had spoken no more than a few words during the day. "Thank you," he said awkwardly. "She is quite a lady. Again, I was sorry to hear about what happened to your wife."

Octavius nodded and showed no emotion on his aged face. "Your wife reminds me of my Lucinda."

"I've been thinking about what happened to your wife since this morning. I don't know how I'd ever get over something like that, or what I would do. I try to put myself in your shoes, but I can't. Sarah is my world."

Octavius exhaled deeply and looked at Nathan. "You don't want to be in my shoes, boy. They've come a long way and stepped through more blood than a man's supposed to see in a lifetime. If you're as wise as I think you might be, you'd take my advice, turn around and go home right now. Take care of your wife. We'll take care of the robbers. She's a good one, and, just so you know if continue with us, I intend on keeping my promise to her."

Nathan frowned, "What promise?"

"To get you home alive."

Nathan laughed and smiled. "That's my Sarah for you; always looking out for me."

Cal glanced back at Nathan and smiled; his first smile of the day. "I swear, if anyone ever blackened your eye in a fight, Sarah would track them down with a switch and give them a licking!" He laughed. "And I thought Ma babied you!"

Nathan smiled proudly. "Yeah, she would!" He smiled at Octavius. "I don't know what I'd do if anyone ever hurt her."

Octavius grinned knowingly. "You'd hunt them down and kill them. That is exactly what you'd do; I can see it right there," he said and pointed at Nathan's eyes.

Nathan grew serious. "Probably so."

Cal said seriously, looking back at him, "You would, because I'd go with you to do it!"

Octavius nodded. "Indeed, you would. I can see it in you," he said to Cal.

"Is that what you did?" Cal asked Octavius.

Octavius looked at Cal for a moment and then stared straight ahead. "I'm thinking our bank robbers are local valley boys pretending to be who they claimed to be. They said they were the Sperry Helms Gang, but most gangs don't make it a point to name themselves like those boys did. I don't think it was them. They were too obvious."

Cal watched Octavius closely. "I thought that myself. So, to change the subject, I'm taking that as a yes; you did hunt those men down."

Octavius glared at Cal. "I buried my wife, and that's all I'll say about it."

Nathan interrupted the growing tension between the two men. "Octavius, you mentioned your children earlier. What happened to them?"

Octavius sighed. "I left them with my wife's sister and her family when I left. I don't know how they fared since."

"Left where?" Cal asked.

Octavius appeared to be growing annoyed. "Cumberland Mountains, East Kentucky."

Cal questioned with interest, "Clinton County?"

Octavius looked at Cal and grew serious as his dark eyes narrowed. His voice took on a low and dangerous tone, "Why?" He stopped his horse to wait for an answer.

"I've read a lot about the war. That area of the Cumberland Mountains was brutalized by both sides. You said your wife died twenty years ago. That would make the year about eighteen sixty-two, sixty-three. I read there were a lot of rebel guerilla forces running around those hills at the time."

Octavius nodded slowly, without taking his hardened gaze from Cal. "There were a lot of union guerillas running around, too, but you probably didn't read about that in your Union books, did you?" He sounded bitter.

"I did. Champ Ferguson was around that area, wasn't he?" Cal asked.

Like an unexpected strike of lightening, surprise and possibly even worry flashed in Octavius' eyes. As soon as the expression had appeared, it was gone. Octavius spoke quickly but left no doubt about his ending the conversation. "Don't ask questions you already know the answers to. Now if you don't mind, we have men to catch!" he kicked his horse and rode ahead of Cal and his brother.

Cal watched him carefully and said nothing more. He kicked his horse as well to get it moving up the mountain side.

Jack had ridden into the small clearing within the trees in which they had stopped to talk momentarily. "Hold up, boys! I think this is a fine spot to camp for the night."

Octavius turned around immediately. He was angry. "What?"

"Yeah, this is good. Let's set up camp, boys. We have a long day tomorrow, so let's rest up." Jack dismounted his horse as did his son, Dustin.

Octavius glanced around him. They were in a dense forest of Douglas fir trees on a slanted incline of a mountain side. Though it wasn't as steep as some they had climbed, it was a small patch of clearing with a dead, rotting log lying across it, surrounded by tall ferns and underbrush. What irritated Octavius most was that there was no grass or water source with which the horses could nourish their bodies for the following day. He was furious.

"Mike," Jack continued, "go ahead and run a string line for the critters. I'll clear a spot for the fire, while Dustin borrows your handy-dandy axe and cuts up some wood for the fire. That dead log right there should supply us with some good wood. In the meantime, perhaps you two"—he nodded at Cal and Nathan—"can dig into the supplies and see what we can cook up. I know I'm getting pretty hungry." He looked at the obviously angry Octavius. "Well, step on down and sit awhile. I brought some cards. We can play few hands to pass the time."

Octavius was dumbfounded. "There's still an hour of daylight left! We could gain another mile on them!"

"Ah, they ain't going nowhere." Jack waved him off. "They're taking the time to blaze the trail. We're running right up their backside in record time. We'll be on them tomorrow early, I figure."

Octavius said heatedly, "They were two hours ahead of

us to begin with because of your talking to everyone in town! Now they're probably eight hours ahead of us, because of your talking on the trail! We're not pressing them. They're escaping us because you and your damned son won't shut up and ride. They'll gain two more hours in the morning by the time you sip your damned coffee or tea! Whatever it is you damned cowards drink! If you want to sit here and tell stories all night, fine, but I am going after my gold!" He turned his horse to leave.

"I'm afraid you're not!" Jack said. Octavius' words angered him. He didn't mind letting folks blow off some steam, but he was sick of listening to Octavius' insults. "Cal, Nathan, Dustin, if he takes one more step, shoot his horse! You see, Otto, I am in charge, and I don't like being yelled at. Now get off your horse, or these boys will shoot it, and we'll leave you here on foot!"

Octavius moved his hand towards his revolver, but he stopped short when he noticed Cal's hand already on his and ready to pull his revolver. Cal had a better angle and could fire his gun in half the time it would take Octavius to unclasp the leather loop around his trigger, pull his weapon, raise his arm and turn it to fire at Cal. Octavius knew he was at a disadvantage and lowered his hand to his thigh. Jack and the others might not even have noticed his actions, but Cal had. He'd not only noticed but acted as if he'd antici-pated them. Octavius looked at Cal and then smiled as he gritted his teeth. He said to the sheriff, "I assure you, I could find those men on foot faster than you can with fresh horses."

Dustin scoffed and shook his head. "That's ridiculous!"

Jack shrugged. "Maybe, but I'm in charge, ain't I? Look, I'm a fair fella, I think. I certainly don't like to be forceful, but I can't have you chasing our gang without us. So, here's what you're going to do. You're going to get off your horse, put your saddle and bed roll over there and enjoy our company for a while."

Octavius shook his head. "Why don't you stay here and me and the boys here will go find the robbers. I won't let them get away just because you're hungry! Come on, boys, let's go get them." Octavius turned his horse to leave.

"Stop!" Jack yelled, "I said you're not going anywhere. Now get down off your horse and unsaddle it. I won't warn you again! I know you don't think much of me, but I'm the sheriff, and you're working for me. Now get off your horse!"

Octavius remained seated and looked at Jack defiantly. He said, "I don't work for you. And secondly, I'm not the kind of man who likes to be ordered around, especially by someone who isn't worth the sweat off my horse's ass. Your boy might think you're a hard man to handle, but I could go through you like a breeze through the trees. You might want to keep that in mind when you're talking to me, Jack. I am not one of your local boys. I have seen more and done more, than you can possibly imagine."

Jack smiled and shook his head as he chuckled. "You might be tough as nails, but five to one is a pretty tall order for anyone to handle. I don't want to fight with you, but we are making camp for the night, and that's all there is to it. Now, I'm asking you one last time to get off your horse and come join us for some grub, cards and some rest before we continue tomorrow. Please."

"If I refuse?" Octavius asked with a mean scowl on his clenched jaw.

Jack shrugged. "Then Cal or my son will shoot your horse, and its ass won't sweat anymore."

Dustin pulled his rifle out of its scabbard and aimed it at Octavius' horse as Jack spoke.

Octavius reluctantly got out of the saddle, knowing he was momentarily defeated in his fight to keep going. "The men we're after are better mounted then we are, and we will never catch them if we don't push through the night. All our horses are exhausted and thirsty. Only someone as stupid as you would camp on the side of a mountain with no grass or water to replenish them! We won't find any water until we get over this mountain and down into a gorge, if we're lucky. Who knows what's on the other side of this mountain? Jack, our horses might drop dead from dehydration before we get to water if you make them wait here all night. Stupid, just plain stupid!" Octavius spoke bitterly while leading his horse over to the line Mike had just finished tying between two trees.

"You can share your canteen with your nag if you want to, but horses are hardy animals, and they'll be fine." Jack turned to Dustin. "Besides, my hind end's aching. I don't think I've sat in a saddle for this long since..."

"Not since coming out west. It's the being bounced around that's killing my butt."

"Well, that was wagon travel coming west. I'm talking about sitting in the saddle. It's been a rugged ride, and I'm not so used to that. I'm sure the robbers are saddle sore too, though," Jack said.

"You ride all the time, Pa."

"Not for no eight or nine hours."

"No, I suppose not, but Huntsville is a couple-hour ride."

"Yeah, but we never ride back the same day, we always stay the night..."

"Seriously?" Octavius asked in disbelief. "You're the sheriff and you're complaining about being saddle sore?"

"I am, too," Dustin offered as he rubbed his backside.

"I'm not surprised," Octavius stated.

"Well, Mister Clark," Jack said, "Loveland isn't too crime-ridden. And it's small enough that I don't need to ride anywhere. Most of the time my horse is in the livery stable eating. Dustin's too, usually."

Dustin said, "I take Lightning Bolt hunting sometimes."

"Lightning Bolt?" Octavius asked and then chuckled at Dustin.

"Yeah, Lightning Bolt. She's a full-blooded Arabian; a whole lot faster than any other horse breed. Arabians are known for their speed, endurance and sure-footedness. I don't know what else matters besides that. I know one thing: Lightning Bolt is bred to go without water, so she'll keep going long after all of your horses give out."

"Your horse is not an Arabian," Octavius said simply.

"She is, too! I bought her from a man who bought her straight from the breeder in Arabia! Her ma was brought overseas with Lightning Bolt still inside her. She's an American-born pure-bred Arabian!"

Octavius chuckled and then looked at Dustin with befuddlement. "You have to be the dullest knife in the west! Do you know that?" He wore a bitter half smile as he set his saddle down at the base of a tree.

Dustin was taken aback by the insult and frowned. "I'm not stupid, mister, I know what my horse is. I'm the one who bought her!"

Octavius shook his head. "Well, that's true. But I wouldn't go around calling your quarter horse an Arabian if I was you. Personally, I couldn't care less, but it might be a bit more embarrassing in front of a lady if she knows anything about horses; and most of them do."

Dustin scoffed. "No, I know what my horse is. Lightning Bolt is not a quarter horse, and anyone who knows what an Arabian is can tell you that! Isn't that right, Mike? No one knows more about horses than Mike. What is she, Mike, an Arabian or a quarter horse?"

Mike Hall looked up from checking the bottom of his mule's foot. "Um, she's as Arabian a horse as I've ever seen, but she's the only Arabian I've ever seen," he said and reached down to check the other foot of his mule.

Dustin wasn't satisfied with Mike's confirmation, so he called out to Cal. "Cal, you know. You tell him!"

Cal raised his eyebrows as he answered. "Well, it's just like the Arabian I saw in San Francisco. It was in a traveling carnival and had a sign saying, 'Ride a real Arabian for five cents'."

"See?" Dustin asked Octavius with confidence. "Maybe you don't know so much about horses after all. I mean, my Pa's been working horses since he was a kid in the fields, so I'd say he knows quite a bit more than you give him credit for!"

"That's probably true," Octavius said. "I'm getting the idea that arguing with you is senseless, because you're always right, huh?"

"No, but I know what Lightning Bolt is. She's an Arabian. What's your horse's name, anyway?"

"I don't name animals. I don't get attached to them like some people do."

"Well, I named Lightning Bolt because she's white and real fast. On Independence Day, I won first place in our town's horse race. She won by almost a length! I won twenty dollars. Next year, I'm taking her to Huntsville for their Independence Day race, and if I win there, I will take her to Branson the next year. She's fast. I'd say faster than most, but she's an Arabian, and that's what they're known for."

"Hmm mm," Octavius said while combing his sweat-lathered horse.

"You should name your horse. I think a good name for yours would be...um...I don't know. Red, if nothing else."

Jack Schwartz walked over to join in the conversation. "I had a horse named Red. Remember that old nag I bought from Ike? His name was Bethel, or some odd name like that; it was a funny name for a horse. Anyway, I renamed him, Red. He was about the same color as yours. A little bigger though."

"I remember Red," Dustin replied. "He was thorough-bred, wasn't he?"

"Thorough work horse, anyway. That old boy got sick, so we had him for dinner!" He laughed. "A little Red steak for dinner!" he repeated himself and laughed again. "We had Red stew the next few nights!"

Dustin added to Octavius when he finished laughing with his father, "Just think, if your horse keels over because he can't keep up with Lightning Bolt, we could have some more red steak!" He laughed at his own joke.

Octavius peered from father to son with no hint of humor on his face. "My horse won't give out going at your pace," he said, and walked past them to Cal and Nathan, who remained by their horses. "His horse ain't an Arabian," he said as a matter of fact to Cal.

Cal shrugged. "It doesn't do any good to argue with him. I just agree and let it be. Otherwise, he'll follow you around until you do agree. In fact, here he comes now."

Nathan chuckled. "Let's ride up to the top and see if we can see anything."

"Let's go," Cal said, and he mounted.

"Where do you think you're going?" Dustin asked as he stopped beside Octavius to hear the brothers' answer.

"Just looking up there. We'll be right back," Cal said and continued to ride away from Dustin.

Dustin spoke a touch louder to be sure he could be heard. "They're not hiding their trail, so you should be able to follow it to the top okay." He turned to look at Octavius, who gazed at him with an aggravated expression on his face. Dustin didn't seem to notice. He continued, "Most outlaws at least try to hide their trail, but not these guys."

"I told you that," he exclaimed irritably. "I didn't say most outlaws; I said if they feared the law coming after them, they'd try to hide their tracks. They're not, because they don't fear you, and I can understand why."

"Oh, and they should fear you?" Dustin spat out, resentful about being insulted again.

"They will."

"Yeah, they will when we arrest them. Pa's and my name will become known throughout the area, and men like them will stay out of our neck of the woods for good, because they will fear us. Who knows? If we get into a gunfight, we might even become as well-known as Matt Bannister. He's the new marshal over in Branson now. You've heard of him, I'm sure," Dustin finished with confidence.

Octavius simply stared at Dustin with a scowl and didn't say a word.

Dustin continued, "We could become so well known that he asks us to move to Branson and be his deputies."

Octavius narrowed his eyes and said indifferently, "I wasn't talking about them being afraid of you. I meant they'll be afraid of me when I catch up with them."

Dustin exclaimed, "I know! They will me, too. I wear a badge, remember? Like I was saying, Matt Bannister has a pretty-tough reputation, but I met him once when we went to Branson about two months ago and, you know, he really doesn't look that tough to me. He's got long hair and a beard, like the Pierce brothers, but he didn't look as tough as they do. He was standing outside of his office in a suit when we stopped and introduced ourselves. I was expecting a giant, I guess, but he's not much bigger than me. I think I could take him in a fight. I haven't lost many fights. He seemed like a nice-enough man, but he wasn't as tough as people say. After Pa and I catch the Sperry Helms Gang, we'll have a reputation like that too. Marshal Bannister would probably offer us a job with him."

Octavius exhaled heavily and rolled his eyes. "I doubt that."

"Wait and see. I might have to shoot one or two of those men, and the newspapers will write about that. I could become famous, just like Matt Bannister. And like I said, I don't think he's as tough as they say. I could take him," Dustin said with confidence.

"You do that," Octavius said and walked away from him.

Dustin followed. "Have you ever been in a gunfight? Because we may get into one with the Sperry Helms Gang."

Octavius turned and faced Dustin. "I asked you that earlier. So why the hell are you asking me, when you already know the answer. For a man who's never drawn a weapon on another man, you sure talk a lot. Tomorrow you may get your chance, but until then, shut the hell up! You have no idea what you're talking about."

"Do you?" Dustin snapped. He then backtracked when he saw the hard eyes of Octavius turn deadly cold as they glared into his. "I mean, we don't know if you have the mettle when it comes right down to it."

Octavius was perplexed. He shook his head slowly and answered, "Son, I have killed more men with a saber than you will ever kill, and that's not counting killing men using my guns, knife and hands. Killing those four men will be no trouble for me. It's what I'm good at."

"Yeah, that's what I'm saying..."

"What?" Octavius asked, raising his voice in frustration. "Huh?"

"What the hell *are* you talking about? You haven't shut up since we've stopped. No wonder you're not married. Not even a used-up nickel whore could stand listening to you talk your nonsense for very long! Now shut up and leave me alone!"

"I don't talk nonsense. I haven't said anything that isn't true. Besides, I think you're rude," Dustin said as his father walked over to them.

Jack said with a friendly smile, "What's going on over here?" He chuckled nervously.

Octavius said, "Get your son away from me, and keep him away from me. I'm not telling you again." He sounded as if he meant it.

Jack frowned. "Why are you so riled up? What'd he do?"

"I didn't do anything, Pa."

"Well, son, why don't you go get some wood cut for the fire like I told you, and I'll talk to Mister Clark."

"Fine," Dustin said and walked toward the horses where the axe lay.

Jack shook his head. "Kids. Well, he's not so much a kid anymore. He's twenty-seven—"

Octavius cut him off "He's a man! And I won't tolerate him any longer. Keep him away from me. I swear; I've never met anyone who talked as much as he does in my life!"

"Well...he may not be the brightest star in the sky, but he's certainly not the dimmest. I suppose that's my fault. I mean, he didn't have much schooling, and I'm no scholar by any means," Jack said and chuckled.

Octavius shook his head with disgust. "Just keep him

130

away from me." He walked quickly away from Jack and into the trees to be alone.

"Where'd Oggie go?" Dustin asked, watching Octavius walking away.

"It's not Oggie, it's...well, let's just call him Mister Clark. He doesn't seem to like us too well, so let's just leave him alone for a while."

Dustin frowned. "I don't like him so well either. He thinks he knows everything, and I don't like people like that."

"I know what you mean. I don't like people like that either. Well, let's make a fire before it gets dark."

12

Pick lay on his blanket holding his head up with his right hand, covered by a blanket not far from the small fire the men had made. The other three men were lying around the fire, talking quietly before going to sleep for the night.

"You know, I was engaged once a long time ago," Pick offered. "I was twenty-five, and Lilly was her name. She was twenty years old and had the prettiest brown hair and eyes you've ever seen. I sure loved her, and she loved me, or so she said. I asked her to marry me and she agreed. It was the happiest day of my life—up to that point, anyway. Some girls are just funny, and Lilly was one of those funny ones. She could make me laugh for sure, and I enjoyed being with her, plain and simple. I suppose that's what makes love... well, love: just enjoying being with that person.

"Anyway, I was hired on to drive a herd up to Kansas City, and it took about three months. When I got paid, the first thing I did was buy Lilly a pretty, yellow dress, some hair things and a wedding ring. I spent a large part of my earnings on her, and I hurried back home as fast as I could go.

"When I knocked on her door, she was all prettied up for another man! She'd done lost her interest in me and moved on. I gave her the dress and hair things, and proposed with the ring, all gentlemanly like. And she said, 'no'. Oh, she was thankful for the dress and hair things; she liked them a lot, but apparently not me. In my absence, she had taken a liking to a barber with nicer hair than me. He knew how to cut hair, too. She broke my heart, fellas. She really did," he said.

He continued, "I kept the wedding ring. There was no reason to give that to her anymore. She got married in that yellow dress I bought her, though, and she wore the hair things, too. In fact, I even sold the wedding ring I bought to the barber so he could put it on her finger when he married her."

Deuce said, "You paid for your fiancé's wedding to another man? That's very gentlemanly of you!" He laughed with the two other men at Pick's story.

Pick nodded and smiled. "I did, and then I was broke and broken-hearted! Boys, stay away from Lillies. They are heartbreakers. I packed up my horse and left town. I went back about three years later to see my folks before they moved on to heaven. I decided to get my hair cut. The barber said they were doing well and had two kids and a third on the way. Then the ungrateful dog had the gall to charge me for a shave and a haircut, even after he stoled my lady, and I paid for him to marry her!" he finished, laughing with the others.

"I would've shot him," young Brent Boyle said with a grin.

"Nah, that's just the price you pay for loving a Lilly. She was too poor of heart, I think. Some people, men and women just can't seem to be by themselves for very long before they start getting lonely and need to be loved. I don't get it, but she was my one true love, nonetheless."

Deuce McKenna offered, "My wife and I have been married for twenty years almost. We've had some tough times, but she's still by my side. Sometimes I don't know why, but she is. Her parents thought I'd be a success at whatever I put my mind to. I suppose they'd be disappointed to know I'm not much more than muscle at the grist mill and a part-time robber."

Pick said, "Well, you can always become a full-time robber."

"Sounds good to me," Brent said with enthusiasm. "I always wanted to meet the Sperry Helms Gang, but Uncle Dick won't introduce me."

Deuce shook his head. "And I am not going to. Morton Sperry is not the kind of man you want to know. It is best to just stay clear of all of the Sperrys and the Helms family." He turned his attention to Pick. "You know the others aren't going to be happy about us doing this?"

"So you've said. Once Morton and Jessie are arrested, the rest will lie low and fade away to keep the law at bay. The Sperry Helms Gang is practically finished; thanks to us."

"What do you think?" Deuce asked Karl Digsby, who had remained quiet, as usual.

Karl shrugged. "I personally can't stand my wife."

"What?" Deuce laughed. "I was talking about the Sperrys."

Karl nodded. "I know. Remember I was with Morton, Jessie and Cass when they murdered that fella called Possum and his wife. I had to drag their bodies into the cabin before they burned it down. I am not saying a word about them in any way, shape or form until they are in prison or hung. So yeah, I can't stand my wife. I've been married for four years, and I've hated every one of them."

"What happened up there at Possum's?" Pick asked.

"I'm not saying a word about it... Not until the gang's in jail."

"Was his wife pretty?" Deuce asked. "Remember we used to wonder why he kept her hidden away so far up in the woods?" he asked Pick.

Pick nodded. "Yeah. Was she?"

Karl frowned and shook his head. "No."

"I didn't know you were married," Brent said to Karl.

Karl nodded. "Like I said, I don't like my wife, and she doesn't like me, so I don't talk about it."

"Do you have kids?" Brent asked.

Karl nodded sadly. "One. A three-year-old daughter named Susan."

Pick suggested, "Since you don't like her, why don't you send her back to her folks?"

Karl rolled his eyes exaggeratedly, "Because she won't go without me."

Pick chuckled. "I thought she didn't like you."

"She doesn't. But she said her vows, and she won't break them. So, like it or not, we're married for the worse."

Deuce asked, "Why'd you marry her if you didn't like her?"

"I did like her back then. It was after our wedding that she changed," he said.

"How'd she change?" Pick asked.

Karl breathed in deeply and then exhaled. "She won't fulfill her wifely duties. It took nearly two weeks after our wedding to consummate our union, and she didn't like it. Far and in between were any kinds of consummations in our union. Once she got pregnant and had a baby, that was it. She won't ever do it again, not at all."

"Huh," Deuce grunted. "Maybe I should be extra thankful for my Mabel. She's never acted that way."

"Uncle Dick, I don't want to hear about Aunt Mabel that way!"

Deuce chuckled lightheartedly. "Maybe not but do yourself a favor and find a woman like your Aunt Mabel to marry. I'm not much, but she sure loves me."

Pick looked at Karl thoughtfully. "Maybe you should try courting her again. I mean, buy her a new dress, maybe some new hair things and take her to the Monarch Hotel for a good dinner. Make her feel pretty. Perhaps that'll spark her fire for you."

Karl looked at Pick seriously. "She doesn't like sex, period. She has no interest in it at all. I've tried that a few times, and it makes no difference. She's locked up as tight as a bank's safe. It's the strangest and most frustrating thing in the world."

Pick smirked. "There's a bright side to that. If you ever get syphilis, she'll never know about it."

Karl gave a sarcastic smile and nod to Pick. "What is your deal with dresses and hair things, anyway? Do you always buy dresses and hair doodads?"

Pick laughed. "My ex-fiancé, Lilly, told me that women always love to feel pretty. She said a man who can make them feel pretty is a man they will fall in love with and do anything for. Dresses and hair things help with that. You know the saying, 'you can't buy love', but love sure does inspire us to buy our women gifts. What's nicer than a pretty dress to make them feel pretty?"

"You're not married," Karl replied simply.

"Never have been, but I wanted to get married once."

"Yeah, you told us," Karl said.

Brent leaned forward with a grin that expressed a touch of excitement. "I would sure like to marry Christine. I swear, she's the most beautiful girl I've ever seen in my life, but I don't know how to win her affections. There are so many guys with more money than me who dance with her at night. That's why I was hoping to get back to Branson quickly, so I can dance with her over and over and try to win her affections."

"From Bella's Dance Hall? That singing girl, Christine?" Pick asked.

"Yeah."

Pick chuckled. "Boy, you better rob a bigger bank than the one we robbed. She's an expensive one, and she won't look twice at a pup like you. She's drawing the men like fleas to a dog, and half of those men got something to offer her aside from their last dollar for a quick dance."

"Do you know her?" Brent asked, a touch of jealousy in his voice.

"Not personally, but does anyone get to know entertainers personally? All those girls are housed there and are watched around the clock, just so no one does get too close to them. They're money to Bella, and she doesn't risk losing them to strangers like you or me. Good luck, boy, but I don't see you marrying her ever happening."

"You should see the way she looked at me. There was something there, something she doesn't see in everyone. I know there was. I felt it, and I could see it in her eyes. Yeah, if I could dance with her a few more times and have the chance to talk to her, I am sure I could court her."

"With what?" Pick asked skeptically. "She's not the kind of girl who will settle into a marriage of hiding from the law. You seem to want it all: the high-class wife and life, provided from the lowest of ambitions. Take it from me: you can't have it both ways. Not in this world."

Karl said quietly, "Oh, let the boy dream. It's good to have something to shoot for. Brent, you just go for it and do your best to win her. The worst she can do is reject you, and that's not so hard to accept, so go for it."

"I will..."

Deuce yawned. "We better get some rest. I want to be moving by sunup. If there's a posse behind us, we want to stay ahead of them until we hit the valley. It's still a far piece of riding to get to Windsor Ridge, but I think we'll get there by tomorrow if we get going early and move fast. Once we get over that ridge line, the rest is all downhill. I reckon we could be home by Sunday night, or Monday at the latest."

Brent sounded disappointed as he said, "Today is Friday."

"One thing's for sure," Pick said, "Karl's wife isn't being unfaithful!" He laughed.

Karl laughed despite himself. "That's for sure."

A wolf's howl echoed through the mountains. It sounded distant, but it still raised the hairs on the backs of their necks in the blackness of the forest. The howl was followed by three more wolves in succession. With echoes, the howling seemed to come from all directions, but all were distant and came from Windsor Ridge.

"Wolves," Deuce said, listening carefully. "I heard three different ones, but there's bound to be a lot more out there. I might be wrong, but it sounds like the howls are coming from the direction we're going. Keep your revolvers handy tonight. Even if a posse doesn't find us, a pack of starving wolves might."

Pick nodded. "With a posse out there, trust me, my gun's already within reach. You boys make sure your weapons are ready to use. If anything happens, we might have to be quick."

Brent said, "Men can't track us at night. I'm more worried about a wolf attack or a grizzly than I am about a posse."

"Best we can do is be prepared for it. Goodnight boys," Deuce said. He closed his eyes to rest his weary body.

13

"Did you hear that?" Luther Fasana asked Adam. He lay on his bedroll watching the fire. "Sounds like we might've caught us a wolf or two," he said of the high-pitched yipping and howls coming from the meadow above them. The echoes created a menacing atmosphere in the otherwise silent mountain air.

Adam smiled as he listened. He lay on his back, across the fire from Luther, ready to go to sleep. "Yeah, I'd say we caught a wolf or two. Maybe all three traps caught one. It's hard to say with all that howling. We should have brought more traps though."

Luther nodded and spat into the fire to hear the sizzle in the red coals. "There's plenty of wolves up here, that's for sure. The traps I set probably caught the bigger ones. Yours probably caught a pup."

Adam grinned. "Probably."

"Listen to them!" Luther said, looking up the mountain. In an instant, the cries and howling seemed to triple in number and rise in volume like a flash flood racing down the mountain after a torrential rain. "My word, there's more than I've ever heard before. Maybe we caught the best-loved pack leader they've ever had."

Adam sat up to look at the black mountainside outlined, by the clear night's sky. He couldn't believe he was hearing so many wolves at one time. He shook his head, but within him, a stirring of excitement began to grow. They had come to hunt elk and trap a few wolves or, if they were lucky enough, catch a mountain lion. Then they'd sell the hides at the Natoma Tannery for a few dollars. However, as he listened to the howling, it was clear there was a multitude of wolves he could hunt and kill. Every pelt brought in that much more money, and a pelt of good size and condition could bring five dollars at the Tannery. If he shot twenty wolves, it was possible to earn as much as a hundred dollars. That much money could be turned into a few new young beeves in the spring. He asked his uncle, "I wonder what we caught up there?"

"Wolves, Adam," Luther said. "They'll still be there in the morning. I suggest we just enjoy listening to them tonight. I've never heard so many of them, though," Luther said, with obvious awe.

"Nor I, but you know we can move our traps tomorrow and set a few snares, too. We may not get out of here for a week or two if wolf-hunting is as promising as it sounds like it could be."

"It could add up to quite a few dollars, couldn't it?" Luther asked without too much interest evident in his voice.

"It could add up, sure enough."

"Unfortunately, we're committed men," Luther said, looking over at his nephew. "You have your family and I have my business, so we can't stay away too long."

"True," Adam replied tiredly as he lay down again.

Luther rolled onto his back and gazed up at the stars.

The moon was partly hidden behind the tops of the trees, but the sky was a clear and star filled. "Adam, have you ever just looked up at the stars and thought about how small we are compared to God? Think about it. God created this whole planet and everything on it, yet we are just temporary little people living on this beautiful creation for a moment, as the Bible says. When our lives are over, we'll be in Heaven, but down here our bodies become dust, just as if we never existed at all. We'll all be forgotten, given enough time, if it wasn't for guys like me who chisel names onto granite tombstones. It doesn't matter if you're the President of the United States, King of England or worn-out old prostitute dying slowly in the street. Eventually, all that's left of us on earth is a slab of granite marking where we were laid to rest with our name and the years between our birth and death carved into it. We're given such a short time to live, you just have to wonder what really matters in life. Following Christ, obviously, and doing what's right comes first, then family, and building a legacy for them to know and follow. Faith, family, love and character, like the fruits of the spirit, are what matter in life—to me, anyway. I don't think the meaning of life is getting rich, do you?"

Adam yawned. "No. I don't know if you remember or not, but when I was young, I worked for Hoyt Crawford over in Natoma. He farms more land than anyone else in Jessup County now—"

Luther interrupted Adam. "I know Hoyt. In my business, you get to meet everyone in the county eventually, at least once." Being the owner of the Fasana Granite Works and Quarry, Luther made all the grave-stones marking where a family's loved ones were laid to rest.

"I suppose so," Adam said. "Anyway, Hoyt had a thousand-acre field of wheat that just goes on for what seems like miles. When the wind blows across it, it's like watching the ocean's waves rolling across the field. I think of my life as nothing more than a single stalk of wheat within the millions of stalks in that thousand acres. If we rode over to Hoyt's tomorrow and picked one stalk of his wheat, he isn't going to care, because it's just one of several million. But to God I *do* matter, even though I am one of several millions of people around the world. A single stalk of wheat has what... forty to fifty seeds per head? Compared to the rest of Hoyt's thousand-acre crop, one head of wheat isn't much. The Bible makes it clear that God doesn't see any of us as expendable like that. He sees us all as individuals, unique and special. He loves me for who I am just as I am, and you for you, just as you are. Unlike Hoyt, God would notice if we were picked out from the millions of stalks of wheat in the field. That is what makes life worth living. That's what life is all about.

"There are so many people hurting in this world, so many people who feel helpless and wanting to give up. Many don't know the Bible says in the book of Mathew, *'a bruised reed He will not break.'* It means that, in His thousand-acre field of wheat, God loves every plant so much that He will heal and care for a bruised or broken stalk and save it. God loves to restore hope in our lives, heal our emotional wounds and give us peace, even during the toughest times. How many people long for a second chance at life, but lie down and die in their own bitterness, sorrow and regret without giving the God who created them a chance to heal them? Hope is a glorious thing many people miss because they refuse to believe in Jesus Christ for whatever reason. It really doesn't matter what the reason. The results are the same. Those stalks of wheat are thrown out because they have no seeds. They have no value, they are nothing but chaff. Yes, Uncle Luther, I think about how small I am compared to God every time I look at the stars. For me, coming into the mountains, holding my children, or watching the wind blow over a wheat field reminds me just how loving, amazing and wonderful God is to me and all his children. As with any wheat field, you know the harvest is coming, and there's no way around it. I intend to spend my life as one of the workers, and not the chaff of the earth."

"I think you missed your calling. You should've been a preacher," Luther said, sounding worn out.

Adam smiled. "No, I was called to be a rancher, a husband and a father. If I do what I'm called to do, then most likely my kids will do what they're called to do. But if I live for the chaff—you know, the trash of the world—what more could I expect of them? We are all called, foremost, to nourish the seeds we grow in our own homes first. Our children are our only legacy that will really matter."

"Hmm," Luther said sadly. "You know, I hate to admit it, but I wasn't such a good father to my children. I worked too much and forced them to work hard, too. I went through having one wife leave me and another dying, and I think I took all that out on my kids. I made them bitter, I think. The boys live far away and seldom write, and my baby girl...well, she's not made good choices either. I think I've failed, Adam. Perhaps that will be my legacy: a failure as a father."

"That's not true, Uncle Luther. Luke and David have both grown up to be good men, and they're doing well in California. They're not thieves, and they run an honest business. They know the truth about the Lord. Whether they live it or not, I don't know, but they know the truth. Yeah, Billy Jo has made some mistakes, but she's still a good-hearted lady who's trying her best to raise her boys right. You didn't go wrong raising your kids, Uncle Luther. You were a father without a wife for all those years and did the best you could with what you had. More than anything else, you loved them, and it showed. You finished the race of being a father. A lot of men don't.

"Again, Uncle Luther," Adam continued, "it's the seeds we nurtured when our lives are over that matter, not the regrets and mistakes we made along the way. In a believer's life, the regrets and shame, the mistakes we make are the chaff that's tossed aside. The meat of our life's work is the legacy that will matter. I'm not talking about your granite quarry, by the way. I'm talking about your interests, conviction and witnessing to everyone around you about the Lord and surrendering to Him. You do that a lot, Uncle Luther and trust me, your words are seeds and they won't be wasted. God will plant them exactly when and where He wants them."

"I hope so," Luther said simply. "I spent my whole life building that quarry into what it is. I always hoped one of my sons would fill my shoes when I left. But Joel's son is taking over the whole shebang, and my sons won't even write to me. I got to tell you, Adam, I don't feel like much of a success. I do pray you're right though, because I'd like to be remembered for more than a hole in the ground and tombstones."

Adam chuckled. "Oddly enough, that's all that will remain of any of us eventually."

"Oh, you know what I mean. I was talking about my quarry," Luther said with a half-smile.

Adam said seriously, "Uncle Luther, I know what you meant. You are a Christian man through and through, and it shows to everyone who knows you. You were called to nourish the seeds you planted, and you have. You're still planting seeds, as evident by this discussion. Your legacy will not be of failure or the biggest hole in the ground, but of being a godly man. What greater legacy for your family could there be? What other kind of success really matters when you stand before Jesus and face eternity someday? Jesus Himself said, *'what good is it to own the world, and yet lose your own soul?'* We just need to nourish our seeds, so they can grow and prosper in the knowledge of Jesus Christ. And that is the greatest legacy known to man. It is the reason we are here; it's the reason we exist, to know and love God."

Luther looked at Adam with a big smile. "All of that from looking at the stars, huh?"

"Oh, that and working in wheat fields for twelve hours a day, day after day on the Crawford Farm."

14

"One time I saw a pack of wolves outside of town. There was about twenty-four or -five wolves running in the pack. They began to circle around me and that's when I shot up in the air and scared them away. If I didn't have my rifle with me, I would've been wolf food," Dustin Schwartz said. He was lying on his bed roll not far from the fire, covered with a blanket. "Yeah, wolves are not like bears or mountain lions. Wolves run together in a pack and attack strategically, like soldiers. They were planning to circle around me and box me in. They would've all attacked at once when the leader of the pack gave the signal. That's probably where humans learned military strategy from. Anyway, it was pretty scary, really. The lead male had red eyes! He was pure white but had red eyes. He was quite beautiful. I would've shot him, but I just didn't have the heart. I mean, a more gorgeous animal I've never seen. He was massive, too! He was the biggest wolf I've ever seen. He was probably close to a hundred pounds or more. But those red eyes were scary. Anyway, I fired my rifle, and they all ran off this direction from town. This could be the same pack I saw that day making all that racket. Wolves are territorial, you know, but they know what a man with a gun can do, so they might've moved way out here to get away from me."

"Will you shut up? I'm trying to sleep!" Octavius yelled from about twenty yards away from the others.

"I'll talk quieter," Dustin said and then added, "you might want to move closer to the fire. It's a known fact that when wolves smell a fire, they come to investigate. They won't come to the fire, but anyone sleeping away from it is fair game, especially at night. You might wake up to a pair of red eyes and big teeth just before you turn into wolf food."

Octavius' strained voice came from the darkness outside of the firelight. "I'm not in the mood to listen to you prattle on about nonsense! Now shut up!"

Dustin grimaced and looked at the two Pierce brothers and Mike Hall. They sat on the ground near the fire, looking at him with a touch of humor. Dustin shook his head and said a little more quietly, "He's not a very friendly feller. But like I was saying, when it comes to wolves, you must keep your eyes open, because they'll sneak right up on you. If you have never been surrounded by a pack of wolves like I was, I swear, you don't know what fear is! But you can't show it. You have to control your fear and not let it control you."

The grumbling sound of bitter cursing came from the bushes behind which Octavius tried to sleep. A moment later, Octavius moved out of the bushes and into the firelight. His gaze burned down into Dustin. He pointed his finger and shouted, "Shut up! Do any of you believe one word of what he's saying?" he asked, glancing at the three men. He looked back down at Dustin. "Wolves do not have red eyes, unless the firelight's reflecting from them, just like a 'possum's or a deer's do! No pack of twenty-five tried to surround you, either, or you'd have crapped your pants and run home like the coward you are! Fear? What the hell do you know about fear? Fear of a woman maybe, but you haven't got the slightest idea of what you're talking about! Not the slightest idea. You don't know fear, but if you don't shut up, I swear you will!"

Dustin sat up on his bedroll and glared at Octavius. His face red with embarrassment, he said in his defense, "I know what I'm talking about! You weren't the one being corralled by wolves. I was. How would you know what fear is anyway, huh? Oh, yeah, you're a dirty Reb, terrified of the color blue—"

Without hesitation, Octavius jumped on Dustin, forcing him to his back. He straddled Dustin's chest, using his weight to hold the boy down in. He then began hitting his face, right fist then left fist, fast and hard. Through a clenched jaw, Octavius spat out the words, "Don't ever talk to me like that, you son of a bitch!"

Dustin tried to get Octavius off him by twisting, bucking and turning, but Octavius' balance was precise and unmovable as he rode the flailing Dustin. Dustin's every effort only resulted in another solid blow to his face.

"Hey!" Cal yelled as he, Nathan and Mike Hall jumped up and grabbed Octavius and tried to drag him off Dustin.

"I'll kill you!" Octavius tried to hit Dustin again, but Mike Hall grabbed his arm. Cal and Nathan wrapped their arms around Octavius and dragged him off Dustin, who rolled to his left side. He covered his face with both hands. A large welt was already swelling under his left eye.

Octavius fought wildly to break free from the two brothers. Nathan held his arms behind his back in a tight lock, while Cal stood in front of him, pushing him back. Octavius cursed them both bitterly while demanding they let him go.

His eyes remained fixed on Dustin like a those of a vicious predator.

"Calm down!" Cal yelled.

Octavius stopped struggling and looked into Cal's eyes dangerously. His lips curled wickedly. "Let me go, or I'll kill you all! I swear I will!"

Nathan spoke said, "Hey, calm down. I understand he can push you to the limits, but we're not here to fight you, Octavius. Calm down, and I'll let you go."

Octavius took several heavy breaths and seemed to calm down. Still angry, he said in a softer voice, "Okay...I'm fine! You can let me go now."

Slowly, Nathan loosened his grip and let Octavius go, prepared to grab him again if he had to.

Mike Hall bent down beside Dustin once Octavius was calm and asked, "Are you okay?"

Dustin slowly sat up with his head down. "Yeah, I'm fine."

Out of the bushes ran Jack Schwartz, his shirt untucked, and his pants mostly unbuttoned, except for the top one. He peered at his son with concern and then at Octavius. "What's going on? Did you hit my son? Did you?" he demanded heatedly.

Octavius took a deep breath and exhaled. "I'm going to sleep now. In the morning, I'm packing my gear and leaving. You men are on your own. I won't ride with him another foot," he said, nodding at Dustin.

Angry, Jack said, "You'll do as I tell you, or I'll leave you here tied to a tree! Now why would you hit my son?" Jack's show of force was soon cut short by the cold-bloodedness gleaming in Octavius' eyes.

"Try it," Octavius dared him, "and I will leave all of you here half-gutted or shot dead. Don't test me, Jack! I'm far more than you and your boys bargained for. That I can promise you. Now stay out of my way, all of you!" he warned as he looked from man to man. His gaze held on Dustin. "And you," he pointed his finger at him, "don't say another word, or I'll slice your throat and pull that tongue of yours out of it!"

Dustin gasped and raised his hands innocently. "I didn't do anything! I was lying in bed and he jumped on me and started hitting me, Pa. What kind of coward does that?"

"Coward?" Octavius went after Dustin again, but was grabbed and held by Nathan and Cal. "Let me go, you bastards! I'm going to kill you! You stupid son of a..." Octavius cursed.

Dustin stood up to defend himself.

"Hey!" Jack hollered, "I won't have you talking to my boy like that! I don't care who you think you are; I won't have it! Do you understand me?"

Octavius fought against the brothers who held him, his face red with fury.

"Enough!" Jack yelled. "The enemy is out there, not here. We're supposed to be working together, not fighting each other." Jack took a deep breath and then continued in a milder tone, "Listen, Mister Clark, we don't know you and you don't know us, so maybe we will get on each other's nerves a bit. But we can't be fighting each other. So, let's let bygones be bygones and get some rest. We're all tired, and we're all fed up for the day, so let it go and start a new in the morning. What do you say?" Jack offered Octavius a half-smile.

No emotion showed on Octavius' face except a cold sneer. "Fine."

"All right. Boys, let him go. Let's put this day to rest, and no more trouble," Jack said.

"Just let go of me so I can get some sleep!" Octavius said bitterly to Nathan, who still held him tightly. Nathan slowly released his arms.

Cal spoke to Jack without taking his attention from Octavius, "Jack, I'd sleep a whole lot better if he was unarmed tonight."

Octavius cast a hard glare at Cal. "I ain't a prisoner, and I ain't giving you my weapons!"

Cal said evenly, "But you did threaten our lives twice, and I don't want to take any chances."

"Oh, Cal," Jack said. "Mister Clark didn't mean that, did you? He was just angry and saying things angry people say. It doesn't mean nothing."

"Hmm-mm," Cal said, still focused on every move Octavius made. "But he meant it. Take his guns away, Jack. I'm not kidding."

Octavius smiled slightly as he stared into Cal's eyes. "I'm not going to hurt anyone. I just want to sleep."

Cal nodded, but refused to turn away from Octavius. He spoke to Jack. "You know, John said the darnedest thing back in town. I didn't think too much about it at the time, but now I am."

Jack chuckled nervously. "Oh, John always has something to say. Now boys, let's break it up and call it a night, huh?"

"Take his guns," Cal said again.

Jack shook his head and said with a wave of his hand, "We don't need his guns. What's done is done, and he's right, he's not a prisoner. So, let him go to bed. We'll all feel better in the morning." Jack tried to sound as friendly as he could to keep everyone calm.

Cal looked at Jack and shook his head. "I'm sorry, Jack. You're the sheriff and all, but I'm overriding you! Mike," he called to Mike Hall. "Put your gun on him. You too, Dustin—"

"You can all go to hell!" Octavius spat out and stepped forward to pass Cal, but Cal stepped sideways into his path and shoved Octavius backwards.

Octavius cursed and clenched his fist to strike back, but before he could, Nathan grabbed him from behind and pinned his arms.

"Let me go!" Octavius yelled. He stomped, hard, on Nathan's foot.

Nathan cried out in pain and leaned forward just as Octavius threw his head back, connecting with Nathan's forehead. Nathan let go of Octavius, stumbled backwards and fell to the ground, dazed. Octavius had spun quickly to watch him fall, then turned back to Cal. A powerful right fist thrown by Cal connected with his jaw, and Octavius fell, dazed by the unexpected blow. He'd pulled himself up off the ground to his hands and knees, when a vicious kick to his gut sent him back to the ground, the wind knocked out of him. He looked up, trying to catch his breath, and saw Cal walking away.

Nathan Pierce then walked to him and knelt down. A red spot marked his forehead where he'd been head-butted.

Nathan looked at Octavius with a hardness in his eyes Octavius recognized and knew well. Nathan said shortly, "I'll give you that one, but don't ever think you'll get away with something like that again. I'm not Dustin," he added, and stood up to walk away.

"What's that mean?" Dustin asked Nathan as he walked past him. He had his revolver pointed at Octavius.

Nathan glanced at Dustin but didn't talk as he walked to Octavius' bedding within the bushes. He spat out some blood from biting his tongue. "I'll get his guns," he said irritably to the others.

"No, you won't!" Octavius exclaimed. He began to stand.

Dustin Schwartz spoke. His face held a vindictive smirk now that he held a gun on the unarmed Octavius. "Better stay put, or I'll shoot you! You're not so tough now, are you, Octopus! You're scared now, huh, tough guy?"

"Boy, you haven't got the goods to scare me. Now get out of my way!" Octavius said and strode past Dustin without concern.

Cal Pierce pulled his revolver, cocking the hammer as he leveled it at Octavius. "I do," he said, stopping Octavius in his tracks. "Now, we'll just wait a few minutes for my brother to collect your guns, and then you can go on to bed."

"Are you going to tie me up, too?" Octavius asked bitterly.

"Should I?" Cal asked just as bitterly.

"You might wish you had."

"Then I will!"

Jack Schwartz stepped between the two men. "Wait, wait... Cal, he's not a prisoner, so you're not tying him up like one. Look, I'll allow you guys to take his weapons, but you're not going to tie him up. That's carrying things too far. We're all tired, and it's been a heck of a day, so let's just settle down and call it a night. We're all on the same side, and the bad guys are out there somewhere." He pointed up the mountain. "Mister Clark isn't here to fight with you boys. This was just a misunderstanding that will be cleared up after a night's sleep. Isn't that right, Mister Clark?"

Octavius sighed. His gaze went to Mike Hall, who stood back a bit, holding a shotgun. He looked at Cal evenly. "Not taking any chances with me, are you?"

Cal shook his head. "No," he said. He watched Nathan walk into the camp carrying Octavius' rifle and gun-belt.

"Got them," Nathan said.

"Okay!" Jack said in a tone of excitement. "Now he's unarmed; so, let him go to bed. And, Mister Clark, we'll see you in the morning, bright and early."

"Yeah, you will," Octavius said to Jack. He turned to Cal and spoke pointedly, a quiet, dangerous rage burning in his eyes. "I'll see you in the morning."

Cal said slowly, "If I catch you sneaking through the brush tonight, I'll shoot you."

"Cal!" Jack exclaimed in horror. "He's not the enemy! What is wrong with you? Now, do as I say and lower your gun, right now! Goodnight, Mister Clark. Go get some sleep, and we'll get this all straightened out in the morning."

Octavius glanced from Cal to Jack, and then looked around the camp. He stepped forward and paused in front of Dustin long enough to smirk at him before he wandered off into the darkness where his bedroll lay.

Cal watched him the whole time. He looked at Jack once he was out of view. "We should tie him up for the night and send him on his way in the morning without his guns," he said.

Jack shook his head and laughed. "He's all right. Let's just get some sleep and focus on who we're here after and not each other. I know I was never in the army or anything, but I do know Abraham Lincoln said, 'A house divided won't stand' or something like that. And that's what we are: divided. We can't go after the bad guys if we fight with each other! Now, I don't know what sparked the fight between him and Dustin, or, for that matter, him and you, but it ends tonight. Right now, okay?"

Cal stared at Jack with irritation. "Sure, Jack."

"Good! Now, let's all get some rest. We've got a long day tomorrow, and I want everyone rested and in a good mood! I've never led a posse before, but damn it, I want to catch those men now that we're out here, before the marshal does!"

Mike Hall laid his shotgun beside his bedroll and said, "By the way, Jack, did you know Dustin said he could take the marshal in a fight?"

Jack shrugged. "We met the marshal, and I can tell you Matt Bannister is not as impressive as you'd think. Dustin probably could take him in a fight. I think I could, if I was a few years younger."

"Yeah, probably so," Mike agreed. "Hey, Dustin, I was pretty impressed with how fast you drew your pistol. You're pretty-fast with that. Have you been practicing?" He smiled slightly at the disapproving expression Nathan gave him.

"I have," Dustin admitted proudly. He smiled, despite the added pressure it put on his swollen left cheek and eye. "Being a lawman is dangerous work. You never know who will walk into town and rob a bank or want to cause some trouble. You know the chances of having a gunfight in Loveland are small, but someone like those men today, or this"—he said, lowering his voice and pointing behind him at the brush—"idiot could come into town and cause trouble. Being a lawman, you have to be ready and expect the unexpected. It goes with the badge. Having a fast draw gives me an advantage over other gunfighters..."

"Not to interrupt," Mike interrupted, "but could you be considered a gunfighter? Aren't all lawmen considered gunslingers?"

Nathan spoke under his breath to Mike, "Knock it off!"

Dustin said, "All lawmen are. It's part of the business of keeping the peace. Sure, Loveland's not Dodge City, but it could be easily enough. Who knows? We could become famous tomorrow, just like I was saying earlier today. I could become as famous as Matt Bannister. I know he's from Willow Falls, which isn't a whole lot bigger than Loveland. I understand that. He had to start somewhere, too, and I think I'm just as good as he is. These outlaws aren't hiding their trail, so I could track them just as well as the marshal could. And I'm probably just as good with my guns, if not better. Oh, he's good! He must be, but all of us lawmen are. We have to be. Our lives depend on it."

Octavius yelled from the darkness, "Shut up!"

In the momentary pause, Cal tapped Nathan on the shoulder and motioned for the two of them to walk away from camp to speak privately. Nathan stood up to follow Cal.

"Where are you guys going?" Dustin asked loudly. "What's the matter, Cal? Are you afraid to pee in the dark by yourself?" He laughed.

Cal looked back at Dustin without any humor. "Yeah, we'll be back," he said, and led Nathan about thirty yards uphill from the camp, so no one could overhear him. Finally, he stopped, looked back at camp and then said quietly to his little brother, "I think Octavius is the Veneta Creek killer everyone is talking about. I can't prove it, but I think he is."

"Could be," Nathan said. "It's probably a good thing we took his guns then."

Cal nodded in the filtered moonlight that made its way down through the thick Douglas fir trees. "Yeah. Dustin's pushed the guy's nerves to a breaking point. Mine, too, actually. But I'm not taking a chance with this guy, and don't you, either. We cannot afford to take him lightly if he is who I think he is."

Nathan nodded in understanding. "Maybe we should

tell Jack. He might allow us to tie Octavius up and take him back to town, or at least send Dustin and Jack back to town with him. That would free us up a bit."

"It wouldn't do any good. Jack would laugh it off like he did a minute ago. The guy's about as idiotic as his son. I don't think they have a clue how dangerous their great tracker is. I don't like Octavius, Nathan. And I really do not like him being free to roam around while we sleep. It's not normal for someone to threaten to cut someone's throat like he did to Dustin. It's normal to threaten someone when you're angry, but not like that. By the way, that is exactly how most of the prospectors on Veneta Creek were killed. Their throats were cut."

"I got his knife, too," Nathan said quickly. "Is that why you think he's the killer?"

"Think about it. He shows up out of nowhere with more gold than most people ever find up here—in recent months, anyway. No one knows who he is, or has ever seen him before. No one knows where he comes from, except the Cumberland Mountains in the early sixties. I am convinced he rode with Champ Ferguson. Yeah, all those men were pardoned for their crimes, but there has never been a bloodier bunch. Not even Quantrill or Bloody Bill were as evil as Champ Ferguson. Those were wicked men, and I read that Champ preferred using a knife to kill people. He even beheaded folks. Octavius, I can almost guarantee you, rode in that gang of murderers. That kind of man will kill anyone at any time. And you saw him tonight. Beware of him."

Nathan exhaled. "What do you want to do?"

"For now, just keep it between us. I'll tell Mike, but don't let Jack or Dustin know. Who knows what they'd say or do? Keep yourself armed and ready tonight. If anything happens, do not hesitate to shoot him. I'm telling you right now, beware and be ready. I don't like him, and I really don't like this setup tonight."

"Well, let's be prepared for the worst, but hope nothing happens. But if he is who you say, he might try something when we're not expecting it."

"Exactly. He's a former guerrilla and knows we were soldiers. So, he'd be wise to try to get us first, since we offer the greatest resistance. Keep your wits about you."

"I will."

"One more thing: let's sleep on opposite sides of the camp in the brush somewhere. He was studying where we were all sleeping before he went to bed. So, let's mix it up and be ready," Cal said.

"I will. Ever notice that he has no intention of arresting those bank robbers? He intends to kill them, which means he'd have to kill us too, now that I think about it," Nathan said thoughtfully. "I'm not liking this either, Cal. Maybe we should have stayed in Loveland like Sarah suggested. She said she had a bad feeling about this." Nathan sounded slightly worried for the first time.

Cal nodded. "Just keep yourself on guard and be watchful. Remember, no hesitation and no mercy if anything does happen. It may not, but just be ready if it does, okay, little brother?"

"You got it. You, too."

"Always. And you know, it might not be a bad idea to pray about it."

Nathan smiled slightly. "Sarah's got me covered on that. You, too."

"Yeah, but it never hurts to get right with the Lord either."

Nathan hesitated and looked at his brother. "Well that seems kind of odd, coming from you."

Cal said seriously, "Nathan, we have never met anyone like Octavius before. If I am right, killing is second nature to him, just as laughing is to you. I love you, brother, so be careful. And pray I am wrong."

"Love you too, Cal."

"Go move your bedding into the brush and get some sleep. I'll stay up and keep watch."

15

Octavius Clark opened his eyes and took a deep breath of the cool mountain air. It was still dark, but as he lay on his back looking up through the treetops, he could see the faint tinge of blue indicating the sun was about to rise upon a new day. He hadn't slept much, but waking from what little he did sleep, his heart was heavy with thoughts of his wife, Lucinda.

Nathan's wife, Sarah, had reminded him so much of Lucinda, she had been on his mind ever since. He dreamed of Lucinda and for a moment, he saw her face with her determined blue eyes and her perfect smile. He had seen her alive, vibrant and well, like she was years ago. He could hear her voice, and it stirred his soul. He felt the sweet reminisce of the greatest time of his life. It was beautiful, but then his eyes opened, and the moment was gone. It was merely a dream, but the empty hole that filled his chest felt as though it was consuming him. He gritted his teeth to fight the tears puddling in his eyes. A man does not cry! His father had beaten that into him many years before.

Octavius had grown up in the Cumberland Mountains of Clinton County, Kentucky, near the Tennessee border. He had grown up poor and living off the land, like everyone else in their little community. When he was older, he married the prettiest girl he'd ever known, Miss Lucinda Parnell. By the time the early sixties came to the Cumberland Mountains, Octavius and Lucinda had three children they were raising on their small farm. Octavius managed to get caught in the middle of growing hostilities and loyalties that varied throughout the borderlands between Tennessee and Kentucky. Some of his relatives were devoutly pro-Union, while others were for the Confederacy.

Octavius and many others were in the middle and simply tried to live in peace while raising their family and crops. As tensions grew, so did violence in the Cumberland Mountains. A peaceful life was becoming impossible. Many folks were attacked, outraged and harassed by gangs of outlaws or bands of guerrillas terrorizing homesteads for the Confederate cause, while guerillas invaded homesteads for the Union cause.

In short, the mountains were out of control with death and wickedness—All for a cause, but neither side in military garb. True, the two would meet and fight each other often, but robbery and murder seemed the most common tactic on both sides. Guerillas hadn't attacked Octavius' home, though, but there was a small detail of Union soldiers looking for a Confederate guerila named Montrose Parnell, Lucinda's brother. The soldiers believed she and Octavius knew where he was hiding, if they weren't actually aiding him in the Confederate cause. They made it known they suspected Octavius of being one the guerillas they were looking for. No quarter would be given to him or to his bride until the guerillas got the answers they were looking for.

They beat Octavius until he was unconscious, urging Lucinda to talk as they did so. But Lucinda didn't know where Montrose was! She told them what little she did know, but the soldiers were intent on beating Octavius to death with a rifle butt.

Lucinda tried to intervene, and in the process, she was stabbed multiple times in cold blood. When Octavius awoke from being knocked unconscious, his beautiful bride was dead, and his life as he had known it was over. Swearing to avenge his bride, he took his kids to his wife's sister, and went to find Montrose. He joined Montrose in the fight against the Union under the command of their leader, Champ Ferguson.

Filled with hatred for any man dressed in blue, Octavius fought for a Union body count, not the southern cause. He killed every union soldier and supporter he could find, and never even considered showing mercy. Every Union soldier might be the man who murdered his wife or had done something similar to another innocent man's family. Octavius owed no loyalty to the Confederate Army or to anything else except his family of guerillas and Champ Ferguson.

Over time, Octavius' began to thrive on his lust for revenge. The more brutal the battles—with a gun, sword, knife or his blood-covered hands—the more he liked it, and the more satisfied he felt. He had become a killer, pure and simple.

When the war was over, Champ Ferguson was hanged for his war crimes, and all his men, Octavius included, were pardoned by the U.S. Government. With a fresh beginning in a new, war-ravaged country, Octavius no longer desired to farm land or to raise his children. He had not gone back to see his children or Lucinda's grave. He never wrote them a letter to let them know he was alive. He simply left the South and came West. He worked in a Nevada mine for a while, and then in another mine in Arizona. He traveled to California and tried his hand with a gold claim, but found it was easier to kill other prospectors and take their gold than dig for his own. He had escaped the law in San Francisco by hiring onto a clipper bound for Europe, and then hired onto another for a five-year stint at sea. Coming home, he went back to prospecting in California, Nevada, and finally made his way to Oregon, where he meandered between Northern California and Oregon, collecting gold from other prospectors who crossed his path. Especially ex-Union soldiers, who were a little too proud of having fought on the winning side of the war. A year before, he had made his way to the eastern side of Oregon to the Blue Mountains. Now he was in the Wallowas. He had earned quite a bit of gold, but now he had been robbed, and no one would stop him from getting his gold and money back; not one person.

Octavius had wanted to collect what he was owed and leave the Oregon mountains for a while. But when the robbers hit him on the head and took his gold and money, they signed their own death sentences, and would get no pardon from him. Against his will, he was shanghaied into leading a posse of fools into the woods; fools a normal man would leave behind. The sheriff, Jack Schwartz, was irritating enough to throw overboard if they were at sea; but his son, Dustin, had pushed Octavius too far with his constant babbling about nothing. Octavius would like to have done far more than just hit the boy; he would've beaten Dustin to death if the two brothers, Cal and Nathan, had not of pulled him off the boy.

Cal was wise to have taken Octavius' guns. It was also a good idea to tie him up for the night. Luckily though, Jack's inexperience wouldn't allow Cal to do it. That error would be to Jack's detriment. The brothers took his guns and his long knife, but they did not check the pocket of his denim pants where his pocketknife remained. Nor did they instruct the know-it-all, Dustin about where to sleep or where to hide his revolver. Those two might be a couple of decent soldiers in the posse, but experience was heavily on Octavius' side.

Slowly and silently, Octavius removed his blanket, reached into his pocket to pull out his pocketknife, and unfolded the three-inch blade. He put the knife handle between his teeth and crawled through the underbrush to the camp. He kept watch ahead, while he listened for the slightest sound. In the silent morning, not even the birds had begun to chirp yet. He knew Jack and Dustin would sleep soundly, without concern. Cal and his brother, who were taking precautions, concerned Octavius a bit. Anything he did had to be quick and efficient, because he didn't know where the brothers were, or if they were awake and alert or sleeping.

What he did know was that he had to be quick. Wisdom would suggest taking out the strongest enemy first but removing the weakest link to get the upper hand in a surprise attack was wise, too. The first few seconds of the attack would be crucial for Octavius to locate the others and efficiently disappear into the brush. There he would renegotiate his plan as necessary, while the other three tried to make sense of the chaos.

Little by little, he moved across the ground over small limbs and layers of fir needles, between the thick tall ferns and other underbrush. He saw Dustin sleeping beside the fire circle and moved to him. He had a personal score to settle with Dustin, and he could hardly wait to do it. His heart quickened and his adrenaline picked up as he neared. Octavius watched the brush line around camp, searching for any sign of the others, but other than Dustin and Jack sleeping by the fire, there was no sign of anyone else. Dustin's revolver lay beside him exactly where it had been the night before, which was exactly where Octavius had expected it to be. He grabbed the knife with his right hand and carefully crawled out of the brush and into position above Dustin. With a sudden motion, he covered Dustin's mouth with his left hand and turned the boy's head away to expose the artery. His knife sliced through Dustin's throat and neck in one slick move.

Dustin tried to scream, but all he could do was gurgle on the blood pouring from his neck and down his throat. Dustin kicked and swung his arms wildly to get at Octavius' throat. Octavius pulled Dustin's face towards him to look into Dustin's terrified eyes. "Shut up," he said, and let Dustin go as he retrieved Dustin's revolver and stood up. He pulled the hammer back and watched Jack begin to wake to Dustin's desperate thrashing about.

It took a moment for Jack to understand what was happening to his son. Suddenly, as panic seized him, Jack began crawling to his boy as fast as he could. "Dustin!" he called out. "Oh, my God...No!"

Octavius aimed the revolver at the top of Jack's head and pulled the trigger. Jack dropped face down close to his son, as Dustin's own life ebbed away. Octavius ran and dove into the tall ferns to hide. He could hear panicked men scrambling to reach their weapons and try to figure out what had happened. Octavius listened to the directions of the sounds and waited for them to reveal who was where. It didn't take him long.

"Jack!" Cal called. "Dustin! Nathan... spread out. Jack!

Dustin!" Nothing but silence answered his cries. Cal shook his head and he leaned against a tree, still in a squatting position. He stood up to peek over the brush into the camp some distance away. "Nathan, you take the right flank. I'll take the left. Mike, stay put and watch out! I think Jack and Dustin are dead. Be alert, boys."

Octavius stayed on the ground underneath the thick ferns and slowly crawled away from camp without disturbing the foliage enough to be noticed. He could hear Cal approaching him. Octavius nestled at the base of some ferns and lay perfectly still, Dustin's revolver in his hand. It was still dark and hard to see into the foliage very far, which was an advantage for Octavius. He waited as Cal passed within ten feet of him without seeing him.

When he felt safe enough not to be heard, Octavius began crawling uphill, away from the camp. His goal was to get higher and put all three men below him, rather than having them spread out around him. He would crawl, pause to listen, and crawl again without making any noise if he could. He knew all three men were also being as quiet as they could be in order to listen for him.

From down at the camp came the voice of Cal. "Mike, Jack and Dustin are dead! Octavius' gear is still here, so he hasn't left us. Shoot anything that moves!"

Nathan Pierce looked at his brother as they met up at the far side of camp where Octavius had slept. "He could be anywhere—on the ground, behind a tree or in a tree."

Cal nodded. "I know. Let's double back but make a twenty-yard wider circumference. I'll take the east this time, and you get the west. And remember, if you see anything, shoot or drop to the ground and roll. We'll back each other up, got it?"

"Absolutely. Be careful, brother," Nathan said, anxiety in

his voice. Suddenly, he remembered Sarah's worry about the posse and felt a chill run up his spine. He took a deep breath and prayed silently for the Lord to be with him, Cal and Mike. He didn't like not knowing where Octavius was, so as he moved forward through the silent forest, he would pause and kneel. The third time he knelt, he noticed that the ground before him had been disturbed by someone crawling. Nathan considered calling out to Cal but decided against it. He now knew Octavius was using the ground and decided to follow the trail quietly and prepare to shoot the man.

Octavius had heard Mike Hall gasp at the confirmation of Jack's and Dustin's deaths and moved toward the sound. Mike was within twenty yards of Octavius. He knew the two brothers were coming up behind him, so he had to act quickly to even the odds for close-quarter combat. Finding a small stone, he picked it up and tossed it over Mike into the brush behind him.

Mike Hall knelt behind a thick Douglas fir tree, holding his double barrel shotgun tightly with sweaty hands. Mike couldn't comprehend what was happening; he was woken by a gunshot a few moments ago, and now two of his friends were dead. It seemed like a crazy dream he was trying to wake up from. He had never been in a situation where his life was threatened by another man. Kneeling in the silent darkness behind the Douglas fir, Mike couldn't care less about the bank robbers or if they got away. All he wanted was for Octavius to leave them and go away, so Mike and the Pierce brothers could take the bodies of their friends back home where they belonged. Mike exhaled as his heart pounded in his chest. The forest was so dark, and the silence seemed uncanny. Beside that tree, Mike began to pray.

Suddenly behind him came the sound of something in the brush. Without warning, he swung around and fired one barrel of his shotgun at the direction of the noise. He fired his second shot in the panic of the moment, and then realized no one was there. He realized too late that the sound he'd heard had probably been a rock thrown into the brush from another angle. With a sense of dread, he turned back around just in time to see Octavius spring up from a squatted position. Octavius ran as he aimed his revolver.

Time seemed to stand still while Mike looked into the black eyes of death. Octavius pulled the trigger, and Mike Hall fell to the ground, dead, with a .44 caliber bullet entering his forehead and exiting out the back of his head. Octavius pulled the shotgun out of Mike's hands and quickly knelt beside the body and searched Mike's body for more shotgun shells.

"Mike!" Nathan yelled. He started running through the ferns and brush to get to his friend. Everything was happening too fast for him to react wisely. "Mike!"

Cal also ran to where he had left his friend, though he was wary of Octavius and held his sidearm at the ready position to shoot in an instant.

Octavius had no time to search, but he flipped Mike's body over to search his back pocket, if he had one. He did not. He looked around in near panic because he knew Nathan was getting close to him. At the base of the tree, four other shot gun shells lay on the ground. Octavius grabbed one and took off running through the underbrush as fast as he could.

Nathan dashed out of the tall ferns beside Mike, glanced down at his friend, and then saw Octavius running through the brush. Nathan yelled in rage, then held the trigger down to fan his revolver as fast as he could aim six shots at

Octavius. He had seen Octavius dive to the ground at about his fourth or fifth shot. He had no idea if he had hit the man or not.

Cal had seen where Nathan was firing and fired two quick shots in the same direction in the same fanning motion, but he chose not to waste his bullets on an unseen target. He walked to where Mike's body lay.

Nathan knelt as he reloaded his revolver. Cal ducked as well and stayed beside his brother. Nathan said with intense anger, "He's on the ground. Shoot low!" He fumbled the bullets into the chamber, his hands shaking.

Cal looked at Mike and gritted his teeth. "Did you hit him?"

"I don't know. I don't hear him screaming," Nathan said.

Cal opened the cylinder of his revolver, ejected his two spent shells and reloaded quickly. "The sun's coming up. He won't be able to hide forever."

Nathan agreed. "Yeah, but that goes both ways. I feel like we're sitting ducks out here!"

Octavius was about thirty yards away, on his back, listening to the brothers talk quietly. He slowly and carefully opened the barrel of the shotgun, extracted the first shell casing and loaded a shotgun shell into the first chamber. He took a deep breath and yelled, "I made a promise. Don't make me break it. Go home now, Nathan, and we'll part ways. You'll never see me again."

Cal immediately stood and fired in the direction of Octavius' voice without saying a word. When he finished, he knelt back down to empty his cylinder and reload. He looked at Nathan and whispered, "Get ready." He then spoke loudly, to be heard by Octavius, "You killed our friends. It's a little late to turn the other cheek now, don't you think?" He looked at Nathan as he listened for Octavius to answer.

Octavius crawled through the ferns as softly as he could towards a Douglas fir not too far away. The spray of bullets Cal fired had missed him, but one bullet passed over him within inches. It was a close call, and he dared not answer Cal until he had some solid cover to protect him from a lucky bullet. He had not expected Cal to fire so quickly without first trying to make an escape while they still could. He had underestimated the fight in the man.

"Give up," Cal hollered over the dark forest. He stared at the foliage for any sign of a man's form compressing the ferns, but there were no signs of him anywhere. "I don't want to hurt you, Octavius."

From behind one of the trees some distance away came the sound of laughter. It was an eerie laugh that sent chills down the spines of both brothers. "I wasn't talking to you, Cal. I never promised you could go back alive, just your brother."

"I'll have to talk to Sarah about that when I get home, but I am her favorite brother-in-law," Cal answered loudly with a small grin and a wink at Nathan. He whispered, "Do you see him?"

Nathan shook his head. "Keep him talking."

"Well, you know where I am. Come get me, and let my brother go home then," Cal challenged.

"No..." Octavius said slowly. "You come find me. Or you and your brother can ride back home, and I'll disappear. Trust me, boys. I'm far better at this than you. I'm a man of my word. Don't make me kill you, Nathan. Go home to your wife and forget about me."

Nathan looked at his brother. "Maybe we should go home, Cal. We can let the law catch up with him."

Cal shook his head. "No, not me. You should, but if we both did, they'd put a bounty on Octavius, and every bounty hunter and lawman will be coming to Loveland and talk to us to learn what they can about him. One of them might recognize you and Sarah. If we go home, there's no more hiding in Loveland for you. And you'd never see Sarah again even if you lived through one of them recognizing you. Her father wants you dead, remember? One of those head-hunters will shoot you in the back of your head in your own home, just like Ford did to Jessie James. At least out here I have a fighting chance to protect you from that.

"If I can bring Octavius' body back to camp, I can take him to the sheriff in Huntsville and keep your name out of it completely." He pointed into the forest. "But if we go back and say we lost him, this whole mountain will fill up with men who might carry your and Sarah's wanted posters in their saddlebags. Think about it, Nathan. We don't have a choice! You go back to Sarah, and I will finish him off before I come home."

"I don't like it. Sarah said she had a bad feeling about this..." Nathan said nervously.

Cal nodded in silence and then looked at his brother. "Sarah is a good Christian lady, and she's praying for you and me both. I believe God will be watching over me. He always has. So, let's trust the Lord to keep me safe, and I'll go get this guy. But you need to leave. You're married; I'm not. You should take the opportunity and go home. He's letting you go."

"I'm not leaving without you."

Cal shook his head. "He's already killed Mike. I can't let him get away."

"Well. I'm not leaving you, so make a plan, and let's go get this guy."

Cal sighed heavily. "Nathan, Sarah will never forgive me if anything happens to you. Don't put me in that situation. Just leave!"

Nathan shook his head with determination. "Forget it. If you're staying, so am I! Now what's the plan? It's better odds if we fight together."

"All right," Cal said hesitantly. "Everything he has done has been in very close quarters, and all he has is Dustin's revolver and Mike's shotgun. He can't have that much ammunition, so he won't waste his shots." Cal paused to exhale and look around before he continued. "We're going to have to try to flank him. You take the east flank and I will take the west. I don't know where he is—he seems to keep moving around, so move slow and use every sense you have. Nathan, use your brain and keep your wits about you! If he shoots at me and misses, I'll pretend I'm hit and call out your name and say I'm hit. That means I'm fine, and you take cover and wait for him to come to you. Once he comes to check on me or goes after you, then I will take him out. Or visa-versa. You call out my name if you're okay. Are we clear?"

Nathan nodded. "What if I am hit?" he asked nervously.

"Then I imagine I'll hear the difference in your voice." Cal looked at his brother. "Be careful, Nathan. This man isn't like any we've ever known before. He is a killer of the worst kind. *Do not* hesitate to kill him if you get the chance. I love you, little brother. I'll see you up the hill. May the Lord watch over us and give us a victory this morning."

"Love you too, Cal. Ready or not, let's go."

Cal nodded at his brother, turned and crawled quickly through the ferns. Nathan watched him go, feeling a hollowness in his chest. The only word he could define the hollowness as was dread. He had seen the three bodies of his friends and the speed with which Octavius moved through the brush. In the back of his mind was Sarah's warning of a bad feeling coming over her. He had no desire to lose his life going after a man he cared nothing about—other than wanting to bring him to justice for the murder of his friends, perhaps. Even then, his greater responsibility was to his wife. He was all she had in the world. Nathan didn't want to risk that for a man the law would catch sooner or later.

Sarah feared he would be arrested and held for the Pinkerton's, who had orders from Sarah's father to kill him. The Pinkerton's were a law enforcement agency, but for the right price, killing a person was just another part of the job. They wouldn't receive their twenty-five thousand dollars if he wasn't dead and Sarah returned to her parents. True, Sarah was an adult woman with a mind and life of her own, but that didn't matter to her father. He refused to lose his only daughter to a simple man of humble means like Nathan.

The great and wealthy railroad man, Louis Beckman, had been humiliated, and that kind of pride was never satisfied until blood was spilled. Nathan would rather face Octavius with his brother by his side than risk being found by a bounty hunter or lawman passing through Loveland wanting information about Octavius. And if they failed to get Octavius, it wouldn't be a matter of *if* bounty hunters and lawmen started coming to his door; it would be when.

Nathan took a deep breath and began crawling on the ground to keep himself low, just as Octavius had done.

Octavius stood on a fallen log hidden in the darkness of the forest, watching the brothers from fifty yards away. If he had the rifle he'd bought at the store, or better yet, his own Winchester, he could have killed them both. But with a single shot in the shotgun and four shells in the revolver, he needed a closer target to make his few bullets count. He smiled slightly when he saw the tops of the ferns moving as Nathan crawled through them.

He called out into the silent forest, "Last chance, Nathan. Go home to your wife while you're able!" He heard no response. "All right, I'm coming for you first!" he yelled. He smirked when he saw the fern tops cease moving. Nathan had stopped to wait for him. Octavius leveled his attention at Cal. He stepped down off the fallen tree and moved to his left.

The forest was silent. As much as Cal strained to hear the slightest sound, all he could hear was his own heartbeat as he crawled through the ferns, still wet from the night's dew. He held his revolver in his hand, crawled a few feet, paused to listen, smelled the air and crawled again. Time passed with every yard he crawled slowly up the mountain side, and it became increasingly brighter above the trees as sun filtered on to the forest floor. A few distant birds began singing in the trees, but other than the sound of another beautiful morning, the silence was complete.

The closer Cal got to where Octavius had been, the stronger became his feeling that he and Nathan were sitting ducks in a small pond. He kept low to the ground to remain unseen, but by doing so, he couldn't tell where Octavius was. He could have climbed a tree, for all Cal knew. Cal might be in clear sight of Octavius even as he crawled along the ground. He knew he was close to his target, but without knowing where the man was, it was hard to flank him. It was the same tactic they used earlier; however, Octavius had out-flanked their flanking maneuver. He might be doing the same thing now.

Instead of being on the offensive, suddenly Cal felt like he was the hunted, exposed and helpless, lying on his stomach and hiding behind bushes. Lifting his head just enough to look around, he saw a fat Douglas fir fifteen feet ahead of him. The anxiety of being caught in the open was becoming too much to bear. He rose to sprint to the tree, where he would have solid cover and the ability to move freely.

After three fast steps, Cal was petrified to see Octavius swing around the tree with the shotgun held up and aimed at him. Cal had no time to lift his revolver. Octavius pulled the trigger, and Cal took a close-range twelve-gauge round in his chest. He fell backwards, dead before he hit the ground. Octavius slithered behind another tree.

Nathan listened for Cal to cry out his name, but the word never came. Birds had stopped singing and silence settled over the forest. Nathan lay motionless on the ground, listening. He grew more and more afraid, not so much of Octavius, but that Cal might be dead. He rolled to his back and, breathing heavily, waited in silence. When he could stand it no longer, he called out, "Cal!" No response. "Cal!" he shouted louder. His breathing grew heavy as his heart beat faster. "Octavius!" he yelled bitterly.

"Go home!" came a reply that sounded farther away than before.

Nathan stood up in panic and began running west to where Cal should've been. He ran across the thick ferns and stumbled over a fallen branch but regained his balance and kept running. "Cal!" he called and pulled to stop to look for his brother.

At last he saw Cal's legs lying behind a tree. "Cal! Oh, Lord, no." He ran toward Cal as fast he could.

Suddenly, Octavius stepped around a tree and swung the wooden stock of the shotgun; it hit Nathan across the forehead and knocked him to the ground. He was dazed and barely conscience when he heard Octavius say, "Tell your wife I kept my promise. Now go home and don't ever leave her again." Then Octavius hit Nathan on the side of the head with the butt of the rifle and knocked him unconscious.

16

Karl Digsby had just slipped his boots on at the break of day when he heard the first shot. For the next twenty minutes to half an hour, the inconsistent gunfire left a very unnerving feeling in his stomach. Just when they thought the shooting was over, there would be another shot and then silence. One single shot, silence for a bit, and then too many shots to count. Then a larger caliber weapon, like a shotgun, fired twice. Then silence reigned. Ten to fifteen minutes later another shotgun blast came, then silence. A few minutes later a single shot that might have come from a revolver sounded, then silence fell again. The inconsistency, time of morning and number of shots fired gave everyone in the camp an eerie feeling.

"It has to be target practice, huh, Uncle Dick?" Brent Boyle asked after hearing the last lone shot. "It can't be a posse, unless they're target practicing."

"Shh!" Deuce McKenna silenced his nephew irritably and listened closely to the now silent woods. "I don't know what's going on, but they're behind us. So, we better move on."

"A posse?" Brent asked.

"I imagine so."

Pick Lawson smiled. "According to that deputy, the Huntsville sheriff and the Loveland sheriff don't get along, so maybe the two posses are fighting over who gets to come after us," he chuckled. "You're right, though. We need to move on."

Karl Digsby shrugged. "Laugh if you want, but there isn't much to do in those little mountain towns. The whole town could be coming after us, and they're not strangers to this terrain like we are. If they are killing each other, though, I hope they even the odds up for us."

"Yeah, there could be a hundred men coming after us!" Brent said. He pulled out his jackknife and began pushing the blade between the trunk of a tree and a large fungus, about twelve inches wide and ten inches tall, growing on the side of it.

"A hundred men would be hard to feed up here," Pick said to Brent. Maybe Brent's statement seemed stupid, or maybe it was lack of coffee or being awakened by gunshots on their back trail, but Pick was feeling mighty irritable.

Brent looked at Pick. "Maybe that's what they were doing; shooting breakfast this morning."

Pick grimaced. "What are you doing, anyway? You should be saddling up your horse, not collecting conks."

Brent pulled the fungus off the tree and held it up to show Pick. It was of common size, but Brent was proud of it. "I know a guy whose wife paints pictures on these. I am gonna have her paint a beautiful peacock on here and give it to Christine. When she says, 'Oh, how beautiful', I will say, 'Its beauty does not compare to you.'" He continued with a smile, "Huh, what do you think? Do you think she'll fall for me then, huh?"

"Well, remember I bought my Lilly a dress, and it didn't matter," Pick said and walked over to saddle his horse.

"What kind of answer is that?" Brent asked anyone who would answer. "Well, I think she'll love it. She has enough dresses, but I will bet you she doesn't have a peacock painted on a conk!"

Karl nodded. "Probably not. I think she'll love it."

"You should grab one for your wife. She'd love it too," Brent advised.

"Not likely. She'd just ask what she's supposed to do with it, other than it taking up

room. But on a serious note, you need to get your gear packed and your horse saddled. We do need to get moving. Those guys aren't too close, but if we loiter, they can be."

Deuce McKenna was looking south at the series of ridges they would have to cross before reaching the back side of Windsor Ridge. "We need to hurry, men. We have a long day of riding ahead, so fill your canteens and let's get moving. I can see Windsor Ridge, and that's where we're heading. Once we get over the ridge, it's all downhill from there."

"Yeah, it's downhill, but still twenty miles of mountains and hills just to get to Jessup Valley," Karl said with a roll of his eyes.

Deuce pointed to the north. "If we stay ahead of them, I don't care how far it is!"

Pick said as he saddled his horse, "They don't sound very friendly, whoever they are."

"We'll ride harder than we did yesterday and make up some ground on them."

Pick looked at Deuce irritably. "If they know this country better than we do, then they'll catch up with us soon enough, because we haven't got a clue where we're going.

We better be watching our back trail. And if I may say so," he added with a hint of hostility, "I don't like this! We are cutting across some of the roughest country I have ever crossed! There isn't a road or a trail in fifty miles of here. The fact is, we have no idea what's around the corner. We could run into a canyon or a cliff and be completely boxed in, for all we know. None of us have ever been here before, and we're supposed to outrun a posse whose only concern is following our trail. I think we might be in some trouble, Dick!"

"We took a chance, and I am convinced it was the right choice. We have a land marker right over there." He pointed at the top of Windsor Ridge in the distance. "We know where we are and where we're going, and if we need to, we'll set up an ambush to slow down the posse or stop them. But rest assured, Pick, we will get home."

Karl added, "If we do, we'd better kill them all. I don't want to be arrested on my doorstep because someone described my horse and me to the authorities."

"There could be a hundred of them," Brent said.

"No, there's not going to be no hundred of them," Pick said harshly. "Ten to twenty at most, probably. Certainly more than we want to ambush, though!" he said pointedly at Deuce.

"I said, if we have to! Now let's get going, so we can stay ahead of them."

"When are we going to eat? We haven't eaten anything since yesterday morning," Brent said, tightening his saddle.

Deuce answered him shortly, "I don't have any pancakes and eggs in my saddle bags. We'll eat when we can."

"I'm starving," Brent stated.

Karl looked at Brent with a slight smirk. "If you were riding with the Sperry Helms Gang, I doubt Morton would put up with you whining like that. Jessie wouldn't either."

"I imagine they get hungry, too," Brent answered.

Pick glared at Brent and said bitterly, "Not when there's a posse running down their necks! You better toughen up, because none of us who ride with men like them take kindly to weakness and whining!"

Deuce spoke with growing frustration in his voice, "He isn't riding with Morton and Jessie. He's riding with me!"

Brent spoke to Pick. "You don't think I'm tough enough to ride with the likes of them? I will lead a tougher gang than them. Watch and see. I will be famous."

Pick shook his head and went about gathering his bedroll and packed it up. Karl looked at Deuce and waited. He didn't have to wait long. Deuce answered immediately, "They haven't been famous since the shootout three years ago, when Barry Helms was killed, and Alan Sperry sent to prison. That's what fame brought them, Brent. Morton doesn't want to be famous—or even noticed. That's why they murdered Possum and his wife, or have you forgotten about that? The Sperry Helms Gang is finished when we get home. I promise you, Matt Bannister and his deputies will go to arrest them, and Morton and the boys will either go to prison or get themselves killed. Either way, they are finished, and we won't have to worry about them anymore. If you want to become famous for being an outlaw, you won't be riding long. I guarantee it."

"We just robbed a bank. I don't know how that's not experience enough to start my own gang," Brent said as he rolled up his bedroll and went to his horse to tie it to his saddle.

Pick sat on his horse waiting impatiently. "You held the horses! By the way, we are far from getting away with it. If those boys back there catch us, we'll hang! By the sounds of those gunshots, it isn't a posse, but a mob thirsty for someone to lynch. And while you're standing here complaining like a woman and dreaming about writing love notes to a female who probably won't notice a whelp like you anyway, they're getting closer. Now get on your horse if you're coming with us, because I am leaving now!"

Karl stepped into his saddle and said, "I'm with you, Pick."

"Let's go," Deuce said and turned his horse to leave. He was followed by Pick and Karl. Brent had climbed up into his saddle, but then jumped down to check his conk and make sure it was secure in his saddle bag.

Pick glanced back and scoffed in disgust.

17

Luther Fasana had some sliced potatoes frying over the fire with a little wild onion, garlic and pepper, along with finely chopped pieces of elk meat. A pot of coffee was ready when Adam Bannister opened his eyes and sat up to a bright early morning.

"Good morning, Adam. I figured if the gunshots didn't wake you, the smell of breakfast would. Or perhaps the howling of three caught wolves. They've been barking, howling and yipping all night. I'm surprised you slept through it all."

"I heard the wolves. They were howling when I fell asleep," he said as he stretched tiredly in the cool morning. The sun was still rising in the eastern sky.

"They didn't stop. About an hour ago, around twenty shots were fired to the north. They weren't close at all, but it sounded like a battle. They wouldn't have woken me up, but I was already awake when I heard them. They were pretty faint."

"Hmm," Adam grunted. He sat on a wood block by the

fire and poured himself a cup of coffee. "Maybe it was a bad hunter with a Gatling gun."

Luther chuckled. "No, they had different sounds."

"Gunshots, huh? Well, with all the people moving into Branson and Jessup County, we couldn't expect to keep our hunting spot secret forever. Now that the buffalo are just about gone, maybe some rich guy like Lee decided to lead a group of city fellers out here to shoot a herd of elk, for a price. No, that's too much work for those city men. Lee and his friends would have better luck raising elk in a pasture for them to shoot."

Luther shook his head with a grin on his face. "No, these shots came from the north side of Windsor Ridge."

"There's a lot of prospectors around too, I guess. Next summer when we come back here, our camp might be someone's claim. Wouldn't it be irritating to find out we've been sitting on a million dollars of gold all this time?"

Luther smiled. "I know you can be a little grumpy before your coffee, but my, you're pessimistic today. I've panned up and down this creek and have never found enough gold to count. I think if we're going to make any money at this camp, it's going to be by skinning those wolves and selling the hides we've collected this time. The probably won't bring more than ten dollars, but at least we're not going home empty handed."

Adam took a sip of his coffee. "With all the jerky we have; I'd call this trip a success. But you know we still have room in the teepee and three wolves to kill. If we stayed another day or two, we could add another ten to fifteen pounds of meat to our total. I'm in no hurry to get home, are you?"

Luther looked at Adam and smiled. "Let's go get them."

Adam led the way up the trail toward the meadow where they'd set the traps the day before. Luther followed on his mule and led a pack mule behind him. They were not concerned about making noise or scaring away game; the wolves would have already done that for them. The terrified yips and barks of the trapped wolves grew louder the closer they rode to the traps. The meadow was empty of life except for a single doe at the far end of the meadow near the tree line.

The first trap staked down just inside of the tree line held a young gray wolf about a year old. It whined while trying to run away to escape the approaching men, but the steel trap was gripped tightly to its hind right leg. The wolf's ears were down, and its tail was tucked tightly. It pulled desperately to break free of the trap, but the effort was useless.

Luther dismounted and tied his lead mule to a tree branch. "Well, how about you finish them, and I'll start skinning." He pulled out his sharp knife and waited.

Adam tied the reins of his horse to a thin tree and pulled his revolver out of the worn leather holster tied to his hip. He stepped close to the frightened wolf, pulled the hammer back, took aim and fired. The animal fell to the ground, dead.

Pulling the hammer back again, he walked wordlessly to where the second trap was located a short distance away. The second trap contained another young wolf about a year old and of similar color to the first. The second wolf reacted differently from the first, though. It yelped and tried to run but, finding itself helpless to escape, it began a series of desperate howls.

Adam was disappointed by another small wolf. "It's another young one; we're not doing well," he called out as he aimed the revolver and fired. The howling stopped as the wolf dropped dead.

Adam heard whining and yips from deeper in the woods and looked up, alarmed. He looked carefully through the trees and saw another wolf pacing anxiously past an opening in the trees. "The pack's still here, Uncle Luther! They're back there," he said, waving toward the woods.

Luther looked up from his first cut into the young wolf he was skinning. "Huh!" he exclaimed. "Normally they don't stick around so close."

"I know. It's weird," Adam responded and started walking toward the third trap. His senses were elevated now that he was aware of being watched by the wolves. He knew the pack was large from the noise it had made the night before, but he couldn't see another wolf anywhere in the trees. They were there, though; he could hear them whining and occasionally pacing. He stopped suddenly in surprise when he saw the third trapped wolf. It was a large adult female that neither tried to escape nor cried out in fear. She faced him fearlessly and snarled, her teeth bared. A deep growl came from within her. Her left front paw was caught securely in the trap Luther had set.

Adam grinned at the threatening wolf as it lunged at him. Adam aimed his revolver and fired. The large wolf fell dead with a bullet through its head. She had obviously given birth to a litter during the past spring. He stepped closer and knelt down to look at the width of her head and count her teats. He rolled her over to begin counting when he heard a deep growl. The growl was far deeper than the female's had been. He looked to his left and froze as a cold chill of fear ran down his spine. He was staring at the biggest wolf he had ever seen, standing not ten feet away from him. It was pure black, with a massive head. More startling, though, was that it stood taller than Adam as he was kneeling. To Adam's best estimate, the mass of the creature put it over two-hundred pounds, easily.

Most frightening, however, was that the massive creature didn't run away, but stared at Adam fiercely with its large fangs bared in a vicious snarl. If the monster charged, it would be on him before Adam could defend himself.

He stared into the eyes of the huge beast, knowing deep down that the moment he broke eye contact, the wolf would be on top of him, tearing at his flesh with the large incisors fiercely bared in its snarl. Fear Adam had not felt since his days in the Cavalry many years before swept through him. He was frozen, in a vulnerable position with no way of shifting his body without inviting an attack. He wished his Uncle Luther would hear the growling, come with his rifle and shoot the beast before it attacked him. Adam slowly pulled the hammer of his revolver back until it clicked. With a silent count of three, he swung his right arm across his body toward the wolf and pulled the trigger. He held the trigger down and fanned the hammer as fast as he could with his left hand. He had only three shots left, and they were spent instantly.

The wolf turned and ran into the trees within those same few seconds.

Adam stood up, emptied his cylinder, and frantically searched his pocket for more bullets, but he had none on him. All his ammunition was in his saddlebag. He ran to his tied horse and spoke to his curious uncle as he reached his saddlebag. "I just saw the biggest wolf I've ever seen!" He opened a box of bullets and began reloading his revolver as quickly as he could.

"Oh? Bigger than this pup, I hope," Luther said as he

pulled the organs out of the open belly of the first young wolf.

"I'm not kidding! It must've been nearly four feet tall and two hundred pounds. I'm not letting that monster get away. I'm going down to camp to get some supplies, and then I'm going after it!"

"Are you serious?" Luther asked, standing from his work to question Adam. He held his knife in his hand.

"Yeah, I'm serious! It was huge! It was as big as a black bear, but a lot more intimidating. Didn't you hear it snarling at me? I'm tracking it. I'm not coming back without it, either."

"What about skinning these beasts and our jerky?"

Adam's excitement beamed in his face as he answered with a smile, "I'm sorry, Uncle Luther, but I just seen the scariest wolf in my life, and I'm going to kill it. It was a monster!"

"Maybe it was standing on a rock and just looked big," Luther suggested.

"It was ten feet away from me! You don't understand. It was huge. Come on. Let's go see if we can find a track, so you can see for yourself."

Luther shrugged. "I've seen big wolves before."

"Not like this one, you haven't."

Luther replaced the knife in its scabbard and watched Adam pull his Winchester rifle out of its scabbard and load a cartridge into the chamber with the lever action. Adam led the way to where he'd been, without taking his attention from the tree line where the wolf had disappeared.

"I was kneeling down by her head and right over there, I heard a deep growl. I looked and couldn't believe my eyes. Right there stood a giant, black wolf, staring at me, snarling. And it was *huge!*"

Luther walked over to where Adam had pointed and looked at the ground. He knelt slowly to look closer at the large prints left in the dust and needles at the base of a tree at the edge of the grass. "Huh!" he exclaimed. He stood up and followed the trail through the grass to find a clearer track. The grass had been trampled and kept low by the herds of elk, deer, wolves and whatever other wildlife lived around there. He knew the track of every critter in the mountains, large or small, and looked for one print in particular. He had walked into the trees a bit and stopped to kneel again with interest. He had found a clear print in the dust near another tree. "I have never seen a larger wolf print! I swear, it's as big as a large mountain lion's!"

"I told you! I had no idea wolves could get so big. This one could kill a grown man easily by itself," Adam stated.

"And you're going after it?" Luther asked, already knowing the answer.

"You bet."

"There's no blood. You didn't hit it once from there? I thought you boys from your Uncle James' unit were crack shots." Luther said in jest of his brother-in-law, Colonial James Ziegler, who had led the Oregon 7th Cavalry Company E during part of the western Indian skirmishes known as the Snake War. Five of Luther's nephews were in the 3rd Company Volunteers under James' command: Adam and Lee Bannister, William Fasana and James Ziegler's two sons, Phillip and Seth Ziegler, who were both now officers in the cavalry themselves. James Ziegler had retired the past spring and moved up north to southeast Alaska to run a trading post and, of course, hunt and fish.

Adam hesitated before answering. "Not with a revolver, I'm not. Lee and William were better shots with a revolver. I was a better with a rifle; still am."

"Yeah, but you were right there! How could you miss it from there, if it was so big? I'm not too good with a handgun myself, but I could hit it from there!"

Adam shook his head and grinned. "I won't miss again."

"It's interesting how it stuck around though, isn't it? Of all the years I've been doing this, there have only been a few wolves that stayed close when we arrived, but none ever stayed here after the first kill shot. Yours did. I find that interesting. Was it a male?" Luther asked seriously.

Adam nodded. "The pack leader, no doubt. We know he has a big pack, so he won't be hard to track."

"A feller might do well at the tannery if he trapped that whole pack. You should take the traps with you and get a few more."

"I just want that one. I may be a while tracking it down. It didn't get so big by being stupid."

"It can't be that smart to stand there growling at a hunter. There is no one up here to hunt it so, like the elk, the animals up here get big. That includes grizzlies, so you be careful of them. That wolf might be huge, but there could be a few much larger grizzlies out there too." Luther warned.

"I know, but I'm only after that wolf this time."

18

"Wait up!" Deuce McKenna said, holding up a hand.

"What is it Unc—"

"Shh! Dammit!" Deuce said heatedly as he listened closely.

They were all on horseback cutting their way through a thick forest of trees on rough ground. Between low limbs, fallen trees, steep hazardous rocks and having to zigzag to get around everything, the pace they traveled was slow. The top of Windsor Ridge could be seen above the trees just beyond another high rolling ridge in front of them. It was increasingly apparent that, no matter how close Windsor Ridge appeared, it was a long way from where they were. They had run into many dead ends and had been forced to change directions to get around a crevice in the middle of nowhere and faced steep grades falling nearly straight down. The going was rough, and the farther they went, the tougher it seemed to get. However, straight ahead of them, beyond another vast rolling ridge, lay the crown of Windsor Ridge. They could see it clearly but getting to it was more difficult than it had looked that morning.

Deuce had heard a faint gunshot in the distance and now listened carefully. He held up his hand to his nephew to be quiet. "Gunshots…" he whispered.

"I heard them, too, but there were a lot more behind us this morning, so let's keep going," Pick said.

"True enough," Deuce agreed and kicked his horse to keep going. He added, "Besides, running into anyone in these mountains is like trying to find a needle in the haystack."

"Not if they're tracking us. And I don't want to get shot in the back," Pick said.

"Actually," Karl Digsby said, "I would be, since I'm the last in line." He rode behind Pick, who followed Brent and Deuce.

Pick looked back at his friend. "Do me a favor and make yourself bigger then."

Karl smiled. "Just remember that all the money is in Deuce's saddlebags, so if they miss me and you and hit Deuce, grab his reins. We can leave him and Brent behind, but not the money."

Pick chuckled for the first time.

Brent added jovially, "Uncle Dick is so big, they couldn't miss him."

"Maybe we should move him to the rear to protect the rest of us," Pick suggested. "I'll hold the bank bag just in case."

Karl added through a yawn, "This would be a very poor adventure if we lost the only compensation we're getting for the trip. I don't mind being away from home. In fact, that's about the only time I get to enjoy life. But I don't particularly like having the law behind me, either. And listening to Pick keep talking about being shot in the back makes me like this situation even less. After all, I am bringing up the rear."

"Karl, that's the most I've heard you say this whole trip," Deuce stated. "It's a good thing you said something, I forgot you were here. I would have cut you out of our earnings."

Karl smiled. "No, you just don't listen. I've been talking this whole trip. I always talk when I'm nervous, and I am nervous. I don't want to be shot in the back," he said pointedly to Pick.

Pick chuckled. "Like I said, put Deuce back there."

Deuce shook his head. "Maybe I'll put Brent back there so you two will quiet down."

"I ain't going back there!" Brent exclaimed quickly.

"Feeling yella-spined, are you, Brent? I saw one of your relatives a little earlier slithering on the ground. It was another yella-spined garter snake—a bit like you," Pick said. "You need to show some salt because, quite frankly, we're all risking death, and we got no room for a coward."

Brent stopped his mount and turned it halfway to look at Pick severely. "I'm no coward! I would've went into that bank, the same as you. You want me to ride back there? Fine, I'll ride back there." He rode past Pick to Karl as a show of his irritation. "Move up there, Karl. I'm taking over as last in line. I am not afraid of being back here."

Karl looked at him without any humor. "You're slowing us down."

"I don't care. I'm not a coward, and I don't take kindly to being called one."

Pick said heatedly, "Then start acting like a man! No one's forcing you to ride last, but you had better find a backbone. Things could get a hell of a lot scarier than riding at the back of the line! Damn, kid, your uncle wasn't serious to begin with, and you damn near had a fit."

"I didn't have a fit, and I *do* have a backbone! I'll show you what a backbone is when the time comes," Brent exclaimed while eyeing Pick angrily.

"If that's a threat, you'd better prove it right now!" Pick said, his voice hard. His breathing grew heavier as he glared at Brent.

To lessen the growing hostility between the two men, Karl said quickly, "We'll find that out if the posse catches up with us. In the meantime, how about Pick and I ride back here so your little sweet cheeks can ride safely behind your uncle."

Brent looked at Karl, annoyed. "Shut up, Karl! I don't need to be saved by my uncle."

Deuce said harshly to his nephew, "You better calm down, boy! These aren't your school chums; these men will knock you out of your saddle if you don't watch it. The only reason they haven't done it yet is because of me, I imagine. Now shut up and ride!"

"No one's going to knock me out of my saddle," Brent said confidently.

Pick shook his head and laughed as he kicked his horse to move past Deuce. "Your nephew's something else, Deuce. Even I wasn't so dumb as to talk that big when I was his age," he said as he passed Deuce to take the lead.

"I don't think you're that smart, either!" Brent said loudly.

"What did I just say to you?" Deuce asked his nephew sharply. "Just be quiet for a while, okay?"

Karl added simply, "It's not smart to get on Pick's bad side, Brent. It might be wise to remember he is a member of the Sperry Helms Gang."

"So what? I could be, too."

"No, you couldn't," Deuce said frankly. He added irritably, "They wouldn't have anything to do with you. Now, if you want a good lesson for beginning the outlaw life, it's keep your mouth shut and just follow us out of these damn mountains!"

"I *am* following. But Pick had no business calling me a coward either. I don't care who he is, no one talks to me like that!"

Deuce shook his head in frustration and wordlessly turned his horse to ride after Pick.

Brent exhaled heavily and then said to Karl, "I may be young compared to you old guys, but there's nothing you can do that I can't do, too. If that posse catches up with us, I'll show you all just what I mean. I can shoot as well as anyone, and there's no cowardice in my bones, I can tell you that. My spine's as solid as an oak."

Karl smirked. "If you keep standing here, they probably *will* catch up with us, and then you can prove yourself as the meanest gunman in our little gang. But until then, turn your horse around and get to riding like your uncle told you."

19

Nathan Pierce opened his eyes to the sight of a tall fern not far from his face. His head throbbed and he felt cold, even though it was mid-morning and warming up quickly. Aside from a distant bird chirping, the mountain where he lay was completely silent. Slowly, he sat up and rubbed his painful temple. He could feel the knots where the butt of Octavius' shotgun had hit him and opened two gashes on his scalp. He felt the dried blood that had run down his face. It took him only a second to remember what had happened and why his head throbbed.

With a sudden spurt of alarm, he stood up and looked around for his brother. "Cal?" he called but received no response. "Cal?" he yelled. He listened as his voice echoed back to him, seemingly unheard. "Oh, no," he said as he remembered seeing his brother's legs lying beside a tree just before he was knocked unconscious by Octavius. With a sense of heavy dread, he turned around to look uphill to his left. There were his brother's legs, still pointing down beside a tree.

"No, no. No. Oh, Lord, no!" Nathan ran to where his

brother lay. He fell to his knees beside Cal and turned his body over. It was obvious Cal had been shot at close range by a shotgun. The shot that had mangled his chest would have killed him, but Octavius had put a .44 bullet through the center of Cal's forehead, as well. Cal's eyes were open, and bits of dust and fir needles stuck to him. Nathan fell to his knees and screamed, "*No!*" He sobbed over his brother's body as his scream echoed through the wilderness.

After a few minutes, Nathan started gaining control over his emotions. He wiped Cal's eyes clean of the debris. He closed his brother's eyes and took some deep breaths, trying to calm down. He looked at Cal's face and tried to memorize it, knowing it would be the last time he would ever see it looking as good as it did now.

He would never see Cal's smile or hear his voice again in his life. Never again would Cal be there for him to count on as a brother, or to confide in as a best friend. He would never be there again. For a long moment, Nathan stared at Cal as tears slowly slid down his cheeks.

Some brothers couldn't stand each other; some carried unresolved bitterness, and some had no idea why there was such hostility between them. Others simply lost contact and became strangers; others lived separate lives but stayed in contact. Nathan and Cal had always been together. Nathan had joined the cavalry so they could be together, they got out together and, when Nathan fell in love with Sarah, Cal was there every single day to support him and encourage him to fight for the lady he loved. Cal had even changed his last name in order to remain in the lives of his little brother and new sister-in-law.

When Sarah's father set a bounty on Nathan, Cal stayed with the couple to help protect and watch over them. Cal was not just a brother; he was the closest person in Nathan's life. Now he was gone; simply no longer there... gone.

He wasn't lost, though. Nathan knew where Cal was; he was in Heaven. It wasn't like when they went to the funeral of Henry Osbourne in Loveland earlier that summer. Henry worked for the logging company and was the victim of an unfortunate accident when a tree splintered, hit and killed him. Henry was known for his aggressive and mean-spirited personality. He treated his wife and children cruelly, and wailing could often be heard coming from their little cabin. Henry drank most of his earnings away and had a foulest tongue in a camp full of foul tongues. He had no fear of or respect for God. When Cal had tried to talk with Henry about the Bible and Jesus Christ, Henry had laughed at him. Only a few days later, Henry met his untimely death and faced his Maker.

At Henry's funeral, Cal and Nathan were taken by surprise how many people said the comforting words, "He's in a better place now." Nathan had his doubts about that. A person does not go to Heaven because he dies; he goes to Heaven because he believes in Jesus Christ as his savior. That was the only path leading to Heaven. Every other way leads to the wide path to hell.

However, Cal was a devoted Christian and, although life isn't fair or easy and isn't always kind, one thing was for sure: Jesus was Cal's savior, and Cal was in Heaven. His life on earth was over, but his life in eternity was just beginning.

Nathan walked down to the camp, grabbed Cal's blanket and carried it back to cover his body. He paused before covering his brother's face to look at Cal one last time. Tears filled his eyes again, as a hollowness seemed to open like a vacuum within him. "I love you, Cal, more than you know. We'll meet again. Greet Ma for me. Don't worry about Sarah and me. We'll be okay. I promise we'll name our first boy after you. Okay, big brother?"

He wiped his eyes before taking a deep breath. "I don't want to leave you," he said in a high-pitched, cracking voice. "I will never forget you, Cal." Nathan looked at the entrance wound in Cal's forehead and a wave of fury rose within him. "I'm going to find Octavius and I will kill him for doing this to you. Rest assured, I will! Until we meet again, I love you, brother."

Nathan covered Cal's face with the blanket. His breathing grew heavy, and he yelled fiercely, "Octavius! I'm coming for you!" His voice echoed through the mountains, shattering the silence. When the echoing stopped, Nathan walked quickly through the trees to find broken limbs with which to cover Cal's body. He could not stand the idea of scavengers in the forest feeding on his brother, so he stacked a thick layer of branches, limbs and ferns on top of Cal's body to protect it.

Consumed by the urgency to track Octavius down, Nathan walked to where Mike Hall's body lay next to their bedrolls. Nathan looked for his rifle, but it was missing, as was Cal's. He walked into the camp where Jack and Dustin both lay in large puddles of coagulated blood. Dustin's revolver and rifle were missing, as were Jack's. For a moment, frustration almost got the better of Nathan. Then he noticed Jack's empty holster a short distance away, where it had been tossed. Nathan walked into the tall ferns beyond the camp with the thought that Octavius must've thrown all the arms into the brush to leave him weaponless when he awoke. It was only reasonable Octavius would have tossed the weapons when he came back to camp to get his horse.

After looking around for a few minutes, Nathan found Jack's old Winchester. He picked it up, confirming his suspicion, and then ran uphill to where he had been struck by Octavius, and started looking for his own revolver. After a few minutes of searching, he found it in the middle of a large fern about thirty feet from where he was knocked unconscious. He checked the cylinder and replaced it in his holster.

He glanced again at his brother's covered body, then forced himself to go back to the camp to the horses. He placed his saddle onto his horse and then tied Jack's scabbard onto his saddle for the Winchester rifle. He pilfered through Jack's saddlebags for more ammunition and gathered his bedroll and all the .44 cartridges Cal had brought along, as well. He took one last look around at his dead friends and then kicked his horse forward. He could follow the trail left behind by the bank robbers and, most recently, Octavius.

Octavius would undoubtedly be moving fast, but Nathan was determined to catch him. He no longer cared about the bank robbers or if they were ever found. His only concern was finding and killing Octavius Clark.

20

———

Nathan rode quickly where the rough terrain would allow him to. He rode up the mountain where they had camped, and down the other side, followed a gulley around a solid rock face. Then he followed the trail into the gulley and up another steep forest trail. The path he followed grew hard to follow at times, but by slowing down and scanning carefully, he could make out the ground that had been disturbed by shod horses.

He had ridden parallel to the mountain for some way before making his way up to the summit. Nathan stopped on the summit and gazed at the view ahead, which showed more rough country and a row of four or five tall mountains that seemed to grow only steeper but weren't quite as tall as the one upon which he sat his horse. In the distance, he could see a long ridgeline that looked like an impassable wall of rock-faced peaks.

Recognizing Windsor Ridge from its back side, Nathan felt a slight sense of comfort. There was no doubt that the view was quite beautiful, but his only thought was about Octavius trapped between the jagged wall of rock in the distance and himself. He put his hands on the saddle horn and sat quietly for a moment. He had ridden quite a distance already and still had a long way to go, but somewhere up ahead he would find Octavius Clark.

"Lord," Nathan prayed, "I know I don't pray much. And maybe I've been discouraged. It isn't fair to live like a rat hiding from a thousand cats. Maybe that's why I can't serve you the way I should. I don't know. Maybe I just don't believe you care, like folks say you do. Cal believed in you, and you let him die! Maybe I just don't see the good in living my life for you when everything can go so wrong and you sit quietly and do nothing about it." His eyes brimmed with tears as the hollowness of his brother's death once again filled him with sorrow.

"God, I don't have any right to ask any favors from you. I don't even know if I'm doing the right thing in going after this man, because he is like a ghost in the trees. He killed Cal and my friends. He killed them all. Help me bring him to justice for Cal's sake, if not mine. If you don't help me, then I probably won't make it out of here alive. And if I don't, then all I ask is that you please watch over Sarah. I pray she will meet someone who will love her as much as I do, and able to give her more than I ever could," he said, then wiped tears from his eyes.

"I could not forgive myself if I went home and Octavius got away. Jesus, if you want me to serve you, then show me that I can trust you. Help me to kill Octavius. Give me just one clear shot to blow that... animal"—he chose the word carefully—"out of his saddle. In your name, I ask this. Amen." He kicked his horse and began descending the steep mountain side.

Before too long, he reached the camp the bank robbers had made the night before. Squinting at the sun, he placed the time at about eleven in the morning. There was no doubt that Octavius would catch up with the robbers in the next hour or two. It was clear to Nathan that if Jack had let Octavius go ahead by himself yesterday, the bank robbers would have been found dead right here in their camp, and Octavius would be gone with the gold and money, never to be seen again. However, Cal, Mike, Dustin and Jack would all be alive, as well.

If it had been any other stranger in the territory, everything might've worked out all right. But Octavius Clark happened to be the most dangerous man any of them had ever met. Yet Nathan was only alive because Octavius had enough humanity in him to keep his word to Sarah. Nathan hadn't feared too many men in his lifetime, but he feared Octavius. He couldn't let Octavius get away, though. Not only would he never forgive himself for letting him escape but killing the sheriff and the deputy would surely bring U.S. Marshal Matt Bannister to Loveland.

The marshal would then come knocking on Nathan's door and perhaps recognize him and Sarah. A ten-thousand-dollar bounty was enough money to cause the marshal to forget all about Octavius, arrest Nathan and send Sarah back to her parents. It might even be enough money to account for an accidental shooting on the long journey back to Branson.

If the marshal didn't recognize him, then the many bounty hunters who came to track Octavius might recognize him and Sarah. Men like Bloody Jim Hexum didn't care about anything except the bounty money. For the price on Nathan's head, Hexum would kill him like a fly on a wall. Nathan didn't fear death as much as he feared losing his wife. He was risking his life by going after Octavius, but the terror of losing his wife would be greater if he turned back and went home to the comfort of Sarah's arms than if he continued his journey.

"Lord, remember to help me," he said, and kicked his horse to forward. The more time that passed, Octavius was getting that much closer to the robbers. With that thought, Nathan suddenly felt a kinship with the gang of robbers, because they had the same common enemy. They didn't know it yet, but Nathan was sure they would soon.

21

Now that Adam had seen the oversized wolf up close, he had no interest in hunting any other animal until he had the monster's hide hanging on his wall. He had found the pack's trail leaving the meadow and traveling up the mountain easily enough. The way was steep, and trees thinned the higher up Windsor Ridge he rode.

As he left the last of the trees, he saw the large, crown-like cliff that had given Windsor Ridge its name. The cliff face was majestic and impenetrable. Below it, a wide field of scree rock flowed under the cliffs. At the bottom of the scree field sat large talus rocks that had tumbled down and accumulated over the centuries. However, to the east was a saddle along the ridgeline that appeared to be the easiest way over the mountain. It was also where the wolves' tracks were leading.

Adam slowly made his way around a few heavy boulders and lose rocks as he worked his horse toward the saddle. The hard climb rose sharply, but when he reached the top, he took a minute to let his horse rest. Looking back at the beautiful view of the miles of forest and rolling hills below him, he saw Jessup Valley in the distance and the smoky blue color that gave the beautiful Blue Mountains their name. It was a beautiful view, and he smiled with appreciation. Very few men had ever viewed the scene he now scanned, but his grandfather certainly would have.

He turned his horse and rode over two hundred yards through the ridges rising on both sides. The way was tough and tight-fitting in some places where boulders had fallen from ridges overhead. Though the natural pass through the ridgeline was fairly-wide, rock debris made it challenging in some spots. When he'd made it through the pass, he stopped in wonder at what he saw on the other side.

Below him spread a large forested valley, separated by wide green meadows with scattered small groves of trees. Running down the center of the valley a high, rolling hill covered with a thick carpet of Douglas fir trees tapered down to nothing on the valley's western side. From his viewpoint, Adam saw three small high mountain lakes, bluer than most any he'd ever seen, including Lake Jessup in the Blue Mountains, separated by miles. He estimated the valley to be at least six or seven miles long and three to four miles wide at its widest, completely encircled by mountains and cliffs as rugged and high as the one he was on.

The beauty of the scene literally took Adam's breath away. His grandfather had mentioned a beautiful valley beyond Windsor Ridge somewhere, but Adam had never seen it until now. He sat still, gazing on the hidden treasure he had heard about years ago, but had never before seen for himself.

The view was indeed breathtaking; however, the way down the mountain and into it appeared to be more treacherous than the trail he had come up. It was no wonder his grandfather didn't hunt in the valley below him instead of where their hunting camp sat. The effort of finding and hauling out an elk or two wouldn't be worth it.

A monster-sized wolf was worth the risk, though. And a risk it would be; the sheer backside cliff of Windsor Ridge ended in a large cascade of fallen rock piled halfway up its height. The mountain was nothing except jagged rock, with walls of granite having no places to climb over or around. The only path into the valley below was on a wide scree field that angled sharply downhill into a large collection of talus rock ranging in size from a pig to a house. Above the scree field, was a tall granite cliff that appeared as unforgiving and formidable as any Adam had ever seen.

It was risky to cross a scree field; one wrong step could start a landslide of rock that would send him and his horse rolling out of control down the steep mountain with tons of rock following. They would not stop rolling until the avalanche slammed them into the huge boulders at the bottom. He would be lucky to come out of the disaster bruised and scraped up. At worst he and his horse would be killed—or wishing they were dead, if they had to lie there with a broken leg or two.

Most people probably wouldn't try to cross the scree field, but Adam looked at the situation a little differently. If he could get across that field and down onto the valley floor, then he would be just fine. He could see the unmistakable narrow line across the field where the wolf pack and other critters had, over time, packed a firm path. It seemed reasonable that if an estimated two-hundred-pound wolf and his pack could walk on the trail, then Adam and his horse could do it.

Dismounting, Adam took hold of his Winchester rifle and led his horse by the reins. With a quick prayer and a deep breath, he stepped onto the wolf's trail. He walked carefully and felt stones adjusting to his weight with every step. His mare followed, though a few stones slid downhill with her every footfall, too.

Step by step, he led her down a narrow path while considering his best course of action if the trail gave way, or if he or his horse began sliding down the scree field. The farther Adam walked, the more confidant he felt that it would hold his two-hundred and fifty-some pounds without too much concern. It was conceivable that heavy use by the wolf pack, and possibly elk, bear or mountain lions had packed the field down tighter than he'd expected.

Finally, after a cautious walk, Adam stepped onto solid ground not far from a tree line. He mounted his mare and followed the pack's trail through the heavy shadows of the trees in a westerly direction, down a gentle slope onto the valley floor and into a clearing of about forty acres, rich with tall grass. There was no lack of life in the valley either. Within minutes, he saw garter snakes, grasshoppers, gopher holes, deer and a large bald eagle. He crossed the meadow and rode in between a series of small clusters of trees that dotted the landscape until finally he entered another wooded area that was thick, but not overly wide, and which opened up into another small meadow. Adam paused and took a drink of water from his canteen.

A badger scurried down a hill near its den, and he had seen two rabbits so far, as well. The thick grass was not only beautiful to look at, but could also be hazardous, if a man wasn't careful where he rode his horse. Some of the gopher holes were plenty wide enough for a horse's hoof to slip into, but a rabbit or badger's hole hidden in the grass could break a horse's leg. The wolf trail through the meadows avoided the holes for the most part, but it also flattened the tall grass, covering abandoned holes. Adam rode slowly and closely watched the ground in front of him while staying alert for wolves. He was in the wolf's territory and might run into one or a feisty dozen or more of them at any moment.

The sound of a pup playfully barking caught Adam's attention, and he turned his horse in the direction of the sound. He rode into the nearest tree line to remain as concealed as possible when he approached the den. As the barks grew louder, he stopped his horse and dismounted. Tying the reins to a tree branch, he pulled his rifle from its scabbard and set out on foot.

Caution filled him; this was the wolves' territory, and he was encroaching as he neared their den. Like any other animal, wolves were protective of their young and the den housing them. Adam had considered riding his horse closer, but horses were easily spooked. That alone could scare off the pack, or worse, invite the whole pack to charge him. Either way, it was wiser to hunt on foot so he could control his own steps, speed, noise, and lie lower if necessary and wait longer without worrying about his horse making unwanted noise. If necessary, he could climb a tree to escape trouble. Of course, his horse was at risk, but he hoped his mare would be all right while he continued his trek.

Ultimately, it was the thrill of the hunt he enjoyed the most. The prey he was after could kill him if it caught him off guard, but there were other predators to watch out for as well. Grizzly bears were the greatest threat he could run into, but mountain lions, black bears, and again, the pack of wolves he hunted were all a threat to him. It was August, and all four predators had young to protect.

The valley he was in had been, to his knowledge, untouched by human hands and as wild as any mountain in the west had ever been. The predators here would be bigger, stronger and less afraid of humans than ones in more populated lower elevations. On one hand, they might not feel threatened by his presence. On the other, they might not hesitate to attack him.

Adam moved forward slowly through the trees with his 1876 Winchester rifle in his hands. He would've liked to have his Hawken rifle, but with an unknown number of wolves in the area, he didn't want to take the chance of having to reload the powder, cap and ball while being attacked. His Winchester was fully loaded with a cartridge in the chamber. His revolver was reversed on his left hip, and his twelve-inch horn-handled knife rested on his right hip. Adam knew very well that wolves were intelligent and alert. He wasn't taking any chances with his weapons in case his hunt became a battle for his own survival. The monster wolf that had growled at him earlier wouldn't hesitate to attack now that Adam neared his den. That wolf had sneaked up on him silently that morning without his knowing it was there, and it might do so again. But this time, Adam doubted it would be content to growl. He knew the risks of stalking such a beast on its own territory, he believed that to skin that monster before anyone else could do it was worth the risk.

Adam moved through the trees toward the sound of playful pups. He was nearing the edge of the woods, where another grass-covered meadow began. It was wide and sloped uphill, where another tree line sat on top. Large gray boulders dotted the meadow floor, but on the hillside, a natural rock formation cave made a perfect wolf's den. Adam saw the pups, running, jumping and mock-fighting with each other outside the den, under the watchful eye of four female wolves lying in the sun.

Adam was about a hundred and fifty yards from the den, hidden in the shadows of the trees. He did not see the monster he was after yet, but he knew it was around some-where. A good hunter must have enough patience to wait for prey to reveal itself, and then have the self-control to make a single killing shot. Adam was gifted with both patience and marksmanship, so he waited silently, alert to his surroundings. He listened for any cries from his horse or any other sound that might indicate he was in trouble.

Within the next half-hour, his patience paid off. The big black pack leader walked out from the den and went up above the cave entrance to lie on a large flat rock over-looking the youngsters playing in the meadow.

Where all the other wolves were, Adam didn't know, but he had found the one he'd come to collect, and that was all he needed to know. Adam grinned, slowly raised his rifle and set the barrel over a sturdy branch at the right height to match his aim. He looked down the sight and aimed care-fully. The big wolf lay at such an angle that a shot to the heart would be difficult, but he had a good bead on the animal's skull. Slowly, Adam pulled the hammer back to lessen the chance of a missed shot due to trigger pressure. The hammer clicked into a locked position, and Adam moved his finger to the trigger. Just as he was about to fire, an unexpected shot echoed across the valley. Startled by the shot, Adam missed his target. The bullet hit the rock just below where the wolf lay and ricocheted.

Adam ejected the spent cartridge quickly and aimed at the fleeing animal, but the wolf sprinted for the tree line above him and disappeared. The quick sound of a gunfight interrupted Adam's hunt and changed his focus from the wolves to the sound of a man screaming in pain. He recog-nized the two sounds from the time he served in the cavalry during the Snake War. He knew those sounds well.

22

"My word, would you look at that!" Deuce McKenna exclaimed.

They had reached the summit of a tall, steep ridge they'd had no choice but to climb. When they finally reached the top, they paused in wonder as they took in the view below them. Their journey across the mountains had led them to a wide valley encircled by a formidable rock-faced ridge line that looked like a wall meant to keep the world away from the oasis they had just discovered.

The valley spread out before them. Miles of rich green grass were interrupted by small groves of trees and a few larger forests. Deuce saw three small blue lakes in the valley. He guessed the valley itself to be six or seven miles long, and four or five miles wide at its widest. A tall, steep hill, thick with trees, ran like a spine through the center of the valley, but tapered at the west end of the valley floor. The back side of Windsor Ridge loomed over the far side of the valley. They would have to climb that peak somehow, but once they got over the ridge, they could split up if they wanted to and race for home at their own speed. One thing was for sure, though, the valley was far more beautiful than anything Deuce or the others had expected to find.

"Would you look at that," Deuce repeated with astonishment as he rested his hands on the saddle horn. "Amazing. Gorgeous!"

"What I wouldn't give to marry Christine and build a house up here. I swear, if I built a nice log cabin up here somewhere and brought her here, she'd never want to leave. That's for sure," Brent said.

Karl laughed and said, "Brent, Christine's the elite dancer and singer at Bella's Dance Hall. Men come from everywhere and from all walks of life to win her heart, and you're bringing her a tree fungus and a promise of paradise? Good luck."

"It's a conk, not a tree fungus. And yeah, if I could marry her, I'd spend every day up here building a log cabin for her. And I don't mean a small one, either. I'd build an upstairs and make it a home as beautiful as she is. A cabin with the best view and a big porch, so we can sit outside and watch the sun going down. And you know what else? Forget painting a peacock on that conk. I'll pay my friend's wife or a painter to come up here and paint this valley on that conk. Whatever the price, that's what I'm going to do with my share of the money."

"It would be a pretty picture," Deuce stated.

Pick Lawson said seriously, "You guys can sit here and drool over the view if you want, but what excites me is the way down into it. It's a hell of a lot easier to ride down than to ride up. But getting over that ridge line over there doesn't look easy, no matter where you look, does it? That saddle beside Windsor Ridge might be the easiest route."

Deuce smiled slightly. A gentle, long rolling slope led

into the valley. There was tree cover most all the way down that ended at a wide meadow of grass with scattered groves of trees and fallen logs. "Well, let's go down, boys. We have a posse behind us somewhere, apparently. All we have to do is get across this valley and over that ridge, and we're almost home."

"Give or take thirty miles," Karl added with a slight smile.

"That will be easy riding compared to what we've been through," Deuce answered. He kicked his horse and moved forward to begin his descent from the high mountain. "Pick's right. Our luck's changing, boys. It looks like maybe five or six miles across the valley, so we'll be over Windsor Ridge today. By tomorrow tonight, if you ride real hard, Brent, maybe you'll be able to see your Christine."

"I'm not stopping until I do! I'm telling you I will marry her."

Pick shook his head as he followed them down. "I already told you, she won't be interested in an adolescent crook."

Brent turned in his saddle to glare back at Pick. "And like I said earlier, I can do anything you can do! I can change my career if I want to, but you're getting too old. So, I'd say I have more potential to make her a nice home than any of you do. I'm still young enough to become anything I want: a banker, lawyer, teacher, or the boss of our gang here."

Pick chuckled spitefully. "You won't be over me in any aspect of life. You haven't got the steel to stand up to any of the men I've known. Hell, even young Tad Sperry would have you shaking in your boots, and he's only fifteen or so. Isn't that right, Deuce?"

Deuce shrugged. "He's a bad seed."

Brent scoffed. "I'm not afraid of any adolescent *crook*, as you called me. Trust me, when the time comes, I'll show you what I'm made of. I mean, Uncle Dick's my uncle. Toughness runs in the family."

Karl smirked. "You're not blood related. He married your aunt."

"Doesn't matter. I'm learning from the best. And we're still family, isn't that right, Uncle Dick?"

"Yep," Deuce replied, a trifle amused by the conversation.

Pick added with a vindictive smile, "Well, your uncle is the Big Deuce, there's no doubt about that, but you're still a little whelp."

Angrily, Brent turned his horse around to face Pick. "I'm getting sick of you calling me a damn kid! I'm almost twenty years old, and I'll fight any man any time, including you, right now! Do you got that, Pick?"

"Hey!" Deuce shouted. "That's enough between you two. Quit picking on him, Pick. And you," he said to Brent harshly, "you better learn how to take a little harassing here and there by your friends, or you won't have any friends at all. You can give it out, but you can't take a little harassing? That's crap! No one will put up with that for long, not even me. He was teasing you! Now cool down, or I'll throw you off that horse and show you you're not so tough after all. Got it?"

Brent grew red-faced with embarrassment but nodded to his uncle. "Yes, sir."

"Good. These men aren't your enemies, Brent. We all watch out for each other, but we tease each other, too. You want to fit in? Then learn to take some teasing! And, by the way, you'd be a fool to want to be the leader of any outlaw gang. With Matt Bannister and his deputies in town, there's too much law around to risk living this kind of life."

Pick looked at Brent. "I was teasing you, but boy, you just keep proving my point. You're just a temperamental kid." He chuckled sarcastically and rode past Brent to continue downhill.

Karl paused to wait for Brent, who appeared humiliated. "If it's any consolation, I believe you can become a very fierce and tough man. Unfortunately, badgers usually don't win against a man with a gun. It's foolishness to fight a man for vanity's sakes. It doesn't take much wisdom to know when something is worth fighting and maybe dying for. I recommend you seek to gain a little bit of wisdom."

"I don't even know what that means," Brent said, sounding annoyed, and kicked his horse to follow behind Pick.

Karl snorted and said, "In short, it means that you really should seek a more stable living than this, Brent. A banker might be a good idea, now that you're a bank robber. I'm pretty sure most bankers aren't experienced bank robbers."

Brent grinned. "I'm sure they aren't. They just rob the working man."

"If you want to win the heart of a lady like Christine, it might be the right path to take. She isn't a low-class-thief's-wife kind of woman. She is high-class and most definitely a Christian. I suggest if you want to marry her or someone like her, find a more respectable life than robbing banks or laboring in a mill. It might be a little late for the three of us, but your life's just beginning. Don't waste it running from the law."

"Why are you doing it, Karl? You're no hardened criminal. Why did you join up with the Sperrys? You have a job at the mill, a wife and a home. Obviously, it wasn't enough, so why did you risk your life joining up with these guys?"

Karl paused to think for a moment. "To be honest, I don't

know. I found my life to be the same dull day, lived repeatedly. I am married to a woman I can't hardly stand and work at a job I hate. I would say my life is a constant downhill cycle of boredom and discontent. I always wanted more, but unfortunately, I married on emotion rather than love. I never became the teacher I wanted to be because my wife had other needs I had to meet. Let me give you some marital advice: if Christine or any other woman you begin to fall in love with starts to control your life, don't marry her!"

"Why don't you get divorced and become a teacher and start seeing one of the other dancers at Bella's Dance Hall? Christine's not the only beautiful one, but she is the most beautiful one."

"I took a vow for better or worse till death do us part. I meant it."

Pick spoke from up ahead of them, "You know the difference between 'I do' and 'I did'? Past tense and now! Leave her and move on. You don't even need to divorce her. It's not like anyone's going to care. She sure in heck isn't going to divorce you, is she?"

"Probably not. But she said her vows, and she meant them, at least to keep her reputation clean, anyway. We made our bed and now we are stuck with it, even if it's unevenly made."

"Unevenly made?" Pick asked. "If your marriage was compared to a bed, it would be an unused one that's been kicked around, rolled over, drug through the mud, soaked in turpentine, vomit and piss. But the blankets are thrown back on there to make it look like a nice comfortable bed. That, my friend, is your marriage. So why not leave that bed-bug-infested room while you can?"

"Pick," Brent said, "for a guy who bought the ring for

another guy to marry your fiancé, you're not sounding very nice."

Deuce laughed despite himself, as did Karl. Pick shook his head and grinned. "Yeah, I don't usually treat everyone that nice," he said. "But he was doing me a favor, I think, after listening to Karl complain about his wife."

Karl shook his head. "If Lilly was anything like my wife, then yeah, he saved your life."

Pick laughed.

They rode down the mountain side into a deep swell and then back up over a rolling finger that ran horizontally across the ridge. Then they continued to the valley. They traveled through trees, patches of grass around fallen trees and rock debris that scattered the area. It was a long ride, but they were nearing the bottom and level ground.

Brent asked after a long spell of quiet riding, "So, when we get back, what do we do with our money? How do we explain it, if you don't want anyone to know about it? I know what I'm going to do. I'm going to hire an artist to come up here and paint that conk for Christine. But what if someone asks where I got the money? What do you guys say?"

Deuce was quick to answer. "You say nothing at all to anyone. And you don't go buying the store out, either. You don't buy anything until I say so, and when you do, it's in proportion. Do you understand?"

"Sure, but what if I wanted to get a new suit and a pair of boots? That's not such a bad thing, is it? My boots are pert' near worn down to nothing. I know I can't spend much, but I need to look good the next time I see Christine."

Karl spoke from behind Brent. "Let me put it this way, Brent. We hope to have framed Morton and Jessie for our crime, but if you suddenly have money for a new suit and boots or whatever else you might buy on *your* budget, the law might get suspicious and start asking questions."

"And if the law gets suspicious and lets Morton and Jesse go, we'll all end up dead. Trust me, fellers, you don't have to worry about Brent. I'll hold his share and give him a little at a time on his paydays," Deuce said as he neared the bottom of the mountain.

"That's the best idea I've heard yet," Pick said as he looked back up the mountain behind them. He couldn't see anyone following them but he had an odd feeling they were being watched. "I'm thinking we need to be on guard. Remember those shots we heard this morning? Some were from behind us. Then, a bit later, some came from this way. I have a feeling we're being watched, and I don't like it."

"From where?" Brent asked and turned back to look up the mountain. He couldn't see a trace of anyone.

"I don't know." Pick said slowly as he gazed around the valley. It was silent except for a few birds in the distance.

"Well, I see a big doe standing over by that tree over there. Maybe that's what you're feeling," Deuce said and rode forward without concern. It wasn't the first time Pick felt like he was being followed or watched after committing a robbery. They had been hidden in thick forests for most of their journey across the Wallowa Mountains so far, and now that they were in the open and entering a valley with a lot of open space, he too felt anxious and vulnerable.

"No, it's not the deer. Let's just get across this valley as fast as we can. I don't like it."

"You seem like too tough a man to be scared," Brent said with a sneer for Pick.

Pick looked back at him and said harshly, "Being scared and being cautious are two different things, and I trust my instincts! We heard shots from over this way just a few hours ago. If you think we're out of trouble and home free, you have another thing coming, because we are not. There's a posse out there somewhere. I don't know what the hell they were shooting at this morning, but it wasn't us. Trust me, that little town back there hasn't forgotten about us. By now, every town around here has heard what we did and will be looking out for us. It wouldn't surprise me if every town around here has sent a posse into these mountains to find us. You had better sit up in your saddle and keep your eye out, because I'm telling you, we're not as alone out here as you all think."

Deuce said, "This was Nez Perce territory just a few years ago. Who's to say there aren't a hundred Indians hidden up here in this valley."

"If there is, we'll never get out of here alive," Karl said. "They won't chance us telling the cavalry about them. Why would you even say something like that, Deuce? Now you have me thinking about it. It had never even occurred to me there might be Indians around!"

Pick sighed. "Well, I'd rather run into Indians right now than a posse, so let's hope it's them. The Nez Perce never meant anyone any harm until the whites pushed them out of here. Let's just hope, if there are any, they haven't forgotten how to be nice. Because a posse sure isn't going to be."

"Will you stop talking about posses?" Deuce said sharply to Pick. "We haven't seen a single sign of human life since we left Loveland. We have outrun them so far and are still ahead of them. We don't even know for sure if they are after us. For all we know, they might have run across four prospectors and shot the hell out of them, thinking they're us. There was a lot of shooting going on, so we have no idea. But so far, we are doing good. Look." He pointed at Windsor

Ridge, which towered above them. "Once we get across that, we're on our way home. They don't even know what our horses look like, so we can split up and ride freely. But the last thing we need is to get spooked by the first open ground we come across. We'll be fine. We just have to keep riding. And I was kidding about the Indians. At least, I think I was." He chuckled.

"Well then, let's run to the next tree line and get out of the open," Pick suggested anxiously.

"What the hell? Do you want to wear our horses out before we even get to Windsor Ridge? We're going to that lake we saw from up there and refresh our horses with some good water and grass for a bit. We can go without nourishment for a day or two, but the animals can't. We need to let them graze and drink; not for long, but for a bit. Besides, it's getting hot enough that I wouldn't mind a quick dip in the lake myself, just to refresh myself a bit."

Pick was perplexed. "Are you crazy?" he asked. "We haven't got time for that! We haven't got time to walk across this meadow, either. Those men could crest that mountain at any moment, and we're in plain sight. If you want to rest by the lake, you do that, but I'm going home! Give me my share right now, and I'll see you at home, if you make it. Really, Deuce, give me my share so I can go." His anxiety was turning to panic, and he wanted to run, and run now, to the farthest edge of the valley. He didn't know why he felt the way he did, but he knew they were in danger and needed to find cover.

"We'd have to count it all up and weigh the gold to make it fair. I can't just hand you some money without knowing what we have. It's not like you to get so worked up, Pick. What's wrong with you? You were fine not even half an hour ago."

"And it's not like you to be so relaxed while on the run. I don't understand you! I don't know if it's because you think you're experienced with this stuff now, or if you're trying to impress your damned nephew! But you're putting Karl's and my life on the line, and I won't stand for it anymore. I want my share, and I want it now!"

"What are you talking about, putting your lives on the line? I haven't done anything of the sort!" Deuce exclaimed.

"You are being a bit complacent, Deuce," Karl said. They had stopped in the middle of wide grass meadow, as evidence of Deuce's complacence.

Deuce said caustically to Pick, "Okay, fine. Do you want me to count it all up now, in the middle of a meadow? I can count the money, but you won't get any of the gold, because we haven't got a scale to weigh it with."

"No! We can do that later, but can we go?" Pick snapped.

Deuce sat back in his saddle and paused to intentionally irritate Pick even more. "Fine," he said at last. "We'll go to the lake and split up our shares and go our own ways. But you see that big hill there?" He pointed to the hill like a spine running down the middle of the valley. It rose sharply for three hundred feet or more. "We have to climb that hill to get to the other side of it. Then we have to climb Windsor Ridge! Our animals are beat. They need water and a full stomach to keep going. I know you're worried, but we won't get home if we don't rest the horses! If there is a posse, they'll need to do the same thing. We can only go until the horses can't run anymore. In this heat and at this elevation, our horses don't have much left in them. We should ride at a steady pace and not run them to death. I know what I am doing!"

"I understand that, but there's no time. We can rest our

horses on the other side of Windsor Ridge, not here! Not in this valley."

Deuce sighed and looked at his longtime friend. "Why not? What are you so worried about—?"

Suddenly a rifle shot shattered the silence. Karl Digsby arched his back and, with a painful cry, rolled from his saddle when his horse jumped with fright. Karl hit the ground hard and rolled to his back. He reached beneath himself and found an entry wound just above his right kidney. He screamed as his horse ran off.

"Go! Go! Go!" Pick yelled as he kicked his horse and leaned low over the saddle. Horse and man raced across the open meadow.

Deuce wheeled his horse toward Karl, but a second shot coming from a different direction changed his mind. For a moment, he thought he was caught in a crossfire, but then realized the second shot was too far away to be shooting at him. Confused, he wondered where the shots were coming from and if he should try to save his old friend. Momentarily overwhelmed, he stood in place, staring at Karl. A second shot from the mountain they had descended zipped past his head. Suddenly, he turned his horse in the direction Pick had run and kicked it hard. "Haa!" he yelled. "Run! Brent!"

Brent had begun galloping after Pick but started having trouble controlling his horse. "What?" he asked Deuce.

Another rifle shot from the tree line went past Deuce and his horse. He leaned over the horse's neck to become a smaller target.

"Run!" he yelled as he passed Brent. Another rifle shot missed his head by inches. Deuce kicked his horse all the harder.

Brent's horse reared up and started crow-hopping,

frightened by the rifle fire. Then the horse bucked. "Uncle Deuce!" Brent shouted as he fought to stay in the saddle. Another bullet sped past Brent's head and made his horse leap into the air. This time, Brent fell off. He hit the ground hard and looked up to watch his horse run wildly away from him. Brent stood and started running as fast as he could after his horse. Another bullet whizzed past him as he ran. He was now a target. His heart pounded as it had never pounded before. He had never known a fear as immediate, consuming and nightmarish as he ran across a wide-open meadow away from an unknown shooter. The more he ran toward his horse, the farther it ran from him.

"Uncle Dick!" he shouted in desperation and came to a stop.

Deuce looked back and saw Brent's horse running toward him. Brent, though, stood like a statue in the middle of the meadow, waiting to be shot while he tried to catch his breath. Deuce turned his horse around to race back for Brent. Another shot barely missed Brent, who waited for his uncle. Deuce pulled the reins hard when he reached Brent and hollered, "Get on!"

Brent reached up and pulled himself into the saddle. He grabbed his uncle, just as another shot sounded from the tree line. The bullet struck Brent's right thigh. He screamed and almost fell off the horse. Deuce reached back to hold on to Brent and kicked his horse to find some cover.

"Hang on!" Deuce yelled to his nephew.

Second by second, Brent expected to hear another shot and feel the bullet strike his back, just as a bullet had struck Karl's. He saw Pick waiting about a hundred yards ahead on the other side of a small creek in a grove of trees.

Deuce ran his horse as fast as it could go toward the trees.

No matter how desperate he was to find cover, and no matter how fast the horse ran, time seemed to flow too slowly for Brent, who was the most exposed. Brent had never been religious, but he prayed like he had never prayed before for them to get to the trees and out of the open. He half expected a bullet to tear into his flesh, but he heard no more shots as they got closer to Pick.

Without slowing, Deuce ran through the creek and into the trees to where Pick waited. He came to a stop and turned to look behind them. His face was hard, and his eyes glared back over the meadow to find the person who had shot his friend.

Brent was the first to speak. "I'm hit! Uncle Dick, I'm hit!" He began to panic. "I'm bleeding! Oh, my god!" he cried out as he stared at the blood dripping down his leg. "They shot me, Uncle Dick!"

Deuce dismounted and walked around the horse to look at Brent's leg. He wore a concerned expression.

Brent continued, "We're going to die! Oh, my lord! I'm too young to die!" He spoke loudly and had tears of fright and pain in his eyes. "Pick! They shot me! They shot Karl, too! What about Karl?"

Deuce grabbed Brent by the collar and shook him hard. He spoke into his nephew's face with a venom Brent had never heard before. "Shut up! Shut up, Brent!"

"I'm shot," Brent said, more quietly but just as urgently. "Am I going to die? I don't want to die, Uncle Dick. I'm scared! And I don't want to hear him screaming anymore!" he said, referring to Karl's cries for them to come back and help him. "Are you going to help him?"

Pick rode out from the trees, leading Brent's horse behind him, his rifle in his hands. He shot a hard glance at

Brent. "He's already dead! Here's your damned horse. Lose him again and you're on your own." He then looked at Deuce with the same hard expression. "I told you we needed to get across that meadow! Karl's dead because of you! I'm not waiting on you two again. I'm going home and staying under cover. If you want to follow me, then come on. And you"—he pointed at Brent—"keep up, or I will leave you behind!"

"I'm shot," Brent whimpered while favoring his right leg and holding his horse's reigns.

"That's your problem," Pick said unsympathetically. He turned his horse and began to ride away.

"What about Karl? Can't you hear him calling you? He's your friend. You can't leave him there!"

Pick looked back at Brent with a stone-cold expression. "He's dead."

"No, he's not! Listen! He's calling you and Uncle Dick! He needs help."

"Then go help him!" Pick shouted through gritted teeth, his eyes burning. He turned his horse and galloped through the grass.

"Uncle Dick?" Brent asked desperately. "What about Karl?"

Deuce was rattled by how suddenly his world had exploded. His friend lay in the grass within range of the posse, yelling his and Pick's names to come help him. His nephew had a bullet in his leg, and they were still far from home. The posse was six hundred yards away, and it was all his fault. Pick was right about that. Deuce took a deep breath to get control of himself. "There's nothing we can do. Let's go."

"You're leaving him? Listen to him," Brent said, anguish in his voice. He liked Karl a lot.

Deuce nodded sadly. "He's dead. Get on your horse and let's go."

"I can't. My leg! I can't even move it, Uncle Dick."

Deuce got out of his saddle to help Brent get into his. As they were leaving, Brent looked back where Karl lay. He longed to help his new friend, but he reluctantly turned his horse and followed his uncle.

23

Octavius had caught up with the bank robbers earlier that morning but followed at a distance in order to study them. He had followed them long enough to decide who to shoot first, second, third and fourth. He took into consideration their mannerisms, the condition of their horses, weapons, and how cautious they were individually. He knew an opportunity would come soon enough when he would have the advantage of better cover while they were in the open.

He had grabbed Dustin's Sharps rifle, the one Dustin had bragged so much about. Octavius knew Sharps were good rifles, but he had never owned one himself. He reasoned that, if Dustin could hit a deer with it, then Octavius, being an experienced hunter, could use it with far greater accuracy. He was wrong.

He followed the men down the mountain to the valley floor, dismounted in the trees and walked quickly to the edge of the tree line. He took advantage of the vastness of the meadow and, as they had done a few times before, the men stopped their horses in the meadow's middle to talk. Taking aim, Octavius first shot at the toughest-looking man in the gang. That shot missed completely and accidentally hit the man riding beside him.

At that point, Octavius knew the gun's sites were off. However, since he'd never shot the rifle before and didn't know precisely how far off they were, he aimed for the largest target available. The big man who seemed to be the leader of the gang had turned back to see his fallen friend, exposing his broad chest. Octavius aimed and fired but missed him. One shot after another missed. He tried to gauge where his shots were hitting so he could adjust his aim enough to hit his target.

The apparent leader of the gang came back to fetch a younger man. When he did, Octavius aimed the Sharps at the horse's heart. The bullet accidentally hit the young man in the thigh. Seeing where the bullet struck, compared to where he'd aimed, let him know how far off-target his sights were.

Once he had a reasonable idea where to aim to hit his mark, he took careful aim to the right of the big man and pulled the trigger. All he heard was the click of an empty rifle. Infuriated, Octavius cursed and watched the three men escape him into another line of trees some distance away at the other end of the meadow.

With a howl of fury, he grabbed the rifle by the barrel and swung the stock as hard as he could against a tree. He swung it again and again until the stock broke off the rifle. With a cry of rage, he threw the rifle, but it bounced off and landed on the ground near him. He bent over to catch his breath and looked over the meadow. There was no sign of the three riders. He suspected the three men were running for their lives and wouldn't be coming back for their friend. He also doubted they would regroup and set up an ambush to kill him, since they were on the run and didn't know if one man or forty were after them.

However, he wasn't going to take any unnecessary chances. He sat underneath a tree to observe the meadow and listen to the injured man cry and whimper as he realized his friends had left him to die in the middle of nowhere. If, by chance, the three men were waiting in the trees for Octavius to expose himself, the cries of their friend would affect them far sooner than they would bother Octavius. So, he sat and waited and listened to the slowly dying man's cries and prayers.

Half an hour later, Octavius stood up, untied his horse from a branch, got into the saddle and walked from the tree line to the whimpering man. He watched the edges of the meadow carefully and listened intently for any other sound, but aside from the man's groaning, no sound could be heard. He dismounted near the wounded man and led his horse by the reins in one hand and held his revolver in the other. He approached Karl Digsby and peered at him carelessly while he knelt beside him.

Karl stared at him and spoke through his pain. "Please, help me. I don't want to die. Get me to a doctor please," he pleaded.

Octavius shook his head slowly. "Nope. It wouldn't do you any good anyway. Where's the gold? On your horse?"

"What?" Karl grimaced. "I don't want to die." He began to cry.

"Where's my gold? Is it on your horse or someone else's? Is it on the big man's horse?"

"Gold?" Karl asked without any interest. "I've been shot. Lord, help me. Please...help me."

Octavius stood up and looked at Karl coldly. "You're the one who hit me in the head back in the bank. It'll be my pleasure to shoot you in yours." He aimed his revolver at Karl.

"Please..." Karl begged, tears streaming down his face. "I don't want to die."

"You don't have a choice," Octavius said and pulled the trigger. The single shot echoed loudly through the valley.

Octavius holstered his weapon and bent down to search the man's clothes. He found little except a small jackknife and a coin dollar in his money bag. He looked at the size of the man's boots, which were in better shape than his own. Sitting down, he yanked off his own worn-out boots and put on the much newer ones he'd pulled from Karl's feet.

He then drew the Schofield revolver from the dead man's holster to see what caliber it was. A .38. Octavius stripped Karl of his gun-belt and put it in his saddlebag. He could sell it in one of the towns he'd pass through for a few dollars more than he'd have if he left it behind. He climbed onto his horse, which had once belonged to Mike Hall but borrowed by Cal Pierce. He started searching for Karl's horse, which had run off after its rider fell off.

After a fifteen-minute search, Octavius found the horse grazing on some grass between some trees. In the saddle-bags, he found nothing but a horse brush and a few shotgun shells. He pulled a shotgun out of the scabbard and cursed himself for breaking the Sharps rifle. That had been foolish of him, and he cussed in frustration for putting himself at a disadvantage, as he no longer had a long rifle.

All he had now were short-distance weapons while he chased after three men who had long guns. He would no longer have the advantage of distance but would have to get near and attack them in close quarters, as he had the men in the posse.

No matter; it was swift and highly effective warfare.

24

"Whoa!" Pick pulled his reins hard to stop his horse. When he heard a gunshot, he looked back, his eyes blazing dangerously.

A moment later, Deuce and Brent pulled to a stop beside him.

Brent asked, "What was that?" His fear shown on his face as plainly as the pain from his bleeding leg. He repeated himself, with more anxiety, "What are they shooting at?"

Deuce looked at the ground and said softly, "I think they killed Karl, Brent."

"Killed him! He was hurt, not dead. They didn't have to kill him! We shouldn't have left him there!"

"Shut your mouth! Don't say another word or I'll knock your teeth out of your head!" Pick spoke heatedly, breathing hard with emotion. "They would've killed us all if we tried to help him. We had no choice but to leave him behind. Karl knew the risks, and now so do you. Leave it at that."

"I liked Karl," Brent said softly.

"We all did," Deuce said. "But let's keep moving."

Pick nodded. "Keep up if you can."

"Uncle Dick, my leg really hurts. Shouldn't we try to stop the bleeding or something?" He was afraid of bleeding to death.

"We don't have time to worry about that right now. Those men are coming after us, and they are bloodthirsty. They obviously don't want to arrest us, so we had better run for our lives."

"What if I bleed out?"

"Then you'll die," Pick shouted irritably. "But die like a man, would ya?" Pick turned his horse and kicked it to run toward the base of the high hill running through the center of the valley. Covered with a dense forest of Douglas fir trees, its steep incline looked nearly impossible to climb.

Pick slowed down as he reached the base of the hill. Then he directed his horse into the trees, zigzagging around them as he climbed. Deuce didn't hesitate to follow him into the trees and up the hill.

Brent hesitated at the bottom and looked at the steep grade. He knew that to climb it, he would have to lean forward and keep his weight centered over the saddle horn rather than his stirrups. Climbing up steep grades was becoming all too common on this journey. Normally he would brace himself in the saddle by pressing his weight back against the stirrups while he leaned forward. However, with a bullet in his leg, he would not be able to hold himself in the stirrup. Gravity and the rough terrain would work together to pull him off the horse.

He knew it would be an excruciating climb and doubted he could stand the pain, but he took a deep breath and tried anyway. He put his boot into the stirrup, kicked his horse forward and began to climb. He cried out in pain when he leaned forward and held on to the saddle horn with his left hand as tight as he could. He tried to relieve some weight from right leg, but that made his body slip to the left side of the saddle with every jarring step his horse took.

He resituated himself squarely on the saddle, but pressure on his injured leg sent a flame of pain through his thigh. It burned like fire until he had to pull his boot out of the stirrup and let it hang free, as he hovered over the saddle horn and hung on as tight as he could to relieve the pain a bit.

His horse stumbled over a broken branch and almost lost its footing. Brent nearly slid out of the saddle but managed to hold on by forcing his foot back into the stirrup, and endured the fire tearing up his thigh. He stopped to regain control of himself and let his foot dangle to reduce the throbbing.

Brent's breathing was as hard as his horse's and sweat poured from him like the lather soaking his horse. He could no longer see his uncle or Pick ahead of him, but he could hear their horses climbing through the trees. They seemed to be making the climb with relative ease, but it was excruciating for Brent. He tried to keep the reins loose, so his horse could climb unhindered, but he found himself pulling the horse to a stop every time he could no longer stand the pain or when he'd nearly slip out of the saddle. Some men might be natural horsemen who would be fine riding up this hill in his condition. Brent wasn't a natural horseman, and he struggled miserably.

"Get up here, Brent!" Deuce hollered down the hill. He sounded angry at his nephew.

Brent sighed and took a deep breath. "Come on!" he ordered his horse and whipped its hind quarters with his reins. The horse jolted forward, and Brent grunted in pain when the movement jarred his leg. If it wasn't for his strong hold of the saddle horn, he'd have fallen out of the saddle. His horse climbed at a constant pace, while Brent lowered his head to go under branches and maneuver around trees, broken limbs and fallen logs, and tried his best to stay in his saddle.

"Hurry up!" Deuce yelled again.

"I can't! My leg hurts!" Brent hollered back.

Up on top of the hill, Pick shook his head in frustration. "I'm not waiting," he said to Deuce and turned to leave.

"He's my nephew. I can't leave him behind."

Pick looked at Deuce and spoke seriously, "Deuce, we've ridden together for a long time now. We have more money than we've ever had before. Brent might be your nephew but he's slowing us down. Leave him for the posse, and let's get away while we still can."

"He's family. My wife would never forgive me if I left him."

"He's going to get us killed, Deuce! You know as well as I do that if he can't make it up this hill, he won't make it over the mountain. He's wasting time we don't have. Give me my share, or most of it, and I'll meet you back at home—if you make it. But I'm not waiting for your nephew."

Deuce said sharply, "I'm not dismounting to count out shares right now. When we stop for the night, we'll count it, and you can go your own way if you want to, but not right now."

"He can't ride!" Pick exclaimed. "He's dead weight, Deuce. Face it. Waiting for him is a death sentence."

"Then leave!" Deuce shouted.

"Not without my share," Pick said.

Deuce sighed heavily. "We can stay right here, set up an

ambush and fight our way out. It's better than getting shot in the back like Karl was. At least we'll have the decency to face them head-on when we shoot them."

Pick shook his head. "No way. I'm not taking a chance on being shot out here. I say we just run and don't look back."

Deuce grinned at his friend. "You keep saying that, but you're still here."

"You have the money! I don't want to go home empty-handed, either."

"I do have the money. And it's going to stay in my saddlebag until we're home or until tonight, when we make camp."

"Deuce, they have no interest in arresting us. You know that, right? Even if we surrendered, they'd lynch us right here. Your nephew isn't going to make it out of here. You know that as well as I do; so why are you waiting to for him? He's going to get you killed."

Deuce said, "He will make it out of here. Here he comes right now." Deuce directed Pick's attention to Brent, who was nearing the crest of the hill. "It's about time, Brent. We can't wait for you like this again. If you can't keep up, then we're going to have to leave you behind. Do you understand me?"

Brent was sweating profusely and looked pale and weak. He looked at his uncle with an exhausted stare. "My leg..."

Deuce's voice rose. "I know it hurts! But you have to toughen up like a man and quit whining about it! For crying out loud, Brent, there's men out there wanting to kill you! So, toughen up, take the pain and ride your damn horse. Do you hear me?"

"Yes," Brent said softly. Trying to stay in the saddle during his journey up the hill had taken a lot of energy out of him. "But I'm feeling weak, Uncle Dick."

Pick rolled his eyes in frustration and turned his horse to keep moving.

"You'll be fine. Just keep up!" Deuce said and turned his horse to follow Pick.

They rode quickly along the top of the hill toward the east, looking for a well-concealed path into the remainder of the valley. The last thing they wanted was to ride into another meadow with an unprotected area where the cowards chasing them could shoot them in the back. If they could find a path with heavy tree cover leading across the valley floor, they could remain out of sight. Unfortunately, the best they could find was a fairly-deep gully running down into the valley below. The gully was not too steep, but it was wide and deep enough to partly conceal them if they rode inside it. It twisted around a boulder and tall Douglas fir trees that had refused to bend to the water after heavy downpours. The only concern Deuce had was that the trees thinned toward the bottom of the gully where it emptied into a meadow scattered with fallen trees and only small, occasional trees for cover. The meadow was open, but it wasn't that far to another tree line. If they raced across the meadow as fast as they could, it was a safe exit off the hill and across the valley. They would be one step closer to home.

"Boys, let's take this gully and get across that meadow. Come on, follow me," Deuce said and turned his horse to the open mouth of the gully.

Pick pointed to the east of Windsor Ridge, which looked close enough that they could reach out and touch it. "Deuce, do you see that saddle? If we get split up, that's where we want to cross over, just so we're all on the same trail, okay?"

"Hear that, Brent?" Deuce asked. "If we get separated,

that's the way home. Don't wait around for us. Just get home, and we'll meet you there. Got it?"

"Don't leave me, Uncle Dick. Please don't leave me behind. My leg hurts so much," he said in a weak voice.

"I ain't leaving you, Brent. You've done okay so far, so just keep it up." Deuce turned his horse and entered the gully. It was steeper in places than he'd thought, and rougher than it appeared. He leaned back and braced his weight against his stirrups as his body bounced with each uneven step his horse took. For Deuce, it was an easy ride, but for Brent, it was more painful than the ride up the hill had been.

Brent kept his left foot in the stirrup, but it was more bearable to leave his right foot hanging loose, despite the extra effort it took to keep himself upright in the saddle. Being jostled around increased his agony, and his leg throbbed non-stop. He had nearly fallen out of the saddle when his mount leaped over a small boulder. Before he had traveled very far down the gully, he couldn't take the pain any longer. He turned his horse to ride out of the gully.

"What are you doing? Get back here!" Deuce said urgently. "Those men are coming, and you're a bigger target up there."

Brent shook his head. "I don't care. My leg is already killing me. I'd rather they just shoot me than ride down there again. At least up here the ground is a little easier to ride on!"

"You will care when they start shooting at you!" Deuce could see the blood running down Brent's pant leg and dripping from his boot. It was the first good look he'd had at the wound so far.

He sighed heavily. Two more days out in the woods, and Brent's leg would be infected beyond saving, if it wasn't too late to save his life. If he didn't bleed to death first. A heavy layer of guilt washed over him. He knew whatever happened to his nephew was his fault. He forced the guilt away and hardened his tone. "Brent, toughen up and get back down here before you give our position away. They could be coming up over that ridge any minute."

"Well, if they're coming from behind us, then who's that down there? See? You wouldn't have known he was down there if it wasn't for me coming up here." Brent felt a little self-satisfied as he pointed into the meadow.

Deuce glanced at the meadow and stopped his horse in a moment of horror. In the meadow, not far from the tree line he had hoped to run into, came a lone man riding toward them. He appeared to be a big bearded fellow with a sidearm at his waist and a rifle in a scabbard. He looked to be exactly what Deuce would expect from a Loveland posse. Fortunately, the rider had not noticed them riding in the gully or Brent riding out of it.

Pick dismounted to be lower and less noticeable from the valley floor. "They obviously split up to cover more ground. They'll have us boxed in if we stay here. Who knows how many more there are?" He drew his rifle from its scabbard and told Brent to watch behind them. He didn't care if Brent remained on his horse in the open; in fact, he kind of hoped he would, so the posse would take notice of him and draw their fire, while Pick and Deuce evened up the odds a little.

"We'll be in a crossfire if we don't get across that meadow! Damn it, Brent, get down here!" Deuce said as he pulled his rifle from its scabbard. "I'm gonna blow this guy out of the saddle, and then we're going to run like hell across this valley. You fellows stay put until he's in range. And keep watch up there. The last thing we need is his friends sneaking up behind us again."

"Uncle Dick, maybe he's not with the posse. Like you said, they're behind us. Maybe he's just a prospector with a cabin and medical supplies nearby. Maybe he can help with my leg," Brent suggested. He did not ride back down into the gulley, but he did walk his horse closer to a tree full of low branches in order to remain hidden. "We should ask him before you kill him."

"Shut up!" Pick glared at Brent, then turned back to watch their back trail.

"Shh!" Deuce ordered at the same time.

"You're not the one shot!" Brent said quietly.

Deuce ignored him. "Brent, take your horse way over yonder and hold him, because he may go wild again when he hears shots. Get down and hold him tight! I'm moving down just a bit to get a better line of sight on this man. You fellows be ready."

25

Adam Bannister rode across an open meadow toward the sound of the shots he had heard. He had no intention of poking his nose into someone else's business, but it was better to know what was happening around him. He might also be of help if a man was hurt.

Far from the nearest town, a fellow wasn't likely to survive if he needed help out here in the mountains. Of course, he had no way of knowing who was shooting or if anyone was injured, but he figured there was probably a reasonable explanation. In all the years he and Luther had come hunting in their old family hunting grounds, Adam had never seen another person. Curiosity eating at him, he rode for a tree-covered high hill running along the valley floor. From the height of Windsor Ridge, he had seen that the hill ran through the middle of the valley and tapering to nothing at the west end. He hadn't realized how tall and steep it was until he approached it, though, and he decided to get to it from the other side.

He yawned and looked up to watch an eagle fly over his head. No sound came from the meadow and everything seemed peaceful, although he experienced the unsettling sensation of being watched. He could see no one, but the being-watched feeling grew steadily. Adam reined in his horse to look into the dark shadows of the trees, trying to locate someone watching him.

Unexpectedly, Adam heard a hollow sound. Drops of blood spattered Adam's face from the bullet that hit his horse's neck. The horse collapsed to the ground as another rifle shot came from the hill.

Pulling his left leg from the stirrup, Adam swung it over the back of the falling horse and landed on the ground to the right side of the saddle and with his back exposed to the shooter. He scrambled over his dying mount and took cover behind it, as another bullet tore into the horse's flesh. As he tried to locate the shooter on the hill, another bullet hit the ground not far from him.

Like lightning, Adam reached over his horse, grabbed the stock of his rifle and hauled it out of the scabbard. He was glad his horse had fallen on its left side, giving him easy access to his rifle. Now, he might have a chance of surviving this sudden assault, if he could locate the shooter.

Another bullet struck the horse's belly not too far from Adam. He dropped down behind the horse and peeked over it again in an attempt to find the shooter. Yet another bullet struck the dead horse close enough to splatter blood on his clothing and hand. His heart racing, Adam swore he could hear a pin drop a mile away, so taut were his senses. His dead horse gave him cover, but it wasn't solid. Shot at the right angle, a bullet could travel right through the animal and into him.

"Lord, I could use some help," he said as a bullet hit the horse's thigh and splattered warm blood across the back of his neck. He slid lower and checked the sights of his rifle, which held six cartridges. He'd already fired one round, though, so he had five shots left until he could open his saddlebag. Suddenly two shots came simultaneously, as a second shooter joined in the first. One bullet hit the ground short of his horse, and the other hit the horse's front quarters.

Adam stayed low, peeked over the saddle and searched the woods for any movement. Another bullet barely missed his foot. He had neither room to move nor enough cover, so he tried his best to make himself a small target. Unfortunately, big men generally made big targets.

Adam knew the two men ambushing him could shoot; eventually they would hit their mark if he stayed put. He gazed around for anything that might offer him more protection than his dead horse. About thirty yards to his right, he saw the sun-bleached remains of a fallen tree in the tall grass. Another shot hit the horse, followed by one that hit the ground close of him.

Taking a quick breath and saying a quick prayer, Adam got up as fast as he could and ran to the fallen tree. Both shooters fired at him as he ran. The sound of the bullets zinging past him reminded him just how helpless he was. Ten feet from the tree, he dove forward and rolled to a stop behind the dead tree.

He heard one of his attackers curse loudly after Adam reached the cover of the dead tree. It sounded like the two men were arguing. In the ensuing silence, Adam tracked the men to a gully running down the hill. He saw two men leaning over their rifles at ground level, focusing on him. Their horses stood behind them higher up the gully.

The two men were about three hundred yards away. Now that he knew where they were, this might be a fair fight. The two men could shoot, but one of them could shoot better than the other and hit close to his target at that distance. Still, it was obvious neither was a military-trained sharpshooter. Adam was.

One of the men hit the top of the log near him and the bullet sheared off. That was the man Adam needed to kill first. He lowered his cheek against the stock of his rifle and looked down the sights. He steadied the rifle on the log, centered the sight on that man's forehead. The man fired and missed again.

"Goodbye," Adam said quietly and pulled the trigger. He watched the man fall backwards against the opposite side of the gully wall and slide down out of sight.

Adam had no doubt the man was dead. He watched the other shooter duck from his sight and then appear at the two horses. The man whacked one horse on its hindquarters to get it out of his way. The horse darted down the gully toward the valley. The man slid his rifle into its scabbard and forced his horse to turn uphill in the tight space offered by the gully. From the shadows, a third rider rode out of the trees toward the dead man in the gully.

"UNCLE DICK!" Brent yelled frantically as he rode forward. "Uncle Dick!"

"He's dead!" Pick exclaimed. He sheathed his rifle and led his horse up the gully to a place where he could safely mount. Pick knew there was no time to spare, and the posse was still coming from behind them as well. "We gotta go, so come on," he ordered while he stepped into the saddle. "We have to go now!"

Brent looked at Pick with an expression of shock, horror and disbelief mixed together. "We can't leave him. Uncle Dick—"

"Stay here then. I don't care!" Pick said and kicked his horse to leave Brent behind.

Brent stared at his uncle's body. He shook his head, and his eyes filled with tears. "Pick, what are we going to do? Uncle Dick's been shot. Where are you going, Pick? We have to help him. What do we do?" His voice quavered.

Pick looked at Brent. "You join him!" He drew his revolver and aimed it at Brent.

"Pick—"

Pick pulled the trigger and watched Brent fall out of his saddle as his horse reared and ran off, bucking. He watched Deuce's horse run into the meadow with all the money in its saddlebags, and shook his head. He turned his attention back to Brent, who was struggling to breathe. He would die, but he might live long enough to identify Pick to the posse before he did. Pick aimed his revolver at Brent's head and pulled the trigger. Then he turned his horse and kicked it as hard as he could to get through the trees.

His two good friends and Deuce's nephew were dead, and the money was all his if he wanted to go get it. But no amount of money was worth dying for. His only goal now was to get over the mountain and go home. No one ever needed to know he'd had anything to do with the robbery and the resulting deaths, and no one would, if he got out of this valley alive. One thing was for sure though; he would never come north of Windsor Ridge again.

26

Adam watched the man who had taken a couple of shots at him ride out of the gulley on a paint horse. Then, after what appeared to be a short conversation, the shooter shot a third man out of the saddle and made sure he was dead before riding away. Adam figured the man on the paint had left the area for good, but he remained where he was for a few moments to watch and listen for any sign of the him. The dead man's horse, grazing about a hundred-fifty yards away, was the only sign of life. The horse carried a set of saddle-bags and a bedroll, and split reins hung freely from the bridle.

After watching cautiously, Adam walked to his dead horse. A twelve-year-old quarter horse he'd named her Cougar. He had bought her from a horse breeder in Washington when she was three, and broken her to saddle himself. An attack by a cougar had a made a large scar on her left flank, so naming her Cougar had been easy enough. During all his years of riding, including those spent in the cavalry, he had never known a better trail horse for hunting.

Sighing, Adam knelt to touch her neck. He shook his head sadly, then stood and gazed at the dead man's horse, which grazed hungrily. Slowly, he walked toward it. The horse had been spooked earlier and might be skittish of a stranger, but he walked slowly and called to it softly. The horse raised its head to peer at him for a moment, then resumed grazing.

A moment later, Adam took hold of the animal's reins and carefully lifted himself into the saddle. The horse side-stepped under his weight, but quickly calmed down and moved forward under his soft nudging and vocal command. He rode the horse over to the log he had hidden behind and tied the reins to some exposed roots. This horse's saddle was in decent shape, but it wasn't as comfortable as his own. Adam went to his dead horse, loosened the saddle and then put it on his new mare. He opened the saddlebags belonging to the stranger he'd killed and began searching inside. The first saddlebag didn't contain anything of significance, except a half box of .44 cartridges. He pulled the saddlebags off the saddle and opened the second bag.

He stared at a white bank sack holding a stack of paper money. Astonished, Adam then opened a metal box to discover it held about three pounds of gold. At the bottom of the sack lay a leather pouch with leather strings. He opened it and discovered it, too, was full of gold.

Adam shot a glance back at the hill, and a chill ran down his spine. He suddenly realized what all the morning's shooting had been about. Evidently, someone had robbed a bank and the robbers were perhaps fighting a posse. The robbers, too, might have been under surveillance. Adam sat on the log facing the hill and stared. He was no longer sure the man who had ridden away in a hurry had run very far. Someone was probably looking for this much money and gold and might even kill for it. Two people had been killed in the last thirty minutes, and the third man might be anywhere.

Huntsville lay northwest of here. It was possible the men had robbed the Huntsville bank. But if they were expecting to find an easy getaway through the mountains to Jessup County, they chose wrong. It wasn't an easy trip at all. Adam decided a posse had been following the bank robbers. That would explain the shooting earlier that day and why they'd shot at him as they had.

If there was a posse out there, they'd be looking for the man Adam had killed, the owner of the horse he planned to ride. He worried he might be mistaken for the bank robber by the posse if they saw him on the horse, but to be on foot in this territory wasn't advisable either. He could ride quickly back to his and Uncle Luther's camp, but he wouldn't know who could be behind him. He might lead a bloodthirsty posse right into his camp and get himself and Luther lynched right there before they could prove their innocence. Or Adam could ride up the hill, look for the posse, and hope they'd listen to him before they shot him.

He sighed and stood. There was only one thing to do, and it was the right thing to do: find the posse, explain what had happened and return the gold and money to the authorities. Adam could use some money, but he was, first and foremost, an honest man. Taking what wasn't his was stealing, even if no one ever knew about it. He would know, and his integrity wouldn't allow him to steal. He was accountable by God. Adam depended upon the Lord to walk before him and make a way for him to return the money and get back safely to Uncle Luther.

Adam put the gold and money in his saddlebag, then walked to the front of the horse and looked at it thoughtfully. "I don't know if you're a blessing or a curse yet. I guess we'll find out, huh? But until then, I think I'll just call you, Jackpot. Because you certainly are a jackpot to the right guy, in more ways than one." He then stepped up into his saddle and turned toward the gulley on the hill.

27

Octavius Clark had looked at the large hill in the middle of the valley and knew the grade and tree cover would give the men he was after every advantage to lie low and wait for him to follow their trail. If the bank robbers were wiser than most Yankees, they'd leave their horses tied a good distance up the trail and come back to lay down a good crossfire and ambush anyone who followed them. Or they could leave one or two men behind to take cover in the trees and wait for someone to follow, then shoot him off his horse.

These were two of the tactics Octavius had learned during in his years of fighting in the Cumberland Mountains and surroundings when he and friends were being chased. Learning to use the ground cover as an advantage had come naturally and had served him well over the years. Experience had made him too cautious to walk blindly into potential ambushes.

As he rode into the valley, he realized the steep hill in front of him was simply that: a long hill that ran some distance but led nowhere, before it dropped to the valley floor again. No matter how long the bank robbers might wait to ambush him, they would have to cross the other side of the valley to get over Windsor Ridge. Undoubtedly, the bank robbers would get across the mountains that way, so there was no reason to chase after them like a blind dog. Octavius turned his horse to the east and followed the base of the hill in order to cross over it a mile or two from where the robbers expected him to.

He had no reason to hurry. By nightfall he would have located their camp. He'd tie his horse a mile or so away, and he could approach quietly. At the first morning's light, he would attack and have three more notches on his belt—and close to thirty thousand dollars in paper money and gold in his saddlebag. That was the amount the banker quoted, but Octavius thought he'd embellished a bit. Nevertheless, it was a good amount of free money to set him up somewhere for a while. He could build a cabin in the woods where no one would bother him and use a few dollars here and there to purchase his goods to live on while he enjoyed the peace and quiet of his golden years. This was an opportunity to have that dream come true once and for all. There was no way he would let those men slip through his hands with the money. That paper money and gold were his future, and he'd never have to work again. Tomorrow, the treasure would be his for the taking. He would finally be able to buy himself a hammock, tie it between two trees outside a cabin somewhere and rest while listening to a nearby stream for the remainder of his days. Nothing could keep him from reaching that dream now.

Octavius rode along the base of the hill, watching the area around him for any evidence of a person either inhabiting or passing the valley recently. He saw not a trace of human habitation. Certainly, old-time trappers would have trapped in this valley, but they'd left no evidence. He had not seen one cut stump or horse track in the whole valley, aside from the ones he was following. There were many signs of wildlife, including the fox and few deer he had seen. He had seen bear scat a few days old, and elk scat as well, but the majestic beauty of the valley impressed him the most.

He had traveled across the country and spent time in woods all over the nation, but he had never seen a wilder and more beautiful place than this large valley high up in the Wallowa Mountains. He'd never have found it if not for the bank robbers. By rights, he supposed he should thank them for leading him to such a beautiful place before he killed them. It would be a beautiful valley to build a cabin in, but the winters would be a struggle. One thing was for sure though: he would never have visitors if he built his home up here.

Reining in his horse, Octavius thought deeply as he considered constructing a cabin in this valley. He could spend the spring and summer months here, and perhaps winter in a lower elevation somewhere. He could imagine the amount of snow that must bury the valley during the winter. Still, there was no more perfect place to spend his days than this valley.

So fixed was Octavius on how he could make his dreams a reality that he was shocked to hear a rifle shot echo through the silence of the valley. He heard more shots, then two rifles seemed to blast simultaneously. He knew the shooting had to come from the bank robbers, but he couldn't imagine what or who they shot at—unless another posse from Huntsville had tracked the robbers down. However, he would expect more shooting if that was the case. Finally, a rifle, sounding different from the other two, shot once and then fell silent.

Overwhelming silence seemed to drag on and on. Then Octavius heard two pistol shots. Then silence reigned again.

Octavius grinned as he pondered the only explanation he could think of. That young man, Nathan Pierce, had probably come after him to collect his brother's blood debt, and had foolishly wandered into the bank robbers' ambush. Octavius shook his head, smiled and sighed heavily. He had given his word to Sarah that Nathan would come home alive, and he had kept his word. He had left Nathan alive and well with every opportunity to go home to his wife and live his life. If he decided not to do it, then it was no one's fault but his own. It made him sad, though. Octavius had liked Sarah, and it was too bad her husband wasn't wise enough to be reasonable. She was too nice a young lady to be left a widow, but Octavius had kept his promise, even though she would never know it.

Octavius turned his horse and began to climb the hill. He would head those men off and kill all three of them before they knew what was happening, just as he had the posse. He would take the money and disappear for a while, and there would be no one left alive to tell the tale of what had happened in these mountains. The bodies found in the Wallowas would be a mystery that would never be solved. He would have enough money to wait a year or two before coming back to build a cabin in the valley.

28

Nathan Pierce paused at the top of the high ridge over-looking the valley and, although he could appreciate the natural wonder of it, he was searching the meadows for Octavius. He kicked his exhausted horse and began descending into the valley. He had pushed his horse hard to make up time and draw close enough to Octavius to take the one shot needed to blow Octavius out of his saddle. He didn't care if he shot him in the heart or in the back, as long as Octavius was dead at the end of the day.

He'd known he was getting close when he'd heard some shooting not long before. Somewhere in the valley he expected to find four dead bank robbers and an unsus-pecting Octavius hoping to ride away with his treasure of gold. Unfortunately for him, Nathan didn't aim to warn him before he pulled the trigger.

The ride downhill wasn't too bad, and Nathan followed the trail fairly-easily. Octavius had been following the four riders who'd cut a trail over the hardened ground and through the trees whenever they could. They clearly knew they were being followed, which meant they may not have been taken by surprise as Nathan and his friends had been.

Nathan arrived at the edge of the tree line on the valley floor where Octavius had broken Dustin's rifle. Nathan saw the rifle plainly and, upon looking closer, he found the empty cartridges lying on the ground. Clearly, Octavius had fired all the shots Nathan had heard, except for maybe one. He searched the large meadow from horseback and barely saw the body lying in the tall grass.

Slowly, Nathan rode out into the open and cautiously approached the body of Karl Digsby. He didn't bother to dismount; he saw the man was dead and missing his gun and boots. He also recognized Octavius' old boots beside him. The man had been killed within the hour; likely when Nathan had heard the shots. He kicked his horse softly and looked for other bodies but found only four trails through the grass heading south toward another dark tree line in the sea of grass. Beyond that a steep hill looked eerily dark and foreboding, like an impenetrable wall. The only bit of comfort Nathan found was that Octavius had missed the other riders and, in a rage, had broken Dustin's rifle. Right now, Octavius would be focused on pursuing the bank robbers, perhaps he was even watching them, waiting for the right moment to attack. One thing was for sure though: Octavius would not be looking behind him; that's all Nathan cared about.

Trails in the grass indicated the three bank robbers had ridden into the small grove of trees and most likely up the large hill beyond it. However, Octavius' horse had turned east to circle around, probably to ambush them down the trail, rather than follow them up the hill. Nathan turned his horse eastward to follow Octavius. Octavius was a dangerous man to follow, especially now, when he could circle back on the hill and see Nathan down below, but Nathan saw no other choice.

While he followed the trail left by Octavius, Nathan cautiously pulled his rifle from its scabbard and laid it across his saddle in case he needed it quickly. There was no way of knowing where Octavius was—a mile ahead of him or sitting in the shade of the next small grove of trees. Octavius wasn't like most men. No. Octavius wasn't a man who would panic, but one who would wait and attack ferociously when least expected. He had an uncanny, almost unnatural, ability to use shadows to his advantage and disappear in the brush. Nathan had never seen his like before. He paused to scan every tree and shadow before moving forward.

Suddenly a rifle shot sounded from behind him to the west. Nathan turned his horse around and listened carefully. Another shot came, and then another. He listened as two rifles fired nearly together. Then a last shot, sounding slightly different from the others, ended the gunfire for a few minutes. Then Nathan heard two final shots from what sounded like a revolver, echo through the valley. Once more, silence descended around him.

Nathan turned his horse and kicked it into a fast gallop toward where shots had come. Octavius must have circled back up on the hill faster than Nathan had expected and ambushed the bank robbers—or had been spotted by the bank robbers.

Either way, Octavius was up on the hill somewhere, and Nathan needed to find him. Tall and steep, the hill was also long and thickly forested. It would be quicker to follow the bank robbers' trail up the mountain and find where the battle took place than it would be to keep following Octavius.

Nathan didn't know what Octavius planned to do after he got his gold: whether he would continue south into Jessup County or what. However, Octavius knew John Riggs had been sent to Huntsville to inform the sheriff there about the bank robbery. A second posse from Huntsville would be coming along. In fact, it was probably only a few hours from their original camp at this moment. Nathan doubted Octavius would chance going back to Huntsville, which only left one reasonable direction for him to go: south into Jessup County. Therefore, Octavius would be going over Windsor Ridge.

Nathan kicked his horse and held the reins loosely to gain more speed. He watched the trees on the hill and glanced ahead of him as he galloped through the meadow to a grove of trees. Suddenly, his horse collapsed with a loud snap. Nathan's body flew over the horse and landed, his left shoulder taking the brunt of his weight. Agony ripped through him. The force of his impact with the ground rolled him head over heels. He tried to get to his feet, but his right foot hit a rock and his ankle buckled. He collapsed and rolled to a stop. Staring at the blue sky above him, he wanted to scream in pain, but knew he could not.

Gritting his teeth, he held his right hand over his left shoulder while he tried to get control of his pain. His shoulder throbbed and, to make matters worse, his left arm hung limp and useless. His right ankle also throbbed, as it was being torn apart. He felt his ankle swelling in his boot, and he knew he would be unable to walk on that foot. He lay still and sucked in several deep breaths, but every breath seemed to pull on his injured shoulder.

Nathan lifted his head and forced himself to sit up. He looked at his horse and sighed heavily. The poor horse lay on its side, helpless to rise. It had a broken front leg. A broken bone pierced the horse's skin. Taking a deep breath to prepare for the pain he knew he'd experience, Nathan used his right arm to push himself to his knees, then forced himself to his feet. A searing pain shot through his ankle and he couldn't keep his weight on that foot. He hopped on his left foot to his horse; every hop sent shock waves of pain through his shoulder. He collapsed onto the ground next to his saddle. He breathed hard and gritted his teeth to endure the pain ravaging him. He glanced over to see what had caused his horse to fall and saw an abandoned rabbit hole covered with dry grass. The horse must have stepped in it and broken her leg.

"Sorry, girl," he said softly. He drew his revolver from his holster, slid on the ground to be closer to his horse's neck, pulled the hammer back until it clicked and then hesitated. It was so silent in the valley, if he fired his weapon, it would pinpoint his location. He was in no shape to fight Octavius now.

Slowly, he lowered the hammer and replaced the revolver in its holster. He pulled out his hunting knife and leaned back against the horse with a heavy sigh. It would hurt like hell to twist his body toward the horse's neck, but he couldn't let the animal suffer anymore. With a silent count and a deep breath, he twisted his body, leaned over his horse, cut its throat and ended its suffering.

Miles out in the middle of nowhere, Nathan's only hope, now lay in being found by the Huntsville posse, if they came this far into the mountains after finding his friends' bodies. He had no chance of being found if he remained with his horse, except by the wolves he'd heard the night before, or maybe a grizzly.

His thoughts turned to Sarah, sitting alone in their little cabin, waiting for him. He should be home right about now.

She wouldn't know everyone else in the posse was dead and that Nathan was deeper in the mountains than anyone would look. If there was any hope of seeing his beautiful bride again, he would have to walk—or crawl—all the way home to Loveland. It would be a long and painful journey, but he had to make it if he wanted to see Sarah again.

Every journey begins with a first step. Nathan dreaded taking his first, but there was no other choice. He untied his canteen from the saddle, then rested against the mare's belly while he drank some water. He replaced the cap and strung the strap over his neck. He struggled to reach into the saddlebag and pull out what food he had: a piece of hard tack and a small slab of salted elk.

He crawled farther to the horse's rear and untied his bedroll. Taking his knife from the scabbard, he cut the leather straps of his saddle and used them to tightly tie his bedroll, using his teeth and right arm to do it. Sweat from the sun's heat and the energy he expended ran down his cheeks. He tried to reach under the horse into his second saddle bag, but the horse weighed too much. He tried to pull it free with one arm, but it barely budged. He continued pulling until the saddlebag broke free from the horse.

Nathan rested for a few minutes before opening the saddlebag and pulling out his flint and striker for a fire, as well as all the ammunition he had, which wasn't much, considering his situation. He scooched to the horse's head and used his knife to cut the two split reins from the bridle. Using one rein, he tied it to both ends of his bedroll and slid it over his neck and shoulders. He used the other rein to fashion a sling for his left arm.

After he pulled his rifle from its scabbard, he sat and peered into the clear blue sky, dotted with beautiful white cumulus clouds. He breathed heavily from pain and exertion. Then, closing his eyes, he shook his head in defeat. He wouldn't be going after Octavius any longer and, in his shape, it would take a miracle for him to get back home to Sarah. A deep well of helplessness filled him, and he took a deep breath. Then he prayed for the first time in...well, he didn't know how long.

"Jesus...I know I've failed to serve you the way I should. You don't owe me a dang thing, but I'm asking you to help me. I'm hurting bad and have no chance of getting home without you. I just want to go home to Sarah, Lord. So, help me if you would. And I ask you to forgive me for my lack of diligence. Sarah always asks me to read the Bible with her, but I never do. If you help me to get back home to her, I swear to you that I will read it with her and live my life serving you.

"I know you're not a deal-maker, but you know my heart and how serious I am. I might fall, and I already have...but now I know why I should be close to you, because I would like to know for a fact that you're listening to me, like you listen to Sarah. Lord, I am sorry for failing in my Christian walk with you, and I ask you to forgive me. I just want to get home to Sarah. So, Lord, if you're willing to, just give me the strength to get home. I don't care about Octavius. I will leave Cal's revenge up to you. I suppose that's how it's supposed to be anyway. I have no choice but to give him into your hands. I just want to get home and hope you'll help me. In Jesus' name, amen."

Nathan wiped tears from his eyes and used his rifle as a crutch to stand upright. His swollen ankle burned like a blacksmith's fire. "Lord, that hurts," he said.

Then, step by step, using his rifle, he slowly limped at an angle back to the mountain he had come down. He figured it was the easiest way to climb out of the valley. Also, if there was any hope of rescue, it would be via the trail the bank robbers, Octavius and he had made entering the valley. He refused to stop or to rest, even though his ankle throbbed almost unbearably. His shoulder ached, too, though his sling helped keep his arm stable. His back ached and his neck hurt as well.

Nathan was miserable, but by pure determination, he kept going, one step at a time, one step after the other. He could see the ridge he had come down and set a goal not to rest until he made it to the tree line where he had found the broken rifle. His ankle had swollen so much, it felt as though his boot was cutting off the circulation to his foot. Every step increased the damage to his ankle, and the pain steadily grew. Little by little, he drew closer to the cool shade and a moment of rest among the trees.

Even though he crossed in a straight line to get to the trees, he still had to walk a long, long, mile. As he drew closer, he could barely step on his foot without screaming in pain. Finally, after what seemed like an eternity of walking, he entered his resting place.

Gingerly, Nathan sat against the first tree and let out a loud sigh of relief. He longed to pull off his boot and relieve the pressure on his ankle, but he knew he'd never get the boot back on if he did; and he had no intention of making the twenty-mile journey back home without a boot on his foot. Nathan slid to the cool ground and put his bed roll under his ankle to elevate it some. Then he closed his eyes and concentrated on ignoring his pain.

Physically and emotionally exhausted, he fell asleep in the cool shade of the peaceful Douglas fir trees protecting him from the hot sun.

29

Adam rode to the gulley and up the hill beside it. He kept his rifle in hand, not knowing what to expect. He paused to observe the dead man in the gulley who had shot at him. A middle-aged man of good size, he wore a blank expression on his face and a bullet hole in the center of his forehead. His rifle lay beside him, and he wore a decent gun-belt carrying a single revolver.

After dismounting, Adam slid into the gulley to fetch the man's rifle and gun-belt. He searched the man for anything else and found a small money bag with about five dollars in it. He climbed out of the gulley and walked over to the other dead man, who turned out to be quite a bit younger, maybe about twenty-years old. Adam also unbuckled his gun-belt off and searched his pockets. All he found was a piece of paper with a poem written on it. It read:

"CHRISTINE, every trickling stream calls your name;
    Every waterfall leads me closer to you.

Christine, the bright blue skies light the way, but the night's starry sky

reveals how many years I'd love to love you.

If love was a stone, mine would be a mountain that towers above you, but

soft like a dove's whistle is my love for you.

If I only had a million dollars, I'd spend my life buying dances with you

Christine, because seeing you smile is all I want to do until my dying day."

ADAM READ THE POEM AND, with a quick smile, stuck it in his shirt pocket. He tied the rifle to his saddle with the ring and shoved the gun-belts into his saddlebags. They were a tight fit. He got into the saddle and continued riding uphill until he reached the top. He turned his horse north and followed the tracks the dead men had made. He was nervous about riding the stranger's horse, as it would surely be recognized by a posse or whoever was looking for the stolen money in his saddlebag. It would be easy to explain who he was and why he had the stranger's horse—*if* he was given the chance to talk. He feared being shot out of the saddle on sight, as he'd almost been before.

He hoped, though, there were some decent, law-abiding men trailing these would-be killers. It was only right to contact the posse and return the money. He followed the men's back trail to a steep hill leading to the other side of the valley and began the long descent to the valley floor.

He had never ridden with a posse himself but remembered the pride he'd taken while fighting in the Snake War. Adam felt the same sense of duty and pride the posse would feel when they caught the bank robbers.

He also remembered being anxious about leaving Henry Creek. He'd expected to be ambushed by the Shoshonis. After the shooting he'd heard earlier in the day, he had every reason to expect the posse to be alert and ready for battle.

Adam aimed to go slowly and watch carefully. He could shoot and fight well, but for now, caution would be his most effective weapon.

30

Adam paused at the bottom of the steep hill and scanned the grass meadow before him. He saw no sign of anyone, except for the back trail the robbers had cut across the meadow. He kicked his horse and began walking toward a small grove of trees and underbrush lining a small stream of clear running water.

At the bank, he paused so the horse could drink. He dismounted to get a drink of the cold mountain water himself. He emptied the warm water from his canteen and refilled it with fresh. He got back in the saddle, rode over the stream, through a small grove of trees and across a narrow strip of grass before having to climb a small hill. Eventually, after what seemed like two miles of nothing except the beauty of the valley, he saw his first sign of life: a lone saddled horse eating grass, with its reins falling free. Adam saw no rider anywhere. He rode slowly, so as not to spook the horse, but it seemed happy enough to see him that it walked to him.

Adam dismounted and spoke quietly to the approaching horse. When the horse got to him, he petted its neck and took hold of its reins. He looked through the saddlebags but found nothing to identify the horse's owner, so he led it back over to his new horse and tied it to his saddle. He stepped up into the saddle and continued riding across the lush grass.

It wasn't long until he noticed the human body in the grass. He rode over to it and peered down. The dead man appeared younger than Adam, perhaps in his early thirties. Adam didn't bother to get off the horse to check the body; it had obviously been plundered by someone. Adam reasoned he must have been one of the bank robbers because his horse seemed to be acquainted with the one Adam was riding.

Looking around carefully, Adam froze when he saw another body leaning against a tree about a hundred yards away Adam pulled out his rifle and laid it across his lap as he rode to the second body. At first, he couldn't tell if the man was alive or dead, but as he got closer, he could see the man's chest moving.

Carefully, Adam dismounted and carried his rifle with him as he approached the sleeping man. He knelt beside him and removed the stranger's rifle lying beside him. Then, cautiously, Adam reached over and opened the leather flap covering the stranger's U.S. Army-issued revolver. He slowly pulled the revolver from its holster without waking the young man. Adam didn't know who he was, but there was a dead man not far away and a broken rifle behind him.

Adam stepped back quickly after he touched the young man, who woke with a jerk and tried to kick him while reaching for his empty holster. The young man rolled onto his left shoulder to get away from Adam and cried out when his shoulder hit the ground. He sat up, holding his shoulder, obviously in severe pain, and said through gritted teeth, "Go ahead and shoot me, if you're going to!" When he opened his eyes, he seemed to do a double take and added, "You're not Octavius."

"No, I'm not. My name's Adam, and I don't mean you any harm. There's been a lot of shooting, though, and there's a dead man over there. I don't know if it was one of your buddies who tried to shoot me, but he's dead, too, if it was. So now you tell me: who are you and what's going on up here?"

"Who'd you kill?" the man asked lifting his head, still holding his shoulder tightly but he squeezed his eyes shut, evidently in an attempt to control his pain.

"I don't know, but there were three of them. They ambushed me, so I shot one of them and then one of them shot their other friend and rode off. Sounds more confusing than it really was, I suppose. Were they friends of yours?"

The man shook his head and grimaced. "No. I'm Nathan Pierce. Those men robbed the bank. Octavius must still be out there."

"My name's Adam Bannister. I figured they robbed a bank. They shot my horse, so I took the horse belonging to the man I shot. I found a bunch of money in his saddlebag. I intended to find the posse and return—"

"You have the gold?" Nathan asked, sounding alarmed.

"Hmm-mm. Like I was saying, I intend to turn it over to the posse if there is one. If there isn't, then I'll take it to the nearest authorities."

Nathan closed his eyes. "Octavius Clark will be coming for that gold. I doubt you'll survive the day with him hunting you. I was trying to trail him, but now he'll be tracking you."

Adam frowned. "Who's Octavius Clark? Is he leading the

posse, or is he one of the robbers? I don't have any reason to hide from a posse, so he can track me if he wants to."

Nathan frowned and shook his head. "I'm the last of the posse. Everyone else is dead. Octavius murdered them all this morning. Including my brother..." His eyes misted over, and he had to catch his breath before continuing, "I tried to track him down, but my horse broke its leg in a rabbit hole. It feels like I broke my shoulder and my ankle in the fall."

"We'll look at that in a minute. So, is the dead man lying over there one of your posse?"

Nathan shook his head. "Bank robber. Octavius killed him from over there." He nodded at the broken rifle behind him. "He must have missed the others with that rifle."

Adam scowled. "It must be a cut-throat bunch to kill your posse and then kill each other, too. Like I said, I killed the owner of that horse. It must've been Octavius who killed that young kid and ran off. It didn't look to me like he had any intention of coming back. Now, let's look at your shoulder," he said and moved closer to Nathan.

Nathan shook his head and said irritably, "It was the Sperry Helms Gang that robbed the bank in Loveland. That's where I live. Octavius was selling his gold when the bank was robbed, and they took it all. Our sheriff forced Octavius to help us track the gang down. Octavius murdered everyone this morning, except for me. When he figures out you have his gold, he will come after you. Octavius is the Veneta Creek Killer everyone's talking about. You know; the one killing all the prospectors and taking their gold."

Adam stared at Nathan for a moment before answering. "Well, first of all the man I shot wasn't Morton Sperry or Jesse Helms or any of their brothers. I don't know Sperry or Helms, but I know who they are. Neither of the dead men I've seen, or the man who shot his buddy off his horse, are in that gang. I don't think it was the Sperry Helms Gang. Second, if Octavius is as dangerous as you say, then we'd better be ready, right? That's the one thing we have on our side. Those prospectors and your friends weren't expecting him. We are. Now, let's see if you broke your shoulder. I noticed you're wearing a cavalry-issued holster. Did you pick it up somewhere, or were you in the cavalry?"

"California 6th Cavalry Company C for four years. You?" Nathan asked, and he noticed Adam's old, worn army-issued holster.

"Oregon 7th Cavalry Company E back in the mid-sixties for three years."

"Snake War?"

"Yeah."

"7th Company E? Wasn't that the one ambushed by the Shoshoni on...?"

"Henry Creek. Yeah, it was."

"Were you there?"

Adam nodded. "Yeah, I was there." He gently touched Nathan's shoulder. "I don't think your shoulder's broken, just dislocated. I can put it back in the socket for you, but it's going to hurt and be sore for a while. Are you ready?"

"I heard that battle was mostly hand-to-hand combat. Seventy or eighty Indians against thirty men, is that true?"

Adam nodded. "We didn't have much choice about the manner of fighting. They attacked and we defended ourselves the best we could using whatever we could. By the grace of God, and by the grace of God alone, I survived. I had an arrow in my leg, my back and my chest. I was stabbed in the back and in the arm but kept fighting and survived. Nine others did not, and sixteen others were wounded as bad as or worse than I was. Only two men walked away un-scathed: my brother Lee and another guy named Howard. It was a tough fight. How about you? Any battles?"

"You had all of those injuries, and I'm complaining about a hurt shoulder. The Modoc War, yes. I was in a few skirmishes with the Modocs and Bannocks, but nothing like you went through. Ahh...Stop! Don't...don't. Ohhh, my word!" Nathan cried out as Adam popped his arm back into the shoulder socket unexpectedly. The operation went easily enough.

"Oh, you're a soldier. Toughen up," Adam said, humored by the young man's pain-filled expressions. He continued, "Now it'll feel better. I picked up another horse right out there, so you'll have a horse to ride. I'll save your ankle until we get back to town. If I take your boot off, it won't go back on as you probably know, and you'll need that boot on to get out of this high country and back home."

Nathan gave Adam a nasty look as his pain began to subside, but it had been excruciating for that moment. "You could've warned me!"

Adam grinned. "I could've, but you were talking, and I didn't want to interrupt. Now, let's get you on that horse and back to my camp. Just so you know, and I'll be very honest with you, I think it's quite a miracle I even found you. I was hunting a wolf when I heard gunshots and came this way. Now, having said that, I hope you're a good guy and we get along well, but I don't know you. So, I'll keep your weapons until we get to town, if you don't mind. I'll give you a warning about me here and now, though, because I am a fair man. If you try anything on me at all, if you try to ambush me in any way, I will cut your Achilles tendons and leave you out here to be eaten alive by the pack of wolves I've been tracking. And there are a whole lot of wolves. Are we clear on that? I'm a nice guy, and I'm more than willing to help you out of here safely, but if you try to harm me, I won't have the slightest bit of mercy on you. You do understand me?"

"Sir, you are the only hope I have of getting back home to my wife. Trust me when I tell you I'd be an absolute fool to betray the only chance I have of getting home alive. I came out here to get Octavius, but now all I care about is going home," Nathan said sincerely.

Adam nodded. "You'll get home soon enough."

Nathan grimaced in agony as he tried to stand. "Listen... I have to get home. If the Huntsville sheriff brings a posse and finds my brother and friends, they'll send word back to Loveland. My wife will think I'm dead and have no choice but to go back to her parents. I'd never see her again. And if I tried to get her, chances are I'd be killed. So please, can you take me back to Loveland? Look, you can tie me onto the saddle if that would make you feel safer. I don't care what you do to me, but I have to get home soon." The thought of Sarah going back to her parents made Nathan cringe inside.

"Don't worry about your wife. We'll send her a message as soon as we get to Willow Falls."

"What is your name again?"

"Adam."

Nathan said urgently, "Adam, if we leave for Loveland now, we might run into the Huntsville posse. They can take me the rest of the way home and return the money for you. But if we stay in this valley or try to go over those mountains"—he pointed at the cliffs and vertical peaks along the southern ridge—"we'll run into Octavius, and he will ambush us. I don't want to die out here, Adam. I just want to go home and spend the rest of my life with my wife. I love her too much to let her believe I'm dead and leave the life we've made together. So please. Help me to get home. I don't have any money to give you, but you have no idea how important it is that I get home!"

Adam frowned. "That's fine, but we need to go to my camp first and let my uncle know. Otherwise, he'll come looking for me. I'll make sure you get home, but first, tell me why you'd be killed if your wife went back to her parents and you tried to see her. Are you holding her against her will or something?"

"Hell, no!"

"Then why are you worried about her going to her parents? Even if she leaves, why not surprise her at her parent's door? Certainly, she'd come back with you if she knew you were alive, right?"

"There are some things you don't need to know," Nathan said sullenly.

"I suppose not. But there are a lot of dead bodies lying around up here, and I don't know anything about you. So, don't beg me to take you anywhere, except to town to see the doctor. Then you can explain everything to my brother."

"Your brother?"

"Yeah, he's the marshal."

"What marshal?"

"U.S. Marshal Matt Bannister's my little brother. I'm Adam Bannister."

Nathan began to perspire. "I can't talk to your brother, Adam. And you can't talk to him about me either. Please..."

"Sounds like you have something to hide. I don't know if you're part of a murdered posse like you claim to be, the killer of the posse, or a bank robber. I suppose that's for the law to figure out, not me. But I am taking you to town and turning you over to Matt. I am a fair man, though, so I will give you a choice: stay out here and take your chances with the wolves and bears—without my new horse—or I'm taking you in. You pick."

Nathan sighed heavily, and fear almost overwhelmed him. "Fine, Adam. I'll tell you why I can't talk to your brother, but I swear to you and the Lord above, I'm not a criminal!"

31

Octavius found the bodies of Deuce McKenna and his nephew, Brent. It wasn't too hard to figure out what had happened from the clues left for him. The blood and brain matter above Deuce's body on the side of the gulley indicated he was shot from the valley floor. A dead horse lay in the gulley about two hundred yards away from a saddle on the ground. The bullet that killed Deuce was perfectly placed in the center of his forehead.

From that distance, it was either the luckiest shot Octavius had ever seen or had been aimed by a skilled rifleman. The boy Octavius had injured earlier wasn't killed by the same gun—he doubted he'd been killed by the same person. Brent had two smaller caliber bullet wounds, one to the chest and one to the head. The lone survivor had probably been scared off by the shooter in the valley and had killed the injured boy so he could keep the money for himself.

Octavius would have done the same thing for a couple of reasons that had nothing to do with money. First, a wounded man slows the others down. Second, a wounded man with a bullet in his leg would need medical attention and would have to account for the wound. The risk of a loose tongue was reason enough to leave the boy lying up here with a bullet in his body.

Now Octavius knew who had the money and would track him down soon enough. First, though, he wanted to find where the unknown shooter had stood when he killed the guy in the ravine. An unaccounted-for person roaming around this deep in the mountains unsettled Octavius. The shooter might have been a prospector with a claim up here or an old trapper who fell in love with the valley and never left it. It didn't matter what or who he was. Octavius only wanted to determine the ability of the man.

He rode to the valley floor and across a meadow to where the horse lay. The horse had been well fed and groomed. Whoever the man was, he had cared for his animal and had been particular about using his own saddle and bridle. He walked to the fallen log and saw, by the matted grass, where the man had knelt and fired the killing shot. Octavius knelt behind the log and looked at Deuce's body. A clear shot, but a very small target. He looked for any empty cartridges but couldn't find any.

Whoever the man was, he had picked up his brass to reload his ammunition himself. Knowing a little more about the shooter, Octavius focused his attention onto the job at hand: simply following the lone rider to get his money back.

32

Luther Fasana had heard faint sounds of gunfire coming from the other side of Windsor Ridge all day long. He became increasingly worried as the hours crept by. Adam was a good tracker and would trail the wolf wherever it led. He was also a superb rifleman and would kill the wolf with his first clear shot, no matter the distance. It shouldn't have taken him so long to get the wolf shot and skinned. Luther had expected him to return to camp hours ago.

He busied himself keeping the fire burning in the teepee, and even sliced up some thin strips of wolf meat to dry over the fire. As time went by and the meat cured, he grew more worried. It wasn't like his nephew to take so long to track down any creature he had set out to find. Wolves could travel for miles, sure enough, but even so, the sound of gunfire worried him. He had never heard nor seen a single sign of another person in all the years he had been coming up here.

Something wasn't right, and Luther didn't think he should wait any longer. He saddled his mule, stuck his rifle in its scabbard and put his revolver in his pommel holster over the saddle horn. He then mounted and followed what little trail Adam had left. Luther wasn't a tracker by trade, but he knew something about tracking. He'd been Adam's first and most influential instructor on tracking game, which wasn't much different from tracking men, aside from intellectual variances between game and men.

Once Luther reached the meadow where they'd hunted elk, he followed Adam's trail. He climbed up Windsor Ridge into the thinning tree line, and then followed the trail east, where a saddle dipped down in the ridge line. It was clear Adam had followed the wolf through the pass of the saddle and had gone down into the wide valley on the other side of Windsor Ridge.

Luther had never been inside the valley himself, but he had gazed upon it years before. He'd never considered it prudent to risk his mount so far from home on the scree rock descending into the valley. If the access into the valley was as navigable as the south side of Windsor Ridge, he'd not hesitate to explore the valley. Unfortunately, it wasn't. If Adam had tried to cross the scree field and lost his footing, he could be lying at the bottom with a broken leg or worse.

As Luther thought things over, it occurred to him that Adam might have fired those shots to get Luther's attention. Sort of a cry for help. With a growing sense of urgency, Luther approached the pass's opening. Then he heard a horse and the cries of a man demanding his horse run faster echoing out from the canyon through the pass. He frowned, alarmed, and stopped his mule about thirty yards short of the opening, curious.

Within moments, an unknown man on a bloodied paint horse galloped out of the pass. The horse had some deep scrapes and cuts on its side that bled heavily. The rider, as well, wore torn clothing and bled from some deep scrapes.

The man saw Luther and wheeled his horse around in a panic. He pulled his revolver and fired wildly at Luther. The shots went wide. He seemed to want to fire again, but when he saw Luther pull his revolver from his pommel holster, he turned his horse and kicked it brutally to force it down a steep incline of hard-packed earth and rocks.

Luther didn't fire a shot but watched in bewilderment as the man kicked his horse mercilessly. Not surprisingly, the horse's feet slipped, it stumbled, its back legs buckled, and it fell to its already-injured side onto the protruding rocks. The rider stayed in the saddle during the fall but dropped his revolver as he reached for the saddle horn.

Instantly, the man cursed and started whipping the horse, wanting it to get up and keep running. The exhausted and injured black-and-white paint forced itself up, regained its footing, and resumed running down the mountain, breathing heavily and soaked with lather.

Luther watched the exhausted animal's back leg limp severely with each step until horse and man disappeared into the tree line below. Luther dismounted and pulled his rifle from its scabbard. He knew the poor horse wouldn't get too much farther before it collapsed. The man would probably want Luther's fresh mule, so he kept the mule between himself and the tree line as protection from a rifle shot, just in case.

Leading his mule to the mountain pass, Luther entered it on foot. He led his mule all the way through the pass until he reached the other side and looked over the valley below. He had forgotten how beautiful it was and for a moment, he stood breathless as he gazed at it. He did not see Adam lying at the bottom of a cliff or on the scree field, but he did see another rider at the bottom of the scree field begin to climb up what looked to be a thin trail angling across it. Luther held his rifle and took a position close to cover, should he need it. He waited for the man to come to him. This time, Luther was ready if the man turned out to be unfriendly.

Octavius Clark had been startled to see a man with a mule walk out of the pass after he heard the shot from the ridge. He knew the man with the mule wasn't the same man he was after, just from his clothes and build. He imagined the man was probably just a prospector curious about hearing shooting in his territory. As he carefully led his horse up the scree field, he saw the man was his age or older, with a thick barrel chest and a long gray beard, holding a rifle in his hands and ready to defend himself. He watched Octavius carefully. The mule had a saddle but lacked saddlebags or a bedroll; the man must have a camp nearby.

"Howdy," Octavius called from past the midway point up the scree field. He had already unsecured his revolver for easy access. His instincts told him the old timer was harmless, but he never took chances when he was at a disadvantage.

"Howdy," Luther said in return.

"I don't mean you any harm. My name's Jones. John Jones. I'm part of a posse from Loveland trailing some bank robbers through here. I'm assuming the shot I heard either came from you or the man I'm chasing. Did you get him?"

Luther seemed to relax a bit and lowered the rifle. "Well, if he was riding a paint, then, yeah, he shot at me and then kept going. He won't get far, though. His horse is on its last leg. Maybe another mile or two before it falls down for the last time."

Octavius pointed behind him. "It looks to me like he

tried to ride it up this scree and slid down it twice before he wised up and led his horse up. His horse is in bad shape, you say?"

Luther nodded. "Yeah, pretty beat up."

Octavius nodded. "Good to hear. He and his gang killed the rest of our posse this morning. Now it's down to just him and me. I'm glad you scared him away. I was worried he might ambush me as I came up this mountain." Octavius walked slowly closer to Luther. He and his horse were both exhausted.

"I didn't scare him away. He was running away when he shot at me. I just happened to be looking for my nephew who came this way."

Octavius peered at Luther as he got closer. "Your nephew?"

"Yeah, he tracked some wolves this morning, and they must've come this way. I've tracked his horse this far."

"Wolves? Are you trappers?" Octavius asked.

"No. Just stocking up on our winter's meat. My nephew's been gone for longer than I expected. I feared he might've got caught up in all the shooting. Have you seen him? He rides a big bay horse."

Octavius nodded. "Did it have a white sock on one leg?"

"Yes," Luther said nervously.

"He's fine," Octavius said. "It seems my bank robbers had a run-in with your nephew. The robbers ambushed him and hit his mare, but he killed one or two of the robbers for me. It was a hell of a shot your nephew made. I found the robbers' bodies on the southwest side of that hill over there. Your nephew switched saddles with a robber's horse and moved north. I can't say I saw many wolf tracks there, but that's the direction he went."

"You saw him?"

Octavius shook his head. "Only his tracks and a dead horse. But he is fine. I can account for every shot fired today, and none of them got him. I would've seen blood if he was shot, so I'm guessing he's fine. Just chasing his wolves, is my guess. Did I already tell you my name is John Jones?" Octavius reached out his hand to shake Luther's.

Luther shook his hand firmly. "Luther Fasana."

"Are you camped around here?"

Luther nodded. "Yeah, down towards the bottom of the mountain. We come up here every August to shoot a few elk and deer to make our winter's jerky."

Octavius smiled. "Mind if I stop in and have some? I haven't eaten much in the past couple days, and that sounds mighty good."

"You're more than welcome to stop and rest a while if you'd like. We have plenty of food. Follow your nose. You'll find us."

"I will take you up on that. Luther, there isn't anyone else up here who can cause your nephew any trouble. You could go try to look for him down there, but you might be better off going back to camp. Your nephew will be along when he's done with whatever he's doing. But as for me, I have a man to catch up with. Have a good day, Luther Fasana."

"You, too," Luther said as Octavius got into his saddle.

Octavius gazed at Luther. "That's a big valley down there, Luther. You might as well ride with me down the mountain and talk some before you go to your camp. Then I'll go find my money."

"I suppose you're right. I'd never find him down there." Luther scabbarded his rifle and stepped into his saddle to ride with Octavius. "So, what do you do for a living in Loveland, John?"

"Oh, a little bit of everything, but nothing particular full-time. What about you?"

"Granite quarry. It's hard work, but it's what I've been doing for a long time now," Luther said with a shrug.

"How long?"

"Most of my adult life. I'm one of those guys who can do it, so I stayed with it."

"Are you a married man?" Octavius asked.

"Nope, you?"

"Once..." Octavius answered. "Were you in the war?"

Luther shook his head. "No, you?"

Octavius nodded. "Yeah. Born and raised in eastern Kentucky, in the Cumberlands. I guess you could say I was in the war before it even started. That's where my wife's buried. Some Yanks came onto our farm looking for her cousin and murdered her for no reason. That was the turning point for me, and I never looked back."

He didn't know why he had opened up so quickly to the stranger named Luther, but there was something about Luther Octavius felt comfortable with. Like an old lost friend. He couldn't explain it. He'd never before felt such a sudden kinship with a man he'd just met.

Luther shook his head. "I'm sorry to hear that. My wife died, too, but she was sick. I married twice. The first one ran off with another man, leaving me alone to raise our two boys. My second wife and I had my daughter, and then she passed away, leaving me alone to raise my girl."

"Did you track your first wife and that man down and kill them?" Octavius asked.

Luther laughed. "No. I had children to raise. I just worked to earn enough to house and feed them. What about you, John? Do you have any children or grandchildren?"

Octavius frowned sadly. "Not anymore. The Yanks took

my family away from me." He didn't mention leaving his children behind and never going back to them. He had no idea if he had grandchildren. He'd never thought about possible grandchildren until now. His sons would be men about the age he was when he left them, and his daughter would be nearing thirty. He had tried to forget so much, but he still remembered their birthdays and how they'd looked when they were young. He dreamed about them occasionally, but he knew, if he saw them today, he wouldn't recognize them. And if he did have grandchildren, he wouldn't be able to pick them out from any other screaming kids on the street. He was sure he was dead to them, and they had moved on with their lives without him.

They were his children, though: his and Lucinda's flesh and blood, and he still remembered. Once in a blue moon, he would be haunted by their memory, but this time those memories hurt. He was riding beside a man who had raised his children alone; a man who had earned the right to be called a father. A man who had no regrets or shame.

Octavius' whole life was filled with regret and shame. He wished he could go back to the time when he was a loving husband and playful father to his children. He longed to hold Lucinda close to him one last time. If there was any way he could go back in time and relive his years, he would pack up his family, leave the Cumberland Mountains, and come west so he could raise his family like Luther did.

"I'm sorry to hear about your family," Luther said.

"Me, too," Octavius said softly.

33

Sarah Pierce worried about her husband while she steamed a pot of mason jars filled with green beans from her garden. Her garden wasn't awfully big, but she grew enough green beans, carrots, beets, and spinach to last through most of the winter. Apples, pears, cherries and various berries she either picked or bought to can, as well. The local mercantile provided other canned and general goods necessary to survive the long, barren winters of the Wallowa Mountains. The work of filling the pantry shelves with canned vegetables and fruit was an act of love, labor and sweat. In August the cabin was already hot inside, even without a fire in the woodstove; Sarah needed a fire to boil the water to seal the cans. The humidity inside her two-room log cabin was nearly too much to bear.

Sarah wore a lightweight blue dress with little bouquets of flowers printed on the fabric. Perspiration darkened the dress around her unbuttoned collar, under her arms and her upper back. She wore her hair in a bun to keep it out of her face, which she wiped with a grayish white rag to clear away the sweat burning her eyes. She sighed tiredly and cut the stems off the next several lines of green beans. She picked them up with her left hand and dropped them in a half-full mason jar. It was her responsibility to make sure there was enough food in the pantry to keep Nathan and Cal fed.

When snow began to fall, the logging camp would close for the winter. Then most of the people would move down to the valley, where the snow was thinner and the temperature a little warmer. Sarah and her two men stayed in Loveland and toughed it out. Winters were hard, but she labored all spring, summer and fall to prepare for those four months. They could move down the mountain where the snow wasn't quite so deep, but they were safer hidden away in the mountains.

Unknown to everyone else in their community, her real name wasn't Sarah. She was born Catherine Eckman, the only child of millionaire railroad tycoon and Sacramento socialites, Louis and Divinity Eckman. She had grown up wealthy and privileged and had the best education money could buy. However, Sarah found certain subjects, such as mathematics, difficult to learn and had no desire to further her education by going to a state university, to her parents' dismay.

She had enjoyed the growing up with wealth, but as she grew older, she started noticing her parents' inconsistencies when it came to moral values. They never missed church, and they tithed regularly. Her father was even on the church board, and her mother was active in many ways, but they only did good works to further their public reputation. They were pillars in the Sacramento society, and the church was an asset in keeping up their flawless personae. They preached publicly what a good Christian family should be, but behind closed doors and away from their church friends, they failed to live like Christians in their own lives. In public, the Eckman marriage was strong, joy-filled and unbreakable. Their apparent love for each other could be seen far and wide. They appeared to be the perfect couple blessed within the perfect marriage.

Inside their home, however, their marriage was dead, silent, cold and miserable. Louis often remained late in his home office or place of business, purportedly to earn money. Sarah found out, however, that her father had a long history of having affairs with other women.

Divinity Eckman, his aging wife, had grown cold, lonely and bitter. She left Sarah home alone with the maid every day in order to attend luncheons, banquets, or other social activities with Sacramento's social elite.

Sarah found her parents' life empty of substance, but full of false piety and hypocrisy. Her one joy was the maid she had been left with for so many years: Jane Montgomery. Jane was an older Negro lady who came to the house every day except Sundays. Miss Jane cleaned an already-clean mansion and tended the flower garden. Miss Jane was paid very little for everything demanded of her, but she did it well.

The quality Sarah always found intriguing in Miss Jane was her constant smile. She never seemed bothered by anything her parents said or complained about. Her eyes always glowed with gentleness and love. Sarah had never met anyone else like Miss Jane. Miss Jane lived in a dilapidated shack in the poorest and roughest part of town but every morning, no matter the weather, Jane walked over a mile to serve the Eckmans. Then she would walk home, just to do it all over again the next day.

It seemed a worthless existence to her parents, but this little Negro lady of no substantial means was the most significant influence in Sarah's life. She found a friend in Miss Jane; a friend who would listen to her every word, and cared enough to answer honestly, even if her answers weren't what Sarah wanted to hear.

Confounded by Miss Jane's sweetness, one day Sarah asked, "Miss Jane, why do you work so hard to please my parents when they treat you so bad?"

Miss Jane's answer struck a chord in Sarah. Her answer separated authenticity from hypocrisy: "The Bible says to work like you're working for God himself. And I'll tell you, child, it doesn't matter what anyone says. God deserves the best work I can give him."

"But...my parents treat you like rubbish."

"Oh, sweetie, I don't work for your parents. I work for Jesus himself! He is my boss, and he says, 'work for them Eckmans'. So, I do."

"They don't pay you enough. My mother tells her friends that you're too stupid to know you're practically working for free."

Miss Jane looked at her kindly. "My payday will come when Jesus himself calls me home. And greater are my riches in Heaven, sweet girl, than everything your parents and their friends have here put together. Remember, we will all stand before Jesus, and we will all have to give an account for every word, deed and thing we say or do. It doesn't matter if you end up rich or poor. What matters is your integrity. Take Jesus by the hand and walk with him, work for him and live for him. And if you treat everyone right—even those who don't deserve your goodness—you will live a blessed life. You'll also have riches beyond your parents' wildest dreams. Riches in here." She tapped her chest over her heart. "And up there." She pointed upwards. "That's where it really matters."

In Sarah's world of imitation happiness within her parents' mansion walls, the words of their poverty-stricken, unappreciated maid revealed a life of unwavering devotion to God. Instead of putting on a pious mask, Miss Jane just lived the Christian life. The line between the hypocrisy of her parents and the authentic devotion of Miss Jane suddenly became a choice Sarah had to make in her own life. That very day she committed her life to serving Jesus as Miss Jane did. She wanted the joy she saw in Miss Jane's eyes, and the gentle smile that was so inviting to a girl who needed a friend. She'd seen enough of her parents faking smiles for others to see, then coming home to live in bitterness. Sarah wanted a real commitment to Jesus or no commitment at all.

When Sarah was eighteen, she had several suitors wanting to court her. However, too often her suitors were cut from the same moral fabric as her parents and were more interested in creating a wealthy future than listening to what was important to Sarah. Then came the day when her parents spoke to her about a young man named Gaius Bertrand. Gaius was the twenty-seven-year-old son of the owner of a large ship manufacture in San Francisco. Gaius had graduated from a prestigious Eastern college with a mechanical engineering degree and would have a solid future at the renowned Bertrand Ship Builders Company. Louis and Divinity Eckman thought Gaius would be a winning match to marry their beautiful daughter, and they were excited to introduce Sarah to Gaius at the upcoming Governor's Ball in Sacramento.

When the day of the Ball came, Sarah was tutored by her parents on how she should act, and what was expected of her as their daughter; they were going to the most important social event of the year, after all. She was also instructed

KEN PRATT

to be interested in the ship building industry and particularly interested in the future owner of Bertrand Shipping, the young Gaius Bertrand. They emphasized how the two of them would be a great match, even though they had never met.

Her parents didn't care about Sarah's feelings. They aimed to make Sarah into a perfect woman and snag Gaius Bertrand as their son-in-law. On the day, the Eckmans took Sarah to a grand ball, dread and helplessness walked with her. She didn't want to meet the man her parents had chosen for her to marry.

As SARAH and her parents neared the door of the capitol building, Sara noticed two U.S. Cavalry soldiers dressed in their blue uniforms with their sabers on their waists, guarding the entrance.

One of the soldiers met Sarah's eyes just as she glanced up from the ground. Their gazes held momentarily. Only a private, the soldier was startlingly handsome. He smiled and nodded at her alone, as he opened the door and held it open for her and her parents to walk inside. His gaze never left hers, nor did hers leave his.

Inside, Sarah's parents enthusiastically introduced her to Gaius Bertrand and his parents. Like so many other rich, pompous men who had courted her, Gaius was arrogant. He blathered on about a new steam engine that would add speed to the newly designed ship fleet his father planned to build.

Sarah lost interest in his conversation within a matter of minutes. Her thoughts went back to the soldier guarding the entrance door. Before too long, she excused herself from the table, left the banquet hall, walked down the corridor and stepped outside the front door to linger on the top landing of the steps. She pretended to be looking over the town in the evening's fading light.

"It's a beautiful evening, isn't it, ma'am?" the young soldier asked politely.

"Very," she said with her back to him. She turned around slowly. "So, you must be part of the king's royal guard here?" She sounded sarcastic.

The young man smiled. "I suppose I am."

The second guard, who was a bit older, with red hair and freckles, said, "You'd better stop talking to the princess or you might be beheaded. You know the rules. We're not supposed to fraternize with the guests."

"I'm just saying hello. It would be rude not to." He turned his attention back to Sarah. "Forgive me, Your Highness. A lowly guard shouldn't be bothering you."

"Who said you were bothering me? It might be nice to have a conversation that's not about money."

The guard chuckled lightly. "Then you're talking to the right fellow, because I haven't got a dime to my name. My name's Nathan Webster," he said, holding out his hand to receive hers.

Sarah let him grasp her hand and said candidly, "My name is Catherine Eckman, the daughter of Louis and Divinity Eckman. And to be honest, I am bored to tears with the conversations in there."

"Nice to meet you, Miss Eckman," Nathan said as he bent to kiss the back of her soft hand.

The red-haired corporal spoke with a touch of authority in his voice, "Private Webster, may I remind you that we are under orders to not converse with the governor's guests."

Sarah said, "I'm not the governor's guest. My parents are. I don't want to be here. So…" She paused to look at Nathan.

"It's too bad you can't talk. We might've had a good chat. I've never had a chance to talk to a lowly door guard before."

Nathan chuckled quietly, and he and Sarah continued their pleasant conversation.

Half an hour later, Louis Eckman stepped outside, looking for his daughter. He was annoyed to find her outside talking to a cavalry soldier rather than to Gaius Bertrand. He forced her back inside, guided her to Gaius' table and sat her down. She was forced to remain inside for the rest of the evening, but her thoughts were with the handsome guard named Nathan.

She managed to tear a page out of the guest book and used the quill to write her name and mailing address thereon. When the ball ended and they walked out the front door, she slipped the piece of paper into Nathan's empty hand. That began a year-long correspondence, as Nathan finished up his last year of military service.

Because her father forbade her from writing to Nathan, Sarah sent Nathan a letter giving him Miss Jane's address. Miss Jane would bring the letters into the Eckman home and hand-deliver them to Sarah.

The more Sarah and Nathan corresponded, the more Sarah longed to be with Nathan, despite her parents' efforts to introduce her to more affluent suitors. After eight months, Sarah realized she had fallen in love with Nathan. When Nathan asked her to be his wife in an unromantic hand-written letter with a ring drawn on the page, she felt grand. It wasn't the way she'd dreamed a marriage proposal would come, but when she read the words, "Will you marry me when I get out of the cavalry?" her heart skipped a beat.

She knew Nathan would never be able to give her the opportunities Gaius Bertrand could give her, or the large home and life of ease her mother knew so well. But she also knew financial gain wasn't as wonderful as many people thought it was. Seeking vindication of her decision before answering him in a letter, Sarah asked the advice of her only true friend, Miss Jane.

"Child, if you have invested in real love, and you've got the Lord, too, then that's all you need to know pure joy in life. Money ain't got nothing to do with it, baby girl."

Sarah, wrote one word in a return letter: "YES!!!!!" And she sent the letter.

They waited until Nathan was out of the military so that he could meet her parents and ask for her hand in marriage. Louis had no interest in meeting the unemployed ex-soldier who wanted to court his daughter. He thought of him a leach hoping to get in good with a rich man's daughter. Louis respected officers of the armed services, but a meager private after four years in the cavalry was a maggot not worth the mud on the bottom of his shoes.

When Nathan asked permission to marry Sarah, Louis laughed and said, "My daughter has too much class to marry a leach like you. Catherine has a bright future ahead of her. She is weeks away from being engaged to a college graduate who will own the largest ship-building manufacturing facility on the west coast." He then scoffed with disgust. "What can you offer her, thirty cents a day picking up coal off the street? Don't waste my time; you have nothing to offer. Now, get out of my house and don't ever contact my daughter again!"

Nathan had smiled and replied simply, "Yes, sir."

What Louis and Divinity did not know was that a wedding had already been planned to take place in Miss Jane's little shack. The couple already knew the only way they could be together was to get married in secret and leave Sacramento and her parents behind. In the years ahead, the

Eckmans would either come to accept Nathan as part of their family or they wouldn't. But once Nathan and Catherine Eckman were married, the Eckmans would no longer matter. Or so Nathan had thought.

Their wedding was not the one Sarah had dreamed of. The only two witnesses were Miss Jane and her pastor, Mr. Cal. Then Sarah mailed a letter to her parents explaining that she was now married and moving to Oregon, where Nathan and his brother planned to open a hardware business in Portland.

Unfortunately for them, Mr. Eckman had hired thugs to kidnap his daughter and her new husband and force them to sign annulment papers. Sarah signed under protest. Nathan only signed when Sarah begged him to do it, because she knew her father's hired men would kill him otherwise.

Sara then became a prisoner in her parents' home. They told her this was for her own good, and that she would soon be married to Gaius Bertrand. Sarah thought she might die of a broken heart.

However, not long thereafter, Miss Jane delivered a letter to her from Nathan. Once again, Sarah and Nathan began corresponding.

Every day when she left the Eckmans' mansion, Miss Jane took few of Sarah's clothes or personal items to her home so Sarah could grab them when she finally left with Nathan. Eventually the fated night came. Sarah waited until three in the morning, then wrote a short note to her parents.

"DEAREST MOTHER AND FATHER;

I am married and leaving with my husband.
You will never see me again.

Your only daughter,
Catherine Eckman."

SARAH AND NATHAN bought tickets using their real names for a train going to Oklahoma, but they weren't on it. Instead, they rode by wagon northeast into Nevada. Nathan and his brother found work in a silver mine, and the married couple settled into a small home. That was when Catherine wrote Miss Jane in confidence and told her where they were.

Not long after that, Miss Jane wrote to tell them Louis Eckman had not only hired Pinkerton agents to find her but offered them—or anyone else—ten thousand dollars upon the death of Nathan Webster and the return of their daughter.

Shocked, the newly married couple moved to Loveland, Oregon. Nathan kept his first name but changed his last name to Pierce. Thus, Catherine Eckman became Sarah Pierce.

Miss Jane kept Sarah updated about her parents and their search for her, but the news seldom changed: they had no idea where she was. Wanted posters with Nathan's name and likeness had been sent out, but the drawing looked very little like Nathan, who had grown a bushy beard. With the beard and by letting his hair grow long, no one would recognize him as Nathan Webster.

The Eckmans had also sent out a poster with Sarah's likeness on it. The likeness favored her, but the Eckmans distributed it as a *missing person* poster with a high-dollar reward if she was returned unharmed. Miss Jane sent a copy of both posters to Sarah and Nathan. Since the photograph used on the poster was old and depicted her as a rich man's daughter, Sarah let her hair hang down and became a lumberman's wife. The two could walk past a bounty hunter holding the two posters in his hand and wouldn't be recognized, although Sarah didn't want to take the risk.

The unsolved murders of several placer miners in the area had raised her anxiety, as more outsiders came to their neck of the woods to find the Veneta Creek Killer. She wanted that killer found; however, she feared her true identity might also be discovered. Neither she nor Nathan had ever done anything illegal, and they had no reason to fear the law. Due to her own father's wicked heart, however, they lived in a state of constant fear.

Now she worried about Nathan and Cal because they'd joined a posse to track a group of bank robbers. The rumor had it that the Sperry Helms Gang had robbed the bank. No one doubted the bad men in the gang would kill at the drop of a dime. Sarah worried that the two most important men in her life were risking their lives for someone else's money.

She had begged both of them not to go. She couldn't shake the uneasy feeling in her stomach. Also, there was no doubt that Marshal Matt Bannister would meet up with the posse somewhere, and Sarah knew he would have their posters, even if no one else in Oregon did. The man's reputation as a killer had reached into the farthest corners of America, even her hidden little town of Loveland. The ten-thousand-dollar bounty was enough to buy a marshal, especially one with Matt's reputation. He would kill Nathan and send her back to Sacramento, shackled and tied against her will. Matt Bannister was one of her greatest fears. She prayed he would never come to Loveland. If he did, she wouldn't step foot outside her house while he was in town.

A knock at the door startled her. The door was wide open to let in the slightest breeze. She glanced over to see

John Riggs in the doorway, a grin on his face. She had no idea how long he had been standing there watching her before he knocked. He held a whiskey bottle that had been emptied and then refilled with some red liquid.

She shrieked. "John! You scared me. What can I do for you? Have you heard anything from Nathan and the others?"

"No, nothing yet. It looks like you're keeping busy."

She wiped some sweat from her forehead with her sleeve. "Of course. I'm always busy. So how can I help you, John?" She wouldn't invite him inside.

He smiled. "Well, I know you're probably worried about Nathan and Cal, so I thought I'd stop by and check in on you."

"Thank you. I am doing fine."

"I'm glad to hear that. I also wanted to give you a bottle of my finest wine. It's a gift," he said, handing it to her.

Sarah smiled kindly. "Thank you, but I must decline. You should know I don't drink alcohol, and neither does my husband."

"Yeah, but as hot as it is, and as worried as you must be, I thought a glass of wine might quench your thirst better than water today."

Sarah shook her head. "I appreciate the offer, but I must decline. Thank you for stopping by to check on me, though."

John looked hurt by her words. "Oh." He sounded disappointed. "Well you're welcome, but I hate to leave with the gift I brought you. Are you sure you don't want to keep it for later? Maybe this evening when it cools down and you rest from your labors? Really, just try a sip and see if you like it."

"No, thank you, John," she said with finality.

"How about I leave it right here and you can have it when you want it?"

"No, just take it back to your saloon and sell it to someone. I don't want anything you have to sell, period. We don't want alcohol in our house. None at all," Sarah said plainly.

John frowned. "Okay," he said, sounding bitter. He turned and walked toward his saloon in the middle of town.

Sarah had ears and living in such a small community made mostly of men, she often heard stories about other men, most of them unfit for a lady. One of the things she had been told about John Riggs was that he had drugged women by putting chloral hydrate into their drinks. The drug caused the women to fall asleep and remain asleep during John's uninvited entrance into their bodies. With Nathan and Cal gone, she suspected John's low morals were the reason he'd offered the bottle of wine. He was known for being cheap, sleazy and underhanded and, oddly enough, had showed up at her door bearing gifts.

Sarah prayed Nathan and Cal would come home soon.

34

Lyndall Swanson was talking to Big Hank Hanson inside his mercantile when he saw John Riggs leave the saloon carrying a clear bottle of red liquid. John walked purposely toward the northern end of town where the lumber company's employee housing, consisting of forty small log cabins, clustered together on a hillside.

"Excuse me a second," Lyndall said to Big Hank, and he walked to the door.

"What? Are Sheriff Jack and his imbecile son back? I betcha they got lost," Big Hank muttered as Lyndall walked off. Hank followed to see for himself. "I don't see the lost posse."

"No, no. I'm just seeing where John's taking that bottle," Lyndall explained as he stepped outside into the dusty street to watch John. He walked to where he had a view of the Pierce's opened front door and frowned when he realized that was where John was going.

Hank stated, "He's probably taking the bottle to the privy to refill it with piss. All of his watered-down whiskey tastes like piss."

"No," Lyndall said seriously, "I think he's got something else up his sleeve, Hank. Look where he's going: straight to Miss Sarah's, while Nathan and Cal are off trying to bring John's money back for him."

Hank watched John walk to the open door of the Pierce home and stare inside for a few minutes before knocking on the door's threshold.

"Why that..."

"If she takes that bottle, I'm going to walk over there and bust it over his head," Lyndall said with animosity.

"Miss Sarah don't drink liquor," Hank said. "Besides that, if he tried to force himself on her, she'd send him home hurting like a neutered pup."

"Not if she's passed out," Lyndall said.

Hank grinned. "She doesn't drink liquor, so I doubt she'd drink that whole bottle down in one sitting, no matter how hot the weather got."

Lyndall looked at Big Hank seriously and explained, "John was run out of Idaho for drugging women. Some time back, John and I went to Huntsville to get supplies and ran into an old friend of his from Boise in the saloon. When John went to the privy, his friend told me to watch over my wife if I had one, and then he told me about John. The woman he drugged was his friend's wife. I didn't think about it until then, but John had me order a bottle of chloral hydrate from the Branson druggist about a month before that. I didn't ask why he wanted it, but I don't think John has a bad back, do you?"

"Lyndall, you've got me perplexed. What'd you order and, what's it have to do with anything?"

Lyndall took a deep breath and then explained. "Hank, for starting a successful logging camp out in the middle of nowhere, you have to be one of the densest men I've ever known. John was putting the chloral hydrate into the women's drinks. Then, when they passed out, he'd assault them. I'm thinking he may have put choral hydrate in that bottle he's trying to give to Sarah. She's not taking it though," he said with a sense of satisfaction as he watched John's disappointed body language. He was pleased to see John walk slowly away from the Pierce's, holding the bottle.

Big Hank's expression hardened. "You mean to tell me he was going to assault Miss Sarah?"

"There's only one way to find out."

"If that's what he did, I'm going to crush every bone in his hands, so he can't ever pour a drink again. Be right back." Big Hank walked into the mercantile. A moment later, he stepped outside with a hickory axe-handle in his hand. His eyes narrowed when John turned the corner and walked their way.

"Howdy, gents," John said with a touch of annoyance.

"What's in the bottle, John," Lyndall asked curtly.

John gaped at him. "Huh? Oh, it's wine."

"Why were you taking it to Sarah? You know she doesn't drink."

John's expression fell as he recognized danger burning in Big Hank's eyes and saw the axe-handle he held. A flash of surprise crossed his face when he realized the two men had intentionally gone into the street to question him about the bottle he held. A deep, sinking fear filled him. He said, "I thought she might like to have some. You know, her husband's out with the posse and all. You two have a nice day," he said and gave a nervous shrug. He took a step forward to walk around them.

"Hold on a minute!" Big Hank said roughly. He stuck the axe-handle in front of John to stop him. "What'd you put in it?"

"I didn't put anything in it. Come on, fellers. I thought it would be a nice gesture, that's all. But she didn't want no part of it, anyway. Now, if you don't mind, I need to get back to work."

"Drink it," Lyndall ordered. "I want to see you drink it, the whole bottle."

"What?" John protested. "I have work to do, I can't—"

"Did you pour chloral hydrate in there? Everyone knows Sarah doesn't drink, so you must've mixed it pretty strong to make it effective with a drink or two," Lyndall stated.

John looked offended. "Are you accusing me of trying to drug her?" He attempted to look appalled by the accusation.

"You're damned right, I am! And there's only one way to prove you didn't, and that's for you to drink it!"

"Oh, this is bull."

"Drink it!" Big Hank hollered, lifting the axe-handle, intending to hit John with it. "You're not leaving here until you do!"

"Hank," John said nervously in a quivering voice, "we're friends. You know I wouldn't do that. I can't believe you are listening to... I mean, I can't believe you're accusing me of doing something like that. We're all family up here. We watch out for each other. For crying out loud, we're all business owners. Why would I want to hurt my customers?" John swung the bottle loosely in his hand as he spoke.

"If that bottle drops and breaks, I'll bust your head open. Second, she ain't your customer. Now drink it, and I'm not telling you again!" Big Hank warned.

"Fine, if it will make you fellers happy, but I'm not losing money on this bottle. It's a ten-dollar bottle of wine shipped in from Europe. Do you think I'm going to waste it just to prove to you I'm innocent of your disgusting accusations? Someone has to pay for it."

"I'll buy the damned bottle! So, if there's nothing else in it, you'll get a free drunk. It's a bargain. Now drink it!" Big Hank demanded.

John stood still, wordlessly looking at the two men. He shook his head and hesitated before saying, "There's nothing in it."

Lyndall answered before Big Hank could. "I'm guessing you considered the fact that she doesn't drink and mixed it stronger than you normally would. So, if there isn't, you have nothing to worry about, but if you did, you might end up dying from an overdose. Now, let's see you pop that cork and start drinking!"

John looked at Lyndall nervously and slowly began to pull the cork out of the bottle. He paused and spoke anxiously, "It's not what you think. I was just trying to help her get some rest."

"What?" Big Hank yelled, raising the axe handle.

John cringed and said in an urgent voice, "Wait! Listen, wait!" he begged as he dropped the bottle to the ground and raised his hands to protect himself from the axe-handle. "I knew she was too worried to sleep. I was just trying to help! I swear, I wasn't going to do anything else. Honest!"

"You're a damned liar!" Lyndall said. He walked up to John and swung a hard, right-handed fist that connected John's cheek. John fell to the street, holding his face. Lyndall followed with a hard kick to John's groin; John curled up into a fetal position, and a small crowd hurried up to watch the unexpected confrontation.

Big Hank took another step and swung the axe-handle, connecting with the meat of John's thigh. John screamed out in pain and rolled back and forth wildly, holding his thigh. He wept from the combination of pain and fear of more pain to come.

Hank was merciless. "Go ahead and scream your damned head off!" Taking the axe-handle in both hands, he whacked John's head, splitting open a wound near its top. Blood flowed down his face. "Listen to me, John. I'm giving you one chance to sell out and leave our town today! Take your losses and get out!" Big Hank spoke through gritted teeth. He pounded John's other thigh with a powerful blow. John screamed and huge tears mixed with the blood on his face. Big Hank shoved the tip of the axe-handle into John's chest and pushed him flat onto his back. Leaning over John to get his attention, he yelled, "Do you understand me?!"

John nodded as he wept.

"Good," Big Hank said. He took a step away and flipped the axe-handle in the air, catching it with one hand, as if he had lost interest in John. "Anyone wanna buy the saloon?" he asked the small crowd that had gathered to watch him and Lyndall beat John.

Lyndall didn't say a word. He only stepped forward and, as John sat up, kicked him viciously in the face. John fell back to the ground and rolled face-down in the street, his body convulsing in pain. Lyndall reached down, flipped John onto his back straddled him.

"Can you hear me?" he asked harshly. "Sarah isn't one of your whores! And we sure ain't going to let you or anyone else hurt her. Her husband's out risking his life to bring our money back, and you tried to take advantage of that! Not in our town, you sick son of a bitch!" He grabbed the axe-handle from Big Hank. He swung it in a wide half-circle and delivered a solid blow to John's crotch.

"Ohhh!" Big Hank cringed. Then he chuckled.

John seemed to freeze from shock. In great pain and finding it difficult to breathe, he rolled to his side and vomited. Nothing came out of his mouth except the disgusting sound of retching.

The small crowd began to talk among themselves. Some folks started crying.

Lyndall paid scant attention to the crowd as he watched John. "Sell your saloon to the bank when you can stand and get out of town! If you're here tomorrow night, or ever again, you'll wish you were dead. Guaranteed!"

"Lyndall," Big Hank said with concern. "They're bringing bodies into town, but it's not Jack and the boys doing the riding."

"What?" Lyndall turned to look at the bank.

Two Huntsville deputies led a string of horses and two mules. Four bodies were tied over the animals' saddles. The crowd recognized the horses as those of Dustin and his father. The other horse they recognized was the one the stranger, Octavius, rode out of town.

"This doesn't look good," Lyndall said, and a sickening feeling swept through him. He walked to the deputies along with the other townsfolk.

"Gentlemen," one deputy said somberly. "We went to help your sheriff capture those bank robbers. We found Jack and his posse about twelve miles south of here. It looks like they camped on a ridge there. All of them had been shot except Dustin, who had his throat cut."

A series of gasps came from the crowd when they heard the news. The Huntsville deputy dismounted and continued, "The sheriff and the rest of our posse are still hunting the murderers. They send their condolences. We could identify the bodies of the men we knew: Jack, Dustin, and Mike Hall. But we don't know who the fourth body is. Maybe you can identify him for us. He was found a short distance from the others and had been carefully covered with a blanket."

The deputy walked to the horse carrying the fourth body, and pulled away the blanket covering, revealing Cal Pierce, his long hair hanging straight down.

Lyndall sighed. "That's Cal Pierce."

Big Hank took a deep breath and exhaled heavily when he saw his employees, Mike and Cal. "Where's his brother? You didn't find any others?"

The deputy shook his head. "No. There were two sets of horse tracks leaving the camp. The sheriff and his men are following them now."

Lyndall looked at Hank. "Then Nathan and that Octavius fellow must be going after the killers." He paused, looked at the ground and shook his head in sorrow. "I probably better go let Sarah know."

Hank nodded. "I'll go with you. Miss Sarah isn't going to take the news well, I'm afraid."

The deputy had seen the men beating John in the street as he rode into town. He nodded at John still lying on the dusty road. "I'll ask. So...did he break the law or just deserve a little justice?"

Lyndall shook his head. "Um, he intended to some dirty work. He's selling his saloon today, if you're interested, and he'll be leaving town by tomorrow. At least he'd better, or he'll disappear."

With tears in his eyes, he looked at Hank and said, "Let's go see Sarah."

SARAH EXHALED SHARPLY when she learned about the massacred posse. She went weak and stumbled to a chair, shocked by Lyndall's words.

"We have every reason to believe Nathan's alive, Sarah. Cal's body was covered with his blanket, and there were two sets of horse tracks leaving the camp. It appears as though Nathan and that old prospector went after the murderers."

Sarah shook her head slightly and said, "He promised me he'd bring Nathan back alive. He gave me his word."

"Who did, Miss Sarah?" Big Hank asked softly.

As if her thoughts were a thousand miles away, Sarah looked at Big Hank and said, "That man. Octavius. I doubt he'll break his word to me."

"He seems to have kept it so far. I'm sure Nathan is fine."

Weeping softly, Sarah said, "No, he's not. Cal is dead. A worse thing could not happen to him. Wherever he is, he's not all right." She spoke as if the news hadn't sunk in yet.

Not knowing what else to do, Lyndall said, "Well, I'm sure he'll be home in a day or two."

Sarah let more tears run down her cheeks and said quietly, "I told them not to go. I looked into Octavius' eyes before they left. He'll die to make sure Nathan comes home to me if he can help it. I know he will. He gave his word."

Hank said, "I'm sure you're right, Miss Sarah."

Sarah stood up and wiped her eyes. "Well, there's nothing I can do except pray and leave my husband's life in God's hands. In the meantime, I have work to do." She sniffled and wiped her eyes again.

"Is there anything we can do for you?" Lyndall asked.

Sarah peered at him with a smile as she forced her tears away. "You could bring me another dozen mason jars and lids. It looks like I will be working longer than I had planned tonight."

"We'll bring you some supper, too," Big Hank said. "Sarah, I just want you to know that we love you folks. Anything you want or need, just let us know, okay?"

Sarah nodded. "Thank you." Again, she had to fight her tears back.

Big Hank walked to her and put his big arms around her. She broke down and cried on his chest. He didn't say anything; he just held her as she wept.

35

Pick Lawson's mare was in bad shape. It was lathered with sweat, covered with scrapes and pock-marked with bleeding wounds. He had tried riding her too fast across the scree field coming up Windsor Ridge when she lost her footing, fell and began sliding downhill.

Pick jumped off and watched as his mare lowered her haunches and regained her footing. She slid the rest of the way down the hill on her rump. Although she'd already accumulated many scrapes over the course of the past two days through the mountain, she now bore a couple of deep cuts that bled profusely. Pick ran down the scree field as quickly as he could, because he knew he didn't have much time to collect his exhausted mare and get up the mountain. He had no chance of escape without her, so he forced her to get up and try the scree field again.

Normally, he would never treat his mare so badly, but he had a posse close behind him, and his life was on the line. Pick knew the only way his mare would make it to the top was if he led her on his own two feet. It was a long climb, but he managed to lead his bleeding horse across the scree and up to the top of Windsor Ridge.

Once they'd achieved solid ground, Pick remounted. The old man on the mule he had run across on the top of Windsor Ridge had startled him. He was sure he had left the posse behind him, but right there in front of him was a man where he'd never dreamed he'd see one. Pick had panicked, and his instincts kicked in. He drew his revolver and took a shot at the man while forcing his injured horse to run down a steep, uneven hill. Pick knew better than to run his horse on rough ground, but then again, his life was the one on the line.

The poor mare lost her footing and fell, hard, onto her knees. Pick lost his revolver during the fall and his struggle to stay in the saddle while he forced the mare back to her feet. Pick and his mare hobbled down the mountain through the thickening forest as fast they could.

Pick smelled the scent of meat cooking over a fire, and it alarmed him. The posse's camp must be nearby. He rode down the mountain, but his horse stopped beside a stream. Breathing heavily, the mare started drinking. Pick got off his saddle to get a drink and refill his dry canteen.

Sitting on a patch of grass for a second, he gazed at his horse. She had been a great girl for the past three years, but he could see she was done. She was not only exhausted and bleeding but holding her rear leg off the ground. Her haunch trembled, as well, from her many injuries.

She couldn't take another step without limping, let alone carry him over the next hill. He had pushed her farther than a man should to get him this far, but now he was on foot. He could not ask his beautiful mare to give him any more than she already had. He watched her turn away from the stream and begin eating some of the grass. A few days of rest, water and nutrition might get the girl's strength back, but it would not heal her injured leg or the cuts slowly dripping blood onto the grass.

Pick shook his head, stood and unsaddled his mare. He took the bridle off as well, and gave her a soft slap on the haunch to let her know she was free to roam. He debated putting her out of her misery, thereby saving her from the inevitable, but he decided that, just like himself, she deserved a fighting chance to get out of these mountains and back to civilization alive. Pick only had his rifle to protect himself now, and he knew he wouldn't have much time until the posse found him. His decision to ride up the scree field had wasted much of his lead on them. He could begin walking out of the mountains, but there were twenty miles of rugged wilderness between him and Jessup Valley. The posse would be upon him before he got a mile from where he now stood.

He couldn't surrender to the posse, or they'd kill him like they had Karl. Even if he somehow convinced them to take him back to Loveland alive, he'd be hung and left hanging as a warning for others. It had become clear to him that the men of Loveland were merciless and there was no way he would survive if they found him alive. He could hide somewhere and hope they wouldn't find him, but those mountain boys seemed to know how to track a man really-well, and he knew they'd find him. His options were few as he sat beside the stream, defeated.

There was no way out of this mess. He was trapped in a losing battle without enough ammunition to fight a posse. He had to do something, though. He forced himself to sit still and think, rather than react to the panic that wanted him to run as fast as he could. There had to be something he could do to survive. With a deep breath and a sense of hopelessness, he looked at his saddle and saw the coiled-up rope he'd used at night to tie his horse.

An idea began forming in his head. He stood, went to his horse, and grabbed the rope. He measured about four feet of rope and cut it off with his knife. About two feet up from the end of the piece he'd cut, he tied a bowline knot that wouldn't let the rope slip. He made a loop with the remainder of the rope and tied another bowline knot. He pulled the loop over his head and shoulders, so the rope was wrapped around his chest and under his arms. Satisfied, he took the longer piece of rope and tied a makeshift noose around the two knots he had tied on the shorter length that wrapped around his chest. Then he tied his noose and hid the shorter length with the knots in the center, so the noose wrapped tightly around the shorter piece, the two bowline knots securing his large loop to the noose.

When he was satisfied that the noose looked authentic and wouldn't tighten around his neck, he removed his shirt and pulled the loop of the shorter rope through his shirt collar, and then over his head and under his arms. He pulled his shirt back on to hide that rope, then pulled the noose over around his neck and looked for a limb thick enough to support his weight.

He found a sturdy branch about fifty feet from his horse and climbed the tree to tie the long rope to the branch. He had to make sure the rope wasn't too long and that it allowed his feet to touch the ground. Sure the length was right, he tied a secure knot around the branch and then carefully positioned himself to drop down and hang. Pick verified that his knife was within reach on his empty gun-belt and then checked it again just to make sure he could reach it.

Taking a deep breath, knowing that once he allowed

himself to fall, he'd be hanging by his armpits until the posse found him. Knowing they could come upon him at any second, he lowered himself and came to a jolting stop as the rope tightened under his arms. It was only then he realized he should've lined the rope with cloth as it began to burn into his skin. Suspended two feet off the ground, his body swayed lightly as he watched his horse eating grass. The longer he hung by his underarms, the more agonizing the rope burns became. It felt like the rope was tearing his skin apart little by little, and the pain was becoming unbearable. However, he knew he couldn't cut the rope to save himself from the pain just to be shot or hung for real when the posse found him. Thirty minutes later, he was tempted to cut the rope, he was in such agony. The rope burned as he had never imagined it could.

Pick was about to reach for his knife and end the torment when he noticed his mare lift her head and point her ears at the forest. Somebody was coming. Pick dropped his head and let his body go limp, like a dead man's would. From this moment on, he would not make a move or sound. If they cut him down, he'd fall heavily and crumple to the ground. If they decided to bury him, he'd endure it. If they tied him over a horse to take him back to town, he'd play dead until the sun went down. Then he'd have a better chance to escape. And if they discovered he was alive he would pretend to be unconscious.

What he hoped, though, was that they'd believe he'd hung himself and leave him there to rot. He just wished they'd hurry, because he couldn't take much more of the burning sensation under his arms!

36

Octavius had ridden down the mountain slowly. He knew Pick's horse was injured. There was no way to know how far it would go before it collapsed for good. It was only reasonable to assume a man on foot and running for his life would set up an ambush and wait for Octavius to ride into it.

Another reason to ride down the mountain carefully was simply due to the steep, tough terrain. Experience told Octavius that if a man ran his injured horse down such a potentially crippling landscape, he was panicking and desperate to get away. Unfortunately for the man on the run, his horse had fallen and was now limping. The uneven terrain even made Octavius' own horse stumble a couple of times, despite the easy pace they were walking.

It was easy to see why the other man's horse had fallen. Octavius wondered how badly the horse had been hurt. Closing in on the last bank robber, Octavius had to reason like the robber would reason and move off the trail to avoid an ambush. Octavius entered the tree line and saw scrapes from horseshoes against the hard ground and occasional dents in the fir needles. The most telling sign for Octavius to follow were blood droplets every five or six feet. They meant the horse was bleeding consistently from its wounds.

As the forest thickened, grew heavier with shadows and scant rays of sunlight beaming through the trees, Octavius knew he was walking into a good ambush area. The light would occasionally blind him for a second, and he had to refocus his eyes through light to shadow. Octavius steered his horse to the left about a hundred yards off the robber's trail and slowly rode down the mountain, listening to any sound he could hear, while he searched for any sign of the man's trail.

When he came to the mountain's bottom, Octavius tied his horse to a tree limb and walked carefully back to the original trail. A stream ran at the bottom of the hill. Octavius knew the robber would have to stop there to let his horse drink some water, at the very least, before moving on. He slowly walked closer and paused when he saw the robber's horse staring in his direction, its ears perked up, listening.

The horse snorted and went back to eating grass. It looked to be quite scraped up and showed deep cuts, but other than exhaustion and a lame back leg, it looked as if it would recover, given time and proper care. The horse was unsaddled and without a bridle.

Octavius knelt low and crawled closer to try to locate the robber hiding somewhere nearby, waiting for him. It was then that he spotted the robber hanging from a tree limb about fifty yards upstream from where he was. Evidently, the man had chosen to kill himself rather than face the posse.

Octavius frowned and stood, his revolver in hand. He placed it back into his holster and walked into the clearing. He gave the horse a gentle greeting as he passed it. He looked at the hanging corpse and shook his head in disgust. No matter how hard the odds were against the man, to fight —or at least *try* to fight—was admirable. Suicide couldn't be respected, couldn't be honored, and it couldn't be anything but weak and cowardly. Octavius walked to the saddle bags and knelt to search for his gold. He searched one bag and then the other, tossing all their belongings onto the grass as he searched. He found no trace of the bank bag with the money and gold in the saddle bags. Furious, he flipped the saddle over to look underneath of it, and then stood and yelled, "Where is it?"

He looked around for anything that might have been set out to be found by chance, but the only other thing he saw was the hanging corpse. He walked to the dead man and patted his pockets, then pulled the man's boots off one at a time to check their insides. The man's loose wool socks came off with the boots.

Finding nothing, Octavius searched the area for anyplace the dead man might have hidden the money. He was growing more aggravated the longer he searched and found nothing. "Where the hell is it!" he demanded to no one as he frantically searched for any freshly dug holes or obvious places where the loot might have been hidden. Finally, he paused and stared at the body, biting bottom lip, furious that he couldn't find his money. He took a deep breath and then yelled at the dead man, "Where'd you put the damned gold!" Then he pulled out his revolver and aimed it at the body.

Watching the stranger through barely opened eyes, Pick immediately held up his hands and hollered quickly, "I don't have it! I don't have the money, I swear! It's in Deuce's saddlebag, every bit of it!" he spoke desperately, fearfully.

Startled at first, Octavius then stood still and dropped

his hand to his side. He couldn't think of anything to say except, "What the hell?" He was awestruck by what he saw.

"The money, it's in Deuce's saddlebag! One of your friends shot him on a hill back over in the valley. All the money's in there, I swear! I know you could arrest me, but I'm begging you to let me go. All my friends are dead, and you'll get your money back. Please, all I want to do is go home. I swear, I will never—"

"Hush!" Octavius ordered. He walked up to Pick and eyed him curiously. "How'd you do that?" He looked at the rope, put his hand on Pick's leg, and turned him around to look at the backside of the noose. "How did you rig that?"

"Um...I tied a loop in the rope to suspend my weight. The noose hides the knot. To make it look like I'm hanging, sir."

Octavius looked at Pick in the eyes. "You come up with that yourself, or did you learn it from somebody?"

Pick said nervously. "I didn't have any other choice, sir. I just thought it might work."

Octavius nodded appreciatively. "I might use that myself someday."

Pick said quickly, "You don't have to arrest me. Just let me hang here and go get the money before the rest of the posse arrives. I know you don't owe me anything, but I'm begging you to have some mercy on me. Please, let me go."

Octavius looked seriously at Pick. "Why did you kill your friend?"

"Huh? I didn't—"

"Back on the hill, you killed your young friend. Why?"

"I didn't kill anyone!" Pick lied.

"You're lying to me. Lie one more time, and I'll shoot you and let you hang here," Octavius said, irritated.

Pick frowned. "He couldn't ride and kept crying about it.

317

He would've slowed me down and would've talked on and on, so, I shot him." He closed his eyes, knowing he would be arrested for murder now too.

Octavius nodded his understanding. "I've done the same thing before. You won't get far on your horse, nor will you get very far on foot. I'll tell you what. I'll go look for my money and if it's not there, I'll come back and find you. I will hang you myself. I don't want to see you again, so if you're lying to me about the money, now is the time to be truthful."

"I swear, I don't care about anything except going home. The money is in Deuce's saddlebag. All of it is, I swear!"

Octavius nodded. "I'm taking your weapons but have a good day."

"Sir, if I'm to walk out of here, I'll need my rifle. There's mountain lions and grizzlies up here!"

Octavius shrugged. "There's a lot more than that up here, including me. The money better be there."

37

Nathan Pierce had taken a chance to trust Adam. He told Adam how he had met Sarah, but when he mentioned being in the cavalry, Adam seemed more interested in discussing that.

Adam shared cavalry stories before Nathan could finish telling him about his engagement to Sarah.

Though Adam had some interesting stories, Nathan had a reason for telling Adam about his having to run away with Sarah to marry her. He told Adam the whole story without missing a detail. Maybe it was his exhaustion, or maybe numbness of losing his brother. Maybe it was the pain that stiffened his body after his horse's fall; maybe it was the fear of being killed by Octavius, or perhaps it was his desperation to get back to Sarah before it was too late. Whatever inspired him, it simply felt good to finally tell someone the truth, even if he didn't have a tangible reason to trust the man. Sometimes, you can just meet a man and know he is a man of integrity and honor.

Adam was that kind of man. He wanted to return the money to the bank, even though he could so easily get away with keeping it. A man of that caliber wasn't likely to sell out an innocent man for monetary gain.

When Nathan finished telling his story, he looked at Adam and said, "So now you know why I need to get back home to my wife. If she thinks I'm dead, she won't wait very long until she has no choice but to go back to her parents. If she does that before I get home, we may never see each other again. My father-in-law, the great Christian philanthropist of Sacramento, Louis Eckman, has a twenty-five-thousand-dollar bounty out to the Pinkerton's, and ten thousand to any other bounty hunters to kill me and return his daughter. Now you understand why I'm anxious to get home, I hope. And what I'm risking by trusting you."

Adam pulled his horse to a halt and looked at Nathan seriously. "I've read about Louis Eckman in the paper and his ongoing search for his kidnapped daughter. It's one of the great mysteries of the west, or so they say."

"She wasn't kidnapped! I swear to you! Take me back to Loveland and talk to her yourself!" Nathan spoke desperately. He now regretted having shared his story because Adam was familiar with Eckman's version. "The only way she'd go back to her parents is if I'm dead or she thinks I am. I love my wife more than anything else in this world, Adam. If she goes back to her parents, old Louis will make sure I'm dead so we could never leave Sacramento together. I don't want to live without her; she is my life. So, I am asking you to help me to get home to her before she goes to be with her parents." He wiped his eyes to hide his tears from Adam. He added, "And please, don't tell anyone about us. I could be killed if the wrong people found out who we are."

Adam frowned. "I'll make sure you get home. But let me ask you: what are you going to do? Just hide in Loveland forever?"

Nathan took a deep breath. "Do I have a choice? Where else can we go? My face could be in every hotel and law office from New York to Alaska. As you said, it's one of the great mysteries of the west, I guess. All I want is to live my life raising a family with my wife; that's all. I haven't done anything wrong except fall in love with the wrong rich man's daughter. And I don't think that's a crime worth a ten-thousand-dollar bounty being put on my head! Do you?"

Adam shook his head. "I have a wife I love, too."

"Put yourself in my shoes then and imagine the risk of losing everyone you care about. All you have to do is tell the wrong person about me, and my life's over. So again, I'm asking you man to man: please keep this between you and me. Don't tell your brother, and just let us be."

"Why doesn't she write her father a letter and tell him how happy she is and to take that bounty off your head? I know that, as a father myself, I'd want my daughter to be happily married above all else. Of course, I'd want her husband to be able to support her and her family but being treated well is even more important than that. My father didn't treat my mother well, so that's a big issue for me."

"All Louis and my mother-in-law care about is their reputation. It doesn't sound very impressive to their friends that their only, highly educated daughter married an ex-cavalry private with no professional skills other than two hands to labor with. If I had been an officer, it might've sounded better, but I wasn't. It's all about their reputation and has nothing to do with what Sarah wants." Nathan paused and then added sarcastically, "But that's what good Christians do, isn't it? They care more about their reputation and impressing others than actually living the Christian life."

"Some Christians, maybe, but not the ones I know,"

Adam said. "I'm a Christian, but I don't particularly care what people think of me. Nor do I judge anyone else too hard when they fall short. But it's not right to spill innocent blood or to pay someone else to do it for you."

"I'm afraid my in-laws have darkened my view of Christians and Christianity in general. I want nothing to do with religion anymore. Well, I didn't until today."

Adam shook his head as he said, "Christians are just people. We all have our struggles and weaknesses. Refusing to believe in or serve God because of what a Christian said or did to you makes about as much sense as saying every brown-haired woman is an adulteress because my uncle's brown-haired wife was. No thinking person would judge all brown-haired women by the actions of one man's wife, would they? But they do the church; they do Christianity. You shouldn't refuse to serve the Lord and risk losing your own soul because of what a person said or did to you. Remember, Jesus is perfect, but no one else is. Men are as individual as women are, and not all brown-haired women are like my uncle's ex-wife, are they?"

"No," Nathan replied slowly. "My wife has blonde hair, though, just in case."

Adam grinned. "Using brown-haired women probably wasn't the best analogy to begin with, but the truth's the same. It's not uncommon to meet someone who is bitter against God because of what a Christian did or said to them. You mentioned your father-in-law's actions made you question your faith, right? I assure you: God will hold him accountable for his actions, but you'll be held accountable for yours, too. Refusing to serve the great and holy God because of what someone else says or does, is exactly what the devil wants you to do. It's best to worry about the plank in our own eye and let those who give the Lord a bad name be judged by the Lord Himself. In other words, there won't be any finger-pointing at the Judgment seat of Heaven. It comes down to two, and only two, answers: you either knew and served Jesus, or you didn't. It doesn't get much simpler than that, but it does have eternal consequences.

"Let's just say if that guy you're after, Octavius, comes looking for us and shoots me, I'm going to Heaven. Not because I'm a nice guy, but because of my faith in and relationship with Jesus. I guess the question really is, if you were shot and killed today, would the bitterness you have for your father-in-law be worthy of not serving Jesus? I don't think we will be able to explain our way into Heaven, Nathan, so get yourself right with God while you can. Nobody lives forever, and no one's promised to live through today, let alone tomorrow, as you know."

Nathan took a deep breath. "I had a bit of clarity on that earlier today. The Lord must have heard me, because you found me. Now I just have to get home to Sarah. But I have to tell you that Octavius could come riding out of any one of these tree lines or over the next hill. So, you had better be ready for the unexpected, because we never saw him, yet he seemed to be all around us. He shot that guy there in the meadow from about six feet back in the trees. It wouldn't surprise me if he did that to us, as well." Nathan looked around anxiously.

Adam nodded. "We have the advantage of knowing he's out here and what he's after. So, what we're going to do is circle all the way around the valley. That way, if he does come looking for us, we won't run headlong into him, but circle around him while he picks up our trail back where I found you. He'll be behind us, but by the time he trails us to Windsor Ridge, it'll be too dark for him to risk going up it. He'll have to stay the night out here. In the meantime, pay attention to your horse. Our horses will let us know if they notice anyone."

"I think you're assuming a lot. We don't know where he is. He could be anywhere out here! And you sure don't want him behind us. He could sneak up and cut your throat without you even knowing it, that I can tell you! My brother and I were both in the cavalry, but nothing we learned helped us against him. I'm just letting you know. Don't take him lightly!"

"He's just a man, not a ghost, and his horse must be exhausted by now, too. He needs to rest at some point. The moon will be bright enough tonight for us to make our way back to my camp fairly-easily if we can make it to Windsor Ridge before it gets too dark. What all do you know about Octavius anyway?"

"I know he's a killer," Nathan snapped bitterly. "He's the one who killed the miners on Veneta Creek everyone's talking about. He fought for the south, and rode with a man named Champ Ferguson during the war—"

"Really?" Adam interrupted suddenly.

"Yeah. My brother figured that out. He always liked military history and knew all about that Ferguson guy. I'm afraid I don't know a whole lot about him, other than he was a killer and was hung for his war crimes."

Adam nodded. "They were guerilla fighters. They were a heartless bunch of men who killed without conscience. And, sure enough, ambushes were their favorite tactic. Hmm, well he probably has some brutal war stories to tell, but I doubt he'll want to sit down and swap lies with us. What do you think?"

"No, he's not going to sit down and swap war stories with us. He'll just kill us if he gets the chance. I set out to follow him, but now he's somewhere behind us most likely, and I am in no condition to face him. I think our best bet is to set up our own ambush and wait to kill him when he comes."

Adam looked at Nathan and smiled. "If you're worried, you'd better get right with God. Because somewhere along the way, we might have to fight before we can get you home. Lord willing, we will get home to our families safely, huh?"

"Lord willing...that's kind of a questionable statement, isn't it?"

Adam shook his head. "No. When you have a relationship with Jesus—I mean a real one—you learn to trust Him. You learn to count on him to help you get through challenges like this one. It is faith, not luck, that is going to get you back home. Wait and see."

38

Luther Fasana looked at his pocket watch and frowned. It was nearing seven in the evening, and Adam still hadn't made his way back to camp. Luther had trusted the stranger he had met on the mountain and had taken his word that Adam was okay. The man had seemed to account for the shooting throughout the day, so Luther had no reason not to believe him. Luther normally took people at their word.

According to the stranger named John Jones, Adam had been shot at, and returned fire, killing one or two of the bank robbers. Then he rode north on a dead man's horse. It didn't make a whole lot of sense to Luther that Adam would go north after being shot at and forced to kill a man. Luther personally didn't think Adam would be in the mood to hunt a wolf after taking a man's life, but it wasn't the first time he'd been forced to take a man's life in self-defense. Adam was an eccentric man in some ways, but he was reasonable. He could be very determined and hardheaded, so if he was set on getting that wolf, which he had seemed to be, he would track it down no matter how far it went or how long it took. At some point, Adam was sure to come back to camp, and that wolf's hide would be strapped to his saddle, Luther had no doubt. Adam was no greenhorn and could take care of himself, so Luther had to believe Adam was fine, and forced the worry out of his mind as he prepared his and Adam's dinner for the night.

He dumped some canned beans into a pot and mixed in some freshly chopped dried venison and other ingredients to make a nice pot of chili to cook over the fire. He heard an approaching horse and hoped to see Adam ride out of the darkening tree line, but he heard the man named John Jones call out, "Hey, Luther, is it all right if I come on in?"

Looking through the evening's fading light, it took Luther a few moments to recognize his new friend, John Jones. He was standing in the shadows beside his horse, holding the reins.

"Howdy, John! Come on over. I got dinner cooking and could use the company," Luther said happily enough.

"Smells good, even from back there a ways. Your nephew's horse isn't back yet?" he asked as he led his horse out of the trees and to the creek to drink and eat some grass. The black-and-white paint belonging to the bank robber who'd shot at him was being led by John's horse. It was limping and had numerous scrapes and cuts that had stopped bleeding.

"Nope, not yet. I was hoping he'd be back by now, but he must be hunting that wolf, is all I can figure, if all you told me is true. I can't imagine he'd be doing anything else."

"I didn't lie to ya, Luther. As far as I know, he's alive and well. And apparently, he's determined to get that wolf." Octavius grinned as he tied the reins to a tree branch beside the creek. He untied the paint and tied it to a tree as well. He turned to walk to the fire but paused. He bent and pulled Adam's metal-bladed tomahawk out of the wood block they used as a chopping block. He looked at it with interest, then flipped it up, so it landed with the blade sticking into the block. "That piece of weaponry is made for throwing and hacking, not splitting wood," he said. He left the tomahawk in the block and walked to the fire where Luther sat, watching him.

"It works for just about anything a man uses it for," Luther said of the tomahawk. "Adam picked that up in the Snake War in one of his hand-to-hand battles. I think it was at the battle of Henry Creek. Yeah, he'll hunt that wolf until he gets it, no matter how long it takes. Have a seat, John, and I'll get you some food."

John sat on a wooden block and watched Luther scoop some chili with venison onto a metal plate and hand it to him along with a spoon. "Thank you. I haven't eaten much the last couple days."

"There's some fresh jerky wrapped up in that cloth there, if you want some," Luther offered, pointing at a folded cloth on the ground. "I've got plenty, so make yourself welcome to it."

"Thanks again," Octavius said through a mouth full of beans. He ate hungrily.

"I see you must've found the man who shot at me? Where's he at?" Luther asked as he took a bite of his food, nodding at the paint horse.

Octavius nodded. "I found him, but he hung himself. Poor guy..."

"He would've been hung anyway most likely, for robbing the bank and killing your posse and such. It seems he was doomed either way."

Octavius looked at Luther wryly. "He wasn't dead. That

crazy fella rigged the rope to look like he was hanging, but it was suspending him from under his arms. It was the craziest thing I've ever seen. And I've seen a lot!" he said with a short chuckle.

"So, did you hang him for real? I notice he isn't here," Luther said.

Octavius shook his head and took a deep breath. "I thought about it. But he didn't have one cent of the money, had lost all his weapons, crippled his horse pert' near to death, watched his friends get themselves killed, and the man was scared to death. He was just a simpleton who got swindled into a bad deal. If I'd taken him back to town, they'd lynch him before they asked his name. So, I thought I'd let him go. The long walk home will give him plenty of time to reconsider his career in life. I don't think he'll ever break the law again," he said with a smile.

"What about the murdering of your friends?" Luther asked curiously.

"He didn't fire one shot at the posse. I can attest to that."

Luther said. "He sure shot at me fast enough. If he had shot at my nephew, he never would've made it to the tree line up there."

"You're not quick to shoot back, huh?" Octavius smiled as he finished off his plate of beans. "Luther, it's been a long time since I've tasted anything so tasty. Mind if I get some more?"

"Go ahead, there's plenty. Thank you, though. Raising three kids on my own, I definitely had to learn to cook."

Octavius' face grew solemn as he asked, "How old are your children? All growed up with families of their own, I suspect."

Luther nodded. "Yep. Now I have a few grandchildren I

get to play with. They're a lot of fun. Do you have any grand-children?"

Octavius' expression revealed a lifetime of regret and lost love. "I don't even know where my own children are, or if they're even alive, Luther. I don't know if I have grand-children or not." He smiled sadly as the words seem to sink into his heart. He continued softly, "I once had a nice little farm and a beautiful family back in Kentucky. My wife's name was Lucinda, and she was the most beautiful lady in the world to me. We had three children—two boys and a daughter—just like you. Jared, Jake and Jessica. Lucinda wanted to name them all J-names, so even if I messed up on the names, I could blame it on the first letter of their names." He smiled at the memory. It soon faded and he continued, "Anyway, the war was coming, and a band of blue coats came looking for my wife's cousin. They beat me near to death. My wife tried to help me, and they stabbed her. They murdered her for no reason. She was just trying to save me. I loved my family, Luther. That day, in that moment, those men started a war with me." Octavius looked at Luther coldly and concluded, "I took my children to my sister-in-law's and went and joined my wife's cousin to fight the Yanks. I killed a lot of them, but I don't know if I killed the ones who murdered Lucinda. I never went back home after the war. I assume my children think I'm dead."

"It's never too late... you could still get to know your chil-dren while there's time," Luther offered sincerely.

"No," Octavius said sadly. "It's best that I let them think I'm dead. I haven't done many good things since then. I was a good man once. I was a lot like you in fact." He shook his head slowly. "But not anymore. Do you have whisky by chance?" he asked to change the topic.

Luther shook his head. "No, I never touch the stuff. I can make up some coffee though."

"In a bit, maybe," Octavius said as he finished his second plate of chili.

"You're welcome to get more if you'd like." Luther nodded at the pot on the fire.

"No, I've had my fill, thank you. It was very good."

"You know, we're about the same age, and I know men about our age often look back over our lives and have our fair share of regrets. I know I do, but you know it's never too late to make amends. Your children and grandchildren might just be thrilled to discover you're alive, no matter what you've done since then."

Octavius shook his head. "Not likely. I'm afraid my regrets will remain my regrets. I would like to say they were few, but if I could relive my life again, I would take Lucinda and our children to the north, where the war couldn't touch them. I suppose that's my biggest regret in a life of regrets: not protecting my family. How's a man supposed to be a man, Luther, when he can't even protect his family? I've been making up for it ever since, though. Have you ever heard of that saying, a new coat of paint covers up a lot of sins? New beginnings do, too, so I'll be heading to Montana soon enough to get a little place to live out what's left of my years."

Luther took a deep breath and said, "It's my belief that a man's hindsight can become a dark shadow if you let it. It's a guilty pleasure, I guess you could say, if you let it control your life. It doesn't have to. The painful shadows of long ago may be there, but that's all they are: a memory. Sometimes you just have to turn away from the past and walk forward in life one day at time. The future has so much more to look forward to than the past does. As for covering up sins, why cover them, when God is willing to forgive them if you ask him to. Even when we can't seem to forgive ourselves, for things we've done or things we have failed to do, Jesus will forgive us if we ask him to."

Octavius held up a hand and said plainly, "I'm not interested in hearing any god talk, Luther. I appreciate your hospitality and enjoy your company, I really do. Which is odd for me, because most of the time I can't stand being around people." He looked at Luther sincerely, "That makes you a rarity. But I won't listen to any religious talk. My Lucinda was a God-fearing Christian and so was I. It didn't do us any good, did it? God sure didn't protect her, and he sure didn't protect my family, so you can keep all of that to yourself, please."

Luther could not help but notice the anger flash in Octavius' eyes. He asked cautiously, "Can I ask you one thing?"

Octavius looked at him and held up one finger. "One thing. Luther, I like you, but I don't want to hear about a good or loving god. If God was loving and righteous, none of the hell I lived through would've happened. My Lucinda and I would have spent our lives raising our family, and I'd be there with them today. So, don't tell me how great or loving your God is, because I don't want to hear it. He wasn't that great to me, now was he? Ask your one thing, and let's end this conversation, please."

"I know what it's like to lose your wife; my wife died, too. Oh, she wasn't killed like yours was, but she died anyway. She was..." Luther paused to smile sadly in remembrance. "She was my second wife, but she was my one and only true love. We had one baby girl before she died. I was married before her, but my first wife ran off with a younger fella and left me to raise my two boys alone. I've had my share of heartaches, John, but I know this world with all its wars, murder, injustice, and pure evil isn't God's kingdom or his will. I don't have all the answers as to why bad things happen, but they do. They happen to everyone at some point or another."

Octavius waved his hand again to stop Luther. Frustration began showing on his face. "I don't want a sermon. I said you could ask one thing, not give a sermon, Luther. We'll get along best if we don't discuss religion or politics. I don't care about either one, so if you have something to say, or feel you must say, then just say it and get it out of the way. But make it short!"

Luther stared at him, taken back by his sudden hostility. "Well, John, if there's one thing to say then it's this. You're too good of a man to live with all of the regret and guilt you carry around. Come back to the Lord and let him take it all away. He's more than wanting to forgive those sins you're hiding under your layers of paint. He died to forgive them. If you served him once, then come back to Jesus."

Octavius looked at Luther oddly. "You know nothing about me."

"I know deep down you're a good man. Maybe you've taken some wrong trails in life, but deep down you are. I believe you are, anyway. Just remember, it's never too late to get right with the Lord. And there's nothing more secure in life than being right with Jesus."

"Yeah, I've heard that before. Now let me ask you something. I see your gold pan over there. Did you find anything in the creek here?" Octavius asked to change the subject.

Luther shook his head. "No, I've never found much up here. However, we come up here to hunt meat, not gold. You know, John, I just want to tell you one last thing, and that is eternal life isn't all we have through Jesus. I don't have to worry about tomorrow or what's going to happen in the future, because I know God has it all figured out for me. There's a lot of peace in that, and even when heartaches come, and we both know they will, there's still a peace that comes from the Lord Himself, even during the pain. So, you see, serving God isn't just about going to heaven when we die. It's about having a relationship with the Lord today, right now and every tomorrow, too—"

Octavius stood up suddenly in frustration. "Luther, it's been a pleasure meeting you, but my welcome has worn out. Thank you for the good food, but I'm heading back. I've got a long ride, to get across the ridge before dark." He held out his hand for Luther to shake. "I hope we meet again."

"You'll find me in Branson. Just look me up." He shook Octavius' hand firmly. "You can stay the night if you'd like. We have plenty of food and room."

Octavius grinned. "I've heard all the god talk I can stand for one day. Maybe one of these days we'll meet again. But I will take some jerky with me, if you don't mind."

Luther collected quite a bit of jerky for his new friend and watched him put it into his saddlebag. "If you run across my nephew, tell him he missed a good dinner, will ya?"

Octavius got into his saddle and nodded down to Luther. "I will. By the way, if you want to take on an injured horse, there it is. It's my gift to you for the food. Take care, Luther."

"Thank you, but won't that young robber be wanting it?"

Octavius smiled. "The long walk out of the woods will do him some good. Give that horse a good home, Luther."

"You take care of yourself, my friend."

Octavius looked back at Luther. "Friend?" he asked, sounding surprised.

Luther nodded. "I hope so. It doesn't hurt to have a friend, does it?"

Octavius shook his head slowly, a troubled expression on his face. "I don't have friends. You can't trust them."

"Well, maybe now you can."

Octavius grinned again and rode away without saying another word.

39

Adam led Nathan to the farthest western edge of the valley at a steady pace. He had talked to Nathan for a good part of the journey, but the farther they rode, the more trouble Nathan was having keeping his head up and his eyes open. Adam decided to let the young man sleep while he led him around the valley. Adam was anxious to explore new territory, and was exhilarated by the new and beautiful surroundings he found himself in.

This was truly a hidden paradise, and it gave him a sense of understanding about what his grandfather and other early trappers must have experienced when they saw it. The stunning beauty of nature could leave a man breathless. He knew he was not the first person to explore this valley, but so few people had been here, the animals had grown huge. Every species of wildlife was thriving and growing older and larger with time. He had seen a huge bald eagle fly over him, a mule deer that looked as big as an elk, and another bull elk even larger than the one he had shot. Even a fat garter snake with a yellow stripe down its back seemed to be twice as large as the biggest one he'd seen on his ranch.

It was the massive grizzly bear tracks he saw in the soft mud of a stream bed that sent a wave of caution through him. Still, they inspired a deep desire to hunt the beast down and take its hide. Somewhere in this valley was a gigantic grizzly that had to stand at least twelve-feet tall on its hind legs, because one track spread twelve inches across. It sure wasn't a grizzly Adam wanted to run across accidentally—or get close to, for that matter. The sense of wildness and danger in the atmosphere made him feel alive as he explored.

The only thing that concerned him was that the sun had crossed over the sky and was disappearing behind the western mountains rising above him. Most men would make a camp for the night and rest by a fire, but that was out of the question. A murderer traveled this valley somewhere, and it was best not to draw attention to himself by making a fire. Adam doubted Octavius could follow his trail in the dark. He would probably stop and make camp for the night, while Adam led Nathan out of the valley.

The moon would soon be bright enough to see the trail up the scree of Windsor Ridge, and that was all Adam needed. It would be risky, but most of the risk centered on the two horses. He didn't know the horse he rode, or the one Nathan sat upon. He had no idea how either horse would react to the feel of loose rock on the long, steep climb up the mountain, or how well Nathan would remain in the saddle when the trail hit its roughest ground. There was only way to find out, and that was to do it. There was a lot to be concerned about, but Adam never worried about much until it became necessary. Most of the time, it turned out there was nothing to worry about in the first place, so why worry at all?

Adam glanced up to his right as he came out of a

wooded area into another clearing of thick grass. He stopped abruptly. The huge black wolf stood midway up the ridge on a patch of dry grass near rock debris that had fallen and built up from the cliff towering above it. The wolf was about two hundred yards away, looking down at Adam. He saw three other wolves with the black male, but he didn't care about them. He wanted the giant black wolf.

It had been a long day, but he finally had the wolf in sight. Before he could fire a shot, he had to tie the horses' reins to a tree, or chaos might erupt when he shot the wolf. He didn't know how either horse would react to the loud percussion of a weapon firing, and the last thing he wanted was for Nathan to be thrown from the saddle by a rearing horse. The young man was hurting enough without being thrown to the ground again. Adam untied Nathan's reins quickly and lead him to a tree where he tied the reins.

"Hey, wake up. I don't know how your horse will react to gunfire, so be ready," he said without further explanation. "Do you want to get down just in case?"

"Hmm?" Nathan asked drowsily. He had been sleeping for a while now. "What are you doing?"

Adam tied his horse to a tree and pulled his rifle from its scabbard. He walked slowly away from the horses and lifted his rifle. "Look at him, standing there like I'll miss again. I won't miss this time, big fella." He aimed the bead of his sight on the center of the wolf's chest.

"Who? Octavius?" Nathan asked more loudly than Adam expected. Nathan was just becoming conscious of his surroundings after a deep sleep.

"Dang it! You scared him away. Now be quiet!" Adam said with frustration. He knelt down. The wolf had disappeared behind some rocks. It reappeared, standing halfway exposed between two large boulders. Adam narrowed his eyes determinedly and stood up slowly. "There you are."

"Wait, what are you shooting at? You can't shoot, or Octavius will know where we are," Nathan said urgently. "You can't shoot!" Nathan said raising his voice again.

Adam lifted his head from his rifle and looked at Nathan, angry. "I'm getting sick of hearing about Octavius," he said. "I've been tracking that wolf since this morning, and I had him in my sights!"

Nathan didn't back down. "If you pull that trigger, we'll become the hunted. You can always come back to get that wolf, but we can't get out of this valley alive if you take that shot."

Adam glanced at the wolf and shook his head. The wolf stood there as if daring Adam to take his best shot. A part of Adam was tempted to shoot the wolf regardless of what Nathan said. He shook his head with a disgruntled sigh and slowly took the bullet from the chamber of his rifle and put the rifle back into his scabbard. He held the bullet up for the wolf to see and said, "This one's for you. Yeah, I'm going to save it for you."

The wolf stared at him, its ears on the alert. It responded to Adam's words by stepping out farther onto the grass and barking at him.

"Yeah, say what you will," Adam said to the wolf, "but I won't miss next time! Your hide will be hanging above my fireplace before long,"

"What are you talking about?" Nathan asked.

Adam pointed up hill with a grimace. "What do you think I've been talking about? That wolf up there."

Nathan had seen a medium-sized gray wolf a few moments before, but now he followed Adam's finger and was startled by the size of the black wolf. "Oh, my...it's huge!

I can't believe I didn't see it. Wow! And it's just standing there, too."

"I know," Adam exclaimed harshly. He pointed his finger at Nathan, "I'm telling you right now, I'll get you out of this valley and back home, but if I have to kill this Octavius fella here in the valley today, you're going to sit under a tree somewhere and wait quietly until I come back with that condescending beast!"

Nathan smiled despite himself. "Condescending?"

Adam pointed at the wolf. "Look at him! I missed him this morning, but it wasn't my fault. An unexpected gunshot came a fraction of a second before I pulled the trigger. It surprised me! Anyway, look at him, sitting there like a condescending...beast. Somehow, he knows I can't shoot him right now. Yeah, you!" he hollered at the wolf. "I will come back for you!"

"That's the biggest wolf I've ever seen," Nathan said as Adam took his reins and tied them back to his saddle. "Wouldn't it just make you mad if we got down the trail aways and heard Octavius shoot it?" he asked, a slight grin on his lips.

Adam looked at Nathan severely. "That would be very irritating, wouldn't it?"

Nathan grinned. "It might be irritating for you, I suppose, but at least we'd know where Octavius was."

Adam got into his saddle and turned his horse to look back at Nathan. "I'd've had that monster skinned and another thirty pounds of jerky in my teepee, if it wasn't for all of the shooting between you men today!"

Nathan was suddenly outraged. "I haven't shot anyone today, but my brother and three of my friends were murdered this morning! I apologize if the gunshots that killed them disrupted your hunt. The opportunity you're so annoyed about missing came at the cost of some of my best friends' lives!"

Adam exhaled and nodded. He'd never felt lower in his life than he did at that moment. He said softly, "You're right. I apologize."

"No apology needed. Just remember that some of us lost more than a chance at a big wolf today."

Adam nodded and continued forward wordlessly, casting a last glance back up the hill at the wolf. It watched him leave with a victorious bark and howl.

40

Octavius had worked his way over Windsor Ridge and down the scree field into the valley. He had not seen any sign of anyone from his higher elevation, and there was no way to tell where Luther's nephew had wandered once he had crossed over the large hill running through the valley. He could have gone east or west or continued north; there was just no way to know unless he went back to where the bodies of the two bank robbers lay on top of the hill and followed Luther's nephew's trail from the beginning.

What Octavius hoped would be a quick meeting by chance had unfortunately turned into a much longer process than he'd expected. It was getting late in the day by the time he found the body of Deuce McKenna lying awkwardly in the ravine. Flies covered it and the other body nearby. Octavius looked down the hill and saw the dead horse on the valley floor not far from a fallen log. From the ravine, a man in the valley wouldn't be hard to hit, but a man's head partly hidden in a ravine would be a small target from any distance.

Octavius had no desire to harm Luther's nephew. He expected to be able to claim he was the last surviving member of the Loveland posse and needed to return the money. If it all went well, Adam would hand him the bank's belongings, and Octavius would disappear into the woods and never go back to Loveland again. He might go to Montana or perhaps to Canada, but he would leave the Pacific Northwest. He'd even decided not to return to the valley he now rode in. He was getting too old to keep moving around, and he was suddenly within reach of being able to retire at last. He didn't expect any trouble getting the money from Adam, but he did need to find him.

As Octavius rode on, he could not help but wonder what life would have been like if he'd stayed in Tennessee, raised his children and now knew his grandchildren. He had no doubt his children had grown up to be good people and probably had families of their own. His sister-in-law, whom he had asked to raise his children, was a Godly woman who would have loved his children as her own and raised them to be honest, God-fearing people. Octavius didn't have much to be proud of in his life, but deep within him, he believed that, somewhere, his children were living lives that would make him proud. He could be proud of his children, even if he didn't know anything about them. He did know one thing: they were Lucinda's, and nothing bad could come from such a perfect lady. Part of him longed to know what his children were doing now. He wondered if they remembered him as a loving father, or a rogue killer fighting a war built upon vengeance.

Life was fairer to some than to others, but he had been given a raw deal a long time ago. Many men had fought and died in the war, but Octavius had died when Lucinda was murdered in their own front yard. That was the day Octavius Clark, the loving husband and father, died, and the bloodthirsty remains of the former family man came to life. The piece of his soul that died with Lucinda could only be filled with the blood of every Union soldier and sympathizer he could find. Man, woman, or child; it did not matter to Octavius. He killed with the same heartless brutality his friend, Captain Champ Ferguson showed their enemies. Champ and his raiders attacked viciously and left no one alive. They became wanted for war crimes against northern and southern forces and homesteaders by both the Union and the Confederacy.

The only people who'd had nothing to fear from Champ Ferguson and his raiders were loyal southerners who had never said a bad thing against Champ or his gang. Even then, a loyal southerner could be in trouble if he had a local enemy who wanted to see him dead. All it took was a slight rumor of his supposed disloyalty to get back to Champ or one of his men. That man would be dead.

Champ and his raiders killed so indiscriminately that many folks at the time began to say the gang "lived to kill and kill mercilessly." When the war ended, Champ Ferguson was hung for his war crimes. Although Octavius had committed many of the same crimes and was one of the bloodiest of Champ's men, he and the rest of the raiders were pardoned and allowed to go home as free men. Octavius couldn't do that because he no longer had a home. The war was lost, the land was ravaged, and Octavius had nothing left of his life to go back to—so he thought at the time.

Octavius took a deep breath and scanned the valley from a top of the high hill. He saw no evidence of another living person, except the tracks of the dead bank robber's horse going down the north side of the hill—the same way the robbers had come up originally. The only explanation Octavius could think of was that Luther's nephew, Adam, now rode the horse and was following the bank robbers' back-trail for some reason, most likely to find the posse. Octavius was tired of riding. Now that he'd eaten his fill, sleep nagged at him. He didn't have much time, perhaps an hour at most, before the sun retired for the night and darkness overcame the valley.

Along with the darkness, cold would come, and Octavius was getting too old to enjoy a cold night without a campfire, and a place to lay his head. He would follow Adam's trail for a while longer, but he and his horse needed to rest up for the night. He had pushed himself about as hard as he could and needed to find an area with good grass and plenty of water to nourish his horse. He could catch up with Adam tomorrow. It appeared to him that Adam had figured out the man he shot had robbed a bank and was now backtracking the robbers' trail to find the posse and return the money. Octavius was beginning to respect the young man he had never met, but one thing was for sure: he had to find Adam before anybody else did.

He rode down the steep hillside carefully, then rode across the valley to where he had shot and killed the first bank robber that day. He followed Adam's trail, which wasn't too hard, since Adam was following the bank robber's back-trail. Octavius rode past the dead body of Karl Digsby and to the edge of the tree line where he had broken the rifle earlier that day.

Confused, he tried to account for all the horse trails in the meadow. Then he remembered Karl's horse had been left to roam free for most of the day. It appeared Adam had claimed the abandoned horse and was taking it with him. It made sense to circle around the daunting hill he had just come down, as both horses he had commandeered were likely to be as exhausted as his own.

Feeling content with what he believed to be the only reasonable explanation, Octavius looked at the fading sun and decided it was time to find a suitable place to rest for the night. He had seen a small lake toward the middle of the valley, so he rode for it. He eventually found it and made camp beside its beautiful, clear water. He didn't have a tent to protect him from the mosquitoes, but he could make a fire and hope the smoke would keep the biting beasts away from him. He would be tucked away under his wool blanket as well, but of all pests to be burdened with, mosquitoes were perhaps the worst.

Octavius gathered enough firewood to last the night and made a decent-sized fire with enough green brush to make thick smoke to help stave off the bugs and any bears or wolves that might come to investigate the only light in the valley. Once he settled down on his bedroll beside the fire, he closed his eyes. It would be good to get a long night's sleep.

In the morning, he would waste no time cutting across the valley, get to Luther's camp and wait for Adam. Octavius knew that, sooner or later, young Nathan Pierce would make it back to Loveland and organize a much larger and better qualified posse to come after him. If he knew young Nathan like he thought he did, Nathan would lead the party and would have no interest in making an arrest. Octavius smiled as he began to drift off to sleep. Nathan would try to find him, but Octavius would never be found.

Nathan and the people of Loveland could say whatever they wanted about him, but Octavius only cared about one thing: to keep his promise to Nathan's beautiful wife, Sarah. Now Octavius just needed to get the money and gold back from Adam, and then he would disappear for good.

41

Adam Bannister knew riding up the north slope of Windsor Ridge in the dark would be full of risks, not only to him and his horse, but also to Nathan and his horse. Neither man knew the horses they rode, and it was dangerous to take an unknown animal over such rough terrain. A skittish horse could panic and slide down the mountain, maiming itself and its rider in a landslide. Adam could lead his horse up the hill by its reins, but Nathan would have no choice but to sit in the saddle and ride. A large pack of wolves, some enormous grizzly bears, and probably a few big cats hunted at night, and a horse tied at the bottom of the mountain would be too big a temptation for a large predator to pass up. If Adam and Nathan were going up the mountain, they would have to risk going up together. He paused at the bottom of Windsor Ridge and looked at the mountain cliffs that seemed to tower above them like a giant black wall against the starry, moonlit night.

He turned to speak to Nathan, who was exhausted and just wanted to sleep. "Nathan, we're going up that ridge. It looks worse than it is, so just relax and stay in the saddle. If you start to slide down the hill, just hang on and enjoy the ride," Adam knew Nathan was too exhausted to care and would sleep all the way up the ridge, if he could.

Nathan nodded. Adam tied a rope from the horn of Nathan's saddle to his own. He took a moment to pray quietly, then took his horse's reins in his hand and started leading his horse through the talus rock at the bottom of the mountain. To the best of his ability, Adam led the horses and Nathan. They hit an area where the trail had broken free, and Adam's horse stumbled a bit to keep its footing on sliding rocks. Nathan's horse stepped on the same area, too, stumbled, and nearly slipped down the steep grade. The only thing saving man and horse was the rope tied to Adam's saddle, which allowed the horse to regain its footing and get back in line with the lead horse.

Nathan had remained calm and seemed to sleep through the momentary scare. The two men climbed higher and before long, Adam saw the valley below him covered in darkness, except for the moonlight reflecting off the small lake like a gorgeous lamp. Beside it, the small orange flame from a fire pinpointed where Octavius had camped for the night.

In spite of the fire and the beautiful view, Adam didn't dare slow his mount until he'd climbed the scree field and made it to the pass through the ridge. He had to holler to Nathan and wake him as they climbed the last seventy feet or so, because a sleeping man could easily roll out of the saddle and break his neck on the steep grade.

Once they were on solid ground, Adam untied the rope from his saddle horn and climbed into his saddle. Leading Nathan's horse, he nudged his own to move a little faster through the deep ravine and get to the southern side of Windsor Ridge. Carefully, he led Nathan down the mountain toward his camp. Adam knew his Uncle Luther would be interested in knowing why it had taken Adam so long to track a wolf. He'd be even more curious about the injured man he brought back with him. There was a lot to tell, but one of the first things Adam wanted was to get something to eat. There was plenty of jerky, and that would satisfy him enough for tonight.

Soon enough, he smelled wood smoke. Soon he smelled the aroma of the jerky he and Luther had made.

"It's about time you got back here! Did your wolf turn into a man on you?" Luther asked, eyeing Nathan curiously as he and Adam rode into camp. Nathan hunched over in his saddle, his left arm in a cut-leather sling. His eyelids felt heavy with exhaustion when he tried to look at Luther.

"Oh, I missed the wolf. Before I saw him again, I found an injured man in the valley on the other side of the mountain. Uncle Luther, this is Nathan. He dislocated his shoulder, so I re-set it. He might've broken his ankle, too, but we haven't taken his boot off to see." He dismounted and walked back to Nathan. "Nathan, do you want something to eat?"

Nathan looked at him and shook his head. "I just want to sleep."

"Okay. Let me get your bedroll laid out and I'll get you down." Adam started untying Karl Digsby's bedroll from the back of the saddle.

Nathan peered at Adam with half-opened eyes. "You left mine in the woods."

"This bedroll will work." Adam walked near the fire to lay the bedroll in an open area near where the other two men would sleep.

Luther stroked the neck of the horse Adam had been riding while he held the reins. "I heard you picked yourself up a new horse. I'm sorry to hear about Cougar. Did you give this one a new dumb name yet?"

Adam nodded. "Jackpot. It's not dumb to name an animal according to the circumstances I found him in. I hit the jackpot with this one, Uncle Luther."

"I understand. How does this one ride? Did you meet up with John, by the way? I'm assuming not, since you have *him* with you." He nodded at Nathan and spoke harshly.

Adam stopped and looked curiously at Luther. "You heard what from who?" he asked.

"I met a guy named John up on the ridge. I was on my way to find you, and he was coming after the bank robber who shot at me. You're not the only one who has a story to tell today. I've never been shot at before, as you know; but this fella saw me, shot at me, and took off down the mountain. I didn't want to chase him, so I went through the pass. That's where I met John. He was riding up the mountain."

"Who's John? And where did you get that horse?" Adam asked, urgency in his voice. The paint horse he had seen leaving the hilltop with the last bank robber on it was tied to a high line beside the camp. It appeared to be in rough shape.

"Well, I'm telling you. The horse was a gift from John. Now John's part of a posse from Loveland tracking a bunch of bank robbers. Your friend"—he pointed at Nathan—"is one of the robbers. I know that, because everyone else in the posse was killed by the gang that robbed the bank. There were no other survivors except for John. That's what all the shooting we heard this morning was about. When you get your friend on the ground, make sure you tie him up for the night. We don't need a killer sleeping beside us. John will be coming in the morning for the bank's money and him—"

Adam interrupted, "What do you mean, he's coming in the morning for the money?"

"Oh, yeah. John's coming back in the morning. You can't keep the money, Adam. John was hoping to run into you on the other side of the mountain, but you apparently missed him."

"I'm no bank robber, mister," Nathan said tiredly. "That's Octavius, Adam."

Adam nodded and then asked Luther, "So he told you about my horse being shot?" He felt unnerved.

Luther shrugged. "Yeah. He said the robbers must have shot your horse and you killed a couple of them. He was impressed by your marksmanship. That's all he said, really. So, it sounds like you had a more interesting day than I did, but I thought I had a pretty interesting day, too! Want to tell me about yours?"

"Sit tight, Nathan," Adam said, leaving Nathan in the saddle. He took a seat on a wood block next to the fire and picked up a piece of jerky Luther had left lying beside where he had been sitting. "This is good meat!" Adam said after taking a bite. "Nathan didn't rob that bank, Uncle Luther. He was part of the posse that was murdered."

Luther shook his head. "No, the boy's lying to you to save his own skin. John was the only survivor. He let the robber who shot at me go, though. He decided to let him go because he hadn't killed anyone, but he was the only one in the gang who didn't. That means your friend there did."

"I was ambushed by two shooters. I killed one. The other rode away on that paint. Before he rode off, the rider shot and killed a third man I didn't see at first. Do you know where that horse's owner is now? Is it John?"

"No. John is the last of the posse hunting those men down. The horse belonged to the robber John let go. It's injured and couldn't go any farther, but I think it'll be okay after a few days' rest."

Adam shook his head and took another bite of the jerky. "Where's John, now?"

"He went back into the valley to find you."

Adam sighed heavily. "I saw his fire from the other side of the mountain. He'll be coming in the morning. Uncle Luther, the man you met is the infamous Octavius Clark I've been hearing so much about today."

"Who?" Luther, a puzzled. "I've never met anyone named Octavius, except for Octavius Vacha. But that was... geez, thirty years ago? He was another one of those old trapper friends of my pa's. Old Octavius had been mauled by a bear and had these deep scars across his face. It played havoc with his love life. He was a lifelong bachelor and died digging a well. It wasn't even his well, but his neighbor's. Geez, I haven't thought about old Octavius in a long time, come to think of it. Yeah, he used to live over towards Natoma, on the creek there, upstream from the tannery. They even say he buried a bag of gold on his property somewhere, but no one knows if that's true or not.

"Anyway, he was helping old Hoyt Crawford dig his first well, way back in, like, fifty-one. The wall collapsed in on him and killed him. I know we always braced the walls when we dug wells, but they must've thought the dry ground would hold. It didn't." Luther finished with a shrug.

Adam stared at his uncle seriously. "Octavius is the one who killed the posse, Uncle Luther. He killed Nathan's brother and the rest of the posse. Nathan was going after Octavius when he got hurt and I found him. Your friend John is after the gold and money in my saddlebag, that's true. But he's not your friend, and apparently, he's a very efficient killer. He'll be coming in the morning. What do you think, Nathan?"

Nathan sat on the saddle in misery, feeling more exhausted, anguished and helpless than he'd ever felt before. He was mentally, emotionally and physically drained and just wanted to sleep. He took a deep breath that sent a painful wave through his shoulder and chest, then sighed heavily. "I think if he sees me, I'm a dead man, and both of you will be dead, too. Octavius killed everyone in the posse, sir, except me. My brother and I were members of the posse from Loveland. He killed them all."

Adam said, "You better make sure your shotgun's loaded, Uncle Luther. I don't know that we're any better gunmen than the bunch he already slaughtered. You might have to kill your friend before tomorrow's over."

"We're not talking about the same person. The guy I met is named John Jones. We talked for quite a while. Shoot, we even had supper together. Like I said, he let that bank robber go free. A man who killed a whole posse would not do that, now would he?"

"The rider of that paint, you mean?" Adam asked.

"Yeah, that's the horse of the guy who shot at me. John was chasing him and let him go, because, like I said earlier, he didn't kill anyone."

Adam took a deep breath. "The man who rode that paint horse tried to kill me, did kill his friend, and tried to kill you. It sounds to me like your friend John is feeding you a line of crap, because no one does that if they haven't killed before. We had better prepare for when he shows up. I think it's best to find somewhere to hide Nathan. The only place I can think of is in the teepee."

"Adam," Luther said, raising his voice a touch. "You don't know if he's the same man or not."

"Uncle Luther, motives and actions speak louder than words, right? Well, let's compare motives and actions. My new friend just wants to go home. His brother and his friends were killed, and all he wants to do is to go home to his wife. Your friend is looking for the gold and money, and that's all he cares about. Who do you think would have the motive to kill? The man who wants the money and gold or the man who wants to go home? When he shows up tomorrow, I won't hesitate to kill him. I promised this young man I'd get him home, and I meant it."

"You'd better make sure your friend's telling the truth and John really is Octavius before you kill anyone!" Luther turned to Nathan. "What's Octavius look like?"

Nathan held his gaze on Luther. "Five foot nine, maybe. Thin. Around sixty-some, with long graying hair and gray in his beard. He's riding a red mare and is wearing a gray flannel shirt. He also wears an old droopy felt hat."

Luther turned back to Adam. "His description is of John. But he could be lying to frame John, too. That fellow could be Octavius, for all we know. I don't know that I feel comfortable with him in my teepee while we're sleeping. What if he's lying, and John's telling the truth?"

"What if he's not?" Adam shrugged. "Their motives tell me everything I need to know. And I know Nathan's telling the truth, because I've been talking to him for the past five hours or so. Listen, we can argue about this all night, or we can make room for a hurt man in our teepee. If Nathan's lying, the law will catch up with him later. Trust me, he isn't going very far, as crippled as he is right now. I can't say that for your friend, so he is the bigger threat. And one I suggest we best not take lightly. Now, why don't you help me get Nathan out of sight."

42

Adam opened his eyes and sat up with alarm. He wasn't sure what awoke him; it might have been the birds' early morning singing or the sun shining through the tops of the old trees surrounding them. It might have been the crackling fire a few feet away from his bedroll. Or it might have been the eggs, potatoes and diced meat Luther was frying up for breakfast over the fire.

"Morning," Luther said with a cheerful grin as Adam gazed around suspiciously.

"What time is it?"

"Almost seven. After breakfast, I'll check the jerky once your friend's up and see how done it is. Then you take your friend and go to town. I'll stay here, finish the jerky and let that horse mend up a bit."

Adam nodded. "Any sign of your friend, Octavius?"

"No, but if my friend John shows up, I'll invite him to sit down for some breakfast like decent folks would. I've been thinking about it, and we don't know who's really who, so I say give him the money and let him go on his way. We'll get your friend to town, notify Matt, and let him figure it out."

Adam stood up and stretched. "We could try that," he agreed with a yawn. "But we had best prepare in case he refuses to part ways with us so easily." Adam bent over and picked up his gun-belt he had laid beside his bedroll.

"And you think you're going to gun him down with that?" Luther nodded at Adam's revolver. "I'll remind you: you couldn't hit a giant wolf ten feet away from you yesterday. And if John is this Octavius fella and he's as dangerous as that young man says he is, then you might be overmatched. Again, I say let's be smart and keep your friend gunless and quiet, hand the money over to John, give him some breakfast and part ways. It's not our money, and none of our business, anyway. There's no reason for us to get more involved than we already are. Wouldn't you agree?"

Adam sat on a wooden block across from his uncle. "Normally. But I'll keep my gun on me, just in case."

"That's fine. Just don't go shooting someone unnecessarily. Now, how about some breakfast? I have some for your friend—I forgot his name—but when he wakes up, he can eat." Luther scooped some breakfast into a plate for Adam.

"Thank you. Nathan is his name," Adam said as he poured himself some coffee. His stomach growled. He hadn't eaten since the morning before, other than a few pieces of jerky. He ate hungrily and spoke with his mouth full. "I saw that wolf again last night on the western side of the valley. He has a nice den about a mile west of the bottom of the mountain. It's a big pack. I'm thinking we could get fifteen to twenty wolves if we spent a day or two over there setting traps, running snares and hunting. Some big grizzlies, too." He took another bite of food and continued. "I had that big wolf in my site, but I heard a gunshot as I pulled the trigger. That's why I missed it. I could have shot it last night, too, but we didn't know where Octavius was, and didn't want to take any chances of being ambushed." Adam grew serious and looked at his uncle. "When he does show up, friendly or not, you'd better be prepared, just in case."

"Like I said, he has no reason to harm anyone if we just hand the money over. But your young friend, Nathan, could be Octavius, for all we know."

Adam shook his head as he ate. "No, Nathan's telling the truth. You'd know he was too, if you talked to him."

"Are you going to wake him up or let him sleep all day?"

"Let's let him sleep. He still has a long, painful ride back to town. He might as well sleep while he can."

Luther frowned. "Well, he isn't going to be much good helping pack up, is he?"

"No. I don't think he's going to be good for anything for a while. Keep your ear open for any sound of your friend coming. By the sounds of it, he was one of those murderers who rode with Champ Ferguson back in the sixties. He's apparently gifted at Indian warfare."

"I can't say much about warfare myself, but I have a little experience hiding in the brush," Luther said with a hint of sarcasm. "I'll tell you what. If he is who you say he is, and he starts by trying to kill you, I'll go hide. Then my new friend and I can play hide and seek until Matt shows up sometime."

Adam frowned at his uncle's attempt at a joke. "Just be careful. I'm thinking about taking my rifle across the creek to that knoll over there. It would give the clearest view of our camp. If John-Octavius leaves peacefully, then maybe I'll let him go. But if anything goes wrong, he'll be dead before he can pull a weapon. Yeah," he said, nodding in thought, "I think that's our best bet."

"If you want to, but I really don't think there's a reason for it," Luther stated. "John's a pretty friendly fella—as long as you don't talk about the Lord, that is. Seriously, Adam, we're not in this battle. We're just hunting elk. There's no reason for us to get involved in someone else's fight."

Adam sighed. "We're involved whether we like it or not. We know who he is and what he's done. We cannot just walk away and pretend we don't. Nathan said Octavius is the one who murdered all those prospectors on Veneta Creek. We have both read about that. Can you walk away, knowing that man is going to kill again? It wouldn't be right to let him go," Adam said. "Now, I'm going to grab my rifle and head across the creek. You just act normal when he comes into camp, okay? That means just be normal."

"Oh, hell, Adam! You're talking about killing a man you don't even know," Luther snapped. "How do you know Octavius isn't your young friend? Like I said, let's let Matt figure it all out. You can't convict a man on mere suspicion, let alone the word of another stranger. You might become the judge and executioner of an innocent man. We need to let Matt and the law figure it out, not you and not me. Not us, not today!"

Adam gazed at Luther seriously. "I have a bad feeling about your friend, Uncle Luther, and I won't take any chances."

Luther raised his voice in frustration. "He left your friend in there alive, didn't he?" he asked, pointing at the teepee. "And that's if he's the right guy, and you don't know he is! That's my whole point, Adam. You don't know who he is or who that kid is!" He pointed at the teepee again.

Nathan spoke from inside the teepee. His voice reflected the pain he was in. "His name is Octavius Clark. I don't know how to make you believe me, sir, but honestly, you can't trust him. He will kill you as soon as you hand him that gold."

"How long have you been awake?" Adam asked.

Luther spoke coldly to Nathan before he could answer Adam's question. "And I can't trust you any more than I can John, or Octavius, or whatever his name is. You could be one of the bank robbers, for all I know. It could have been you who killed the posse! And that's the problem, Adam: we don't know!"

Nathan groaned in pain as he sat up inside the teepee. The fire had died down to barely an ember, and the two trappers had opened the smoke flap when they put him inside the preceding night. Nathan had slept soundly, except for his throbbing ankle and shoulder waking him from time to time. His body had become stiff and sore from being thrown from his horse, and it hurt to move. "My name's Nathan Pierce," he began. Then he told Luther the story about what happened and how he came to be in their camp.

"I'm telling you the truth, and you'll find out soon enough that I am. Will you please trust me on this? Octavius is a killer, and he will kill all of us. I can't do much, but could you give me back my revolver to protect myself? I don't want to be helpless when he sees me."

"If you were part of the posse, why didn't he kill you?" Luther asked cynically.

Nathan sighed and spoke softly, "Because he promised my wife I'd come home alive."

"That doesn't make any sense. Why would you leave with someone who wanted to kill you?"

"I didn't," Nathan answered sharply. "Look, I don't..." Nathan paused to take a deep breath. Every moment was a moment closer to that one when Octavius would enter their camp and discover him, unarmed, in the teepee. "He liked my wife. He said she reminded him of his own. Sarah made him promise that I'd come back home alive, and he agreed.

That's the only reason I'm alive. Now if you would give me back my gun."

Luther shook his head. "No, but I will get you some breakfast."

"I need my gun," Nathan said loudly.

"Quiet down!" Adam demanded. "We don't need your voice echoing across the mountains, do we?"

"No, but I need my gun."

Suddenly the teepee's door flap flew open, and a big man with gray hair and beard knelt to look at Nathan as he held a plate of food. It was the first time Nathan had seen Luther clearly.

"You're not getting your gun back; do you understand me?" Luther asked, no friendliness in his voice. "I suggest you eat your food. You've got a long way to go to get home, and you'll be glad you ate later today."

"Thank you..." Nathan said quietly. "I'm Nathan." He held his right hand up for Luther to shake.

Luther shook his hand and then handed him his plate of food. "Luther Fasana."

"Luther, listen to me," Nathan pleaded. "Octavius could be here any time. All I'm asking for is my gun. I should have some way to protect myself. Please! I know him, and I've seen what he can do!"

Luther shook his head and waved a hand. "If John comes, you just sit in here and be quiet until he leaves. Everything will be fine."

"Excuse me, Mister Fasana, but you don't know him."

"Young man, I've been dealing with people for over sixty years now, and I've never had to depend on a gun to get out of scrapes in my life. I don't plan to start now. Like I told you, you just stay quiet, and everything will be fine."

"Luther...can't you see I'm telling you the truth?

Honestly, I'm not a killer! I just want to protect myself." He sounded genuinely sincere. "I just want to go home to my wife."

"Are you a Christian, by chance?"

"I am."

"Then pray," Luther advised him simply. "The Lord's your best protection. Pray." Luther closed the door flap as he stood up and left the teepee. "And you..." he started saying to Adam, but Adam was standing beside him holding Nathan's gun-belt. "What are you doing?" he asked sharply.

"I'm giving him his gun-belt," he answered and knelt to peer at Nathan through the teepee flap. "Here," he said and tossed the gun- belt to Nathan. "I already warned you about trying anything on me. I believe I can trust you not to shoot my uncle or me. But if you do, I will blow your knees away and use you for wolf bait a hundred yards from their den. Do not shoot unless you have eye contact, face to face, in self-defense. I don't need you shooting my uncle acciden-tally through the canvas of the teepee. Am I clear?" It was clear Adam meant every word he had said.

Nathan nodded. "Thank you. I won't shoot at you fellows. I consider you my friends."

"Just understand," Adam added, "if you shoot at us, I will give you a chance to ask the Lord for forgiveness, but then you're wolf bait. If the wolves don't kill you, I will. You understand the consequences of shooting at us, right? I just want you to know what's going to happen if you do."

Nathan was stunned by the sudden distrust and hard eyes in a man he'd believed to be a trusted friend. "Yes, I understand," he said quietly.

Adam nodded. "Be quiet, like my uncle told you, and pray. It will all be fine." He closed the flap. "Uncle Luther, Nathan will be all right."

Luther exhaled and shook his head in frustration. He stood outside the teepee and watched Adam walk to the top of the knoll and lie down on the ground between a rock and a large bush. Adam made himself as small as he could, but to Luther's untrained eye, Adam appeared quite noticeable. Of course, he had watched Adam take his position. After a few more moments, Luther went back to the teepee doorway and opened it. He took the plate and fork from Nathan, gathered Adam's plate and the frying pan and carried them to the creek to wash them. He grabbed a towel hanging from a tree branch and dried his face after rinsing it off, as well. He picked up the dishes he'd cleaned and carried them back up the small hill. He passed the chopping block where Adam's steel-bladed tomahawk was still stuck to its top.

He considered taking a moment to split some more kindling to restart the fire in the teepee. He'd hated having let the fire die down overnight and, even more, he'd hated having to open the smoke flap when they put Nathan in the teepee. He doubted the meat was as well-done as he'd hoped it would be by now. He had never let the fire cool down and the smoke escape as he had the night before. He hoped the change in temperature for a few hours wouldn't affect the meat too much. He feared it might begin to spoil, because consistent heat was the key to good jerked meat.

He would relight the fire to make it hotter than usual and add more green wood to make the smoke heavier than usual after John left camp and everything was back to as normal as it could be. He had to stay in camp and watch the meat when Adam took Nathan back to town. This hunting trip was becoming downright disappointing. His first chore, though, would be to split some more kindling. Thinking

363

about it, Luther went into the teepee to check the progress of his jerky.

"Luther, honestly, I just wanted my gun in case I needed it. I would never raise it against good people like you and Adam," Nathan said as soon as Luther entered the teepee.

"Good to know," is all Luther said. He checked the meat at various heights on the rack. "It's not done. I need to build up that fire and close the smoke flap. I knew I shouldn't have opened it last night," he said, sounding disappointed. "You know, if you weren't hurt, Adam and I could probably stay out here for a few more days and pick up another dozen wolf skins, including that giant Adam saw. And we'd have double the amount of jerky this year than most."

Nathan sat with his head down, in a defeated position. "Luther, if we survive this day, I will come back next year with you and Adam and help you skin every wolf on this mountain. I promise. But I really think you need to take me seriously and at least put your gun-belt on. I am a Christian, but I don't think God's going to strike Octavius down with a bolt of lightning in order to save us."

"Have you looked outside?" Luther asked sarcastically. "I think I can trust you on that, because there's not a cloud in the sky. Relax. You'll be fine."

"You have no idea what Octavius is like."

"No, I suppose not. But if it's the same fella I spoke to, then I'd say he was a decent fellow. I think we should we give him a chance before we kill him, don't you?"

Nathan peered up at Luther. "No, I don't. Remember sir, that he killed my brother and my friends. He is an animal, and he needs to be put down like a rabid dog. If a rabid dog bit your daughter, would you trust it with your son or shoot it? He'll get no mercy from me!"

Luther gazed down at Nathan. "That's quite an ironic

statement coming from a man who's relying on the mercy of my nephew and me. I'm sorry about your brother and friends, but we may not be talking about the same man. And even if we are, let's just give him what he wants and send him on his way..."

"A man in his sixties, with long, graying dark hair and beard. Riding a bay horse and wearing a gray..." Nathan began saying, but Luther cut him off rudely.

"Don't interrupt me! If you would've let me finish what I was saying, you'd know Adam took his rifle across the way, just in case anything happens. Now just relax." He continued in a softer tone, "My nephew Matthew will track him down and bring him to justice; that's not our job. But just so you know... it does sound like we are talking about the same man. Maybe it's a good thing Adam's across the way after all. Just be quiet when he shows up, and all will be well."

"I'll be as quiet as a mouse, Luther."

"You can trust Adam. I can vouch that he can't hit a wall six feet away with a revolver, but he won't miss with his rifle, and that's a fact. You can rest easy on that score. That man won't be here long, either way," Luther said and turned to the teepee door. The man calling himself John the evening before bore some bitterness from the war—and for good reason, it seemed to Luther. But Luther had not seen one inclination that John was anything other than a good-hearted man. He'd certainly never figured him for a cold-blooded killer. He didn't believe that John and Octavius were one and the same.

He experienced an eerie feeling, thinking he might have had dinner and talked to the Veneta Creek Killer everyone had been talking about. If the man who'd sat in front of him talking about the loss of his wife was a coldblooded killer, it made Luther wonder why he was still alive.

"Luther," Nathan said, stopping Luther at the door, "He's not your friend. Protect yourself."

Luther saw the genuine warning and sincerity in Nathan's eyes as he stood in the doorway. He nodded, and said, "You just sit tight."

"Morning Luther. I hope I'm not too late for breakfast," Octavius said out of nowhere. He was leading his horse into camp by its reins. He was nearly to the teepee already when he spoke. He looked to be happy to see Luther again.

"Hello...ah, John," Luther said, surprised by his sudden appearance out of nowhere. Luther stood awkwardly in the door flap and then quickly closed it to hide Nathan from Octavius. "No...I mean, yeah, we've already had breakfast. You should've been here about half an hour ago. I just finished washing the pans. I got some jerky though. I won't send a friend off hungry," he said nervously.

Inside the teepee, Nathan's heart began to pound when he heard Octavius' voice. Helpless to defend himself, he did the only thing he knew to do; he began to pray with more fear and desperation than he had ever done before.

Octavius instantly noticed the nervous edge to Luther's mannerisms and voice. He grew wary as he looked around the camp for anything that might account for his friend's anxiety. At first glance he saw nothing except two horses that hadn't been at the camp the night before. Both horses had belonged to the two dead bank robbers lying on the other side of the valley. Luther's nephew must have been the person Luther was talking to when he stepped out of the teepee. "Your nephew must be in the tent there. I heard you talking to someone," he asked.

Luther seemed to have been taken off guard. He stuttered through his answer. "Ah...no. It's a...the fella you let go yesterday. He fell from a tree and broke his ankle and dislocated his shoulder. He's a pretty beaten up."

Octavius' smile grew wide. "Well, that guy has no luck at all, does he? Why was he climbing a tree?"

Luther hadn't expected to be questioned. "Ah...I never asked."

Octavius stared at Luther uneasily. "So, where is your nephew?" he asked as he scanned the tree line around the camp.

"Oh, he's around somewhere. He went to find a privy out there somewhere," Luther explained with a wave of his hand. His gaze darted to Adam's position, and away again.

Luther's quick glances sent chills of caution down Octavius' spine. He forced himself to not turn and see where Luther's eyes had betrayed the location of the cavalry-trained sharpshooter nephew. Octavius instinctively knew he was being watched through the sights of a rifle; he just didn't know why. There was no way Luther and his nephew could have found out who he was or what he had done.

"Hmm. Well, do you know if he found the bank's payroll or not? He might not even know he has it," Octavius said, a friendly note in his voice.

"I didn't have a chance to ask him, actually. But his saddlebags are over there if you want to look." Luther pointed at Adam's saddlebags.

Octavius didn't move for a few seconds. Rather, he stared at Luther. He had been taken off guard, and he wasn't used to being taken by surprise. Caution permeated every fiber of his body.

He needed to make a defensive plan immediately, because he had no chance to outrun, outmaneuver or escape a bullet fired from Adam's rifle. He had no idea how they might have found out who he was, but he felt trapped and knew any wrong move would end his life. He needed time—just a few seconds more, a minute, perhaps—to gain an advantage somehow and save his own life.

"Oh, I don't know if I want to rummage through another man's saddlebags. He might not react too friendly if he comes back and sees a stranger digging into his property. I might just get shot or something." Octavius' hostility grew hotter with each passing second.

"I can look," Luther said with a shrug. He walked over to the saddlebags, bent and opened the saddlebag containing the money and gold.

Octavius let go of his horse's reins and took a strategic step in front of the teepee's door flap to wait for Luther's return.

"Here it is," Luther said. He stood up carrying a bank bag of money and gold along with a smaller leather pouch full of gold.

Octavius grinned at the sight of his leather pouch. "Perfect. Well, I won't be troubling you any longer." He offered Luther a friendly smile. "The bank's going to be mighty happy." He glanced toward the knoll where Luther's gaze had gone to a moment before. There, overlooking the camp, lay Luther's nephew, well camouflaged within the brush. Adam held a rifle pointed at him. Octavius gritted his teeth beneath his posed smile.

"Well, I'm glad to hear that," Luther said, a hint of relief in his voice. He neared Luther to hand the bags to him. "Here you go. Sorry about not making any breakfast, but I can spare some jerky for your trip back home."

"That would be great," Octavius said. When Luther got close enough, Octavius darted behind Luther, pulled out his revolver, held it to Luther's head and pulled the hammer with his right hand. His left arm hooked across Luther's throat and pulled the big man to Octavius' chest. He turned Luther's body towards the knoll where Adam waited in one smooth motion. Octavius' his body and head fitted behind Luther's wide body quite well. He spoke mercilessly into Luther's ear, "Don't move, or I'll blow your head open! Call your nephew, now!"

Luther took a deep breath as he tried to calm down. "Ah… just don't shoot, okay?" he asked Octavius.

"Call him!" Octavius ordered.

"Adam!"

Adam lay on the ground with his rifle sighted on the edge of Octavius' forehead, which peeked out around Luther's thick neck. Octavius wasn't a big man, but he was quick and coldblooded. Adam had a shot, but with the revolver's hammer cocked, the chances of Luther being shot was almost certain. He sighed in frustration. "Let my uncle go, and I'll let you ride away. I don't care about the money. Take it and go," He yelled from the knoll.

"That might've worked earlier, but not now!" Octavius hollered back. "You have one chance to save your uncle's life, and that's to leave your rifle up there, and you come down here."

"If you kill my uncle, I'll kill you!"

"I don't want to kill your uncle! I want to ride away, but I don't trust you with a rifle. I've seen you shoot. I know what you can do. All I want you to do is come down from there without your rifle. Come down here by the stream, and I'll let your uncle live."

"Then I'll be at your mercy."

"Young man, if you value your uncle's life, lay the rifle down and get down here. Otherwise, shoot now, because on the count of three, I'm killing your uncle. Yeah, you'll kill me, too, but you'll never get over knowing his death was your fault. You have three seconds to choose. One, two—"

Luther bellowed, "Don't you dare come down here, Adam! I'm going to Heaven, and I'm fine with that, but you be sure to kill him, so you and Nathan can go home to your wives and children."

"Nathan?" Octavius asked in surprise, nearly letting Luther go so he could turn around and look into the teepee. But he only pulled Luther closer to the teepee door. "Is that how you knew who I am? Is that why your nephew is up there waiting to shoot me?" Octavius was careful to stay behind Luther and out of Adam's line of fire when he pulled the teepee's flap to look inside. He was shocked to see Nathan sitting upright on the ground with a revolver pointed at him. His left arm was in a homemade sling. To Octavius, Nathan looked as nervous, yet as dangerous as any man Octavius had ever seen before. "Throw the gun away." Octavius demanded of Nathan.

"I will not! Let him go and face me like a man," Nathan said.

"Nathan, you're already hurt. Just throw the gun away and go home to Sarah. All right? I don't want to kill any of you. Just toss your gun away."

Adam yelled from the knoll, "Lay your gun down, Nathan!"

"See?" Octavius asked. "Unless you want to be responsible for Luther's death, I'd lay the gun down."

Nathan grimaced. He finally had Octavius in his sights and could kill him with one shot. However, Octavius had his gun cocked and pointed at Luther's head. If he fired, Octavius most likely would too. Adam's warning was fresh in his mind as well. Nathan closed his eyes, slowly lowered the hammer of his revolver and laid the gun on his blanket.

"Toss it over there," Octavius demanded, pointing.

Nathan tossed the revolver across the teepee.

Octavius grimaced, then pulled Luther into the teepee and let the flap close on its own. He forced Luther down to his knees in the cramped space. He looked fiercely at Nathan and yelled, "I told you to go home to your wife!"

"You don't have to do this, John." Luther said. "You can take the money and go. We don't care about that. Just let us all go, and we'll part ways like friends."

"You know my name's Octavius, not John. I just want you to know that I meant no harm to any of you. I just wanted my gold back and to be left alone to live my life the way I wanted to. I did not want any trouble, but you all forced me to do this. You've given me no choice but to kill you all. I am sorry, Luther. I thought you were different than the others. You said I could trust you just last night. I wasn't expecting you to betray me. But that's why I don't have friends, Luther. I can't trust anyone because of men like you."

Luther turned his head to glance at Octavius. "I'm the same man you talked to last night, John. I didn't think you meant us any harm, and I said as much. I said you'd come and get your money, eat some breakfast, and leave as friendly as you were last night. But Adam didn't want to take any chances. We weren't trying to ambush you, or you'd already be dead. He was just protecting us in case..."

"In case what?" Octavius demanded.

"In case you decided to kill us like you did the posse."

Octavius turned to scowl at Nathan. "This is your fault. I told you to go home to your wife, didn't I? Well, you've made your choice, and now you're gonna pay for it. Why are you coming after me, anyway?" he asked bitterly.

As Nathan stared at Octavius, determination and hatred overrode his fear. "You murdered my brother!"

Octavius grinned. "Yes...I did." He turned back to Luther. "I wonder how long your nephew will last up there when he hears Nathan screaming." Octavius then went to Nathan and kicked the back of his left shoulder. Nathan cried out in pain and rolled to his right side, trying to hold his shoulder with his right hand. He rocked back and forth in agony. Octavius kicked the back of his shoulder again, then dropped to one knee, grabbed his left arm and gave it a powerful jerk, dislocating it again. Nathan screamed; the pain was nearly unbearable.

Luther stood up and reached for Octavius, but Octavius pulled his revolver from his holster and pointed it at Luther. "Sit down!" he shouted, pulling the hammer back until it clicked. "Sit down, Luther, or I'll send you to that God of yours right now!"

Luther glared at him. "You leave that boy alone! I swear, if you touch him again, you will have to kill me."

Octavius gave a slow smile. "You're right. You will. But not until your damned nephew surrenders his rifle. If I killed you now, he'd fill this tent up with lead."

"I could tell Adam to let you ride out of here. He's already said you could. We could just part ways," Luther said again.

Octavius chuckled through a cold grin. "No, we can't. You all know my name."

Luther shook his head. "You could change it anywhere you go, and nobody will know. If you need a longer time to get away, then kill our horses. It would take us a week to carry Nathan out of here. But don't end this young man's life, or my nephew's. Adam's got a wife and children back at home who depend on him. And this man has a young wife too. Don't do to them what those men did to you and your family. You're a better man than that."

"You have no idea what kind of a man I am, Luther. No idea at all! What about you? Are you going to beg me to spare your life, too, or are you going to take a bullet like a man?" Octavius held his revolver an inch away from Luther's face with the hammer pulled back. "Well?"

Luther gazed into Octavius' hardened eyes and said softly, "My children are grown. If you want to pull that trigger, go ahead. I won't complain. But do know you don't have to. You can still ride away and start over somewhere else. You can go back home and get to know your children and your grandchildren before it's too late. Life's too important and too wonderful to throw away on things that don't really matter. So, take your gold and go. All of us will just look the other way."

For a moment, Octavius held the revolver at Luther's face, then lowered it slowly. He looked at Nathan and sighed. "What about you? Are you going to keep coming after me? Are you going to leave your beautiful wife at home and spend your life looking for me?"

Nathan glared at Octavius while holding his shoulder. "If Luther could have gotten away from you, you'd already be dead. But to answer your question, if I ever see you again, I won't hesitate to kill you."

Octavius gave a slight nod of his head. "Fair enough." He turned his attention back to Luther. "Okay, I'll tell you what. Call your nephew down. Tell him to leave his rifle where he is and come down where I can see him. I'm giving you all one chance, and that's all. If anyone tries to do anything, I'll kill all of you. Do we understand each other?"

Luther sighed. "Yes and thank you. I think you're a good man, John. I really do."

"You know my name's not John, so why are you still calling me that?" Octavius demanded angrily.

"Because maybe that's who you really are. It's never too late to start over again," Luther said kindly.

Octavius grimaced and his eyes grew harder. "Just call your nephew down. My life is none of your affair!"

Nathan suddenly said, "He's not going to let anyone live, Luther. Our only chance is Adam blowing his head off."

Octavius turned and slammed the butt of his revolver into Nathan's separated shoulder, making Nathan cry out in pain and roll to his left side to hold his throbbing shoulder.

Luther reached to grab Octavius' shoulder and yelled, "Leave that boy alone! He didn't do any—"

Octavius swung his revolver and hit the side of Luther's head with the barrel, knocking the big man off his feet. Luther fell onto the wooden racks holding the meat. The rack collapsed on top of him. Octavius leaned over Luther and hissed through gritted teeth, "I won't tell you again. Get out there and tell your nephew to come down here where I can see him. Now!" He grabbed Luther's arm and tried to yank the big man up.

Luther stood up at his own slow pace and touched the blood running down the side of his face. He had a deep gash about an inch long above his right temple. He looked at the blood on his fingers and reached out to show it to Octavius. "Even if you kill me, I won't call Adam down here. I'm not afraid of dying, John. What about you? If you kill me or that boy, you won't get out of here alive. One minute we are here, the next we are standing before the judge of our souls for an eternity in Heaven or Hell. I didn't do anything to deserve you busting my head open, but this is my blood. Jesus shed his blood for you, too. He loves you enough to let his blood be spilt for you on the cross, just so you can go to Heaven. It's so simple, and so complete. The free gift of eternal life.

He's knocking at your door. All you have to do is let him in. Say yes to the Lord, John. It's not too late."

Octavius scoffed and shook his head. "I know what the Bible says! It's just a book, written by men. By men, Luther! Just like Shakespeare or any other of those other writers in the world. If there's a god, and I am sure there is one, then he'll understand me when I see him. And we'll get along great, with a drink in one hand and a gun in the other." He paused for a moment. "I resent you trying to preach at me again. Like I said last night, I don't want to hear it! Now get your ass outside and get your nephew down here, before I kill all three of you."

Luther's eyes teared up. "Give me one minute," he said and lifted a finger. "My nephew Adam, Nathan, and I are all going to Heaven for eternity if you kill us, and that's the worst it gets for us: Heaven. But if you're killed today without Jesus, you'll be condemned to hell for eternity. Don't risk it! Please, submit your life to Jesus Christ today."

Octavius grimaced, but seemed to consider Luther's words. Then he shook his head hard and sneered a rage-filled grimace that left no doubt about his murderous past. He hollered, "I told you I didn't want to hear any more of that, didn't I?" He hit Luther's head hard with the butt of his revolver. Luther fell and covered his head with his hands.

Octavius knelt and shoved the barrel of his revolver at Luther's forehead. He pulled the hammer back until it clicked, "I will put a bullet in your head. You wanna go to Heaven, I'll *send* you to Heaven! But don't ever mention that crap to me again! Now if you want to live, call your nephew down!"

Blood rolled down Luther's forehead and dripped onto his cheek. "You won't get out of this teepee alive. Just remember, it was your choice to reject Jesus when you were dying, not mine."

Octavius sneered in frustration. He let go of Luther, and turned to Nathan, grabbed him by the neck and shoved his revolver at Nathan's head. "Call Adam down, or I'll kill Luther!" he snarled viciously.

"Don't do this. Come on, you can take the money and go. You don't have to kill anyone. Just go!" Nathan spoke despite his shoulder. "You promised Sarah—"

"I gave her my word, and I fulfilled it when I spared your life and told you to go home! I gave you the chance to live. Any promise I made, I kept. You came after me. I don't owe your wife anything anymore."

Nathan sneered. "Then kill me. Come on, do it!"

"Don't!" Luther called out. "Please, let him go."

Octavius screamed at Luther, "Call your nephew, or this man's dead!"

From outside of the teepee came Adam's loud voice. "Hey, I'm outside now. Why don't you come on out?"

"Stand up!" Octavius ordered Luther, yanking him up and forcing him through the teepee's flap door first, Octavius hiding behind Luther's large body. He saw Adam standing beside the creek down a hill, aiming his rifle at them. He also wore his gun-belt. Adam was bigger than Luther was and looked even stronger, with his bushy brown hair and a thick beard.

Octavius hollered, "Throw your rifle away from you, and your revolver too. Do it now, or Luther's dead!"

Adam looked at the blood running down Luther's face and knew he hadn't thought things through very well. Now he was standing in the open while Octavius hid behind Luther. He could not throw his rifle away and leave himself defenseless, or he would surely be killed. It felt like he was in a chess game that was at a draw, and the next move would win or lose the match. Octavius had gained the upper hand, but the next move was Adam's. "I can't do that. Just let my uncle go, take the money and leave. I won't shoot."

Octavius chuckled. "I don't believe you any more than you believe me. So, what are we going to do? You'd put your hand on a Bible and tell the truth, wouldn't you? You're a Christian, yeah?"

"I am."

"Then swear to me on the Bible that you'll keep your word and let me go."

Adam nodded. "I swear it. What about you?"

"Sure. You throw your rifle away, and I'll lower my revolver. You throw your pistol down, and I'll put mine away."

"You swear it on the Bible?" Adam asked.

"Sure, I do. We have a deal, so toss your rifle and pistol."

Adam hesitated, then lowered his rifle and tossed it to his side. Octavius lowered his revolver from Luther's head. Taking a deep breath Adam casually stepped to the left and slowly pulled his revolver out of its holster and tossed it to his right.

Octavius suddenly pushed Luther away, raised his revolver, aimed it at Adam and pulled the trigger. Adam dove to his left over the chopping block and pulled his tomahawk out. He hit the ground and rolled to one knee just as Octavius fired a second shot at him.

Adam stood and threw the tomahawk as hard as he could, saying a silent prayer that he'd hit his target. The tomahawk's blade sank into Octavius' shoulder, to its hilt.

The power of the throw spun Octavius around to face the teepee's door. His finger pulled the trigger, sending a third shot into the ground. He raised his left arm to catch himself on the canvas frame and stopped. It took him a moment to realize he had been hit by the tomahawk, and that his right arm had been nearly severed. Blood poured from the wound. He stared in disbelief at the tomahawk and didn't seem to notice Nathan painfully crawling to the door to grab the pistol on the ground four feet from him. Octavius saw Nathan grab the pistol and hold it in his right hand. Nathan pulled the hammer back aimed it at Octavius.

Adam's voice called Octavius from outside the teepee. "Turn around and step away from the tent! I don't want to shoot you!"

Octavius focused on Nathan. Slowly his face took on a wild, murderous expression and a cruel sneer formed on his lips. He might be injured and cornered, but there was no giving-up in him. He pulled his knife with his left hand and took a step toward Nathan.

Nathan pulled the trigger. The bullet hit Octavius in the chest. The force of the shot made him step back. His expression turned to one of shock and fear. Then a second shot, louder and more powerful, hit the back of Octavius' head, spraying Nathan with fine droplets of blood.

Octavius' body fell, lifeless, into the teepee. Nathan sat in shock and stared at the drop of blood on his arms and hands. Then he turned his attention to the dead body a few feet away from the gun.

"Are you all right?" Adam asked as he peered inside the teepee.

"Yeah," Nathan answered. He then said to Octavius' corpse, "I hope you burn in hell."

Nathan's words made Luther angry. "How dare you say something like that? How can you wish anybody to burn in hell, Nathan? I thought you said you were a Christian. If so, then you know God himself wishes no man to hell! The reason Jesus was crucified was so we don't have to go to hell. And you hope this man goes to hell? Really? Aren't we supposed to warn him, maybe try to tell him about Jesus so he won't go to hell? Don't you get it, Nathan? God himself does not want to send him to hell. How can you, being a Christian, say such a horrible thing?"

"He murdered my brother. That's how!" Nathan, then suddenly choked on his own emotions. His eyes filled with tears, and he fought to contain them.

Luther exhaled and said in a softer voice, "And my heart goes out you, Nathan. I understand your point of view, but I did my best to reach him. Unfortunately, he chose to reject Jesus. John 3:16 makes it clear. *'For God so loved the world that he gave his only begotten son for whosoever believes in him, shall not perish, but have eternal life'*. It never means more than when you want someone to accept Jesus, give him the reassurance of salvation, and he refuses to accept it. You may get your wish, Nathan, but trust me, it breaks God's heart to send Octavius to hell. Who in the world are we to hope anyone goes to hell? Even those we think deserve it the most."

"Uncle Luther, are you all right?" Adam asked after a moment of uncomfortable silence.

Luther nodded. "My head hurts a bit." He looked at Adam, clearly shaken by the events of the morning. "How did you know he wouldn't keep his word, but would try to shoot you?"

Adam frowned. "In combat, you kill the greatest threat first. I knew you'd be safe until he got me. The tomahawk was there to use until I could grab my rifle. Not a bad throw, huh? You can thank the Lord for that. Normally, I just knock the bark off trees with it; I never stick it in anything."

Luther nodded sadly as he gazed from the dead body to

the blood splattered on Nathan. "I'll go get some water to get you cleaned up. Adam, let's pull this body out of my teepee."

Adam grinned. "Yeah, Nathan needs a bath. How are you doing?"

Nathan shook his head as he exhaled a deep breath. "I just want to go home to my wife."

It was over.

EPILOGUE

Loveland, Oregon.

Sarah Pierce gazed at her husband while he said grace over their evening meal. It wasn't very long ago when it would have been Cal or Sara herself who would say grace before their evening meals. Nathan had always believed in the Lord but had been struggling for quite some time with the "why's" in his life. It had never seemed fair to him that he should love someone as purely as he did Sarah, and for them to have to hide in the mountains to live a semi-normal life.

They both knew they might be recognized on any day, and their semi-perfect world would be torn apart by guns, chains, possible death and a forced kidnapping to take Sarah back to her prison of wealth, power and the corruption of her father's home. Nathan would be imprisoned for thirty years or killed for the bounty his father-in-law put on his head. Perhaps if it hadn't been for her parent's maid,

Jane, Sarah would feel as Nathan did, but Jane had shown Sarah what grace was, and what the love of Christ was, in spite of her parents' blasphemous example of righteousness.

Her relationship with the Lord had nothing to do with her parents or their idea of Christianity. Sarah was a Christian, and that depended solely on her relationship with Jesus. No one else could affect that. She had tried to reason with Nathan, but he couldn't understand why their life together had to be threatened and made harder, while the most unrighteous people claiming to be Christians lived with ease. The injustice of their situation caused bitterness to take root in Nathan's soul. He held tightly onto his bitterness and was unwilling to let it go and move forward.

Somewhere between leaving Loveland and coming home a hurt and broken man, Nathan had reconnected with Jesus. He had committed the remainder of his life to Him. The weeks since he'd come home had been hard in many ways, but he felt the loss of Cal most deeply. He and Sarah both knew Cal was in Heaven, and it brought them comfort because they knew they'd be with him again.

With a small smile of gratitude, Sarah watched Nathan finish his prayer and said, "Amen."

"What?" he asked, noticing her staring at him.

"I just love you. I was thinking how nice it is to hear you pray like you used to and be serving the Lord again."

Nathan smiled. "It feels good."

"And how lucky I am to have married you," she said.

He frowned. "I wish I could do more for you. I know living in a lumber camp in the middle of nowhere isn't every girl's dream."

She shook her head. "I've lived on the other side of that coin, and this life is far better."

"I only wish I could give you more, Sarah. A warmer

house, a softer chair, a nice dress and somewhere to wear it. I always thought I'd be able to give you more. I suppose no man ever dreams of being poor and having to labor so hard for so little. Especially when he's in love with the most beautiful lady in the world. I always dreamed of giving you a nice home and living a good life until we're old and gray."

She smiled softly. "Nathan, you already know we have everything we need to be content and happy. You have supplied everything we need: a home, food, clothing, friends, and a wonderful love. What more could I ask for, really? A dress? It would just become rags eventually anyway. I have everything I need. I have you, and I am very thankful for that. Because the Lord knows, I could have lost you."

Nathan nodded solemnly. "Freedom, Sarah. That is the one thing we don't have. There will always be a bounty hanging over our heads. It feels like we're living in a bubble paradise, but the bubble's small, and we try not to see how fragile it really is. Any day, maybe years from now, but someday, our little bubble will pop and our whole life together will be torn apart just like that," he said with a snap of his fingers.

"And maybe it won't!" she said. "We don't have a choice but to accept that risk. But I'll be damned if I will just sit back and say, 'Okay, take me to my parents.' No way! That will never happen. I will fight for my family. You and I are the only family we have! So, snap yourself out of your 'pity me' attitude and quit worrying about it. Nathan, we live in Loveland, Oregon... do you really think anyone will ever come here to look for us?"

"Yes," Nathan said quietly. "Ten thousand dollars is a lot of money."

"And you think we are the most wanted people in America, I assume? Don't be ridiculous. Bounty hunters have far more important and dangerous people to catch than two young people whose only crime was falling in love and getting married."

"Sarah, it isn't what we did or who we are that motivates bounty hunters, sweetheart, it's the money and only the money. Ten thousand is a fortune to some men out there, and that leaves us trapped here."

"Trapped, Nathan?" Sarah asked with a frown. "I think we're doing fine, thank you."

Nathan gave a discouraged shrug. "We are doing fine, but this is it! While I was recovering at Adam's house—his sister's husband died recently, like I told you—but despite that, his sister still had plans for the future. She wants to start a horse company, and Adam's going to incorporate his business with hers. If we didn't have this dark cloud over our heads, we could help them with that. We could plan a future with the hope of becoming prosperous enough with them so that we wouldn't have to work so dang hard for so little pay. Sarah, I can't push and pull a saw and swing an axe all day anymore. My shoulder hurts all night long. My ankle turns on me all the time on the uneven ground out there. I'm young, but my body has hurt ever since I was injured. I can't quit what I'm doing, but I don't have a future anywhere else. That's what I mean by freedom. I can't quit and find easier work in other towns, because I'm too afraid of being recognized and losing you! Losing you is not an option for me."

Sarah frowned and spoke with a hint of frustration. "So, what do you want to do, Nathan? Your body hurts, but you have to work. We live here, so you have to work here. Oh, we could move somewhere else where you could find a better job, but you're too afraid of being recognized. So, we're stuck living here." She paused and then continued, speaking sharply, "You're talking in circles, and I don't know which way is up anymore! Do you want to go work on a horse ranch? Then do it! Do you want to move to a bigger town? What do you want to do, Nathan? I know what would happen if we were discovered by the wrong people, and I pray we never are, but maybe we need to quit being so afraid of what *might* happen, and trust the Lord to keep us safe while you do what you want to do. I know you never wanted to be a lumberman your whole life. There are more opportunities in larger towns and, if you want to go, then let's go. But make up your mind and stop complaining. We'll always have that bounty hanging over our heads no matter what. So how about we just enjoy being outlaws and make the best of it."

Nathan gazed at Sarah fondly and smiled. "Sarah, I'd rather stay here and do what I have to do just to be able to come home to you. I love you, and that's all that matters to me."

Sarah sighed with relief. "I'm actually glad you said that, because as much as I want to encourage you to reach for your dreams, I don't want to take the chance of you being shot and killed. Like I told you before, heaven to me is just being here with you. But if you must, find easier work. You can talk to Big Hank about becoming a muleskinner and drive the wagons. He'll give you an easier job to do if you just talk to him."

Nathan nodded. "I will talk to Hank tomorrow."

She looked at him lovingly. "I know it's hard, but just think of the story we will be able to tell our children and grandchildren someday."

He smiled and was about to say something when someone knocked on the door. It was a Monday evening, and it was most unusual for anyone to come around at this time of the evening. Nathan stood up from the table and walked to the door. "Who is it?" he asked cautiously.

"Adam."

"Adam?" Surprised, Nathan opened the door. "What are you doing up here, Adam?" His eyes widened with concern, and a cold chill ran down his spine when he saw the man standing beside Adam.

Adam said, "I came up here to give Sarah this jar of mincemeat Hazel made and to check up on you. This is my little brother, Matt."

Nathan's gaze hadn't left Matt since he opened the door. Somehow, he had known who the man was. Perhaps it was his long hair and beard, or the features similar to Adam's, or maybe it was the gun-belt at his waist as naturally as a pair of boots on a man's feet. The man reached out to shake Nathan's. Nathan swallowed hard and faced the fear that his life with Sarah might be coming to an end this minute. He extended his hand to shake and forced himself to say nervously, "Nice to meet you. Your brother is...an interesting fellow," he said with a small smile.

Matt nodded as he shook Nathan's hand. "He keeps me entertained." Matt could read the uneasiness on Nathan's face and was about to say more, when Nathan's wife walked to the door.

"Adam," Sarah said pleasantly. "Come in, for goodness sakes. Nathan, where are your manners? Good evening. I'm Sarah Pierce, and this is my husband, Nathan. You must be Adam's brother. You look like him," she said to the stranger as he and Adam stepped into their home.

"That I am. My name's Matt."

"Are you two hungry? I have supper on the stove, if you're hungry." Both men wore guns tied low, like gunfighters. She was not accustomed to such weapons worn by anyone in her town and fear began to churn in her stomach. She trusted Adam, though, and forced the uneasiness away. "Adam, why don't you and your brother sit down at the table, so we can visit? How about some coffee? I'll get you both some coffee," she said politely and added, "Nathan was just telling me that you're starting a horse ranch, is that right?"

"Hmm, partly," Adam said as he took a seat. "My sister is starting a horse company. I will still be raising cattle, but we're combining our properties and making it one ranch with two separate businesses. Which is why I came up here. I was wondering if Nathan wanted to hire on as one of my ranch hands. What do you think about that?"

Nathan looked at Adam, faintly irritated. "I'd have to think about it." He was too quiet and troubled for Sarah not to notice.

She said, "Well, it's an offer worth considering, don't you think? Adam did come all the way up here to ask you. I'm sure he's offering a fair wage too. The least you could do is inquire about it. Here's your coffee, Adam. And yours, Matt. So, Matt, are you working on your brother's ranch too?"

Matt smiled and shook his head. "No, but I ranched growing up, before I struck out on my own. I just rode up here with Adam to meet you folks."

Nathan said, "Adam's brother is Matt Bannister, Sarah. The U.S. Marshal."

Sarah seemed to freeze suddenly. "Oh...you're very well known. Very famous, indeed," she said quietly as she took her seat. A recent story of his gunfight in Louden, Idaho, had reached town a week ago. Now Matt Bannister, the deadliest lawman alive, was sitting at her table looking at her. She prayed silently but desperately that he would not recognize them. Her hands began to shake, and her breathing quickened. She refused to look at Matt in the eyes at that point but sat still over her cup of steaming coffee. She had been scared to death when Nathan went missing a few weeks before, but now she was terrified of being taken away from the man she loved.

Matt took a deep breath and spoke into the uncomfortable silence that suddenly filled their small home. "I would prefer to stay in my office a bit more, to be honest. I've been traveling lately, but it's nothing I'm not used to. I've spent my whole career on horseback tracking people down here and there. Not to brag, but I've gotten pretty good at it actually. I understand your husband's a pretty good tracker too." He spoke to Nathan, who was obviously uncomfortable with the conversation.

Sarah chuckled awkwardly and stood up, "Well, if you'll excuse me, I'll let you men talk..."

Matt said in a serious voice, "Actually, why don't you have a seat. I'm afraid what I have to say involves you, too."

Sarah froze in place. A sudden panic washed through her as her world seemed to crash down around her. She turned back to the table and sat down slowly as her eyes filled with tears. Her right hand reached out to Nathan's, and he took it lovingly.

Nathan said, "How can we help you, Matt?"

Matt took a drink of his coffee and then began. "Well, as you may or may not know, I am the U.S. Marshal in Branson. Some time back, I went to Idaho. In my absence, someone murdered a married couple who lived in a cabin out in the woods. Whoever murdered them—and I do have an idea who it was—burnt the cabin down with the couple's bodies inside. It's rumored that they were affiliated with some bad people around the valley. So, putting a name to the killer is tough to do at this point. The bodies were burned, and no one seems to know who they were. Even if they did know, they aren't saying. One thing is known for certain. The couple weren't local, and they weren't known by many." Matt paused, waiting for Nathan or Sarah to say something, but neither did.

Matt took another sip of his coffee before continuing, "Some people, including myself, believe the murdered couple were hiding from the law and got involved with the wrong people. I personally think they were the missing daughter of Louis and Divinity Eckman, named Catherine, and her so-called kidnapper, Nathan Webster. Now, I think they were married legally, but Louis Eckman is a millionaire in California who has offered an illegal ten-thousand-dollar bounty for her return. It's a big bounty. Ten thousand dollars is a lot of money, and there are lots of folks looking for his daughter for him. Like I said, though: I think they're dead and buried under tombstones that say 'unknown' in our cemetery. Unfortunately, I haven't found anything that might prove it was them. You know, like something I could send to her parents to prove that their daughter and son-in-law are both dead. Something like—I don't know—let's say, a personalized Bible. Something her parents would recognize and that would let them know without a doubt the dead couple was them. Something I might've found in the rubble to send them. You know, if I had something like that to send, they could quit searching for their daughter and end that illegal bounty. Mister and Missus Eckman could get on with their lives and put everything behind them. And their daughter and her husband could rest in peace finally. Do you know what I mean?" he asked pointedly.

Nathan looked at Adam and scowled. "You told him!"

Matt said, "Adam didn't tell me anything. All I said was I

believe that couple who were burned beyond recognition might have traveled a lot. They might even have been *one* of your neighbors or *stayed* with you. Perhaps they *left* something behind that maybe could be useful in proving who *they* were," Matt said, emphasizing his words. "If you *can't* help me find something to *send* to the Eckmans, then I'm wasting my time trying to *help* them."

Sarah looked at Matt through tear-filled eyes and smiled as she began to understand what he was saying. "I may have something that might help. But I don't know if I can trust you. You are a lawman," she whispered in desperation.

Matt nodded and spoke softly, "I am. But an occasional illegal wrong can be, slightly illegally, made right for the right people in the right circumstances. I believe it's about time to let the Eckmans move on with their lives and let their daughter and her *husband*...live in peace. I mean, rest in peace."

A tear fell from Sarah's eye. "Are you saying what I think you're saying?"

Matt shrugged. "All I'm saying is if someone had *something* I could use to prove it was Catherine Eckman in that cabin, then the search and bounty would be over. Nobody would ever be falsely accused of being them, nor would another young couple who might harbor *similar features*. Let's just say that other couple could move to Branson or anywhere else they wanted to go and do it without worrying about being mistaken for a dead couple."

Nathan said, "Ten thousand dollars is a lot of money. Some men can't be trusted when it comes to that much money."

Matt looked at Nathan. "You're right. It's too much money for me. So, if you'll trust me, I will write up a report and send the evidence to the Eckmans. When their curiosity is settled, they'll have to end that bounty. If they send me the reward money—and I *will* try to collect it for finding their daughter—well, let's call it a late wedding present from your parents. I mean from the Eckman family to some deserving young couple new to our town. Anyway, you two think it over. I'll be outside."

A few minutes later, the door opened, and Sarah and Nathan stood in the doorway. "Marshal Bannister," Sarah said, "I *found* this can of personal pictures, and a marriage license belonging to someone named Catherine Eckman in the house next door. The couple moved out about a year ago, I think it was. It may help prove that she *was* Catherine Eckman. And also the chess game her father bought her for her eighteenth birthday. It was handmade in Greece. My father bought it there for me. I mean *her* father. my name is Sarah Pierce."

Matt smiled warmly as he took the small metal box and placed it on top of the ornamented chess board he took from Nathan. "Is there anything here you'd like to keep?"

"I kept Jane's letters and a picture of my parents... I mean, *her* parents," she said.

Matt smiled. "Don't be afraid, all right? You'll be fine. Nathan, I understand you can track a bit. If you don't want to hire on with Adam, think about hiring on as one of my deputies. I have three now. Two are inexperienced city boys who don't know much, and I just hired the man I went to Idaho to track down." Matt chuckled. "I need good men, so if being a deputy marshal sounds appealing to you, let me know."

"You don't even know me," Nathan said awkwardly.

Matt looked Nathan over closely. "Sure, I do. You're a good and honest man who knows how to treat people fairly. You're meek when you need to be meek and tough when you have to be tough. I have no doubt you'd fit right in with my office. Think about it. I'll have to burn the chess set and char the pictures to make them look damaged, but I will contact the Eckmans and get them sent off. I will let you know when it's safe to come down from here. Your lives are changing for the better, though. Until we meet again—say the first of December in my office, for your first day on the job—if you accept it."

"Why so far off?" Sarah asked curiously. "We might want to move to Branson a lot sooner. Like today!" she laughed.

"Wait until it's clear. I'll let you know when. But it won't be long," Matt said.

"Thank you," Sarah said with a big smile. "Thank you!"

"My pleasure. It really is. See, Nathan? You could be changing your lives for the better, too."

He smiled. "I'll think about it, but I have to be honest. I kind of like the idea of pushing livestock and breaking horses and working with Adam, too."

Matt nodded. "Understood. In fact, you might talk to Adam about moving to the ranch any time. You'll just have to stay around Willow Falls until the Eckmans are satisfied with my findings. However, I will warn you that you'd better be careful working for Adam, because he has a habit of using people for wolf bait when they make him mad." He laughed.

"He told you about that? He scared the heck out of me. I believed him!" Nathan grinned.

Adam nodded and smiled. "It kept him quiet, and Octavius didn't shoot at us. You should've seen him, Sarah. It looked like he was going to cry when I told him that. He's apparently afraid of wolves."

Matt shook his head. "Wolf bait. Only you would come up with that."

Adam said to Nathan, "Give me two weeks, and then come on down to the ranch. I'll have a little something put up for you to live in until you decide if you want to stay on the ranch or move to town. If you want to stay on the ranch, we'll build you a home. But if you break one of our horse's legs by not paying attention to the ground right in front of you and hurt yourself again, then you will become wolf bait, because you're too much trouble to save!" He said the words with a friendly wink and a chuckle. "We'll be glad to have you the Big Z Ranch with us."

A few minutes later, Sarah stood in front of Nathan, their arms around each other, as they watched Adam and Matt riding away from their home. She turned to look at Nathan while he still held her and tried to speak but couldn't. Tears filled her eyes, and she held Nathan close as she sobbed.

He held her tighter and felt his own eyes grow moist. "I cannot believe it. My Lord, thank you. Thank you, Jesus. You're always so...amazing! Even when I don't deserve it."

Sarah took a few deep breaths and tried to control her sobbing. "I'm never going to see my parents again."

"Did you want to?"

"No...but I always hoped they'd be happy for me some-day. I hoped they'd be grandparents to our children. I hoped someday we could all just be a normal family. But it's never going to happen now, and it never would've anyway. I just hoped."

"Well... it's not too late to stop Matt from sending your things. We can keep hiding until they find us."

Sarah smiled. "No. But wouldn't it be fun to sneak into their big old house in the middle of the night and pretend we're ghosts? Promise me, once we're officially dead, we'll sneak down there and do that to them." She laughed.

"I bet they'd really be crying out to the Lord then, wouldn't they?"

"We're going to be all right, aren't we?"

Nathan gazed into her eyes and smiled. "We would be all right even if we stayed right here. My loved one, we are going to be more than all right. We are going to be...wonderful!"

"To Branson we go?"

He nodded. "Willow Falls, Branson; time will tell. But we, my dear, are out of Loveland, out of hiding, and we are now free and out of here!"

AT LOOK AT THE ECKMAN EXCEPTION (MATT BANNISTER WESTERN 5)

WELCOME TO BRANSON, OREGON WHERE NOT EVERYTHING IS AS IT SEEMS.

U.S. Marshal Matt Bannister has returned to identify two dead bodies burned in a cabin as Catherine Eckman and her husband Nathan Webster. However, Pick Lawson does not trust Matt and is on a mission to prove he is lying for his own personal gain...

Matt Bannister is looking forward to a spending a weekend with Felisha Conway who is coming to town for a wedding. His weekend is turned upside down when his dear friend Christine goes missing, and he finds himself under investigation by a Pinkerton Detective for intentionally misleading the missing persons case of Catherine Eckman.

Death, kidnapping and lies is just the start in book five of the best-selling western series by Ken Pratt!

NOW AVAILABLE ON AMAZON

ABOUT THE AUTHOR

Ken Pratt and his wife, Cathy, have been married for 22 years and are blessed with five children and six grandchildren. They live on the Oregon Coast where they are raising the youngest of their children. Ken Pratt grew up in the small farming community of Dayton, Oregon.

Ken worked to make a living, but his passion has always been writing. Having a busy family, the only "free" time he had to write was late at night getting no more than five hours of sleep a night. He has penned several novels that are being published along with several children stories as well.

Made in the USA
Columbia, SC
14 May 2020

97181773R00243